HYPERION'S FRACTURE

ALSO BY THOMAS KELSO

Fractured

HYPERION'S FRACTURE

THOMAS KELSO

JOLLY ROBIN
PRESS

HYPERION'S FRACTURE. Copyright ©2019 by Thomas Kelso.

ISBN: 978-0-9994561-2-5 (ebook)

ISBN: 978-0-9994561-4-9 (hardback)

ISBN: 978-0-9994561-3-2 (paperback)

 Created with Vellum

To Vicky

"I believe God made me for a purpose, but He also made me fast. And when I run, I feel his pleasure."
—Eric Liddell

HYPERION'S FRACTURE

ONE

Tocumen International Airport, Panama City, Panama

HIS LEFT EYE wandered over her body. The right one didn't move. The mustache reminded her of a fat black caterpillar perched above thin cruel lips. Claire ignored the sweat trickling down her neck and the ache in her shoulders. She stood tall and returned his stare. It wasn't easy. She wanted to turn away. The scar marred the right side of his face, producing a permanent half grin and a milk-white cataract. Their eyes locked and he blinked. She wondered what violent act caused this cycloptic face as she pushed her passport over the counter. A shiver jolted her. The caterpillar bristled as the customs agent smiled.

"Eres bella." You are beautiful, he said.

"Gracias," Claire replied.

He stamped her passport and slid it back. The tension ebbed as she shrugged off her backpack, unzipped the main compartment, and stowed the papers.

"Enjoy your stay in Panama, señorita."

She nodded then merged into the jostling crowd flowing through the terminal. Fleeting snatches of multilingual conversations slipped past as she moved upstream against the human tide. A few moments later she spotted a man standing by an escalator wearing a green shirt and khaki trousers. He held up a notebook-sized white piece of paper with *Dr. Claire Hodgson* printed in black block letters. Next to him stood a petite woman in her midthirties with raven hair cut in a pageboy style. She wore a floral print skirt with a pink blouse and began waving.

"Claire! Over here."

"Meera." Claire darted through the throng of travelers and they embraced.

"You made it."

"I almost didn't recognize you." Claire stood at arm's length looking at her friend. "You cut your hair. It's so cute."

"I had to."

"It looks so good on you. I love it."

Dr. Meera Jindal laughed and flipped her head from side to side. "It was too long, like wearing a turban in a sauna."

"Why didn't you post a picture?"

"I've been busy *and* it looks terrible."

"Nonsense—you're gorgeous."

"Not after a few hours in the jungle," Meera said. "A haircut and makeup can't fix that."

"Has it really been three years?"

"Almost. Madrid, remember?"

Claire shook her head and smiled. "It doesn't seem that long ago."

"A lot's happened since then. Anyway, thanks for coming. I need some company. It gets lonely when you're banished to an outpost."

"Outpost?" Claire glanced at the people streaming past.

Meera laughed. "Not here. Panama City is awesome. I'm talking about where I live and work. Tonight, we'll stay downtown.

Tomorrow I'll take you to the lab." Meera reached for the handle of her luggage. "You'll see what I mean."

The man standing next to them cleared his throat and extended his hand.

"Oh, forgive me for being rude." Meera placed her hand to her forehead. "This is Dr. Alvarez, my research partner and director of R&D at the institute."

"A pleasure, Dr. Hodgson," said Alvarez. "I've heard wonderful things about you."

She shook his hand. "Thank you, but please call me Claire."

He nodded and smiled. "If you'll call me, Rafael."

"Deal."

"Your accent, it's Australian?"

"From Sydney originally, but I live in the States now."

"Where?"

"The Raleigh-Durham area, North Carolina."

"Welcome to Panama." He hoisted her backpack, and the three of them walked toward the exit.

CLAIRE SCANNED the modern skyline and tapped the tinted window as they approached the outskirts of the city. "I count fifteen high-rises going up. This is a metropolis."

Rafael glanced at Claire in the rearview mirror while maneuvering their vehicle through late-afternoon freeway traffic. "Panama is no longer third world. Today we're the center of Central American banking and finance."

"Thanks to the canal expansion, it'll remain a focal point of global trade for the next century. What do you think of our giant corkscrew?" Meera asked as they passed the spectacular helical F&F Tower.

Claire craned her neck. "Too bad you don't have a wine bottle to go with it."

Rafael chuckled. "That would be nice." He navigated the SUV through a maze of urban streets lined by glass-and-steel skyscrapers. "Welcome to the jewel of Panama, Latin America's finest city." A few minutes later, he parked in front of the hotel. "Checking in," he said in Spanish to the valet and handed him the keys.

In a short while, they were registered and stepping out of an elevator onto their floor. "I have a call in ten minutes," Meera said when they stopped in front of Claire's room. "Relax and freshen up. I'll meet you in the lobby at six. We have reservations at my favorite place in old town."

"See you then." Claire opened the door and walked to the window across the room. She flung open the sheer drapes revealing the turquoise splendor of Panama Bay. Twenty-two floors below, the beach was variegated by umbrellas and palm trees, while figures scurried like ants across the white sand. Exhausted, she flopped on the bed and closed her eyes. *How will Meera take the news? Will she be mad . . . jealous . . . hurt?* She hoped not. Too many lives depended on her cooperation. As her mind drifted into sleep an image of Hyperion flashed. She bolted upright. *Hang on boy, don't give up.*

CLAIRE HELD UP HER WINEGLASS. "Congratulations. Bill must be proud of you."

Meera's smile faded as she touched her glass to Claire's and shrugged. "I wouldn't know."

"Really? What happened? I thought you two were serious."

Her head turned from side to side. "Haven't heard from him in months."

"That doesn't sound like the William Plunkett I remember."

"I guess a long-distance relationship was more than he could handle." The tip of her index finger circled the rim of her glass. "I'm wasting the most important years of my life hunting flowers in a rain forest."

"Trust me, you're not wasting anything. I guarantee he's going to take notice, along with a lot of others. You're doing incredible work, and those flowers are really important," said Claire.

"I doubt if the jerk has any idea what I'm doing. The great professor is too busy charming coeds half his age to think of me."

"He's not the first man with that problem."

"How could I have been so naïve? He won't even answer an email."

Claire sat up straight. "I'm surprised. He didn't seem the type."

"I've heard he's dating a graduate student. Can you believe that?"

"Well, weren't you one when you first got together?"

"That was five years ago and I was a post-doc."

"Do you miss him?"

"I'm over it. There was a time I thought we had something, but not anymore." Meera drained her glass and reached for the bottle.

"Well, you have to admit he's brilliant," said Claire.

"And gorgeous but, that's no excuse for ignoring me."

"He'll come to his senses, and he won't be ignoring you much longer."

Meera tilted her head. "What do you mean?"

"You'll see." Claire paused and sipped her Viognier while several diners walked past their table. "Where's Rafael?"

"With his family in Ancón. It's a suburb," Meera clarified. "We're borrowing some equipment from the Smithsonian Tropical Research Institute at Gorgas Hospital. He'll pick it up then get us in the morning."

They were seated around an outdoor table at a rooftop restaurant near the Presidential Palace, overlooking buildings dating to the origins of the city. An expanse of brick and stucco structures with acres of terra-cotta roof tiles sprawled below them. A tropical breeze ruffled the edges of the tablecloth and blew strands of Claire's long golden hair across her face. In the distance, across the shimmering bay, skyscrapers in the modern part of the city cut into the horizon like giant jagged peaks backlit by the setting sun.

They ordered after the waiter refilled their glasses. When he walked away, Meera glanced around and looked at her friend. "I'm not complaining, but why the surprise visit?"

"I hope I'm not imposing."

"Not at all, I don't mean that. It's wonderful, but the Stanford reunion *is* in two months."

Claire put her wineglass down. "I know. I'll be there."

"You better be. I may need help dealing with Plunkett."

"You'll have no problem." Claire folded her arms on the table and leaned forward. "I'm here because of your research. Remember your lecture in Madrid?"

"The Pharma Conference? Sure. I presented the results of our first antibiotic project."

"Exactly. I was stunned. You'd discovered the solution to a problem we were having with our patients. We needed a long-acting antibiotic."

"Seriously? Why didn't you say something?"

"I wasn't sure at the time, but I am now. That's why I'm here. You're on to something incredible."

Meera's face brightened. "You really think so?"

"I'm one hundred percent certain." Claire tucked a wayward strand of hair behind her left ear. "Science is so serendipitous—I almost didn't go to that meeting. I remember your presentation like it was yesterday. You talked about an experimental drug that was showing promise. It didn't have a name back then. You called it compound SP-84 or something like that."

Meera smiled and nodded. "I figured this visit must have something to do with Endovancin."

"That's right. Do you remember I cornered you afterward?"

Meera sipped her wine. "You wanted to trial it. Use it in your bone fracture experiments . . . preventing post-op infections. What happened with that?"

Claire nodded. "I've been working with an orthopedic trauma

surgeon, Mark Thurman. We've developed methods to speed up fracture healing using 3D-printed bone and stem cells."

"I read somewhere it's working."

"It is, but we've hit a few snags. Early on, there were too many post-op wound infections. After surgery, the experimental subjects were returned to an NIH monkey colony on an isolated island off the coast of South Carolina. We couldn't keep close track of them in the wild. They were too hard to locate. Daily medication was impossible. We needed a longer-acting antibiotic, one that lasted weeks, not hours. After watching the Madrid presentation, I knew your drug would solve our problem, and at the same time, we could help you with clinical trials."

"That was a long time ago." Meera swirled her glass, watching the legs run back into the bowl. "Back when Bill Plunkett knew I was alive. So why didn't we do it?"

"We have been."

Meera's eyes narrowed as she stared at her friend. "What are you talking about?"

"We needed help. I was getting desperate. So, I approached Jim Roberts."

Meera's head turned. "You talked to my boss? The CEO of Electra?"

Claire pursed her lips and nodded. "We . . . Mark and I, asked him if we could try it."

"He let you?"

Claire nodded.

"Why didn't he tell me?"

"I don't know. Please, don't be mad. He wouldn't let us say anything to anyone. It was part of the agreement. He wanted to keep everything compartmentalized for security reasons. He's super paranoid and didn't want any information about Endovancin leaking out. For good reason."

Meera brushed her bangs back from her forehead. "He's psycho paranoid. I think it's why he keeps the laboratory so isolated."

"Electra provided us with enough for several experimental trials with our rhesus monkeys. I'm sorry about the secrecy. We weren't trying to keep anything from you. We believed Endovancin would reduce bone infections in our patients. The properties are perfect. It's temperature stable and its long half-life means one dose is effective for two weeks after surgery. We were right. It worked. It prevented infections and kept us from having to round up the monkeys every day." Claire stopped and smiled at the waiter as he placed the first course before them.

"Any fresh ground pepper?" he asked, holding up the large wooden cylinder. The women shook their heads and he retreated.

"Go on," Meera said.

"Like I said, we tried it. It worked better than expected, zero infections."

"Great, but you didn't have to make a trip here to tell me that."

"There's more. Everything was fine, until a couple of months ago when we began noticing problems. Some of our earliest patients began developing tumors."

"Cancer?" Meera asked.

Claire nodded. "Osteosarcoma."

Meera's eyes widened. "Any ideas why?"

"The stem cells within the bone graft are hyperstimulated to differentiate into osteoblasts. A ton of cell amplification is occurring. We think there's a transcription error either knocking out a tumor suppressor gene or activating an oncogene. Whatever the cause, since then, more cases have been diagnosed." Claire leaned toward her friend and lowered her voice. "Here's the interesting part: the tumors occurred before we started using Endovancin."

"*Before* you started using Endovancin?" Meera repeated.

Claire nodded. "The lesions were in patients who didn't get your drug. Patients who received Endovancin have been normal. Not a histologic hint of cancer."

"What are you saying? It may prevent . . . ?"

"Not so loud," Claire interrupted, looking around.

Meera leaned forward and whispered, "Endovancin prevents osteosarcoma?"

"Not only that; we think it's a cure."

Meera's fork clattered to the table. "You're kidding?"

"*That's* the real reason I'm here. The early experimental subjects didn't get Endovancin. They were given vancomycin. They began showing signs of tumor formation around two years after the original surgery. When the tumors began showing up a few months ago we biopsied them and the results confirmed the diagnosis. But this time, after the biopsy procedure, they received Endovancin. It was chance, pure luck. We just wanted to avoid a post-op infection and had switched to giving all the patients Endovancin. To our surprise, the monkeys showed an immediate response. They perked up and within a few days the tumors began shrinking. A month later we took more biopsies, this time, the bones *were normal.* X-rays were normal, tissue samples were normal. They were cured. The tumors were gone. And . . . they've remained in remission."

Meera sat slacked-jawed, stunned by what she'd just heard. "How many?"

"Seventeen, so far. Get this, no subject who originally received Endovancin has developed tumor symptoms, *and* no infections *and* no side effects."

"That's miraculous," Meera said.

"I want to try it on other cancers."

Meera became quiet and looked down at her plate.

"What's wrong? You should be jumping up and down."

Meera blinked. "I know. I should be. It's just that my nephew, Aaray," her eyes glistened as tears welled up, "he passed away two weeks ago."

Claire placed her hands in her lap and became quiet.

"Neuroblastoma."

"I had no idea."

"He was seven when it was finally diagnosed. I watched it destroy him. It was relentless."

"Oh, Meera," Claire reached across the table and touched her forearm. "I'm so sorry."

Meera smiled and touched her napkin to her eyes. "I arranged for my sister to bring him to Houston for treatment. They tried all the newest immunotherapies. At first there was hope, and he responded well for six months, but then he relapsed and died."

Claire watched a tear tumble down her cheek and splash onto the tablecloth.

"Now you're telling me I was working on a drug that might have saved him."

"Possibly, but we don't know, we just figured this out a few days ago. You can't blame yourself for anything."

"Excuse me, I have to go pull myself together," Meera said and rose from the table. Five minutes later she returned. "I didn't mean to fall apart. I thought I had it under control. Forgive me."

"I understand. It's my fault for bringing it up," Claire said.

"No, no, it's okay. You didn't do anything wrong."

"You didn't either. They are different tumors. We have no idea if Endovancin would have any effect on a neuroblastoma. Don't beat yourself up."

"If I'd known I could've tried."

"Stop. Listen to me, we just analyzed the data and put the pieces together this week. You couldn't have done anything to save him. You can't change the past. I *do* know Endovancin may be the most important drug since penicillin. It may save millions of lives someday, but it's not going to bring your nephew back."

Meera blinked and dabbed her eyes. "God, what a mess. I'm sorry. Do I look like a raccoon?"

"You look fine. Stop apologizing and drink some more wine. This is a celebration. We have to continue testing. If we're lucky it could help others like Aaray. Right now I need more. We still have experimental subjects who need treatment. Can you increase production? Mark and I are in the middle of several experiments and we've run out. We want to try it in other species but can't proceed. I'm begging you to help us."

Meera took a breath then drank long and deep from her glass. The white wine was cool and crisp. It washed away the salty taste of tears. She nodded and sniffed. "Of course I'll help."

Claire reached across the table and squeezed her friend's hand. "Thank you."

"We can boost production, no problem but, you'll need to get approval from Electra. Did you ask Roberts?"

"That's why I'm here. He recommended I come down and take a look at your facilities."

"I think you'll find BCI unique. It's changed a lot in the last few years."

Claire squinted. "BCI? What's that?"

"My lab," Meera said and took another sip of wine. "That's where we're headed in the morning, Barro Colorado Island in Lake Gatún. It's the only place on the planet we've found that produces the active ingredient for Endovancin."

MEERA AND CLAIRE sat in the lobby drinking coffee when Rafael emerged from the revolving doors of the hotel entrance.

"Good morning," said the Panamanian as he pushed his wide-brimmed hat from his head so that it hung from its drawstring on the back of his shoulders. "Ready to hit the road?"

"All checked out," Meera said. He grabbed their bags and began walking toward the door. The valet helped him place them in the back of the Land Rover. Claire noticed the large crate. "Is that the equipment?"

"An HPLC. Ours is on the blink," said Rafael. "We need it to isolate the antimicrobial molecules from the plant extracts."

They climbed in and Claire donned her sunglasses. "You run high-performance liquid-chromatography in the rain forest?"

"Every day," replied Rafael. "Except when the machine isn't working. This should keep us in business until Electra sends a replacement."

"How long will that take?"

"A couple of weeks," said Rafael.

"Impressive," said Claire. Despite the heat, she and Meera were dressed in lightweight long pants, long-sleeve shirts, and canvas hiking boots. She had an Australian bush hat in her lap, and her hair was pulled back in a thick braid. Technically, it was the dry season but they were prepared for the rain forest. Rafael drove through the congested streets of Panama City and onto the highway. Soon, they were cruising east on the Panama-Colón Expressway. Twenty miles outside the city, Rafael exited onto a two-lane road with canebrake up to its shoulders. A few minutes later, they rounded a curve and could glimpse the canal in the distance.

Meera looked at her friend. "Our boat is docked at the dredging piers. We'll take it to the island. Rafael has a few more items to pick up in Colón. He'll catch a ride from there."

"I thought boating in the Canal Zone was restricted." Claire said.

"It is," replied Rafael. "Very restricted."

"The government granted the Smithsonian rights to build a laboratory to study the canal's impact on the rain forest shortly after it opened."

Claire looked over her sunglasses. "A hundred years ago?"

"The institute has conducted research on Borro Colorado Island almost since Lake Gatún was created in 1913," Meera said. "Don't worry, I'm a licensed pilot. Enjoy the ride."

They crossed a bridge over the Chagres River and turned toward the docks. The steel-blue water of the canal was before them. The waterway was several hundred yards wide at this point and stretched east and west as far as they could see. Rafael parked by a pier. The humid air enveloped them like hot breath when they stepped from the air-conditioned vehicle.

"Whoa, now I understand why you cut your hair."

Meera and Claire grabbed their luggage and followed Rafael. He walked down the dock and stepped onto the Smithsonian's twenty-five-foot center console Boston Whaler and took the bag Meera handed him. Claire passed him hers and stepped on board as Meera stood at the console lowering the engine unit into the water. The three-hundred-horsepower Mercury Verado roared with the first turn of the ignition key and idled like a giant purring cat. Rafael stepped back onto the pier and loosed the lines. He stood holding the bowline as Meera put the engine in gear.

"See you back at the island," he called out and tossed the rope to Claire as the boat motored away from the pier. Meera guided the vessel slowly into the waterway while Claire pulled the fenders over the gunwales. Once in the canal, Meera opened the throttle and they surged forward. In a few seconds the boat was slicing through the water on plane.

"It's about a thirty-minute ride," Meera shouted over the engine noise and rushing wind. She accelerated until the speedometer read thirty miles per hour. Behind the center console the air was less turbulent, but on either side the wind whipped their hair and pressed their clothes tight to their skin. Claire shoved her hat into the overhead storage compartment and gripped the railing. Canal traffic was moving eastward, and Meera stayed on the right side of the waterway, well clear of the giant ships navigating the channel. She turned into the wakes and cut speed when crossing the large swells.

"Good Lord," said Claire as they overtook a Panamax vessel. She tilted her head upward as they passed fifty feet on the starboard side. "Look at the size of that thing. It's a floating warehouse."

"More like a city block twenty stories tall," Meera responded. "Hang on." The bow rose and slammed down the other side of the wake. "You all right?"

"Tough on the knees," Claire said, easing her death grip on the hand railing.

"Don't go overboard."

"No worries." They had traveled about ten miles when the

waterway opened up to the immense expanse of Lake Gatún. Sunlight glinted off ripples on the water's surface. Meera steered a northeast course and pointed straight ahead to a small speck in the distance. "That's BCI," she yelled. Ten minutes later they'd reached the island, and she turned into a sparkling blue cove surrounded by emerald hills. She cut speed as they passed several moored vessels and glided up to a floating dock. Meera put the engine into neutral while Claire threw the bowline to a young man who caught it and guided them alongside the structure. He secured the line and the women disembarked.

"Got it, José?" Meera asked.

"Yes, Dr. Jindal. It's good to have you back."

Claire stopped and took in the scene. It reminded her of a small college campus built into a jungle mountainside. They carried their bags up the long steep flights of stairs to the research facility. Without a headwind and cooling effect of the water, the heat began taking its toll. Claire's heart rate doubled and drops of perspiration rolled down the center of her back as they ascended. She wiped her face with a shirtsleeve and counted five buildings that made up the remote enclave. Two of them were new construction. The other three were being renovated. Scaffolding had been erected and workers were making repairs to the façade.

When the scientists finished their climb Meera turned and swept her arm over the tropical panorama. "This island was once the peak of a mountain. When the Chagres Dam was built, the river flooded the valley and created Lake Gatún, and we're standing on what's left above the surface. The plant and wildlife were trapped on this summit. The result is a unique ecosphere we've been studying for decades."

"It's beautiful," Claire said.

"And full of botanical treasures. These are our newest facilities, courtesy of Electra Pharmaceuticals." They continued walking to the side entrance of the nearest building. Meera flashed her ID badge over a sensor and the door slid open. "The laboratories were finished about six months ago, funded by a ten million dollar donation from Electra to the Smithsonian."

"Based on antibiotic research?"

"Not *just* antibiotics. Did Roberts have you sign an NDA?"

"Yes, he wouldn't say anything until he had it in his hands."

"We have a number of products under development. EndoV is just the first of several long-acting antibiotics effective against methicillin-resistant staph. The newer drugs are ten times more potent than vancomycin and last for weeks and months. One of our postdoc fellows is working on a new treatment for C. diff. A single dose of a compound we call AQ-327 cures it in our animal model."

"Incredible," replied Claire.

"We also have several promising chemotherapy compounds."

Claire smiled as she stopped and peered into a laboratory through the door window. "This place is a pharmaceutical Garden of Eden."

Meera smiled. "C'mon. I'll give you the tour. We'll start with the labs in the new buildings, then the garden." She led the way down the hall. "These labs are for product testing. The building next door is where we produce the compounds. Everything from plant processing to purification and packaging is done there. It's small scale but perfect for product development."

Forty-five minutes later, they exited a door on the third floor and walked across a footbridge to the hillside plateau behind the building. "You've thought of everything," Claire said. "What does the Smithsonian get out of this?"

"You mean for letting us into this Garden of Eden?"

Claire nodded. "Couldn't it spark a massive search for compounds and harm to the rain forest?"

"Like a pharmaceutical gold rush?"

"Something like that."

"That's another reason why Roberts is so security crazy. He doesn't want to start a stampede of exotic-plant poachers in the region. However, like most things, there's a financial interest."

"Of course," said Claire.

"The institute thinks of it as partly an altruistic role in helping mankind." Meera pushed a clump of branches to the side as they walked on a path toward the rain forest. "Also, they'll collect a big chunk of drug royalties. Several could be blockbusters. Plus, Electra is helping them by renovating the original buildings and supplying new labs and office equipment."

"What about the Panamanians?" Claire asked.

"They get a percentage of the royalties, and BCI will be the primary ecological research center for Central America. The Smithsonian has a long-term lease, but just like the canal and the Canal Zone facilities, it will eventually be turned over to the Panamanians."

"Like Gorgas Army Hospital?"

Meera nodded.

"Is it all biomedical research?"

"Not at all. The canal requires immense amounts of water. So much that some scientists are worried about the effects on the rain forest. The institute is interested in the long-term ecological consequences and preventing any adverse outcomes." Meera began walking toward an opening in the vegetation that led into darkness. It was like walking into a cave.

"This is a Hobbit hole." Claire chuckled.

"More like a Hobbit tunnel," replied Meera. After a few yards, the dense foliage opened up into the rain forest. The overhead canopy greedily absorbed sunlight, and only a few rays penetrated. The ground was a carpet of plant life. Buttress-rooted trees lined the path, towering hundreds of feet above. A network of vines crisscrossed overhead while a steep cinder-block staircase dating to the Second World War led up the mountainside. At this time of year, the climate in the forest was reasonably dry, and the insects were tolerable. They had gone only halfway up the staircase when Meera put out her hand to halt the ascent. "Look, do you see it?" she whispered, pointing into the canopy.

"See what?"

"Shhh. The toucan. Up there to your right."

The yellow face turned in profile, revealing its enormous beak. "Spectacular," Claire whispered.

The bird watched as they marched along a ridge overlooking the lake. A moment later, the hair on Claire's neck rose. She stopped in her tracks. A primal wail came from above and increased in volume. A few moments later the guttural roar engulfed them.

"What the *hell* is that?"

"A pack of howlers," Meera said. "They're on the move."

"Those are monkeys? Bloody terrifying."

"They're harmless."

"They sound like hell-bound banshees."

"Relax. They're moving on." The cacophony diminished as the pack of monkeys moved through the trees high above them. "It's not far." A quarter mile later Meera came to a stop. "We're here."

Claire looked around. She could detect no change in the terrain. "This? What are you talking about?"

Meera squatted. Her finger touched the petals of a small flower the size of a buttercup. "Bees."

"You've been in the jungle too long."

Meera chuckled and waved an insect away from her face. "They're tiny orchids related to *Ophrys apifera*. The blossoms look like bumblebees. They grow here because they have a symbiotic relationship with a particular fungus found only on BCI. So far, they haven't been identified anywhere else."

Claire inspected the ground and noticed several more. "They're all over."

"The active ingredient isn't in the flower. We don't harvest the entire plant; we just pluck a few leaves. It doesn't take much. A four-ounce jar full will make enough drug to conduct all your research trials."

"Have you identified the active molecule?"

Meera nodded. "That's why Rafael borrowed the HPLC. We

can isolate and purify the compound, and we've almost worked out its molecular structure."

"Can it be produced on a larger scale?"

"That's what I mean. It's not complicated. I'm putting the finishing touches on a process to synthesize it now. As soon as the HPLC is set up, I plan on purifying my latest batch." Meera bent down and tickled a bee blossom with the tip of her finger. She stood and began walking back along the trail. "Rafael should be back by now."

"Who else knows about this?" Claire asked.

"The location? No one. The people who work here don't know the active ingredient. They just make the product."

"I mean its properties," said Claire.

"Not a soul, unless you've told someone about your results."

Claire shook her head.

"No one can know about this. We're the only ones who know the true potential."

"What about Rafael?" Claire asked.

"He probably has an idea. Endovancin is a special product. He knows it's a great antibiotic, but that's it. He doesn't know I've been tinkering with it. I've worked out ways to alter the chemical structure. It's been modified to be more potent. It's not the same drug I talked about in Madrid three years ago."

"Whatever you did, it works," Claire said.

"If what you say is true, then you and I are the only ones who know it may cure cancer."

"You've applied for the patent?"

"Electra has. For the earlier version. This derivative binds to a different G-protein receptor."

Claire's hand came up to her face. "But it's covered in the application, right?"

"It should be." Meera shrugged then swatted a branch away from her legs. "I'm not sure what the original patent filing covers. I just develop the products."

Claire stepped over roots and tangled vines trying to keep up as they trekked down the narrow path. "You have to check, right away before anyone gets wind of its potential."

"I'll talk to Roberts. Who else could possibly know?"

"My postdoctoral fellow and our histology technician have seen the data, but I'm sure they don't know the full implication," Claire said. "Mark Thurman, my research partner, knows everything I do, but he's not a worry. I was referring to big business. If information about its effects leak, there will be a lot of people wanting that formula."

"It's too early to speculate. There's a ton of work to do before the FDA gives its approval," Meera said as they descended from the hills. "Electra is a small private company. No one on Wall Street knows about them."

I wouldn't bet on that, Claire thought.

Meera loped onward like a gazelle. Claire's thighs quivered as they negotiated the last steep cinder-block staircase in single file. She paused and pulled a handkerchief from her back pocket and wiped sweat from her face and neck. They were almost down the mountainside when Meera stopped.

Claire caught up and stood on the step behind her. She put her hands on Meera's shoulders. "What is it?"

She pointed at an opening in the foliage permitting a view of the water far below. In the distance two boats were approaching. "We don't have any deliveries scheduled this late."

"Maybe it's Rafael," Claire said.

"He should have been back an hour ago, and he would be in one boat. Not two."

They hurried off the mountainside and entered a building. Meera jogged down a hallway to her office facing the bay. They stood at the window, gazing two hundred feet below at two forty-foot boats with official government markings being secured at the docks. "What are those?" Claire asked.

"PCA. Canal Authority. What are they doing here?"

"That's what I'm supposed to ask," Claire said.

The desk phone began to ring. Meera picked up the receiver. She held the handset to her head and listened. Seconds later she hung up. "Come on. We have to get out of here."

"What's going on?"

"That was Rafael. The people on those boats aren't the Canal Authority. We're under attack."

Claire looked bewildered. "*Attack?* This is a research lab." They heard the staccato sound of automatic gunfire.

Meera returned to the window. "They're coming."

"There are at least thirty men down there," Claire said, now standing next to her.

Meera bolted across the room and opened the top drawer of a filing cabinet. She grabbed several files and stuffed them into her backpack. The gunfire sounded louder. She went to the back of her computer and yanked the thumb drive from a USB port.

"Come on! We have to get out of here. Follow me." She ran to the door and peeked into the hallway. She stepped back and shut it.

Meera turned and put her finger to her mouth. Down the hallway, the sound of men shouting commands in Spanish penetrated the walls. Pistol cracks followed the crash of doors being bashed open. The sound of boots tromping in the corridor grew louder.

Claire almost didn't notice her cell phone ringing. She pulled it from her pocket and saw Mark's picture on the screen. She swiped it and held it to her face. "Help, we're in trouble."

The office door imploded, striking Meera. She hit the floor and slammed into her desk. A half dozen uniformed men burst into the office, brandishing guns.

"Don't move!"

Claire palmed the phone and placed it on the desk behind her. She stepped toward Meera and helped her up.

"I said halt!"

The women stood frozen as the armed men surrounded them. A civilian dressed in a linen sport coat and panama hat strode through the doorway. He removed his mirrored aviator sunglasses and smiled.

"Good day, Dr. Jindal." He stopped and looked at Claire. "Dr. Hodgson, what a pleasant surprise. So nice of you to join us."

"Who are you?" Claire asked.

"An admirer."

"What is this?" Meera said, caressing her bruised cheek. "You have no right. We're here under the authority of the Panamanian government."

"Save it, Meera. They don't care," Claire said.

"You're right. I'm here for one thing. The Endovancin files, Dr. Jindal. The ones you *stole*."

He reached across the desk and picked up Claire's phone. His eyes widened and he flung it across the room. It bounced off the far wall and came to rest near Claire's feet with a shattered screen. He walked over and stamped it into the carpet. He leaned his face close to hers. The odor of stale cigarettes and cheap cologne assaulted her like a pesticide.

"Try a stunt like that again and you'll regret it," he hissed. He turned toward Meera, holding out his hand. "The files, please."

"What are you talking about? I'm no thief. This is *my* work."

"Liar," he said, sneering. "You helped yourself to others' research. You fled and set up shop with Electra. Pathetic."

"You're crazy. I discovered it!"

"That's not the way we see it. I'm taking it back. You're a common thief. An academic fraud."

Meera marched up to him. "It's my work, my research. Electra owns the rights. I'll see you in court."

"I wouldn't worry about that," he said and pushed her backward. She stumbled and tripped over a chair and fell to the floor. "There's not going to be any lawsuit. No one knows about it."

"Jim Roberts knows. He will sue your ass."

"You haven't heard?"

"Heard what?" Meera asked.

"Roberts was killed in a bicycle accident yesterday. Struck down by a car. Such a terrible tragedy." He turned to the uniformed leader. "Pack up the computers and the filing cabinets." He nodded to Claire and Meera. "Bring them with us."

THE BOAT SURGED from the dock and accelerated across the bay. Claire and Meera were seated on the deck with thick zip ties binding their hands and feet. Rags had been crammed into their mouths and sealed shut with duct tape. Claire struggled to free herself. It was pointless. The Hunter S. Thompson look-alike held Meera's backpack and glanced at his watch. Thin wisps of black hair fluttered from under his hat, and a cigarette dangled from the corner of his mouth. It bounced up and down as he spoke.

"Say goodbye to your research," he said, laughing. Ten seconds later, a series of blasts ripped through the buildings, followed by the sounds of explosions heard from a half mile away over the rushing wind and engine noise. Flames poured from the second- and third-floor windows. BCI faded into the distance as the boats sped onward. Several minutes later smoke billowed above the treetops.

The two women were shoved flat on the wet foredeck and covered with a tarp. Their bodies bounced and rolled like a load in a clothes dryer as the high-speed vessel skimmed the lake's surface. The boat flew over the water for half an hour. Then they skidded forward as the engines were cut. The tarp was ripped away. Brilliant sunlight made Claire squint, but she recognized the towering bow of an anchored freighter. Their boat idled into the dark shadow cast by its enormous structure. She could make out the letters FESCO written in ten-foot-tall white letters down its side. A rope ladder was lowered from the main deck while the women's hands and feet were cut free.

"Up you go, and don't slip." She felt a stabbing pain in her ribs as someone prodded her with the barrel of a rifle. "Get moving."

Claire grasped the swaying ladder and began the fifty-foot ascent with little feeling in her hands and feet. The rope bounced and shook against the metal hull. Halfway to the top she looked down into the black shadows. If she fell her body would be crushed on the boat below. She wiped the image from her mind then reached upward and grabbed the next rung.

TWO

SATURDAY, MARCH 18TH

Oaklawn Park Race Track, Hot Springs, Arkansas
Five days earlier...

MARK THURMAN SPOTTED his friend leaning against a stall. The horseman was halfway down the far side of the crowded corridor. Mark waved and clenched Claire's hand as they maneuvered through the throng. The scent of hay and horses filled the stable complex. Hundreds of race fans wandered about discussing the equine athletes. Their conversations blended into background noise as Mark focused on avoiding a collision. They passed penned Thoroughbreds, who every now and then looked around with indifference as they munched alfalfa and clover. Most of the horses had several assistants tending to their race-day routine. The couple weaved around the final group of pedestrians and hurried across the aisle.

The man standing next to the stall watched them. He was about Mark's age and wore a camel hair sport coat, starched white shirt, bolo tie, and jeans. At a little over six feet he was almost Mark's height but looked taller because of his cowboy boots and Stetson. A broad grin spread across his face as they approached. He barked a laugh then reached out and embraced Mark. "Well, well! It's about time you dragged your butt down to these parts."

Mark smiled and stepped back, feigning a left hook to the ribs. "It has been too long. I don't have any excuse."

"Me either. We suffered and did too much scut to not see each other more often."

"It was a long five years, but we made it."

"The last time we were together I had my doubts. I thought we were going to lose you."

"Don't remind me."

"You look damn good. What a comeback." He looked at Mark from head to toe. "You're more fit than you were in residency. What have you been doing?"

"Same as you. Working and trying to take care of myself." Mark stepped sideways. "I'd like you to meet Dr. Claire Hodgson. She's the brains behind our recent research."

He stepped forward, tipped his hat, and held out his hand. "Pardon me, ma'am. I'm Mike Rhodes, but call me Dusty. Most everyone else does."

Claire laughed and shook his hand. "All right, Dusty. It's a pleasure to meet you."

"Likewise," he replied as the horse behind him stretched its neck over the rail and nosed the brim of the Stetson, tilting it downward over his face. "Hey boy, cut it out." Claire covered her mouth stifling a laugh as he readjusted it. "That rascal always does stuff like that when I'm talking to someone. He's trying to make me look bad."

Mark reached over the rail and rubbed the horse's nose. "That's easy. Is this your all-star?"

"Meet Hyperion, the fastest three-year-old on the planet," said Dusty with a broad grin. He stood next to the stall where a diminutive horse with bay coloring and a white patch on his forehead pawed at the wood shavings and hay carpeting the floor. The horse leaned toward him and snorted. Dusty stepped back. "I said stop."

"He's got a mischievous streak," Claire said, reaching up and scratching the horse's ears. "Maybe he wants some attention."

"He'll have plenty in a couple of hours." Dusty turned to face Claire and in a solemn tone said, "I want you to know that no matter what others may tell you about the guy you're with he really is a decent human being. Don't believe those rumors; he's not wanted by the authorities."

Mark laughed.

"Thanks for clearing that up," replied Claire with a smile.

"No, really, in all seriousness, if it weren't for Mark, I wouldn't have made it through orthopedic residency, and we wouldn't be standing here today. I owe him a lot."

"Don't believe that for a second," said Mark. "We endured it together. Without him I might have rung the bell and given up medicine."

"That wasn't going to happen," said Dusty.

Claire tilted her head and looked at Mark. "What's scut?"

"It's medical slang for the phrase, some common *unimportant* task."

"Otherwise known as a menial job given to a med student or junior resident," Dusty added. "When you first begin clinical rotations you know just enough to be dangerous."

"So you're given a ton of scut in order to be useful and kept out of trouble," Mark explained.

"Things like keeping up with labs, reporting on test results, looking up journal articles, starting IVs, drawing blood cultures. Stuff like that," Dusty said.

Claire folded her arms. "Isn't that important?"

"Sure," Mark answered, "but it's no fun when you're doing it every day for your whole service, month after month."

"That's usually for thirty or forty patients. It gets old fast. Whatever unpleasant hospital chore that needed to be done, you can bet Mark and I were asked to do it."

Mark leaned his arm on the top rail of the stall. "I think it's a rite of passage for doctors in training but it was frustrating. When you're in a surgical residency you want to learn how to operate. We wanted to be in the OR."

Dusty nodded, "Those first few years I think I slept in the SICU more than my apartment."

"We didn't appreciate how much we were learning about pre and post-op patient care. How to get them out of the hospital and safely back home. That's just as important as operating, probably more important. But it sure seemed like the attendings were trying to make us quit. Those were miserable days. Don't bring that stuff up. I've been trying to erase those memories."

"All right, change of subject. Did you place your bets?"

"Twenty bucks at four to one," Mark said.

Dusty slapped his thigh and laughed. "A double sawbuck! That's all? Need a loan?"

Mark's eyebrows arched as a grin stretched across his face. "You know I'm not a gambler."

"Well, I am," Dusty declared. "I put down a lot more than that. What about you, Claire?"

"You know it. I plan on leaving with more money than I came with." She reached up and touched the white patch on Hyperion's forehead. "I love his star."

"His celestial birthmark," Dusty said.

"Hi there, fella." She rubbed the horse's nose then felt his soft fuzzy lips nibble at her fingers. "I don't have any mints," she said. A second later, she snatched her hand away as the animal gave a snort and shook his majestic head. She released the bridle as he stepped back in the stall. "Skittish."

"He knows it's a big day," Dusty told her, leaning over the rail and rubbing the beast's neck. "This will be his toughest competition. We're about to find out if he can deliver."

"He looks . . . a little small compared to the other horses. How tall is he?" Claire asked.

"Fifteen."

"Fifteen hands? Is that normal for a Thoroughbred?" she asked.

"He's a wide receiver. Not a defensive end. Don't worry about his height. Worry about how big his heart is. This guy's a scrapper. He's feisty. His grandfather was Risen Star."

Claire looked at him. "Who?"

"One of Secretariat's line. He won the 1988 Preakness."

"Still, he looks small," she said.

"That's what they said about Seabiscuit. And he can run just like him, you watch." He reached over and patted the horse's neck. "He's slender and sleek." There was an awkward pause for a few moments then Dusty looked in Mark's direction. "How was the Arlington?"

"Great hotel. Thanks for making the reservation."

"No problem. It's a landmark in Hot Springs. I tried to get you in the Al Capone suite."

Claire brushed her long hair behind her shoulders and placed her arm around Mark's. "It's just down the hall. There's a sign on the door."

"A lot of interesting guests have stayed there over the years."

"I think the hotel is booked full. Sorry we were late. I didn't expect the traffic."

"The population doubles this time of year. Race season is a big ticket in Hot Springs. The Rebel Stakes is a Kentucky Derby qualifier."

"Hyperion's first meeting against Rampage," said Claire.

Dusty nodded. "Otherwise known as the Black Plague."

Claire's eyes widened. "Really?"

"That's what I call him. He's a big nasty bastard."

"The newspaper said they're the favorites."

Dusty tipped his hat to her and looked at Mark. "The lady knows more than she's letting on."

Mark nodded. "I figured that out a while ago."

"If you're into horse racing, Oaklawn racetrack is the place to be this weekend."

A blonde woman in a pink designer dress, matching high heels, and a large brimmed red-and-pink hat came over and placed her arm around Dusty's. She looked at Mark.

"Who's your friend?"

Mark smiled. "Laura, you look lovely, as usual. I'd like to introduce you to Claire Hodgson, my good friend and research partner. Claire, this is Laura Rhodes."

"You must be quite a woman," she said, extending her hand. "I've wondered for years if anyone was going to distract Mark from his work."

Claire grasped her hand and smiled. "Sometimes I wonder the same thing. It's nice to meet you."

"Unfair," Mark pleaded. "I had a few medical issues to deal with."

"Point well made, but I'm tired of that excuse. You work too hard," Laura replied. "It's not good for you."

Claire turned to her companion. "Mark's told me about the fun you guys had in New York."

"He exaggerated. Residency wasn't a whole lot of fun," Dusty answered.

"Come on. There were a few good times," Mark replied.

"Now that most of the bad memories have faded, I guess I can think of one or two, maybe," he agreed.

"You met me," Laura said and kissed his cheek.

"That was the highlight."

"You're a radiologist?" Claire asked.

"Part time now," Laura replied. "Twin ten-year-old boys and a soon-to-be teenage daughter complicate a career."

"Just think, if Hyperion wins the Triple Crown, we can retire from medicine and concentrate on horses," Dusty told her.

"Dreamer," Laura said. "You're not quitting your day job."

He smiled. "Let's get lunch and watch the races. This guy doesn't run until about four o'clock."

"Good luck, fella," Claire said to Hyperion. The four walked out of the stables to the walkway near the clubhouse turn. As they approached the grandstand, the next race started. At the far end of the straight, the horses burst from the starting gate and thundered toward them. The crowd roared as they raced down the stretch.

Claire stood transfixed as the pack blazed into the turn a few yards from where she stood. The air reverberated. Twenty-five tons of contracting muscle and churning dirt streaked by in a blur. She held her breath. "Magnificent."

"Now you know why we got into this sport," Dusty told her. "Come on, let's get to our seats."

"Sorry we couldn't meet up with you this morning," Laura told Claire.

"No worries. We enjoyed the hotel."

"We weren't prepared for all the press interest," Laura continued. "They're acting like Rampage is the next Man o' War, saying he could win the Triple Crown."

"Could he?" Mark asked.

"Sure," she answered. "But Hyperion's undefeated, too."

"That's why they run the race," Dusty said, holding the door as the group entered the glass-enclosed facility. "We couldn't meet you earlier because of a press conference with the owners and trainers. A television crew is filming a segment for one of the major networks. The reporter couldn't stop gushing about Rampage. What a moron. It made me want to puke."

"He's supposed to be a great horse," Claire said.

"Let him prove it," Mark replied.

"Man o' War, my ass," Dusty muttered. "He's co-owned by a young hotshot drug company CEO and an agriculture conglomerate out of Bogotá. They wouldn't shut up. Worth only got two questions."

"Who is Worth?" asked Claire.

"Hyperion's principal partner," Dusty explained. "He controls eighty percent. Laura and I are part of the group that owns the remaining twenty percent."

"Relax," Laura said as she slipped her arm around her husband's. "It's not worth getting wound up over. Hyperion will get his chance."

"Thanks for inviting us," Claire told them.

"You're welcome. I thought it would be a good way to celebrate Dusty's birthday," Laura said.

Mark smiled and held Claire's hand. "We're glad you asked us to be part of it."

"Don't be getting sentimental on me," Dusty said. "What did that chemo do to you?"

"It made him better in more ways than one," Claire said, then kissed his cheek.

"Ouch," yelped Dusty as Laura gave him an elbow.

The group found the way to their box in the enclosed grandstand. The red-and-white twenty-foot tall obelisk marking the finish line was directly across from their seats. Twenty yards beyond the track, in the infield, was a sign that said OAKLAWN in huge letters carved from green box hedges. Next to it, video boards flashed race information and betting odds. Two hundred yards to their left, the starting gate was being maneuvered into position. The horses from the previous race had cleared the track, and tractors were circling the course, grooming the surface for the next race. Between the starting gate and the grandstand was an opening that led from the paddock onto the racetrack.

Dusty stood and waved to an attendant who arrived with a round of drinks. "Cheers," he said, raising his glass. "May Hyperion win by seven lengths."

"Or more," Mark responded.

They ate lunch and watched the remaining races on the card. Before the second to the last race, Dusty rose and motioned everyone to follow. "Come on, let's go to the paddock. I want to see Hyperion before he runs." He led the way to a building next to the grandstand. They entered and walked to a railing. As they approached the guardrail, Mark realized they were standing on a viewing platform. Six feet below, on the ground floor, were two parallel rows of eight stalls where the horses for the next race were being saddled. Several jockeys stood nearby in their colorful riding silks. Dusty showed his credentials to an official, and they were allowed down a set of stairs onto the floor. He led the way to Hyperion's stall.

A trim man in khaki trousers, sport coat, and tie approached from behind Mark and Claire. "Hello," he said with a nod. "Edgar and I were discussing strategy." He looked at Dusty. "Hyperion's as ready as I can get him."

He smiled. "You've done a great job and have my complete confidence. Travis, these are friends from Raleigh, North Carolina. Doctors Mark Thurman and Claire Hodgson."

"Nice to meet you," he said. After shaking hands he opened the gate and stepped into the stall. "Pardon me."

"Travis is Hyperion's trainer," Laura explained to Claire then turned to Travis. "Where is Edgar?"

The trainer attached a rope to the horse's bridle. "In the locker room putting on his silks. He'll be here in a minute. It's almost time for this guy to show us what he's made of."

The activity level was picking up around the stalls, and Dusty took his cue. He rubbed the horse's head and spoke a few words into his ear.

"What did you tell him?" Claire asked.

"Nothing," he said.

"He does that before each race and won't tell anyone what he says," said Laura.

"He's undefeated. It seems to be working," Mark said.

"C'mon. Let's get a drink and get ready for the race," Dusty spoke as he led the group back to the grandstand. A few minutes after they were seated, they watched a rider with a bugle dismount and walk to a microphone. The "Call to Post" blared across the grounds. As the crowd stood the post parade began. Each horse and jockey was led through the paddock gate onto the track by a horse and a uniformed track rider. The racehorses and colorfully clad jockeys paraded down the homestretch. Some walked calmly while others pranced, tugging at their lead.

"There's Edgar," Laura said, pointing to the track.

"Where?" Claire asked.

"He's wearing the blue jersey with the white X and green sleeves. We're in the number eight position."

"Is that good?"

"I don't know. He's not really a frontrunner, but the closer to the rail the better."

"Which one is Rampage?" Claire asked.

"The big black, number seven with the orange saddlecloth, right in front of Hyperion. The jock with the yellow and black silks."

"Now that's a big horse," Claire said.

"Size isn't everything," Dusty replied.

Mark raised an eyebrow. "What a beast."

"He's not that big," Dusty responded while looking through binoculars.

The starting gate was in position, and the horses were at the far end of the homestretch, making their way back. A few minutes later they passed behind the starting gate. The jockeys maneuvered their horses into position as track attendants began loading them into the blocks. Dusty took a gulp from his cup. As the last of the sixteen-horse field was coaxed into position, a hush settled over the spectators. Several seconds later a bell rang, and the gates burst open. The horses and riders lunged onto the track.

"They're off!" The voice came from the speakers. The track announcer began calling the race, but Mark couldn't hear the words over the cheering. He followed the horse with the pink saddlecloth and the rider wearing the blue jersey with the white X and green sleeves as the pack stormed by and leaned into the clubhouse turn. Ten lengths separated first from last. The horses rounded the first turn and entered the backstretch. Rampage ran second. Hyperion was jammed in the middle of the pack. They cruised down the far straightaway. Hyperion was trapped on the rail six horses back. Rampage looked comfortable on the haunches of the lead horse.

"Damn, they have him boxed!" Dusty screamed. "Get him out of there, Edgar!" Hyperion fought to move off the rail. A gap opened and the jockey guided him to the outside where he had room to maneuver. "Let him go, Edgar. Let him run!" By now they were halfway home, and Rampage was a half-length behind the leader.

"Run, boy, run!" Claire screamed. The crowd swayed and yelled. Claire's hands were pressed together in front of her mouth as she stood on her tiptoes, straining to see over those in front.

The horses were spread out over a dozen lengths. The gaps were getting larger as more horses fell off the pace. Rampage pulled even with the leader as they entered the final turn. Hyperion followed in fifth, three lengths behind. He maneuvered for an outside run and burst forward. The little bay with the white star closed the gap and was a length behind the third horse. Rampage now led. His jock looked back. The dark beast shifted sideways, almost contacting the outside horse. The challenger bore out directly in front of Hyperion then surged even with the leader. Hyperion closed the gap.

"Interference!" screamed Dusty, "He's impeding!"

Rampage moved toward the rail. His jock gave him the whip. Then it happened. The challenger jerked. The horse and rider collapsed in an explosion of brown dirt. Hyperion and Edgar catapulted over the downed horse, somersaulting to the turf. Equine and human bodies cartwheeled, coming to rest as the trailing pack scattered. Edgar rolled into a ball with his hands over his helmet.

"Oh my God!" Laura yelled.

Dusty blinked and shook his head to be certain of what he'd seen. The crowd gasped then stood hushed. Two horses were down, and several others struggled to stand. The remainder of the pack rounded the turn into the homestretch. Mark watched the jock with the blue-and-white jersey and green sleeves get to his feet and grab Hyperion's reins. The athlete resisted and tried to run, but Edgar held tight and settled him. The other horse lay still on the turf. His rider was on his hands and knees trying to stand. Men were already running to their aid as Rampage crossed the finish line victorious. Dusty left the box and hurried to the exit. Mark looked back and watched a white truck pulling a white trailer with a red cross painted on its side drive onto the track, heading toward the wreckage.

———

THE TWO ORTHOPEDIC surgeons stood looking at an x-ray screen in the racetrack medical facility. Hyperion was in the middle of the room surrounded by the veterinary staff. He stood on three legs, holding his right rear leg off the ground. A splint had been placed on the injured limb incorporating his hoof.

"That doesn't look good," Mark said as he inspected the radiographs.

"It's a pile of shit," Dusty snapped. "He's broken both the canon and pastern bones and maybe a sesamoid."

"It looks like a bag of cracked ice," Claire said. "Fragments everywhere. Is that fixable?"

"I've seen horses put down for far less severe injuries," Dusty responded."

Claire put her hand to her face. "They're going to try, right?"

"Worth and Jennifer Hobbs are the general partners. It's up to them and the doctors," Laura explained.

"What happened to the other horse?" Claire asked.

Dusty shook his head. "He was too far gone."

"They euthanized him? Out there on the track?"

Dusty nodded.

Claire closed her eyes and shook her head.

A trim middle-aged man with a mustache and rimless glasses approached them. "Drs. Rhodes, I'm Dr. Bill Herbert, the director of equine medicine at Oaklawn." He paused and shook hands. "I don't think I need to explain the severity of the situation. This is rare. We don't have the capabilities to care for Hyperion here in Hot Springs or anywhere in Arkansas for that matter. We don't treat injuries this catastrophic. Horses hurt this bad are typically euthanized."

Laura put her hands to her face and bowed her head. "Please tell me you're not going to do that."

"We're not," Herbert said. "I've spoken with Mr. and Mrs. Hobbs. At their request I've made arrangements for him to be transferred to one of the premier hospitals in the country, the Wilson Andrews Equine Research Center outside of Roanoke, Virginia. Dr. Warwick Grant is the chief of surgery at the facility. He has agreed to accept him as a patient. If anyone can save him, he can. Hyperion will be flown there tomorrow morning. Now if you'll excuse me, I have a press conference in five minutes."

Mark put his arm around Claire's shoulder and pulled her close. The operating room–style lighting had been turned on and the medical staff was making adjustments to the Kimzey Splint on Hyperion's injured leg. A veterinarian had inserted an IV into his jugular vein on the right side of his neck. The blood on his coat looked like a streak of red lipstick on a piece of mahogany. The vet wiped it away with a surgical sponge. Claire smeared a tear across her cheek.

"What a beautiful animal."

"Did Dusty tell you how he was named?" Laura asked her.

Claire shook her head.

"It was Jennifer Hobbs's idea. She got it from the white star on his forehead. In Greek mythology, Hyperion is one of the twelve children of Gaia and Uranus, the Titans of earth and sky. Hyperion was the son called the Titan of Heavenly Light. She thought the star on his forehead was a symbol of that light."

"A fitting name," Claire whispered.

"So much promise," Mark said. "Like Barbaro." He felt a tap on his shoulder and turned his head. Dusty stood next to him.

"Can I have a word with both of you? Away from the press." He started walking through the crowded room. Mark and Claire followed. He went through an exit door and down the pathway to the fence bordering the track. The stands were almost empty as the last race fans headed to their cars. Attendants were picking up trash in the grandstand. A tractor pulling a harrow went by, grooming the track for tomorrow's training runs. Dusty leaned on the railing. He pulled a flask from his coat pocket, unscrewed the top, and took a long tug. He offered it to Mark and Claire, who both declined. "You two know as well as I that unless a miracle happens, Hyperion will die. Even if everything goes perfect in surgery next week, all we can hope for is a fused hind leg. Then we have to pray he doesn't develop laminitis in his other hooves. The best-case scenario is he'll be put out to pasture for stud fees. His racing career is over. Hell, he'll never run again." He took another drink from the flask, put the top back on, and slipped it back into his coat pocket. "I swear Rampage swerved into that horse on purpose. Bastard."

"I'm sorry. It's a tragedy," Mark said. Claire remained silent.

Dusty looked out over the track. "Maybe not. You two might be Hyperion's miracle. I've followed your research and read your latest articles. I watched the Broadcast Med video of the surgery where you rebuilt that guy's leg. He was walking on it in a couple of days and was healed in a few weeks. If that could be done for Hyperion, you could save him."

"I don't know, Dust. We've never tried anything with an equine model. There would be a lot of obstacles."

Claire turned her head and looked up. "I've never cultured equine stem cells."

"You can do it. That can't be much of a problem for the world's leading expert."

"It's not that easy, but not impossible," Claire responded.

Mark gripped the seat in front of him and stood up. "I don't know. He weighs over a thousand pounds, for God's sake. We've never dealt with those types of stresses. Would the graft be strong enough?"

After a moment, Claire answered, "I need to speak with Evelyn about that."

Mark looked at her. "I'm pretty damn sure we haven't tested bone graft strength on subjects that big."

"That doesn't mean it won't hold up," Claire replied.

"Can we talk about this later?" Mark answered.

"This could be an opportunity," she said. "What do we stand to lose?"

"Just our reputations," Mark replied.

"My gut feeling is that we should give it a shot. The odds are long, but this horse, this beautiful creature, has no chance without us. I vote we try it."

"Who's going to pay for it?"

"Let me worry about that," Dusty assured them.

Claire looked at Mark. "What do you say, mate?"

"I said we'll talk about this later." He looked at her and smiled.

"C'mon, don't be a blouse."

His brow furrowed as he met her stare. She had an irresistible force over which he had little control. He turned to Dusty. "The veterinarians may not want any help. There are a lot of technical obstacles. We can't give you an answer right now. Please, try to understand."

"What do your partners want to do?" asked Claire.

"I'm not sure, I haven't discussed it with anyone," said Dusty. "I wanted to run it by you two first."

"Mark has a point," Claire said. "Dr. Grant and his staff at the Wilson Andrews Center have to be fully cooperative. We can't very well barge in and take over their medical plan."

"I'll talk it over with Mr. and Mrs. Hobbs. Please consider it. I know it's risky and the odds are long, but there's no alternative. If you say no, we might as well put him down."

"Give us twenty-four hours to figure this out," Claire said. Mark remained silent.

Dusty began walking back to the medical treatment room with them following behind. "Let me introduce you to Worth and Jennifer."

THREE

MONDAY, MARCH 20TH

Stem Cell Research and Regenerative Medicine Laboratory, Durham, North Carolina

MARK ENTERED Claire's office on the fourth floor of the Althouse Medical Research Building and sat in the wooden chair with the Stanford University seal engraved across the crown. "Sorry I'm late. I got here as fast as I could. What's the emergency?"

Claire looked up and frowned. "We've got problems."

His smile disappeared as he sat perched on the chair with elbows on knees. "You're leaving me for Martin?"

Dimples appeared in her cheeks as she looked over her glasses. "I'm being serious."

"So am I." He leaned to one side and caught the crumpled sheet of paper that came whizzing like a curveball from across the desk.

"Dr. Mile is an outstanding department chairman and supporter of our research. He's a perfect gentleman."

"I know what he'd like to support."

"There is no personal interest."

"He wears a toupee."

"He does not. Mark Thurman, are you that insecure?"

He leaned back with his hands behind his head and smiled. "He has a schoolboy crush on you . . . it's embarrassing."

"You don't trust me?"

"Of course, but you don't know him like I do."

"I think I'm a pretty good judge of character," she said. "I can handle myself around men, so don't patronize me."

"I wouldn't do that."

"You're trying."

Mark sat up straight. "And I thought we were getting along so well."

"We are. At least, I think so."

"Then what's the problem?"

"It has nothing to do with our relationship." She swiveled in her desk chair to face the computer sitting on her credenza. A file opened and the screen filled with histology slides in shades of pink and blue of varying density. "These are the problem."

"Histology slides?"

She nodded. "They were prepared this morning. They're biopsy specimens from one of our subjects. Stephen Sayre obtained them last Friday."

"From Morgan Island?"

She nodded and clicked on an image. "See anything unusual?"

He walked around the desk and looked over her shoulder. "Should I? They're bone samples."

"Look close." She magnified an area of a slide filled with a dense cluster of dark blue dots.

"Pleomorphic anaplastic cells."

She nodded. "Tons of irregular cells at the bone graft site."

He leaned over and focused his gaze on the darkest area. The wide variation of cell shapes combined with bizarre cell nuclei and bits of new bone formation made it an easy call. One he was familiar with. "Osteosarcoma," he murmured.

"I thought you'd recognize it. It's a high-grade osteogenic sarcoma. Meghan brought these to me this morning. She's been analyzing biopsies from a patient we did two years ago. Dr. Sayre noticed another one limping last week."

"That would be from the first experiment . . . there've been others?"

She raised an index finger and continued. "He captured him and brought him to the lab at Yemassee for x-rays and biopsies. The tissue samples arrived yesterday, and the slides were ready this morning."

Mark pinched the stubble on his chin while staring at the image. "This is from a subject we treated two years ago?"

She nodded.

"Show me the x-rays."

She brought up another window displaying the image of a femur, much smaller than one from a human. The bone had an expanded half-inch area in the middle of the shaft that looked like a black hole. Thin white rays radiated from the lesion, penetrating the surrounding soft tissues like a sunburst. Several tiny cracks in the outer layer of bone interrupted its otherwise smooth surface.

"Damn. That looks bad. Exploding bone."

"This poor bloke has been suffering. It's aggressive and probably metastatic," she said, pointing to the cracks in the bone's cortex.

"Thousands of monkeys live on that island. Have only our patients been affected?" Mark rubbed his right thigh and remembered his experience with bone cancer. It was a nightmare he preferred to forget.

Claire watched the motion of his hand. "It's probably a weird coincidence."

"How many others?"

"A few, so far, but Stephen says they're improving. It's strange. They initially looked as bad as this one, but they're acting normal now."

"How many?"

Claire looked at the screen. "This is number eleven."

"A dozen?"

"Almost."

"There's no coincidence. What in the world is going on?"

Claire clasped her hands together on her desk and leaned forward. "We may have caused osteosarcoma in our subjects."

"Why am I just now hearing about this?"

"I didn't want to say anything until I was sure."

"A dozen tumors and you weren't sure?"

"Eleven . . . I didn't want to scare you," she said.

"Too late for that. We must have over a hundred research animals down there."

"One hundred and forty-four, to be exact."

"Lord, have mercy. Have they noticed any more limping?"

"This is the only new case we've come across since last week. Let's hope it stays that way."

"Since last week? Almost ten percent of our patients are affected. What a damn disaster."

"He was the fourteenth subject in our first experimental group."

"What about the other experiments?"

Claire nodded. "There have been several from the other trials, too."

Mark raked his fingers through his hair and let out a deep breath. "We caused this?"

"It's possible. I hate to think about it, but we have to. I'll call Sayre for an update this afternoon."

Mark looked at his watch and returned to the chair. "When is Dusty supposed to call?"

"He's late already."

"I hate to disappoint him," Mark said.

"You won't."

"What are you saying? You really think we can save Hyperion?"

"I know we can," Claire answered.

"We can't treat him after what you just showed me. We have to fix that problem first."

"We will. Have faith."

Mark crossed his arms. "Sometimes your confidence borders on arrogance. You know that?"

"I can't help it."

"Well, I disagree. We can't do this. It's too risky. Our methods may be causing one of the worst types of cancer."

"We don't know that," Claire retorted. "And we know for a fact that our methods heal fractures so fast we might save Hyperion's life."

"There are too many unknowns."

She shook her head. "It's not too risky, and we have nothing to lose."

"Do you have any idea what you're talking about? If Hyperion can't bear weight on all four legs in two or three weeks, he'll develop laminitis.

"I know."

"His hooves will start separating from his legs. There's no cure."

"I know what laminitis is."

"It's what killed Barbaro and Secretariat."

Claire nodded. "That's my point. If we don't help, he's going to die."

"We're not ready. Even if it works he could end up with osteosarcoma."

"Listen to me. We can heal his fracture. Meghan and I have been working on this. Culturing equine cells isn't much different from culturing other mammalian cells. I know we can do it. She's running experimental trials as we speak."

"What about bone graft strength? A thousand-pound horse will crush it as soon as it stands. Even if it holds his weight while standing, think about the pressure across the graft at a full gallop. The bone graft won't tolerate that."

"I disagree. I've discussed this with Evelyn. She thinks we can do it."

"What does Heinricht know?" Mark immediately regretted his words.

Claire rolled her eyes and looked toward the ceiling. "You're a bloody wimp. If anyone in the world knows how strong Bioglass bone graft is, it's Evelyn Heinricht. She says it's strong enough to support the weight. They've created bone blocks that have withstood over five thousand pounds of pressure. Plus, we just need the fracture to heal; we're not replacing any major segments."

"Two and half tons, really?"

"Yes, really." She stood up, crossed her arms in front of her chest, and walked toward him.

"What about cancer? What if he ends up with osteosarc?"

"We'll figure out how to prevent it."

"I don't believe this." He stood and began pacing.

"You better start believing it 'cause we're doing this. Now, when we talk to Dusty and Dr. Grant, you're going to smile and we're going to tell them to get ready because we're coming to save that horse. If you're not on board, now's the time to tell me. I'm doing it myself. With or without you."

Mark looked at the floor and rubbed his forehead.

"*And* I just might take Martin up on that dinner invitation."

"Now you've done it, Dr. Hodgson. You just crossed the line." Mark glared down at her.

"What are you going to do about it?"

He burst out laughing. "A bloody wimp? You really think so?"

Just then Claire's computer screen flickered and an image of Dusty Rhodes appeared. His voice came from the speakers. "Hello, Mark? Claire? Is anyone there?"

Claire leaned close and whispered, "Don't disappoint me." She returned to her chair facing the computer screen, pushed her glasses up her nose, and entered a password. "Mark and I are here. Can you see us? We can see you fine."

"Yes. I can see and hear you. It's a good connection. We're waiting on the Hobbses." Another man appeared next to him on the screen. "I'm with Dr. Warwick Grant," Dusty said. "He's the chief of surgery here at the Wilson Andrews Equine Research Center. I've tried to give him some background regarding your work, but I'm certain I didn't do it justice."

Another window appeared on the screen, and Hyperion's majority owners, Worth and Jennifer Hobbs, settled into their seats. "It looks like we're all accounted for. Any video or audio problems?" No one responded. "All right, let's begin." Dusty made introductions and started the discussion.

Claire moved over as Mark pulled up a chair next to her in front of the screen. "Dr. Grant, did you get a chance to read the articles I forwarded?" she asked.

"I did. Thank you. I wasn't aware so much progress had been made in three-dimensional tissue bioprinting."

"Excuse me," Dusty interrupted. "Not all of us have a medical background. Claire and Mark, can you give Worth and Jennifer an overview of your research?"

"Of course, I'd love to," Claire responded.

"Remember, we're businesspeople," Jennifer said.

"If I get carried away, stop me. My research background is in cell biology, and I specialize in stem cells. These are precursor cells that haven't been biologically programmed to turn into a specific cell type. Stem cells have the potential to become any type of tissue in the body once they are set on a course of development. We call this cell differentiation. I've been studying this process for a long time. About five years ago, we figured out how to make a stem cell mature into a cell that makes bone. These are called osteoblasts."

"She also figured out how to make artificial bone in any desired shape using 3D biological printers," Mark added.

"What's that?" Jennifer asked.

"Specialized printers that are similar to commercial 3D printers that print plastic or metal objects, but instead, Dr. Hodgson's print with biological cells and fluid, creating living tissue."

"You're kidding?" Jennifer responded.

"She's serious. It really happens," Mark told them. "A couple of years ago, Dr. Hodgson gave a lecture on bioprinting at the medical school where we work. Afterward, I approached her with some ideas about a project. I'm an orthopedic trauma surgeon and was frustrated with treating complex fractures in patients with missing pieces of bone. It's a huge problem. I saw many injuries like this when I was on active duty as a military surgeon in Afghanistan and Iraq. I asked if she could make real bone that I could implant into fractures in trauma patients."

Claire spoke up, "I told him I'd try. He convinced me it was possible, and we started working together." She looked at Mark and smiled. "Then, we got the idea that if we increased the number of osteoblasts in the printed bone graft, we might be able to speed up fracture healing.

"We began using rhesus monkeys as experimental subjects. The National Institutes of Health has a colony on a private island north of Beaufort, South Carolina, called Morgan Island. They gave us permission to use a group of them and funded a large part of our early experiments.

"As you might imagine, the Departments of Defense and Veterans Affairs have also supported our research efforts."

"With the help of an NIH veterinarian, Stephen Sayre, and his assistants, we created an experimental model using the femur bone. We treated the animals with our 3D bioprinted bone methods, and they healed remarkably fast."

"How fast?" asked Grant.

"The first subject healed in weeks, instead of months," Claire answered. "Later, we tweaked the formula until healing time was accelerated from weeks to days."

"You didn't hurt them, did you?" Jennifer asked.

"Our subjects? None of us would have intentionally done that," said Claire. "Dr. Sayre used modern veterinary anesthesia protocols during the surgical procedures. After their operation, they were given pain medications and antibiotics, just like you or I would have been treated."

Grant leaned closer to the screen. "Excuse me, did you say days? You're telling me the bones healed that fast?"

Mark nodded. "They would climb trees and jump branches as soon as we released them back onto the island."

"Have you tried this on anything other than monkeys?" Dr. Grant questioned.

"Last year, we started human trials. Thus far, we have almost twenty subjects. Fracture weight-bearing healing time on lower extremity fractures has been lowered to an average of four point five days," Claire said.

"Remember, these are still early results," Mark warned. "We don't have long-term follow-up, but the early findings are encouraging."

"What's weight-bearing healing time?" Worth asked.

"The number of days until x-rays show adequate healing and the patient can walk without pain," Claire replied.

"Let me get this straight," Grant spoke up. "You're saying someone with a fractured leg and missing bone can be healed in *less than a week?*"

"Without infection or complications," Mark added. "We present our latest results next month at a national conference. It should create quite a stir."

"I don't believe it," Grant said.

"How does it work?" Jennifer asked.

"It's a three-step process," Claire explained. "Mark brings me biopsy samples from the patient. I isolate the stem cells and culture them in the laboratory for a couple of days. After that, I put the cells in the 3D tissue bioprinter and program it to create the desired segment of bone. When it's completed, Mark implants it into the fracture site using standard orthopedic surgical techniques. Also, we prime the patient's body with infusions of anabolic drugs and antibiotics. Patients have actually walked on their injured leg twenty-four hours after surgery."

"Will it work for Hyperion?" Worth asked anxiously.

"We've never tried it on horses," Mark said.

"But there's no reason it shouldn't," Claire said, looking at Mark. She pinched his thigh and his eyes widened. "If it works on monkeys and humans, there's no reason it shouldn't work on horses."

"Except the weight of a Thoroughbred horse is five or six times that of a human," Grant cautioned.

"True. We don't know if the bioprinted bone graft will withstand that amount of stress," said Mark.

"But we think it will," added Claire.

"Have you seen Hyperion's x-rays?" Grant asked. "The degree of comminution in the canon and pastern bones is shocking. If he weren't a Kentucky Derby contender, he would have been put down on the track. How could you possibly fix those fractures without them falling apart as soon as he stands up? Horses have to stand. They can't lie around in bed for six weeks."

"Did you say some of your patients were walking a day after surgery?" Dusty questioned.

"Several have. If you can keep Hyperion off his feet for a couple of days after the operation, it might work," Claire answered.

"We have a new anesthesia pool recovery system," Grant said. "We could keep him sedated and floating awhile. Maybe for a day. One of our researchers is working on a computerized suspensory sling system for horses designed to keep them off injured limbs. We could probably use it."

"It's still a long shot," Mark cautioned.

"I say we try it," Worth said. "There's not much to lose."

"We owe Hyperion that much," Jennifer added.

"Then we need to get started," Grant said.

"All right, then, all in favor?" Dusty questioned the group.

"Aye," came the unanimous reply.

"Any opposed?" Claire asked as she looked at Mark. No one responded.

"All right. We're all in agreement. Step one," Claire said, "biopsy samples. Mark and Dr. Grant need to harvest bone marrow from Hyperion. It has to be collected and transported back to my lab within a six-hour time frame. Can this be done?"

"I can have the horse and facilities ready by this afternoon," Grant said.

"Can you be at the Raleigh-Durham airport in two hours?" Worth asked.

Mark looked at Claire. "Let me make some calls. I'll need to clear my schedule for a few days."

"Get your equipment and meet me at the general aviation terminal at noon."

"Okay. We can start processing the samples this evening," Claire said.

"I'll see you at the airport, Dr. Thurman. We'll eat on the plane," Worth said. The call ended and Mark and Claire faced each other.

"You got your wish," he told her.

"It's the chance to save a life and pioneer a way to save hundreds or maybe thousands of horses every year."

"Or it becomes a distraction and a humiliating failure," Mark said.

"You really have to stop being so negative."

"I'm being realistic. We need to stay focused on current projects. Those histology slides you showed me suggest problems we don't understand. All I'm saying is we don't need another obligation that will divert attention from where it should be focused."

"It's too late. We have a horse to save." She reached her arms around his neck and kissed him. Her warm, soft lips parted. He pulled her to him, pressing their bodies together. A stir went through him like a shock. She broke off the kiss and leaned her head back, then touched his lips with her fingertip. "Now, I'm going to check on the cell cultures. You need to get the bioreactor ready." She turned and headed to the lab.

THE GLEAMING white-and-blue Gulfstream G550 was waiting when Mark walked through the terminal door onto the tarmac. The soft whine of the twin turbines indicated the aircraft was ready to leave. In his right hand he carried a red twelve-inch square container that looked like a cooler with a white cross on each side. It was an incubator, also known as a bioreactor, with an inside environment mimicking cellular conditions. The device was designed for maintaining the viability of biological samples and was constructed to withstand a ten-foot fall. In it he would store Hyperion's tissue specimens and transport them back to Claire's lab later that afternoon. Worth Hobbs waved from the jet doorway as Mark and the pilot approached the plane. The pilot stood aside and Mark ascended the steps.

"Welcome aboard, Dr. Thurman. Allow me to secure that for you." Hobbs took the bioreactor and handed it to the cabin steward, who stowed it aft. Mark settled into a soft beige leather seat and fastened his seatbelt. Hobbs sat facing him on the other side of a varnished maple table with walnut inlay. The elderly gentleman smiled, revealing fine pearly teeth and deep crow's feet at the corner of each eye behind his wire-rimmed glasses. The white hair and beard needed trimming. He reminded Mark of the British actor who played the industrialist-financier in *Jurassic Park*. The resemblance was striking. *What was his name?* The cabin steward returned.

"May I get you something to drink?"

"Diet Coke, if you have it," Mark requested.

"Water for me," Hobbs said then looked at Mark. "The quest to save Hyperion begins."

"Sir Gawain had it easier."

Hobbs chuckled, remembering the legend. "There's no Green Knight to contend with."

"It's worse. We have to save a mortally wounded horse."

"One that's depending on all your skills," said Hobbs.

"He'll get all I've got. However, there are no guarantees."

"Of course."

The steward returned with the drinks then took his seat. Mark looked up at the video screen above the windows across the aisle. It displayed their highlighted route on a map of the United States. The engines began to wind up, and the jet rolled away from the terminal. The plane taxied onto the runway, and after several minutes, it was in position for takeoff.

"We're number two and should be in the air in a few minutes," said a voice over the intercom.

"Hold on to your drink," Hobbs said.

Mark looked out the window and thought about the next few hours. With luck he would be back before dinner. The engines surged while the brakes held the plane in place. A few seconds later the aircraft began to move forward. Then, it accelerated like a fighter jet catapulted from a carrier.

"Whoa," Mark said as he was pressed firmly into his seat. The plane sprinted down the runway and the landscape blurred. His glass slid across the table like a hockey puck. He grabbed it just before it landed in his lap. In a matter of seconds the wheels were up and Raleigh was receding. "Thanks for the warning," he said, raising the glass.

"Cheers," said Hobbs.

"Good afternoon, folks. This is your captain. We'll be leveling off at thirty-five thousand feet and cruise at five hundred knots. That should get us to Roanoke in about twenty minutes. The weather service predicts a smooth ride."

Hobbs placed his elbows on the table and leaned forward. "What do you know about the Wilson Andrews Center?"

Mark replaced his drink on the table. "Never heard of it until last weekend."

"I think you'll be impressed. It's a state-of-the-art equine medical facility on two hundred acres of land outside Roanoke. It's the newest addition to the Virginia-Maryland College of Veterinary Medicine. Mildred Wilson and James Andrews wanted to design a facility that would surpass the most modern equine hospitals in the world. The operating rooms, patient wards, and research laboratories have been spared no expense."

"How well do you know Dr. Grant?" Mark asked. "Hyperion is his patient. If this works, you're asking him to let us steal his spotlight. Is he going to get bent out of shape?"

Hobbs sat back in his chair and laughed. "If it works? Do you have doubts?"

"A few, but Claire is a genius. She'll get it worked out."

"Then, don't worry about Warwick. He's a practical man. He wants what's best for his patients and the institution. If Hyperion is saved, we all benefit. He'll support you with every resource available."

"Don't kid yourself, Mr. Hobbs. Academic ego wars are brutal. I've seen university program directors who make dictators look like Eagle Scouts."

"Grant has little to lose. He knows your methods are the only chance for Hyperion. You and Dr. Hodgson are taking some of the heat off him. Without you Hyperion will, in all likelihood, end up like Barbaro. If you're successful he comes out smelling like roses . . . Kentucky Derby roses."

"He still might end up like Barbaro."

"At least he'll have better odds. Grant's ego won't get in the way. He has a lot to gain. If you and Dr. Hodgson can teach him your techniques, he could revolutionize equine orthopedic surgery. Fractures in horses *are* mortal injuries. Your methods could save hundreds or thousands of horses every year."

"I get it. Still, it's a long shot. Even if the surgery is successful, you can't give a horse post-op instructions or expect it to obey a physical therapy plan. It can't be reasoned with. It's a prey animal that instinctively runs from any perceived threat. You can't ask it to stay off its broken leg. It wants to put full weight on it without a thought. Full weight is a half ton supported by four twigs. This isn't going to be easy."

"No one said it would be. I'm just grateful you're willing to try," Hobbs said.

"For the record, if it were up to me, we wouldn't be sitting here. Thank Dr. Hodgson. She's the one with the faith and conviction. I think it's crazy."

Mark leaned back and looked out the window as the plane descended into a cloudbank and a minute later emerged a thousand feet above the ground. In the distance he could see a city. The houses and roads became larger as they decreased altitude. Finally, the runway was below them and the plane touched down with an almost imperceptible bump. It taxied to the terminal and the ground crew secured the wheels. The steward brought Mark the bioreactor and opened the cabin door.

"My car is waiting," Hobbs said as he put his phone into his pants pocket. A man wearing sunglasses and a dark suit resembling a Secret Service agent greeted them at the jetport terminal entrance.

"Good afternoon, Mr. Hobbs."

"Hello, Alex."

"Any bags?"

"Just this." He took the bioreactor from Mark and handed it to the driver. They walked through the building and exited into the afternoon sunlight. A dark sedan was waiting at the curb. Alex held the door while Hobbs and Mark entered the back seat. Then, he opened the trunk and placed the incubator inside. In a few minutes Mark saw a large green sign indicating they were merging onto Interstate 81. The landscape swept past as the car was driven away from the city. Small green buds were sprouting on tree branches, indicating the Virginia countryside was awakening from winter. They passed an exit for Salem and continued southwest.

"We'll arrive in a few minutes. The center is located on land that was owned by Mildred Wilson's family. She donated it and Mr. Andrews put up a sizable portion of the funds for construction of the main medical buildings. The hospital was completed two years ago and is modeled after the New Bolton Center outside of Philadelphia and the Rood & Riddle Equine Hospital in Lexington." White fencing lined both sides of the roadway after the car turned off the interstate. They stopped at the security gate for a moment then continued.

A large three-story building with a glass front and stone porte cochère was straight ahead. The car stopped underneath and the men exited. Mark collected the bioreactor. As he closed the car trunk, he saw Warwick Grant striding toward them through the front doors. He was dressed in jeans, work boots, and a denim shirt covered with a full-length starched white lab coat. The veterinarian stood about six feet tall, and Mark estimated his weight at just under two hundred pounds. His angular face was marked with deep laugh lines. His skin was a permanent rich leather tan acquired from years of outdoor labor. The narrow-set piercing glacial blue eyes were highlighted with tear troughs and chiseled crow's feet. A salt-and-pepper crew cut covered his scalp, and his overall appearance reminded Mark of an aging rodeo cowboy who never met a bronc he couldn't break. All that was missing was the hat.

"Gentlemen, so good of you to come." Grant extended his right hand, and Hobbs shook it. Mark switched the incubator to his left and did the same. "How was the flight?"

"It would be easy to get used to a private jet," Mark answered.

"Worth and Jennifer live in a world a lot different from ours. Let's go to my office and we can discuss the surgical plan. I've arranged for the biopsy procedure to take place in about an hour. Is there anything special that you need?"

"Just a knife and a few basic instruments to collect the sample. I need a few cc's of bone marrow. The collection vessels and culture medium are in the bioreactor." Mark held up the red container. "Have the CT scans been done?"

Grant nodded. "Did them this morning using the new robotic 3D CT scanner."

"Excellent, both legs?" Mark asked.

"We followed your protocol to a T."

"Perfect. The fracture comminution is so extensive we may need to create a large piece in order to replace the small fragments. Hyperion's not making this easy for us."

"Why both legs?" Hobbs asked.

"The uninjured one serves as a template so our computer can tell what the bones should look like," Mark said.

"If you'll excuse me, I'll let you two do your work. I'll be back in a couple of hours," Hobbs said and returned to his car.

Grant led the way down a long corridor that passed through an open cafeteria and into a wing of offices. They walked up a flight of stairs and entered Grant's corner suite.

"Nice," Mark said, admiring the view overlooking the green fields partitioned with white fencing.

"Directorship has its advantages. Something to drink?"

"Sure."

"Water or soda?"

"Water's fine."

He went over to a small refrigerator built into the cherry cabinetry and removed a plastic bottle. As he turned around, a five-by-seven framed photograph fell from the countertop to the floor. Mark reached over and retrieved it. It was a picture of a younger Grant and a boy of about ten. "You and your son?"

Grant nodded, taking the photograph. "Many years ago."

"Nice buck."

"Twelve points. One of the biggest I've ever seen in these parts."

"Where did you get it?"

Grant smiled as he replaced the picture. "Not far from here. That was taken at a hunting cabin in Jefferson National Forest."

———————

THIRTY MINUTES later Mark followed Grant out of the surgical locker room. The scent of Timothy hay and horses contrasted with the aseptic hospital environment he was used to. They were dressed in surgical scrubs and walked into the anesthesia preoperative staging area. Hyperion stood in a stall on three hooves. His right rear limb was held off the ground protected in the Kimzey Splint. Mark watched as Grant opened the gate and approached the patient.

"He looks different. His coat still has its shine, but the fire in his eyes is looking dim."

"It's understandable," Grant replied.

Hyperion's head hung and the white patch on his forehead was no longer difficult to see. His ribs were more clearly defined. "He's lost weight. Did the pharmacy prepare the Bethesda infusions?"

"Just as you requested," said Grant. "He received the first dose an hour ago."

"The anabolic drugs are critical in order to counteract the effects of stress. It's imperative he gets adequate calories, especially protein."

"He will," Grant said.

A vet technician entered the stall and rubbed the horse's face. He administered a medication through the IV catheter protruding from his jugular vein. Grant and the tech slowly led the horse out of the stall. The metal hoof holder of the Kimzey clanged like a bell clapper on the concrete floor as the horse hobbled toward the anesthesia area. The "leg saver" splint held the hind limb in a stabilized position that transferred the horse's weight up the canon bone, bypassing the fracture. As they walked Grant turned to Mark.

"He's been prepped for surgery. We removed his shoes and cleaned his hoof. The anesthesia team washed his mouth while we were changing."

After an agonizing ten minutes the horse was in position against the well-padded wall in the anesthesia room. The anesthesiologist administered the induction agent. Several moments later, Hyperion wobbled and was allowed to slowly slide downward to the floor with five people assisting him. One carefully held the injured leg. Then, the anesthesiologist inserted an endotracheal tube four times bigger than what was typically used on humans.

"That's a damn radiator hose," Mark stared.

"A sterile one," Grant replied with a laugh.

A blood pressure cuff and EKG leads were applied. Mark watched as the splint was removed and the limb shaved and washed.

"Ready to hoist?" Grant asked the anesthesiologist.

She checked the monitors. "Whenever you are."

Mark's eyes widened as the scene unfolded. Ropes were lowered from a winch suspended from the ceiling.

"Careful, careful," said Grant. "Make sure they are firmly attached. We don't need another injured limb." The ropes were looped around the three healthy hooves, and Hyperion was slowly hoisted into the air. He hung upside down with his broken hind limb gingerly supported. After that, he was moved along the overhead rail system into the operating room and placed onto the padded six-by-eight-foot OR table. Once he was on the table, the sliding doors were shut.

"That's how we handle patients that weigh half a ton," Grant said.

Mark rubbed his chin with his index finger and thumb. "You do things totally opposite from what we do in human surgery. We bring the patient into the OR and position them on the table, and then anesthesia is induced."

Grant tied his surgical mask behind his head. "With unpredictable animals that can weigh over two thousand pounds, there's really no other way. If we brought them into the operating room before they were anesthetized, they might freak out and wreak havoc in the OR."

"The proverbial bull in the china shop."

"Exactly."

The surgeons scrubbed their hands and were gowned and gloved. Hyperion's damaged leg had been sterilely prepped and isolated with surgical drapes. The assistant stood dressed in OR attire beside a draped table. The instruments were neatly displayed like jewelry in a display case.

Grant turned toward the assisting surgeon. "Dr. Thurman, this is Roger Coleman, my chief resident."

"Pleasure to meet you." Mark extended his gloved hand.

"Glad to have you as part of the team," Coleman responded, completing the handshake.

"Roger is one of our superstar surgical residents. We're going to miss him."

"Where are you going?" Mark asked.

Grant answered the question. "I offered him an assistant professor position in the department of surgery, but I'm afraid he's been lured away from academics. He's done such a great job directing several research studies that he's been offered a lucrative position with a pharmaceutical company. We can't compete with the corporate world in terms of compensation."

Coleman remained silent.

"That's true everywhere in academics," Mark agreed.

"I suppose you're right. Let's get started." Grant requested a scalpel and cut into the swollen area of injury.

"I hate opening a closed fracture," Mark said as he watched Hyperion's blood ooze from the incision. "But I'm not sure there's any better place to harvest the bone graft."

Dr. Grant dabbed and cauterized bleeding skin vessels. "We have no choice." Coleman placed a small self-retaining retractor in the wound.

"Do you call that a Weitlaner?" Mark asked.

"Yep, you ready?" With the instrument spreading open the incision, Grant pried the fracture fragments a half inch apart. "Get your samples."

"Good Lord, that bone is stout. The cortex must be a half inch thick."

"You should try drilling through it," Grant said.

"I hope we get the chance."

"It's like drilling marble."

Mark picked up a curette from the Mayo stand and scooped half a shot glass of marrow from the core of the broken bone, then placed it in a sterile plastic specimen cup and screwed on the lid.

"That should be enough. I need one of the fracture fragments, too."

Grant looked at him and tilted his head. "What for?"

"I'm going to make a replacement part."

"But we need it to reconstruct the fracture. If you take it we'll be missing a key piece."

"Trust me, you'll get it back better than it is now. This fragment is stripped of periosteal tissue and wouldn't heal anyway. We'll bioprint a replica loaded with stem cells. If it works the way I hope it does, it'll heal like gangbusters." Mark took a pair of forceps and plucked a two-inch curved piece of bloodstained bone.

"Store your specimens and I'll close the incision," Grant instructed.

Mark transferred the bone samples into sterile containers filled with culture medium. He passed them to a nurse, who stored them safely in the bioreactor. He looked at Grant, who was rolling sterile bandages on Hyperion's leg.

"Almost ready for the pool," Grant said.

"I gotta see this."

"We've made significant improvements using the anesthesia pool recovery system over the last several years. A horse has to be brought out of anesthesia with great care. They'll kick and flail about like a lunatic trying to stand and run. Ten years ago, we'd bring a patient through a difficult surgery only to watch it damage its limbs thrashing about. I've seen uninjured legs broken and operations ruined. It was damn discouraging."

Grant finished with the post-op dressings and began ripping the sterile drapes from the surgical field. Several surgical techs lent a hand and crammed the blood-spattered material into a large trash can. Next, he replaced the Kimzey Splint and pulled off his gown and gloves. He signaled to a man standing by a control panel, who pressed the keypad. The room was filled with a low rumble, and the far wall began to slide upward like a giant garage door. A rush of warm humid air enveloped them like a tropical breeze. The smell of chlorinated pool water flooded the operating room.

"Hoist," Grant shouted over the sound of the moving wall. Mark watched as Hyperion was raised a few inches off the OR table by his hooves so that a belly sling could be slid under him. The leg shackles were removed, and Grant checked the animal. The anesthesiologist guarded the endotracheal tube like a mother protecting her baby. When Grant was satisfied, he once again signaled the man standing by the panel. Hyperion was elevated off the table, this time in an upright position with legs dangling downward, and moved toward the pool.

"You're going to lay him on that raft?" Mark asked as he moved closer to the water. The recovery system looked like an in-ground pool with dimensions roughly twenty by thirty feet and deep enough that Mark couldn't see the bottom. In the middle floated a huge rubber raft. "We used those on training missions when I was in the Navy," Mark said.

"Not like this one. Firestone engineers helped us design it."

As Mark approached, he noticed the four submerged rubber cylinders attached to the floor of the raft, one for each leg. On one end of the raft there was a large rubber bolster.

He pointed to it. "A pillow?"

"It cradles his head so we can control it and remove the endotracheal tube when it's time."

Mark looked at the sweat accumulating on his forearms and felt his scrubs starting to stick to him. "It feels like a sauna in here."

"We have to keep him warm. The water is kept close to core body temperature during a recovery." Several vet techs maneuvered the raft so it was under the unconscious Hyperion. It was raised so that his legs fit into the tubes like fingers into a glove. They guided the limbs into the leg wells and held his head as it came to rest on the rubber pad.

"How's he doing?' Grant yelled to the anesthesiologist, who was holding the respiratory tubing next to Hyperion's head.

She held her thumb up. "Perfect." The crane lowered the twelve-hundred-pound rubber-encased patient into the warm water.

Grant turned back to Mark. "Just like with humans, she'll keep oxygen flowing as she decreases the anesthetic gases."

"How long will this take?"

"We'll take our time with this one. Forty or fifty minutes. Maybe more."

"I should get these samples back to Durham," Mark said.

"Don't let me keep you. Hobbs should be waiting. When will you be back?"

"In a couple of days. I want his body primed with the anabolic infusions, and Dr. Hodgson will need the time to expand the cell cultures." They shook hands and Mark left carrying the bioreactor. As he walked to the entrance lobby to meet Worth, his phone rang. It was Dusty.

"Where are you?" he asked.

"Just leaving the Wilson Andrews Center."

"What did you think of Money?"

"What are you talking about?" Mark asked.

"That's Grant's nickname."

"Money?"

Dusty laughed. "What did you think of him?"

"Seems nice enough. What's with the name?"

"How do you think he got his position?" Dusty asked.

"I assumed he's the best equine surgeon in the country?"

"He's the best at raising funds for the institution. His colleagues refer to him as 'Money,' short for 'Grant Money.' I don't think he likes it. There are others with more intellectual and surgical skills, but this guy can turn lead into gold. He's brought in tens of millions in research funds in the last few years. He's doing some big-time cancer research with several of the pharmaceutical giants looking for their next blockbuster drug. 'Money' makes more than both of us combined, and he's worth it to the center. I wasn't thrilled when Hobbs decided to send Hyperion there."

"I don't care about the politics. I want this horse to heal," Mark said.

"His chances are a lot better with you and Claire around. Keep your eyes open, and take the knife away from him if you can. Ask him to let you do the cutting."

"How can I do that? It's his show."

"You'll figure something out. Good luck and keep me posted." They ended the call and Mark realized he was lost. A couple of vet students directed him to the front of the building, and he found Worth sitting in the lobby with his driver. They stood as he approached. Once again his mind searched his memory for the name of Hobbs's doppelgänger. He resisted the urge to retrieve his phone for a Google search. Then the synapses connected and Mark smiled. *Richard Attenborough, that's who he looks like.*

Alex took the bioreactor and led them to the car.

"EXCUSE ME, sir. Dr. Sorenson is here. Should I show him in?" Jeffery Mullion was glancing over the pages of the latest edition of *BloodHorse* magazine when his secretary opened the door to his office. It was Mullion's rule that no one entered his inner sanctum at Telos Pharmaceuticals until they were scrutinized and personally escorted by her. She was his wall. As CEO, he had the authority to make just about any rule he wanted.

"Of course, Rhonda. Show him in." Mullion put the magazine on the desk and sat up. A few moments later the door reopened and Neil Sorenson, doctor of pharmacology, his director of research and development, strode across the room. Mullion stood up.

"Good of you to come by. What do you need?"

"Congratulations on Rampage's victory."

"Thank you. He was magnificent."

"Can you spare a few minutes of your time? I've been trying to catch up with you since last week."

"Sorry, sport. Before the race I was in Paris. God, I miss it already." He smiled and adjusted his European-cut jacket. He extended his hand toward a chair. "Sit down, Neil. What's on your mind?"

"Have you seen this?" He produced a print copy of the *Journal of Tropical Medicine*.

Mullion laughed, raised his eyebrows, and glanced down at the horseracing magazine on his desk. "In case you haven't noticed, my horse is demanding a great deal of attention these days."

"I've noticed, but it's my job to keep up with this stuff."

"What's so interesting about tropical medicine?"

"This is a report about a new class of antimicrobial compounds."

Mullion drummed his fingers on the desktop. "Get to it, Neil. I'm getting bored."

"The lead investigator, Dr. Meera Jindal, is reporting on a substance with long-acting antibiotic properties derived from a plant source. Thus far, it's found only in a rain forest somewhere in Panama. I think she's discovered what we've been after."

Mullion stopped drumming.

Sorenson continued. "She's developed an antibiotic that lasts for over two weeks and kills the nastiest bacteria we know of, including MRSA."

"Do you have any idea what that's worth?"

"Of course I do. Get this, she's an ex-student of Plunkett."

The CEO blinked. "Our consultant?"

"Dr. William Plunkett. He was the chairman of her PhD committee at Stanford," Sorenson said.

"So, have him talk to her." Mullion stood and placed his palms on the desk, leaning forward. "Hire her, for God's sake."

Sorenson removed his glasses and rubbed his eyes. "Give me some credit. I'm working on it. Plunkett says he'll talk to her. He says he knows her well. Apparently they had a relationship for a few years that was more than just professional."

Mullion walked over to the large window and gazed at the Philadelphia panorama. He stood in silence for a moment. "They *had* a relationship? You're saying whatever was going on between them, it's over?"

"That's my understanding."

"That's probably not good."

Sorenson's fingertips drummed the arms of his chair. "Yes, sir, but he says she owes him her career. He gave her the break she needed a few years ago."

"In exchange for what? His attention?"

"Hell hath no fury . . ."

Mullion pivoted away from the window and faced his guest. "Yes, I agree, but money talks. Make her an offer."

"I'd love to, but she's handcuffed by an ironclad noncompete clause in her contract. She's at some godforsaken jungle laboratory on a sabbatical funded by grants from the Smithsonian and a start-up company called Electra Pharmaceuticals."

"Probably a bunch of idealist yahoos. They'll want to give the damn drug away."

"This could be the blockbuster Telos needs. It would be the perfect addition to our antibiotic pipeline." Sorenson picked up another journal and thumbed to a marked page. "There's more. This is an abstract reporting on the drug's use in another study. It was being tested in clinical trials to prevent postoperative infections in monkeys. The preliminary results are spectacular. No infections even after the animals were released back into the wild for months."

"Who did the study?"

"The lead author is Dr. Claire Hodgson at Duke University. Her team has started human trials, and they have a couple more ongoing projects."

"Can we hire *her*?"

Sorenson shook his head. "Hodgson is one of the world's leading experts in synthetic biology. She's too well established to risk getting her hands dirty."

"We need that formula," Mullion said. "Get it. I don't care what it takes."

"Let's start small . . . see if we can turn one of their lab techs."

"A spy . . . I like it." Mullion returned to his desk and sat down. "We need information. Contact some of the technicians in Hodgson's lab. See if they're interested in coming to work for us at a substantially higher salary. Be sure you're discreet."

"I've been working on that. The latest papers published by Hodgson and her group acknowledge the work of a histology technician. A young man named Robert Ard. I checked his social media accounts and had some of our people investigate his background. He wants to go to medical school *and* he's broke."

Mullion smiled. "Excellent. Find out what he knows. If he has information, make him an offer." He tilted slightly in his high-backed chair and placed his feet on the desktop.

"You have something in mind?"

"A male in his early twenties. What else but the timeless temptations?"

Sorenson laughed and rubbed his hands together. "Cash and sex."

"Exactly. Keep me updated."

FOUR

MONDAY, MARCH 20TH

Stem Cell Research and Regenerative Medicine Laboratory, Durham, North Carolina

THE FAINT SOUNDS of a pianist playing the *Goldberg Variations* greeted Mark as he pushed open the door labeled Department of Stem Cell Research and Regenerative Medicine. He proceeded down a short hallway lined with framed covers of *Scientific American* and *Nature*. The volume of the aria increased as he strode past an empty administration office and entered the next door on his left. The music of Bach filled the empty spaces of the main laboratory. He stopped and glanced around.

"Hello? Anyone here?" After several seconds without a response he walked to the back of the room, passing bench tops crowded with scientific instruments, and stopped at the area where researchers had their cubicles. He peered over a chest-high partition. A young woman occupant was absorbed reading an article. Her ivory skin contrasted with thick ebony hair twisted into a tight bun. An ink pen stuck from the neat bundle like a knitting needle from a ball of black yarn. Her left hand cupped her chin as the right manipulated a mouse. She was hunched close to a computer screen, and the collar of her starched white lab coat came almost to her ear. He noticed the gold earring dangling from her lobe lying against the white cloth, gleaming like a newly minted coin. He tapped on the barrier and cleared his throat. "Meghan." The woman sat bolt upright and turned her head.

"Oh, Dr. Thurman. You startled me."

"Sorry, I didn't mean to sneak up on you. That must be some article."

"It's the latest from Evelyn Heinricht's lab. Dr. Hodgson is one of the coauthors. They're proposing a method to bioprint chondrocytes into a cartilage matrix."

"I'm familiar with the work," he said, then smiled.

"Of course, you're one, too." Her cheeks turned a light pink. "An author, I mean."

"It would be something to create a joint surface. We're not far from it."

"It would cure arthritis," Meghan said.

"In some cases, maybe."

"I've heard Dr. Heinricht's learning new techniques while she's visiting the University of Edinburgh. Stuff about physeal structure and bioprinting articular cartilage. She wants to bring them back to WFIRM." She pronounced the acronym *W-firm*, the Wake Forest Institute for Regenerative Medicine.

"That would be great, but it's a ways off. Right now, we have a few other irons in the fire."

"Claire . . . Dr. Hodgson mentioned the accident."

"And the tumor problem," said Mark.

"That too," she said, nodding. "We should have more slides soon."

"Keep up the strong work, and you're going to be able to write your ticket when you finish Claire's fellowship."

Meghan flashed a grin. "I couldn't have asked for a better postdoc advisor. She's the best."

Mark chuckled. "You're lucky." He held up the red container. "I brought the biopsy samples. You think horse cells will behave like humans and monkeys?"

"According to what I've seen thus far. There's no reason they shouldn't." She stood and moved out of her cubicle. "It's a mammalian cell. The genetic code is a little different, but the membranes and organelles are the same. Let's find out."

She took the bioreactor from Mark and they proceeded across the room and entered the adjacent lab. The space felt cool, and a faint chemical antiseptic odor greeted them. On the other side of the room next to a cell culture hood stood Claire talking to a young man. A loose white lab coat that extended almost to her knees covered her tall lissome frame. She held an auto pipette in her right hand. Mark recognized the technician from previous visits but couldn't remember his name. They stopped talking and turned toward them as he and Meghan approached.

"The mission was a success," Meghan said, lifting the bioreactor to waist height.

"Excellent," Claire said as she replaced the pipette under the hood. "Let's get the samples cooking. I've just finished making a new batch of bio-ink."

"What's that?" the technician asked.

"This stuff," said Claire, holding up a half-full liter-sized Erlenmeyer flask.

"The extracellular fluid we use to culture the cells," Meghan added.

"In the bioreactor, you'll find a fragment of Hyperion's bone from the fracture site," Mark said, looking at Meghan. "Can you print a copy of it? I want to implant it at the next surgery."

"What are you thinking? Like a seed?" Claire asked.

"More like a catalyst, a fragment with a high concentration of osteoblasts to act as a nidus for fracture healing," Mark said. "Did the CT scans arrive?"

Claire nodded. "The printers are programmed. We can make

reproductions of all the fractured bones or fragments. Just tell me which ones you want. I'll scan this one and add it to the program. We'll print some trial samples on Wednesday or Thursday."

"I'll let Grant know so he can prepare the patient and the OR. I'm thinking Friday may be best for the surgery. Hyperion needs more priming with the Bethesda therapy. He's looking depressed, stressed, and atrophied."

"Poor boy," Claire said. "It amazes me how fast unused muscle wastes away."

Mark crossed his arms and cleared his throat. "With total-body inactivity, skeletal muscle strength and mass can be lost at up to two percent a day."

Meghan raised an eyebrow and looked over her glasses.

He noted her expression and raised an index finger. "But there's a limit, and those losses slow down drastically after two weeks and max out once you hit a reduction of about twenty-five to thirty percent. In orthopedics we call this *disuse atrophy*."

Meghan smiled and gave a golf clap. "Bravo, Dr. Thurman."

Mark winked and gave a deep bow.

"That sure seems like a lot," said the young man standing next to Claire.

Mark turned to him and extended his hand. "It is, and it's been extensively studied in space flight research. Pardon me, I don't think we've met."

"I'm Robert Ard." He looked to be in his midtwenties, about Meghan's age. His most distinguishing characteristic was a bulbous shiny nose pitted with a field of black ink dots. His thin black beard had patches where hair refused to grow. Three inches of untamed curly black hair sprouted from his head like sheep's wool. He pushed up his round wire-rimmed glasses and shook Mark's hand with the grip of a grandmother.

"You've never met?" Claire asked.

Mark shrugged. "I don't think so. Have we?"

"Nope," Ard replied.

"Robert is one of our laboratory technicians on loan from the pathology department. He specializes in histology. He's made most of our specimen slides for the last year," Claire explained. "Robert's been working here while trying to get into medical school. I'll hate to lose him when he gets accepted."

"I've admired your technical work for a while. Excellent job with the H&E slides. It's good to finally put a face to a name," Mark said. "Good luck with med school. You should be hearing something soon. This is about the time of year the acceptance notices come out."

"Nothing so far. I'm keeping my fingers crossed," Ard said.

"I'm glad you'll be around for a few more months. We're going to need your talent," said Claire. She turned toward Mark. "I spoke with Dr. Sayre while you were in Virginia. He's found several more monkeys that are showing signs of limping. I'm driving to Beaufort tonight. Want to come?"

Furrows appeared in Mark's forehead and his eyebrows moved closer. "Let me make a phone call. My clinic and surgical schedule should have been cleared for the rest of the week, but I want to check with Ryan." He walked toward Claire's office and placed his phone to his ear. A few minutes later he returned.

"I'm good to go. Ryan and Martin are covering for me. Maybe you're right about him."

"I told you," she said. "I'll pick you up in an hour."

"Let me drive?"

"Why?"

"You're probably too tired," Mark said.

"I'm fine."

"My pickup is bigger."

"What are you talking about?" Claire asked. "You don't want me to drive?"

"Don't take this the wrong way, but I've ridden with you and survived . . . so far. You have trouble remembering this is America, *not* Australia. We drive on the right side of the road, *and* the speedometer is in miles per hour, not kilometers per hour."

"I'm offended." Claire set her chin and folded her arms.

"Sorry, but it's true. Right, Meghan?"

Meghan's eyes bounced back and forth between her mentors. "No comment, Dr. T."

"Plus, you can't afford another speeding ticket," Mark said.

"Bloody rubbish."

"He has a point," said Meghan, taking a step back. "Another ticket and I'll be taking you to driving school."

"You can show them your police badge," she said to Mark, putting her arm around his. "You'd get me out of trouble. Wouldn't you, darling?"

Mark shook his head and raised an eyebrow. "Not if there are injuries or property damage."

"Ridiculous, but I'll meet you at your place," she said.

"I'll be waiting. Drive carefully."

"Oh, shut up."

———

ROBERT ARD INSERTED the brass key into his mailbox in the department office. Three letters leaned against the inside of the box. His hand shook as he retrieved the envelopes. He discarded the first into the trash can by the secretary's desk. His heart rate increased as he read the return address on the second. The University of North Carolina School of Medicine. He refrained from opening it and put the two letters into his lab coat pocket and went back upstairs.

Once seated in his cubicle, he brought out the envelopes. He held the medical school letter in front of him and thought of his journey. His wasn't a life of privilege with parents who were affluent. He was an only child of a single mother who worked two jobs to make enough for him to go to college. He'd never met his father. His mother pushed him and didn't tolerate poor grades. He worked two jobs during the school year in order to make ends meet and learned to make histology slides while working part-time as an assistant in the pathology laboratory at a local hospital. During the school year he worked nights, but it hadn't taken a toll on his grades. They had been stellar. His MCAT scores were in the top ten percentile. He knew it wasn't a long shot for him to gain admission. It should be a sure thing. He couldn't understand why he'd been rejected two years ago. But he played the game and spent another year and a half working in research labs and completing his master's degree in histology and bolstering his CV. The three other schools that had granted him interviews had all rejected him. This was his final chance. He *had* to get in. With trembling hands he opened the letter, careful not to tear the flap. He pulled the white paper from the envelope and unfolded it. The letterhead had the embossed seal of the school of medicine across the top. The paper shook.

Dear Mr. Ard,

Thank you for considering the University of North Carolina School of Medicine. Your application has been given careful consideration and was found to be outstanding. However, this medical school receives over ten thousand applications each year for one hundred and sixty seats. It is with much regret that I have to inform you that you were not one of those selected in this year's class . . .

He stopped reading as a hollow feeling expanded in his belly. A chill swept through him, and his hands felt clammy. "Not again, how is this possible?" he whispered as he dropped the letter in the trash. *My application was perfect. The interviews went well. There's only one explanation. My letters of recommendation. I was sabotaged.* As he sat, his mind in confusion, minutes slipped by while his disappointment transformed into rage.

The other letter lay on his desk. He glanced at the return address. Telos Pharmaceuticals, Inc., Philadelphia, PA. He left it unopened and walked out of the lab. He needed a drink. As he walked he thought about the three people who had written his letters. He dismissed Dr. Hodgson as a possibility. She was too nice to do something like that. She believed in him. She knew he was going to be a brilliant research scientist physician. His biochemistry professor had encouraged him to not give up and reapply after the first rejection. "Most people applying to medical school don't get in the first time if they don't have experience working in the medical field," Ard had remembered him saying. That's why he took the job in the pathology department. He was good at making microscopic specimen slides.

Since he'd worked in the pathology lab, he was obligated to ask Dr. Patel, the chief of the department, for a letter of recommendation. *It has to be him. The saboteur. He thinks I'm lazy. I've worked my ass off for him, and he refused to put my name on his latest research paper.* That could've been the difference. His name on the author line of an article published in a prestigious journal could have pushed him over the top. Patel's words were burned into his memory: "You're a paid technician, not a research scientist. Employees do not get credit for scientific work. It's their job." At least he'd been listed in the technical acknowledgments paragraph before the references.

After three pints of Crosscut Lager and a burger with fries, he returned to the laboratory and sat at his desk. "Maybe I should quit and apply to graduate school," he said to no one. He'd heard of students who spent years doing research and never got their PhD. The idea of scraping for grant money for the rest of his career was not appealing. On top of that he was terrorized at the thought of getting up before a classroom and having to teach students. He folded his arms and put his head on the desktop and stared at the unopened letter. Telos Pharmaceuticals, Inc. He opened it.

ARD ENTERED the laboratory the next morning twenty minutes late with a queasy stomach, the result of several more beers before bed. There were dozens of specimens waiting for him from Dr. Sayre, but they could wait. He'd been thinking about the proposition all night. His coworkers were at their lab benches and Meghan was at the BioFab facility. He found the letter in his drawer, took out his phone, and dialed the number.

"Telos Pharmaceuticals," said the woman.

"This is Robert Ard. Is Dr. Sorenson there?"

"Who?"

"Robert Ard, A-R-D," he repeated.

"May I tell him what this is in reference to?"

"He sent me a letter and asked that I call him."

"Hold, please. I'll see if he's available."

Minutes went by and Ard thought about hanging up as the same music played on an endless loop. "Mr. Ard? Are you still there?"

"Still here."

"Excellent. I apologize for the wait. I was in a meeting when my secretary told me you called. You're at Duke in the pathology department?"

"Yes. What about it?"

"You've been working with Claire Hodgson?"

"For over a year," Ard said.

"Then we need to talk."

Ard paused. "Isn't that what we're doing?"

"I meant face-to-face. I'll be in the Research Triangle for the next few days. I'm flying in this morning; can we meet for lunch around noon?" Sorenson asked.

"Today? Sure. Where and when?" He gave him the name and address. "Can I ask one more thing?"

"Go ahead," Sorenson said.

"Who are you and what do you do?"

Sorenson laughed. "I guess that would be helpful. I'm Neil Sorenson, vice president and director of research and development at Telos Pharmaceuticals. I hope to entice you to do some work for us."

Ard perked up. "See you in a couple of hours, sir."

HE WALKED into the Bull and Bones Gastro Pub at five minutes to twelve. It was a popular lunch spot and happy hour hangout for those who worked in the Triangle. He stood by the entrance and spoke to a receptionist, who glanced at the seating chart behind the counter.

"Robert? Are you Robert Ard?"

Ard turned to face a man of medium build with a balding pate and slicked-back black hair at his temples. He was dressed in a navy blue blazer with charcoal slacks and a light blue shirt open at the collar.

"Yes," Ard said, shaking his hand.

"I'm Neil Sorenson. We have a table in the back." He turned and began walking to the rear. He slid into a booth next to a window, and Ard sat opposite. "Thanks for coming. I'm short on time so I ordered for both of us. I hope you like the Angus burger."

Ard shrugged. "Thanks."

"You're probably wondering why I contacted you."

"By snail mail. I didn't think anyone used the postal service anymore. I almost chucked it," Ard answered. "The letter, I mean."

Sorenson leaned back and smiled. "All we had was the laboratory address from the journal articles. There wasn't any contact information listed for you, and we'd prefer not to use social media."

"Why not?"

"Let's just say we have our reasons and leave it at that."

Ard shrugged. "Okay."

The waitress approached with a tray and set glasses of iced tea and plates of food in front of them.

"Back to my question. Were you wondering why I contacted you? It would be natural."

"It crossed my mind a few times last night," Ard said with a mouth full of cheeseburger. He dabbed ketchup from the corners of his mouth.

"I've been following the work your laboratory has been producing over the last several years. Incredible stuff."

"It's not my laboratory. I just work there."

"Of course. However, my company, Telos, has a pipeline of several pharmaceutical agents that are similar to what you've been working with. In particular, we are interested in a drug called Endovancin. It's like one we're planning to market in the next year or two. We'd like to bring you over to our team. Team Telos. Are you interested?"

"I've never heard of Telos."

"Really? As a scientist in our industry, you're familiar with the drug, correct?"

"Sort of. It's some experimental compound Dr. Hodgson is testing for another company. She's talked about it in a couple of lab meetings. Look, I'm just a histo tech. How can I help you?"

"Nonsense. You're much more than a mere histology technician. You have superb talents that are severely underappreciated. You should receive the full recognition you deserve." Sorenson took a sip of tea. "Robert, do you think you could get them to give you more responsibility? Perhaps participate in some of the data collection?"

"Look, Mr. Sorenson . . ."

"It's Dr. Sorenson, but call me Neil."

"Okay. Neil, I just want to get into medical school."

"I can help you. We have connections at several prominent medical schools. Have you thought about Hershey or Thomas Jefferson? How about Temple?"

"You could do that?"

"Well, you'd have to be a qualified applicant, but if you are, I think it could be arranged. Plus, in the meantime, you will be considerably better compensated," Sorenson told him.

Ard leaned forward, rubbing his hands together under the table. "That would be awesome. I'd love to work for Telos. When do you want me to start? I'll give them my two weeks this afternoon."

"Don't do that." Sorenson clasped his hands in front of him on the table and leaned forward. "You misunderstand. We need you to continue working right where you are. What we need is information."

"You want me to give you *information*? You mean like a spy?"

"No, no, I wouldn't call it that. You'll be helping to advance antibiotic research that will cure infections and save millions of people's lives. We want to get our drug to market to be used by people who need it. We're capable and ready to proceed, but there are a few key things we need to know. We need you to provide that information."

"I don't know, Neil. I could get into trouble."

"Nonsense. You'll be helping to foster healthy business competition. Plus, no one will be the wiser, and next year you'll be in medical school with money to pay your tuition. Your dream of a career in medicine will come true. Besides, the drug isn't even approved. It's just started phase two trials. You wouldn't be doing anything illegal. At least think about it. Will you?"

"Give me some time. A day or two."

"Done. Call me tomorrow." Sorenson handed him a blank business card with a phone number printed on one side. "I don't think I need to tell you, this is strictly confidential. Don't mention our conversation to anyone. The last thing we want is for you to get fired."

"I won't say anything."

During the meal Sorenson told him more about the company and their visionary CEO, Jeffery Mullion. "You know, we have plans to take Telos public in a few years. Part of your compensation will be in pre-IPO stock options. They could be worth a fortune one day."

"That's awesome," Ard said as he took a break from sucking iced tea through his plastic straw.

"This company is going to disrupt the pharmaceutical industry. Who knows? In five or ten years, we may be acquired by one of the big boys. That would be a real payday."

"Sweet. Do you think I could do an MD-PhD program in med school?"

"Nothing would please me more. Then, after you graduate, if you decide you like research more than clinical medicine, you can come back and work for Telos. You'll always have a position waiting for you."

After lunch Ard felt as if he were floating to his car. This was the break he'd been waiting for. The break he deserved. He opened the door to the late model Honda Accord and saw a manila envelope laying on the driver's seat. He felt its weight and peeled open the flap. He pulled out two bundles of ten one-hundred-dollar bills. A yellow sticky note was stuck to one. On it was written in freehand black ink:

Regardless of your decision, keep this as a token of our appreciation for considering the offer. I hope it leads to the start of a career in medicine for you and big things for T.
Regards, N

FIVE

MONDAY, MARCH 20TH

Beaufort, South Carolina

THE FULL MOON rose with a gossamer halo illuminating the Lowcountry marsh like a spotlight. Ancient live oaks with tangled limbs draped in Spanish moss stretched over the two-lane blacktop. Palmetto fronds and sweetgrass waved in the breeze along the sides of the highway.

"I don't remember any of this," Claire said as they sped into the night.

"It's been two years since we've been here," Mark replied.

"None of this is familiar. Please, tell me you know where you're going."

He tapped the display on his phone clipped to the dashboard. "You realize who you're talking to?"

"That's why I asked."

"Ye of little faith."

Claire let out a long breath and tugged on her shoulder strap. "We've been driving for five hours. The last bit through some godforsaken swamp. My rear end is sore and I'm desperate to get out of this truck."

"Hang in there. It won't be long. We just crossed the Coosaw River."

Claire looked at the map on the screen. "How much charge is left in that thing?"

"Seven percent."

Claire's head turned. "That's our lifeline. Without it we're lost."

"Relax," Mark said.

"I'll relax when we're back in civilization. Seven percent. I can't believe it. Where's your charger? And who doesn't have a built-in GPS these days?"

"Waste of money. The phone is way better. Plus, this truck's ten years old. I couldn't afford it back then."

"I knew we should've taken my car." She pulled her phone from her purse.

"Everything will be fine. The charger is in my suitcase. We'll use yours if mine runs out."

"You're lucky," she said while thumbing a text.

He leaned closer to the steering wheel. "This place is strange at night. Wouldn't you say?"

She stared out the window at the mist clinging to the marsh. "It's creepy."

"Reminds me of Poe."

"What?"

"It reminds me of Edgar Allan Poe."

"It's close to midnight. We've detoured into the Twilight Zone and you're thinking about Poe?"

"He wrote a short story set in Carolina Lowcountry, "The Gold Bug." The main character goes insane after being bitten by a yellow beetle while looking for buried pirate treasure."

"You've been bitten by one. Hurry up and get us out of this bayou or whatever you call it." She looked at her phone. "Bloody hell. I don't have any reception."

He tapped his phone a few seconds later. "Five percent."

"Damn," she said and swatted his shoulder.

They rode in silence for the next quarter hour. "There," said Mark as a glow appeared over the trees. They rounded a corner and a pair of flashing yellow lights signaled a stoplight ahead. A sign read BEAUFORT 5 MILES.

She leaned over and kissed his cheek. "You're a lucky man."

He smiled and squeezed her knee. "I know."

"Let's hope it's a nice hotel."

"I didn't ask Stephen. It's called the Anchorage Inn on Bay Street. He said to take the last right before you get to the bridge." He glanced around as they drove through town. "We'll be heading over the Beaufort River onto Lady's Island if we miss it."

"There," Claire said, pointing to a lighted street sign. They turned right and drove along the Beaufort Waterfront.

The Anchorage Inn was a renovated Greek-revival-style mansion built in the late 1700s. It had been recently restored for the second time and converted into a bed-and-breakfast. The landscape lighting illuminated white Doric columns lining the front porch and the light gray stucco façades. A large brick staircase led from the walkway to the entrance.

"It looks nice from the outside." Mark turned into the entrance and followed the signs to the rear parking.

"Good evening," said the receptionist at the check-in desk. "We were getting worried. Dr. Sayre thought you'd be here by nine."

"We got away later than expected," Mark said.

"He left you a message." She handed him an envelope.

"Lovely place," Claire said, glancing around.

"Thank you. We have you out back in the upstairs dependency."

"The *what*?"

The receptionist smiled. "The cottage in the rear. It used to be the kitchen. It was built away from the main house to protect from fires. It was extensively renovated two years ago. I think you'll find it quite nice and private. Our bell staff will assist you." A young man in shorts and a golf shirt embroidered with an anchor logo followed them to Mark's truck. He took their luggage through the rose garden to the cottage in the rear of the main house. He unlocked the side door and they ascended a private stairway, emerging into a spacious room.

The bellman placed the suitcases onto foldout stands next to a four-poster king bed. "This is nice in the morning when you're having coffee." He walked to the French doors and then swung them open. Mark and Claire walked out onto a second-story patio that overlooked the garden.

"From here you can see the river and the boats going by."

Claire slipped her arm around Mark's. "Lovely."

"Can I get you anything?"

"No. That'll be all. Thank you for your help." Mark handed him a tip and followed him to the door. When he returned Claire lay sprawled on the bed.

"What time is Stephen coming by?"

"I don't know. I thought he'd call by now." Then he remembered the note and pulled the folded envelope from his back pocket.

Kiddos,

Glad to have you back in town. Hope you like the Anchorage. It was being renovated the last time you were here. Better than the No-Tell Motel! I'll meet you at the marina at nine. There's a bottle of Oregon pinot noir in the fridge. Enjoy!

Stephen

He went over to the small refrigerator. "Brick House from the Willamette Valley. Steve's got good taste."

"He prefers to be called Stephen," Claire reminded him.

"I'll call him whatever he wants if he keeps buying me wine like this."

"After that drive I need a drink."

Mark removed the cork and found two glasses on the dresser. He half filled them and handed one to Claire.

"You'd think he'd be a little less festive about the situation."

"He's just being a good host, but you're right, it makes me ill thinking about it."

"How many has he rounded up?"

"Almost all of the original cohort," Claire said as she opened her suitcase. "They've done x-rays and biopsied the bone graft sites. He and his assistants have been making daily trips to the island rounding up the second group." She carried her makeup bag into the bathroom.

"That's where we're headed tomorrow?"

She turned and looked out the doorway. "Yes. Morgan Island. I want to see them in their natural environment."

"I know what they're going through. I've been there." He rubbed his right thigh where a Ewing's sarcoma had grown large enough to almost burst his femur. That was five years ago. It ended his military career and began a nightmare odyssey of chemotherapy and radiation treatments.

"We have to figure this out. We can't move forward with any experiments until we understand what's going on."

"And cure it." She came out of the bathroom and refilled her glass.

As she put the bottle down, he arose from the bed and stood behind her. His arms wrapped around her waist and pulled her to him. "I hope that's possible. We have to do something."

"You survived, Mark. They will, too." She placed her wine glass on the dresser and put her hands over his as he leaned over and kissed her neck.

"Having you in my life has made a big difference."

She turned around and leaned her head back. "Does your leg ever hurt anymore?"

"No."

"I want to see your scar," she said and began tugging on his belt.

He removed his shirt. "Which one?"

"Where the tumor was . . . on your thigh."

"Then, I want to see yours."

"I don't have a scar."

"Prove it." A moment later she lifted her shirt over her head as his pants fell to the floor. She released her bra and shook it free.

He exhaled. "You are so beautiful."

"Be quiet and show me."

AFTER BREAKFAST THE NEXT MORNING, they walked down the front steps and crossed the street to the Beaufort seawall. Scattered patches of cirrus clouds dotted the cerulean sky. Saltwater lapped against the pilings, carrying an organic scent like fertile soil. A shrimp boat, getting a late start, motored down the river with its nets and outriggers up. The temperature was in the midsixties and was expected to reach into the seventies later in the day. In spite of this, Mark and Claire wore blue jeans and sweatshirts knowing it would be at least ten degrees cooler out on the water. They strolled along the waterfront and stopped at the marina. In the public parking lot behind them, horse-drawn carriages were being prepared for their daily routine of pulling tourists through the historic downtown. At ten to nine, Mark spotted a boat approaching and they made their way to the pier near the boat launch. Dr. Stephen Sayre, DVM waved as he snuggled the thirty-foot Parker Sport Cabin against the dock and put the outboard motors into neutral.

"Welcome aboard," he said. They stepped over the gunwale and Mark pushed off as Sayre maneuvered back into deeper water. Once clear of the marina, he increased speed and headed toward the swinging drawbridge that spanned the Beaufort River.

"I'd forgotten what a gorgeous place this is," Claire sighed. They passed under the bridge.

"My little piece of heaven," he said. "What time did you make it in?"

"It was late. Thanks for the wine. We put it to good use," Mark said.

"You're welcome," he responded, smiling.

"Yes. That was very thoughtful."

"I'm glad you enjoyed it. It's one of my favorites. My daughter lives near Portland, and we've been to the winery several times." He turned the wheel a few degrees and adjusted their heading. The Beaufort Waterfront was disappearing behind them as they made their way downriver. Salt marshes and maritime forests were on both sides.

"You know where we are?" Claire asked.

"No idea," Mark replied. "Stephen, last time we were at the lab, you never took us to the island."

"I should've. We were too busy." They stood in the cabin as Sayre navigated the waterways and narrated the scenery. "Did you ever see the movie *Forrest Gump*? They filmed the shrimping scenes right over there. The boat crashed into that dock." He pointed to a dilapidated pier coming into view on the port side.

"Let's not do that," Mark said, looking out the window at the blue sky.

"Agreed. We're headed to Morgan Island, also known as Monkey Island. It's an interesting place with a lot of local folklore. The NIH took it over in 1959 and established one of only two US colonies of rhesus monkeys."

"Where's the other?" Mark asked.

Stephen shrugged. "Somewhere in Florida, I think. The government keeps them on the island to study the effects of experiments. Every now and then, one will turn up on the mainland, and the local press has a field day."

Claire laughed. "I can imagine. Headlines about Dr. Moreau's island and such?"

The veterinarian chuckled. "It's the furthest thing from that."

"How many on your team?" Mark asked.

"We have a staff of four veterinarians, all simian specialists, and ten vet techs who care for them daily."

Claire turned around as they heard the bone-rattling roar of jet engines at low altitude approaching. The cabin windows shook as the noise increased. "My God," she yelled, placing her hands over her ears. In a few moments, the thunder of afterburners reached a crescendo then began to diminish as two fighter jets disappeared over the horizon. "What was that?"

"The sound of freedom," Stephen said with a smile. "The Marine Corps Air Station."

"Those were two F/A-18 Hornets taking off for a training run," Mark said, looking up at the sky.

"Deafening," Claire said.

"Music to my ears," Stephen replied.

"You were saying . . . about the island?" Mark urged him on.

Stephen scratched his head and replaced his ball cap. "There are about three thousand five hundred rhesus residents. Your fellas all have GPS-locating devices implanted for easier retrieval. We make runs to the island daily to feed the population and make sure they're not up to mischief. There're no predators and they roam free. They've divided themselves into a number of smaller groups, each run by an alpha male."

"They seemed friendly when we were doing our experiments," Claire said.

"Oh, they're friendly enough. Just don't get stranded on the island at night."

"Why?" Mark inquired.

"One of my young colleagues thought she would spend a week on the island collecting data. The first night they almost beat the cabin door down trying to get at her. She lasted one day and said she'd never do it again. Feared for her life. The little buggers are territorial."

They left the protected waters of the Beaufort and Coosaw Rivers and entered the expanse of the St. Helena Sound. The wind was calm and the water smooth.

"Dolphin!" Claire called out as several dorsal fins broke the surface.

"Always a good omen," Sayre said as he pointed to land on the horizon. "That's where we're headed. I'll approach from the other side."

A quarter of an hour later, he guided the boat into a fifty-foot-wide inlet that snaked through the mud flats. Three-foot-tall green marsh grass surrounded them and waved in the breeze like a field of winter wheat. Sayre steered the boat back and forth, keeping it in the center of the winding channel as the island grew closer and the waterway narrowed.

As they approached land they saw many of the trees along the banks were uprooted and blown over. "A hurricane came through last year. It took us a while to clean up the mess. The animals were fine, but these trees didn't fare so well," Sayer explained.

Mark pointed to another boat tied up at the landing dock. "Who's here?"

"Our assistants. I sent them out early to start the round-up." Sayre cut the engines and drifted to the pier. He tossed the fenders over the gunwales and stepped onto the gray sun-bleached dock. He secured the bow while Mark handled the stern. "Come on. They'll be on the other side of the island this time of day."

MULLION STEPPED on the accelerator and the Porsche responded. The pressure on his spine increased as he was pressed into the rigid seatback. Chester County's scenic rolling hills became a blur in his peripheral vision. The tension in his forearms relaxed as the car rose and dipped over the country road and the speedometer held a steady seventy-five miles per hour. He imagined Rampage performing like the GT3, then stepped on the brake pedal as the turn approached. The calipers bit into the disks, and he felt the restraint of the chest strap as the car slowed. He turned right onto the tree-lined lane. Five minutes later, he parked in front of the main building of Devon Stables. The call he'd been expecting came before he cut the engine.

"Ramon. How are things in Bogotá?"

"Fine, my friend. Any problems with the shipments?" The man spoke with a deep Spanish accent, raspy from decades of tobacco smoke.

Mullion disconnected the Bluetooth. He pressed the phone to his head and covered the other ear. "None. The items were received without difficulty. I'm at the stables now."

"Excellent."

"Look, Ramon. I'm hamstrung. I'm at maximum capacity. Demand is outstripping supply. The DEA and FDA have dried up street inventory. We're practically the only show in town."

"That's a problem, Señor Mullion?"

"We need to increase production."

"We will," Ramon answered.

"When will the Bogotá facility be ready?"

"Next week. The inspections have been completed and permits granted." Ramon paused to catch his breath. "Now, we need to expand the product line, or soon you will have a pharmaceutical company producing only prescription narcos. That will not go over well with DIRAN. It will draw more attention than we desire."

"We are a pharmaceutical company, for God's sake. We have legitimate permits to make them," Mullion said in agitation. "I'm not worried about the anti-narcotics directorate."

"You should be."

"I'm working on a solution. We have an interesting possibility. An amazing antibiotic called Endovancin. I'll have the formula soon. Then, I want to start production at the new plant. I've talked to colleagues in Beijing. They're interested."

"Good . . . very good. If all goes well, this could be the beginning of a long and prosperous relationship."

"Nothing could please me more. I've had this dream for years. It's the perfect cover and way to wash millions of dollars. Once the new plant is fully operational, we'll make hydrocodone and oxycodone in Colombia and smuggle it all into the US. That fixes the supply problem. At the same time, we'll be producing the latest and greatest antibiotic that we will sell to the Chinese. Pablo Escobar laundered his money with his taxi business. We'll clean ours with pharmaceuticals and make a legitimate product while doing it. Drugs as a cover for narcos. Don't you love the irony?"

"I'll love it when it happens," Ramon wheezed.

"It will, and soon. I'm ready to put the first phase in motion, but I need your help."

A low-pitched gurgling sound spewed from the phone followed by an emphysematous, chest-rattling wet cough.

"Everything okay?" Mullion asked.

"Sí, señor. My apologies. What can I do?"

Mullion explained his plan.

"Perhaps you *are* a visionary. Time will tell. I will make the arrangements."

"Thank you." He almost added, "Don Corleone."

"Now, tell me how our great black beast is doing," Ramon commanded.

"Rampage is excellent," Mullion responded. "I'm about to watch his afternoon workout."

"No medical problems?"

"The doctors at the New Bolton Center said he checked out fine. They are some of the best equine veterinarians in the world. You were worried over nothing."

"That makes me happy. I look forward to his return home."

"You'll have him back tomorrow. Will we speak again Friday?"

"Sí, same time as today."

"Goodbye." Mullion ended the call and walked to the dumpster. He extracted the SIM card and ground it into the gravel parking lot. Then he tossed the phone into the bin and pocketed the card.

"LOOK." Stephen pointed to a monkey seated on the ground at the base of a tree. "He's hurt. There's no way he'd be there if he could climb." He shouldered the tranquilizer gun and steadied his aim. A second later the muffled sound of escaping compressed air came from the rifle. The monkey jumped and scrambled a few yards away. Thirty seconds later he lay still on the sandy ground. They hurried to the animal and Mark turned him on his side.

"Here's the surgical scar." He inspected the limb. "Feel this," he said, placing Claire's hand on the creature's thigh.

"It's warm and swollen," Claire said.

"Probably a tumor," Mark replied.

"Come on, get him back to the cages before he wakes up," Stephen said.

Mark placed the unconscious monkey on his shoulder and jogged back to the dock, where wire cages were stacked on the pier. The containers resembled a smaller version of the one he'd used to train his black Lab. He'd given the dog to his brother when his white count had all but disappeared during chemotherapy. He paused for a second, thinking of his old friend, then selected a cage and opened the door. He wrote the monkey's ID number on the label then secured the sleeping subject inside. He passed Claire carrying another on his way back.

"They have several more, straight down the trail on the other side of the island," she said.

"Don't forget to write down the ID number on the door."

She nodded. "See you back there."

Mark came upon the veterinarian and three staff members gathered around a laptop. Stephen was pointing to a concentration of flashing dots on the screen.

"There's a pack of them heading to the north end. Ron, take Melissa and Jim and bring back as many as you can. Try to fill the remaining cages. It'll take a few more days to capture all of them."

"Yes, sir," one of the men said. He picked up a tranquilizer gun and the three technicians began jogging down the beach toward the north end of the island.

Stephen turned to Mark and pointed at the computer screen. A group of dots were moving southward near the opposite end of the island. "This pack is about a quarter mile away. We'll capture several then return to the lab. I want you to see how we collect the biopsy specimens before you go."

"How many do you think are affected?" Mark asked.

"It's hard to say. I'd guess fifteen to twenty percent are showing symptoms," Stephen replied. "They've been behaving strangely, more aggressive."

Mark kicked at the sand. "Damn. I've caused this."

"It's my fault, too," Claire said emerging from the thicket.

"Look, this is why we do research. There'll be time for feeling sorry later. Let's round them up and get back to the lab," Stephen said. "I'd like to get them settled before the tranquilizer wears off."

Then came the screams.

Claire's head whipped around. "That sounds like a woman."

Stephen jumped to his feet, "Melissa," he shouted and sprinted down the beach toward the frantic sounds. Screams of panic grew louder. Melissa burst through the tree line onto the beach a few yards ahead of them.

"Help!" Her eyes were the size half dollars. She stumbled and fell. A plume of sand burst into the air as her body tumbled on the beach. She lay curled up, sobbing as the others reached her.

"We've got you. You're safe. What's happened?" Stephen helped her to her feet.

Crimson streaks stained her neck and collar. Blood streamed from her forearms and hands. A red gash ran from her right jaw to her collarbone. Her khaki shirt was torn. "Help Jim. They're attacking!"

"Who's attacking?"

Melissa pointed back into the woods. "The monkeys. There's a pack of them. Down the trail."

"Show us," said Claire.

She shook her head as pink tears streaked her scratched face. "I'm not going back in there."

Stephen took off running into the trees. Mark and Claire followed. The veterinarian began screaming and grabbing at bushes as they ran deeper into the forest. "Make as much racket as you can," he yelled over his shoulder.

The three of them sounded like a war party as they ran single file into the darkening network of trees, vines, and bushes. Wet green leaves and branches slapped their faces as they ran down the trail. Then, they broke into a clearing where a man lay on a layer of pine needles.

"Jim, are you hurt? Talk to me," Stephen said.

A bloody face looked up from the ground. "Those little sons a bitches attacked me like a pack of hyenas. Tried to take off a finger or two." He extended his fingers and several of the tips were bleeding. "Vicious bastards."

"What the hell happened?" Mark said as he helped him up. Stephen held the tranquilizer gun and looked upward into the trees.

"I'd just taken down that guy over there." He pointed to a monkey lying near a bush. "As soon as Melissa and I approached, they started screaming and dropping from the trees. They grabbed and scratched, bit my fingers and face like a bunch of berserk chimps. Melissa started screaming. I told her to run."

"We heard her," said Claire as she scanned the trees. She squatted and gripped a fallen branch about the size of a truncheon in her right hand.

"Is she all right?"

Claire nodded, "scratched and frightened."

"I held them off for a few minutes, but there were too many. I tried to run but tripped. I curled into a ball, covered my face, and made fists. They took off when you started yelling and coming this way."

"I've never seen rhesus monkeys act like that," said Stephen.

"I didn't know they could," said Jim. "They're pissed."

"Most likely scared and in pain," Stephen said.

Mark dabbed blood from Jim's face with a handkerchief. "If you have a first aid kit, I'll treat your wounds. Most of these look superficial. Are the monkeys vaccinated?"

Stephen nodded. "I have a first aid kit on the boat. Grab that one on the ground and let's head back."

Claire cradled the tranquilized animal in her arms but held onto the tree branch.

THEY FOUND Melissa seated by Rob next to the laptop. Four more monkeys lay in a drug-induced sleep on the ground at their feet.

"Back to the boats," Stephen ordered.

Each shouldered a monkey, and Melissa carried the computer and a supply container that resembled a tackle box. At the dock, Mark cleaned the bites and scratches and applied bandages. Then he administered an intramuscular dose of ceftriaxone to each. "When we get back I'll write you both a prescription for a week's worth of Augmentin."

Stephen boarded the twin engine Parker. Mark and Claire followed. "See you back at the lab," he shouted at the technicians as they walked down the dock to the other boat. "Next time you come out here, bring more manpower. No more ambushes."

Claire looked at the cages stacked on the stern. "Where do they go from here?"

"We have a receiving facility close by." Stephen stepped into the cockpit and started the engines. A half hour later they tied up at the Warsaw loading dock. The dozen crates were transferred onto the veterinary transport truck, and they began the drive to the Yemassee laboratory.

Sayre stopped the vehicle at the gate. A ten-foot-high chain-link fence topped with razor wire encircled the compound. Keep Out No Trespassing signs were attached to the fence every thirty feet.

"You've stepped up security," Mark noticed.

"Had to. The Army moved several of its biological research labs here about a year ago."

"Where?" Claire asked.

"I'll show you in a minute." He lowered the driver's window and stuck his arm out. He pressed his thumb onto the glass of a device about the size of a cell phone. The gate slid open. The research facility was made up of several single-story buildings. Stephen drove to the rear of one of the structures and backed up to the delivery platform. He pointed to a building about the length of a football field away.

"Over there. It's part of the new Army biological defense program. They relocated it here from Fort Detrick."

"What do they do?" Claire asked.

Stephen shrugged. "I'm not entirely sure. They don't advertise their work, but I know one of their scientists. He's a world-renowned virologist."

Mark and Claire exchanged glances. The three got out of the truck as a young man approached from the back door.

"Good afternoon, Dr. Sayre. More specimens?"

"Straight from the island," he said, unlocking the latch and lifting the rear door. The animals remained sedate, but several were awake, and their little faces peered through the stainless steel bars. "Come on. Let's move them inside. Don't let them nibble your fingers." A couple more vet techs appeared from the back door to help move the experimental subjects into the lab. After a few trips, the cages were stacked in an animal containment room. Stephen spoke with one of his assistants then approached Mark and Claire. "Vince and Jerry will transfer the monkeys into their permanent cages while we get the operating room ready. We'll change into scrubs then x-ray them. I'll biopsy a few of the specimens so you can see how I do it."

Claire hung her head and wiped a tear from her cheek. "I can't believe it's come to this. We wanted to cure disease, not cause it."

"Chin up, Claire," said Stephen. "Look, you don't know how this is going to work out. There's no other way to do research. You can't animate medical progress through computer programs. Scientific discovery is about taking risk. This story isn't over. These guys aren't dead. We're going to take care of them. You both may be playing a role in a fantastic discovery. Possibly a miraculous cure. Stop feeling sorry for them and yourself. Buck up and let's get to work."

"You're right. I'll be positive." Claire ducked her cheek to her sleeve.

An hour later, the x-rays were completed and the first subject was anesthetized on the operating room table. "This is the first one we found today," Stephen instructed. "The one on the path who wouldn't or couldn't climb." The anesthesiologist adjusted his machine while Stephen began shaving the thigh and washing the patient's skin. When he was finished, they rolled the monkey on the anesthesia cart and into the operating room. Stephen pointed to a computer screen in the corner. "That's his thigh x-ray."

They walked to the viewing screen. "That's aggressive," Mark said. "The cortex is ruptured, and the tumor is spreading into the soft tissues."

"It's at least a centimeter in diameter," Claire added, shaking her head. "Damn it."

Stephen looked at the anesthetist. "Has the patient received pre-op antibiotics, the Endovancin?"

"I gave it when you were prepping the skin," he responded.

"Let's begin." Stephen called for the tourniquet to be inflated, and he made a straight incision through the skin. Bleeding was efficiently cauterized and the mass exposed. "Feel how firm this is."

"Feels like a golf ball," Mark said.

Claire nodded as she felt the firm nodule with her gloved fingers.

"The bone graft dowel was six millimeters in diameter. I can't tell where it was inserted," Mark said.

Claire turned and pointed to the imaging screen. "You can't tell from the x-ray either. The graft has been completely incorporated into the native bone."

"Pick a couple of sites. I'll get three biopsy specimens. We'll fill the holes with demineralized bone graft."

"Here, here, and here," Mark said, marking the selected sites with a surgical pen. Stephen took the two-millimeter-diameter core biopsy needle and inserted it into the tumor. He twisted it, driving it into the bone. He removed the needle and inspected it to make sure the bone material was in the cylinder and then placed the needle over the specimen container and pushed the plunger down, expelling the biopsy. The little tube of tumor material was placed in formalin and labeled. Stephen repeated the process two more times while Mark packed the sites with bone graft. He used a dental pick to press it into the biopsy holes to staunch any bleeding after the tourniquet was released.

Once this task was completed Stephen began closing the wound. "This is what I've done on all the monkeys." He finished tying a knot and held up the suture limbs. "Cut."

Mark snipped the excess material. "Good technique. I'd do it the same way." When the incision was closed they began applying bandages.

"Meghan and Robert will prepare the slides as soon as we get back," Claire said.

"I'll email the x-rays," Stephen replied.

"We can't thank you enough."

"You're a good friend. Thanks," Mark added. "We need the specimens as soon as you can get them to us."

"Let's finish the samples collected today and you can drive them to your lab tonight. I'll send the rest as soon as we get them. We'll work around the clock until we're done."

Claire turned to Mark. "No more 3D bone printing experiments until we figure out what's happening."

He nodded and gripped his right thigh. "What about Hyperion?"

"He's on hold. You better call Dusty."

SIX

WEDNESDAY, MARCH 22ND

Stem Cell Research and Regenerative Medicine Laboratory, Durham, North Carolina

MEGHAN TURNED the knobs of the microscope and the pink-and-white field came into sharp focus. Uniform purple osteocytes occupied the lacunae. *Normal bone. Nothing unusual on this slide,* she thought to herself. This was in stark contrast to the previous slide. On that specimen, she didn't even have to use the fine-focus adjustment. Even blurred, it was obvious she was looking at a full-scale neoplastic battlefield. Healthy cells were being invaded and terminated by mutants invading like a horde of cellular locusts. It made her sick to look at the tissue carnage. *It's a brutal world even at the microscopic level,* she told herself.

She noted her observations in the hardbound research ledger lying next to the scope. *Subject 70165, DOS 8/19/16, right femur specimen #57, normal lamellar bone.* This was one of the last subjects in the first round of experiments. There had been twenty-four patients in the first phase of the research project. Five more remained to complete the analysis of this group. She removed the specimen and carefully stored it in her slide box.

She reached into the tray of remaining slides and selected one at random. She slid it onto the microscope stage and dialed in the focus. *Nothing subtle about this one.* Meghan turned the page in her notebook and made an entry. *Specimen 28356, DOS 8/23/16, right femur, specimen #62, abundant anaplasia, characteristics consistent with aggressive sarcoma.*

She continued examining the slides. Claire wanted the results as soon as she was finished. They had a meeting scheduled for later that afternoon. She looked up when she heard the door open. Robert Ard walked toward her carrying several trays stacked neatly on top of each other. His white lab coat was buttoned and covered most of his T-shirt and blue jeans. His high-top Converse sneakers made no noise on the industrial floor covering.

"How's my technique? They look good, don't they?" he asked.

"It's beautiful, as usual. How are we going to replace such talent? You are the histo king," Meghan teased.

"Glad they're up to your standards. Anything interesting?"

"No pattern. Some have unmistakable sarcoma, and others look completely normal."

"Anything in between?"

"*Everything* in between. Some slides have only a few weird-looking nuclei while others have definite precancerous cell clusters," Meghan told him.

"Why some and not others?" Ard asked.

"No idea." Meghan shrugged. "Let me finish up."

"I come bearing gifts," he said, smiling. "The last slides."

"Goodness." Her eyes widened as he set the new trays next to the microscope. "Were you here all night?"

"I couldn't sleep. Too much stuff running around in my head. Now I'm hungry. You want to grab something to eat?"

"No thanks. Look at all these." She pointed to the trays, as big as cookie sheets, filled with rows of histology specimens.

"Can I get you anything at the cafeteria?"

"Thanks. You're sweet. Tea would be nice."

"Green or black?"

"Either. It doesn't matter."

"I'll surprise you," Ard said as he closed the door.

She placed another glass slide onto the microscope stage and twirled the dials. *Good Lord, this one is really far gone.* After noting her observations she filed the slide and reached for another. She stared at tissue specimens for the next thirty minutes before being interrupted by vibrations from her phone. A message flashed; it was from Ard. *The special today is Sencha.* She replied with a smiley face emoji and went back to work. He returned with the warm paper cup before she'd finished her notes.

Meghan grinned when he placed it on her desk. "You're the best."

"Any theories about what's going on?"

She took a sip before replying. "I told you, no, we don't have any idea."

"What is going on? Some of them look pretty bad. That's an aggressive cancer."

Meghan looked up and tilted her head. "How do you know about that?"

Ard shrugged. "I look at the slides, you know. I can tell."

"Why the sudden interest?"

"Just curious about all this extra work."

"I'm trying to assemble the data so we can come up with an explanation. Now let me get back at it. Thanks for the tea."

"Sure. Let me know if you need anything." He turned and retreated from the lab.

Three hours later the last specimen had been logged and the slides stored. Meghan held her data book like a schoolgirl and walked back to her cubicle. She removed her lab coat and opened her laptop. She began transferring data from her notebook into the spreadsheet while an Emerson String Quartet fugue streamed from her phone over the desk speaker. Each experimental subject had three samples from the affected thigh. The microscopic biopsy results were entered for each specimen along with other pertinent data. It included the date of surgery, right or left femur, height, weight, gender, age, and other information such as type of anesthetic and pre-op antibiotic. Meghan entered all the information. Afterward she leaned back in her chair, put her hands behind her head, and reviewed the columns of data.

She began looking for a pattern. *It would make sense that the earliest subjects might have the worst histologic results because the tumor had the longest time to develop,* she thought. She sorted the data according to DOS, the date of surgery. She blinked at the result. The first fourteen subjects all exhibited signs of osteosarcoma. However, the last ten were cancer-free. She was confused. *How is that possible?* She went back to the original research notebooks and double-checked the subject ID number with the date of the surgical procedure. There was no mistake. The earliest subjects had the worst results, but then something happened and the last ten were cancer-free. *What's going on?* she thought.

"Any theories?" Ard asked.

Meghan's head snapped around. "Robert, what are you doing?"

"Nothing. How was the tea?"

She exhaled and her shoulders sagged as she sat back in her chair. "It was good, thank you. You startled me."

"Sorry. Did the slides help? Did you find anything?"

"It's weird. The earliest subjects have neoplastic transformation but then it stops. Subjects fifteen through twenty-four, the last ones, are normal."

"That is weird. What's different?"

"You think I'd be sitting here if I knew that?"

"Don't get testy. I'm just saying that something must have changed."

"Sorry. Let me think," Meghan said.

"How about dinner later?"

Meghan shook her head. "Not tonight. I want to figure this out. I have a meeting with Dr. Hodgson in an hour."

"I'm going for a run. Call me if you change your mind."

She peered at the spreadsheet and the columns of data. *There's an answer in here somewhere.* She copied the column headings onto another area of the spreadsheet and began to enter the data from the second experiment. This series took place three months after the first, in October and November of the same year. Again, she sorted by DOS and the results mystified her even more. The first ten subjects were clean without signs of cancer. The next five all exhibited tumor growth at their biopsy sites. The final nine subjects were cancer-free. Dr. Thurman performed all the surgeries. The protocol called for him to drill a six-millimeter hole in the middle of the femur followed by filling the defect with a bioprinted, stem cell–impregnated, bone graft dowel six millimeters in diameter, exactly filling the hole. Any excess dowel protruding from the femur was removed so the bone graft was flush with the surface. The tolerances were tight enough that the dowel had to be pressed firmly into the drilled hole. He called it press fit. Next, he sutured the incision and splinted the limb. She made a mental note to ask him if he could recall any change in his surgical technique. She wondered, *Had there been any change in the bone dowel fabrication recipe?* Her phone vibrated on the desk, and the fugue stopped when she answered it.

"Are you okay?" her mentor asked.

"Yes, I'm fine. I was going over the data."

"Care to share the results with me?" Claire laughed.

"Am I late?"

"Just a few minutes."

"Sorry." Meghan closed her laptop and stood. "I'll be right there." She slipped her shoes back on and tossed the empty paper cup into the trash.

"I'VE BEEN WAITING for this all afternoon," Claire said excitedly as Meghan sat in the chair next to her desk. Meghan opened the laptop and displayed the spreadsheet. "After looking at the data, what are your initial thoughts? Any theories?"

Meghan shook her head and explained what she had done and the unusual findings. "It makes no sense. The earliest subjects should have the worst results. They've had the longest time for the tumor to grow and spread."

"I agree, and the data supports that conclusion up to the fourteenth patient," Claire replied. "Something happened starting with subject fifteen. Let's consider other possibilities."

"Were there any changes in Dr. Thurman's surgical technique?"

Claire shook her head. "I observed every surgery. He did the same thing for each one. It became so routine it was boring."

"What about bioprinting? Were the bone graft dowels all made the same way?"

"Exactly the same way. I made them all myself and used the same cell culture line," Claire answered.

"Can you think of any breaks in protocol?"

"Identical methods."

"Subject gender, size, or age?"

Claire drummed her fingers on the desk. "No pattern there. The data look completely random based on those parameters."

"What about this?" Meghan asked, pointing at the empty last column with the heading ABX.

Claire studied the entries. "Those are the antibiotics, vancomycin or Endovancin." She folded her arms and pinched her lower lip. "Let's fill it in." She suddenly stood and walked across the room to a filing cabinet and retrieved a lab notebook from the top drawer. "Nothing like keeping original data the old-fashioned way." She opened the hardbound ledger and scanned the recorded entries. "Hmm. That's interesting."

"What? What are you thinking?"

"You may be onto something."

"What about them?" asked Meghan.

Claire sat with the ledger open on her desk. Her left index finger held her place in the notebook while the other hand entered either a *V* for vancomycin or an *E* for Endovancin into the column on the screen. After several minutes she looked at Meghan and pushed the ledger in front of her. "This is too inefficient. Read me the data and the antibiotic given for each patient. Start with the first patient in the first experiment. I'll enter it in the spreadsheet."

Specimen 28473, date of surgery August 5th, vancomycin. She repeated the process until the fifteenth subject. *Specimen 35987, date of surgery August 22nd, Endovancin.*

"Keep going," Claire said.

Meghan continued and a few minutes later she said, "It's the antibiotic, isn't it?"

Claire's heart was racing. She read the data for the third time and grinned. "I think so."

"Spill it. Don't hold back on me."

Claire leaned back in the desk chair. "Just before starting these studies I attended a conference in Madrid and became aware of a new experimental antibiotic. Meera Jindal, a pharmacologist I studied with in graduate school, was developing a compound with long-acting antimicrobial properties. When we were alone I asked her about it. After I returned, I called the head of the company Jindal works for and asked if they would be interested in testing it in clinical trials."

"*After* the fourteenth surgery," Meghan interrupted.

Claire nodded and glanced at the spreadsheet. "That's how it happened. We used it until it ran out after the tenth subject in our second group. I remember because there was a delay in production and we had to go back to the original antibiotic." She put her finger on the computer screen. "See? These five were given vancomycin. The next batch must have arrived because the last nine were administered EndoV."

"EndoV?" Meghan looked at her quizzically.

"Endovancin."

"Whatever you call it, the subjects who received it are cancer-free," Meghan said. "Every last one of them. Who would have imagined it might have antitumor properties?"

"All we cared about was preventing post-op infections." Claire reached for her phone.

"You calling Mark?"

"Not yet. I'll put this on speaker."

"Hello."

"Stephen?" asked Claire.

"Claire?"

"Have you checked on the patients from yesterday?"

"Of course. I just got back. They're doing quite well, actually. Much better than I expected."

"They all received a pre-op dose of antibiotic, right?"

"Of course," he said.

"Which antibiotic?"

"The one called for in the protocol. Your Endovancin," Stephen replied.

"No other treatments, right?"

"Just pain meds."

"Give them another dose. Make sure every patient gets two doses of Endovancin twenty-four hours apart," Claire instructed, "and check on them twice a day."

"You want to tell me what's going on? We haven't had any infections."

"Meghan McKenna, my postdoc fellow, examined the histology specimens this morning. All of the experimental animals that received Endovancin are tumor-free. The others developed osteosarcoma."

"Good God."

"That he is," Claire agreed. "I want to biopsy those monkeys again next week."

"We're going to need more of the drug. We might have enough

for the rest of this week, but one hundred and forty-four animals, two doses each? We don't have enough."

"Keep giving it. I'll get more . . . and Stephen? Keep this to yourself."

"I signed an NDA, too. Remember?"

"Right. Sorry. This is so shocking it makes me nervous," Claire said. "I'll call tomorrow for a progress report. Is this a good time?"

"It works for me. If I don't answer it means I'm doing rounds. Call back an hour later and I should be free."

"Talk to you then." She hung up and looked at Meghan. "Better let Robert know we plan to do another round of biopsies. Make sure we have enough reagents."

"WHAT'S WITH THE BIG MEETING?" Ard asked.

Meghan closed her lab book and put down her pen. "Pardon me?"

"You've been gone almost two hours talking to the boss in her office with the door closed. What's up?"

"Nothing's up, Robert. We were discussing plans for some experiments."

"What about all those slides I just finished preparing?"

"What about them?" Meghan asked.

"Did they tell you anything? Dr. Hodgson wanted the results as soon as possible. They must have been important."

"More than you can imagine."

"They're biopsy samples from the bone graft trials."

"That's right," she said.

"Was it the drug? The new antibiotic? It worked, didn't it?"

"Who told you we were testing a drug?"

"You did. I remember you mentioned it a while back," Ard said as he pushed his glasses up the bridge of his nose.

"I don't remember that."

"I do. Well, did the slides tell you anything?"

"Yes. They were very helpful. Dr. Hodgson said to tell you that there would be another round of biopsies at the end of the week. Order any slide prep reagents if we need them. Now, if you'll excuse me. I have a few errands to run." Meghan rose and hung up her lab coat. "I'll see you in the morning." She picked up her purse and walked to the door. Ard followed her and sat down at his desk in the cubicle near the front of the lab.

"Drive safe," he called out as the door closed. Fifteen minutes later he rose and opened the door and looked up and down the hallway. He walked back to Meghan's desk and picked up her lab notebook. He opened it to the last page and scanned the data columns. He'd helped her collect and record much of the histological data from the experiments and understood her codes and abbreviations. He smiled as he read the summary at the bottom of the page.

In every case, the experimental subjects given preoperative doses of Endovancin did not develop any physical, radiographic, or histological signs of osteosarcoma. All subjects who received vancomycin as the preoperative antibiotic showed some indication of developing osteosarc. It must be concluded that Endovancin either cures or prevents osteosarcoma.

Ard turned the page.

Electra Pharmaceuticals, Barro Colorado Island, Smithsonian Tropical Research Institute, Panama.

He took out his phone and photographed the data and her conclusions. He smiled as he closed the notebook and replaced it on Meghan's desk. *The price of doing business just went up.*

SEVEN

WEDNESDAY, MARCH 22ND

Wilson Andrews Equine Research Center, Roanoke, Virginia

WARWICK GRANT LEANED FORWARD in his desk chair and reread the title of the scholarly article, "The Use of Stem Cells Implanted Within 3D Bioprinted Bone Graft in the Treatment of Complex Fractures" by C.E. Hodgson, PhD and M.A. Thurman, MD. He'd read it three times and was almost convinced they could rebuild Hyperion's broken limb and have it heal fast enough to prevent his other hooves from becoming diseased. It was the only hope.

He clenched his fists then spun his chair away from the computer and glanced out the huge glass windows. In the distance, white fences and green pastures spread over the Virginia countryside. Several mares nibbled at the ground while their foals pranced. He pinched his chin and realized he'd forgotten to shave after Thurman's phone call. The news of Hyperion's delayed surgery had cast a pall over his mood. The clock on his bookshelf chimed. It was time for afternoon rounds.

"How's he doing?" Grant asked the man spreading fresh straw on the stable floor. Hyperion stood in the rear corner holding his splinted limb off the ground.

"Not good," Roger Coleman replied. He stood in the stall wearing blue jeans tucked into tall green rubber boots and a khaki work shirt with his name and the Wilson Andrews logo embroidered on his left pocket.

"He looks depressed. Is he getting worse?"

"I think so. Wouldn't you be? Those infusions aren't doing much. What does Thurman call it? Bethesda therapy?"

Grant nodded. "It's supposed to prime the body for surgery."

"How? By preventing muscle atrophy?"

"They claim it halts catabolism and accelerates recovery. We've modified it by adjusting the dosage and changing the hormones to the equine variants."

"What's in it? Anabolic steroids?"

"That. Plus some other hormones, amino acids, and growth factors along with a few additional metabolites."

"Ponce de León's elixir," Coleman scoffed.

"Straight from the Fountain of Youth. Thurman says it speeds healing by about thirty percent after surgery."

"It doesn't look like it's doing a damn thing."

Grant opened the gate and stepped into the stall carrying a white tackle box. "How are the other legs?"

"I checked this morning. No signs of laminitis."

"Good. He'll have to stand on them a while longer," Grant said.

Coleman stopped spreading hay and looked up. "Why?"

"The procedure has been put on hold. Thurman called this morning. They're having problems. Some of their early patients are sick. Some type of complication from the treatment. They want to delay the surgery for a few days."

"They better figure it out fast. Three-legged horses don't last long." Coleman stood and rubbed the great animal's nose then handed him a mint. The horse took it from his hand and flicked his head.

"We have no choice. Let's change this dressing." Grant placed the bandage container next to the horse and retrieved several items. He tore an alcohol swab and wiped the IV catheter protruding from the horse's gigantic jugular vein. He took a syringe and injected a dose of morphine into the tubing. Within several minutes Hyperion's head hung lower and his eyelids began to droop.

"He's ready," said Coleman and began removing the aluminum splint. He unrolled the bandages and lifted the soiled gauze, exposing the wound. The incision was intact and dry with only a few brown flecks of dried blood adhering to the staples. The leg remained swollen. Coleman was careful to avoid any unnecessary movement. Even with the opioid in his system, any motion at the fracture site would cause discomfort. Grant handed him a stack of saline-soaked gauze sponges. He wiped the staple line with the moist gauze then reapplied fresh bandages and the splint. "You really think this is going to work?" he asked.

Grant shrugged. "Have you read their studies?"

Coleman nodded. "It's a long shot."

"It's the best one we've got."

"You didn't answer the question."

"I honestly don't know," Grant said.

"Well, I'm pretty sure it won't."

"Why?"

"C'mon. You really believe a shattered leg in a half-ton horse can heal in a couple of weeks?

"It's worked in other species."

"What have you been drinking? That's impossible. It's gonna fail, and eventually, we'll put him down," Coleman said.

"At least we'll have tried."

Coleman stepped out of the stall and closed the gate. "He's due for the next infusion in an hour. I've got other things to do. See you later."

Grant stood next to Hyperion and stroked his face. He ran his fingers over the star-shaped patch of white hair between his eyes and gently spoke into his ear. "You're a good fella with bad luck. It's been a tough three years. Orphaned at birth and now this? It's not your fault your poor mother died bringing you into this world. Did you even know that? A lot of people are pulling for you. Stay strong, fella. Don't give up. Remember when they said you were too small . . . not enough heart to be a winner? You shut 'em up and you'll do it again. We'll find a way, ole boy."

MARK THURMAN TURNED his pickup truck into the parking lot and found an empty space. He was early and looked forward to seeing his friend, Jimmy Ward, the owner of the Old Oaks Tavern. Inside, the dining room was dim. After a few seconds, his eyes adjusted to the lambent light and he could make out the twin mammoth fireplaces at each end of the great room. About a third of the tables were occupied, and there were several empty stools at the bar.

"How things goin', Doc?" asked the bartender.

"Good. Jimmy around?"

His head jerked over his right shoulder. "In the pantry. What can I get ya?" He pointed to a tap handle. "We're tryin' a new lager. It's brewed in Asheville."

"Pour me a pint. I'll stick my head in the kitchen and be right back." As he meandered around tables through the rustic space, he glanced up at the reclaimed ancient wooden warehouse beams. They brought memories of bygone summers spent working shirtless in North Carolina tobacco fields near Jacksonville where they hung fresh-cut leaves like laundry in curing barns. The sweet hay and rose petal scent of the summer harvest was recaptured for a moment and seemed almost real. He pushed open the swinging doors and walked into the bright kitchen. Several employees stood with their backs to him, preparing food. "Anyone seen Jimmy?" A woman turned and smiled. She pointed with her large knife.

"He was in the walk-in a minute ago."

Mark made his way through the maze of stainless steel tables and shelving to the back of the kitchen. A floor-to-ceiling metal freezer was just beyond the ice machines. As he approached, the door sprung open, gushing fog that hovered briefly over the floor before disappearing. Jimmy closed the door and the large chrome handle snapped, sealing it shut.

"Marcus! Man, it's good to see you."

"You too." He walked up and embraced his companion.

"The iceman cometh," Jimmy said, taking off his frosted sweatshirt. "You caught me checking inventory."

"If you can spare a few minutes, I'll be at the bar checking your beer inventory."

"Gimme five."

The pint of amber ale was half gone when his compadre reappeared. Jim Ward had proven to be Mark's closest friend. He'd walked the walk. They'd met when both were freshmen recruited to play baseball at Wake Forest University. Mark pitched. Jimmy played second. After graduation, Jimmy began managing restaurants while Mark went to medical school.

A dozen years later Jimmy owned this place, and Mark was given a medical discharge from the Navy after being diagnosed with Ewing's sarcoma. He returned to Raleigh alone. His parents were gone and siblings lived far away. That was when he discovered the true character of his friend. One day, Jimmy appeared at his front door asking if he could help. He stuck by him through all six months of the cancer war. He was there when the odds were long and the light dim. He drove Mark to every chemotherapy session and radiation treatment. When Mark's body shriveled and hair fell out, Jim asked only that his friend continue the fight. "Don't ever give up," he would repeat. Neither one did.

These days, the sixty pounds of body weight lost during treatments had been rebuilt. His six-foot-two frame packed two hundred and ten pounds of cordlike muscle. His Mr. Clean baldhead was now covered in a shock of brown curls. Mark could never repay this debt of gratitude. Jimmy never even thought about it.

"Where's Claire?"

Mark glanced up from his phone on the bar. "She's on her way. I'm a little early and thought we'd catch up. Did you make a decision?"

Jimmy pulled up a barstool. "Why can't *she* get here early and catch up with me?" He smiled.

"Don't I rate?"

"Not like her, buddy." The bartender handed Jimmy a bottle of water. "If you're referring to the new place, I can't decide if it's worth the risk."

"Would it have the same name? Like a franchise?" Mark asked.

"I don't know. I'm more worried about the location. Winston-Salem is a good town. We both know that. There's a definite need, but the restaurant business is fickle. What works in one city may not work in another. I'm going to check a couple other locations in the downtown area and think about it for a few more months. How were the horse races?"

Mark retold the events of last Saturday.

"You're going to fix him?" Jimmy asked in surprise.

"I hope so, but keep it to yourself. We don't know for sure, and I can't say anything else right now. I'll give you an update in a couple of days."

Mark signaled the bartender for another round. He watched in the bar mirror as the front door opened and a backlit silhouette of a woman removed her sunglasses and stood scanning the patrons. Mark raised his hand and Jimmy sprang to his feet. The woman saw them and approached the bar.

"Hello, boys," Claire said as Jimmy kissed her cheek.

"Will you marry me?"

"Now, James, we've been over this and the answer is still–no," Claire said.

Jimmy placed his right hand over his heart and looked toward the ceiling. "Had we but world enough and time, this coyness, Lady, would be no crime."

"I think it's 'were no crime,'" Mark said.

"Huh?"

". . . this coyness, Lady, were no crime," he corrected. "Plus, she wasn't very coy."

"It was a straightforward rejection. Sorry." She patted his cheek.

"Can't blame a guy for trying." A waitress approached and whispered in Jimmy's ear. He smiled and turned to Mark. "Your table is ready. I'll come find you after my broken heart mends." The woman led Mark and Claire into another room and sat them at a booth near the back.

"How's this?"

"Perfect," he said as they slid into their seats.

"YOU'RE SURE?" Mark asked.

Claire nodded. "Statistically, it's significant to the .001 level. Meghan and I ran the data analysis this afternoon. Endovancin is a great antibiotic and a better chemotherapeutic agent."

"How can that be?"

"What do you mean?"

"How does it have *both* effects?"

She unrolled her silverware from the cloth and placed the utensils next to her plate, then slid the linen napkin onto her lap. "There are several examples of antibiotics that have anticancer effects. The entire fluoroquinolone family is a good example. They interrupt DNA replication."

"It's been a while since I've thought about biochemistry."

Claire smiled. "I know. You've got other things on your mind when you're operating. Also, there's another class of antibiotic drugs based on Streptomyces that have been used to fight cancers for decades."

"Like Adriamycin?"

"Unfortunately, they have a lot of unpleasant side effects."

"That one I know *all* about. It made my hair fall out and made me puke for two days after each dose. I hated that crap."

She reached across the table and tousled his hair. "It grew back and you're here with me."

"Then, it was worth it."

She smiled and squeezed his hand. "I didn't mean to bring up bad memories. My point is . . . Endovancin could be the first in a new class of anticancer *and* antibiotic drugs that don't appear to have a lot of side effects. It's miraculous."

"Okay. Let's say it is. How does it work? Got any theories?"

"Meghan and I came up with a few ideas. I think it has to do with the Wnt cell signaling pathway."

Their waitress stepped up to the table. "Any questions about the menu?"

"I'll have the tuna tostadas," Claire said.

Mark looked over the top of his menu at the waitress. "The rib eye, medium rare, and bring a bottle of the Amon-Ra Shiraz."

"Good on ya," Claire said, holding her fist up over the table. "Jimmy's upping his game."

Mark touched her knuckles with his. "I mentioned it was your favorite. He ordered a case."

"He's a darling. I may have to reconsider his proposal."

The waitress repeated their orders while collecting the menus. Mark glanced across the table. "So, you think it's a Wnt protein effect?"

Claire nodded. "I'm pretty sure. When we print the bone, the extracellular fluid is fortified with a boatload of Wnt proteins."

"A boatload?"

"Yes, a bloody boatload. They bind at receptors on the stem cell membrane and start them on the path to becoming osteoblasts."

"Is it a membrane receptor problem? Maybe a G-protein coupled receptor?"

She shook her head. "It's a receptor problem, but not GPCRs. The Wnts bind at Frizzled receptors, which allows ß-catenin to enter."

Mark interlocked his fingers on the table and leaned forward. "So, what's the big deal?"

"The ß-catenin concentration is too high. Probably by a couple of orders of magnitude."

"A hundred times too high. How is that possible?"

"We've created a situation where the Frizzled receptors are saturated with Wnt proteins. They open up and let a massive amount of ß-catenin inside the cell. The destruction complexes can't keep up."

He rolled his eyes. "Destruction complexes? Sounds like something Ingram and I would shoot at on the firing range."

She ignored the look and shook her head. "They're enzyme complexes that hunt proteins tagged for destruction and chew them into amino acids. That's how the ß-catenin levels are regulated. However, in this case, the surge is overwhelming. The cell is swamped."

"And gene transcription goes into overdrive," he commented.

"Yes! Exactly."

Mark and Claire stopped talking and turned their heads. The waitress looked at them like they were speaking a foreign language. She presented the bottle to Mark. "2010 Amon-Ra," she said. She placed two wineglasses on the table and poured some into Mark's. He inspected the color, inhaled its aroma, and swallowed the sample.

"Excellent."

She filled the glasses as Claire continued. "It's our worst nightmare."

"I can see why you like this. It's really good." He sipped the shiraz and twirled the glass, whipping the plum-colored liquid into a frothy vortex. Then, he stuck his nose into the glass and inhaled. "Earth, blackberries, and a hint of cinnamon. A definite ninety-seven points on the Parker scale."

"Will you be serious? You wouldn't know a ninety-seven-point wine if it bit you on the butt."

The corners of his eyes wrinkled as a grin spread across his face. "So gene transcription and protein production get turbocharged. How does that cause a sarcoma?"

"Remember your intro to biology? The cell cycle?"

"Haven't thought about it in at least a decade."

"You remember the four phases of the cycle leading to cell division. The stem cells are stuck in G_1 phase waiting to copy their DNA. Millions of proteins have to be produced. Once this happens, the cells can begin replicating. Then, they move into S phase where they copy all their DNA."

"So what goes wrong?"

"Mutations. Transcription errors. Probably in tumor suppressor genes. Cell division is happening much faster than it normally would. If a suppressor gene is knocked out, the proteins that find and repair genetic mistakes are lost. The risk of an error not being detected and eliminated skyrockets. If the right mutations occur, all it takes is one cell to be transformed into a cancer cell. Slowly, over time, it will keep dividing and a tumor develops."

Mark held up his hand. "I get that part. Should we have anticipated this?"

"Maybe. Hindsight's always twenty-twenty."

"Say you're right. And a tumor starts to develop. How does Endovancin cure it?"

"More, please." Claire held out her wineglass. "This is the silver lining. I don't know, for sure. We'll have to figure out some experiments to prove it, but there's only one or two places where it can work. In order for the cell to replicate, it has to move from G_1 into S phase of the cell cycle. For it to do this, it has to get past several replication checkpoints."

"I forgot about the old checkpoints." He raised an eyebrow and raked his hair with his fingertips.

"Pay attention. This is the important part." She took another sip of wine. "One of the many things ß-catenin does is to increase the production of cyclin D."

"Huh?"

"Cyclin D. It's a protein that regulates cell cycle progression. It's like a traffic light. It allows a dividing cell to get past the replication checkpoint and move from G_1 into S phase."

"Endovancin prevents cyclin D from being produced," he stated.

"Very good. You get an A-plus for paying attention." Claire smiled and tossed her napkin at him. He snatched it from the air. She continued without a pause. "*I think* Endovancin blocks cyclin D production. That's how it stops the cell from continuing through the cell replication cycle and kills off the cancer cells."

Mark smiled and handed her linen back. "Then why do the fractures heal so fast? Without cyclin D, nothing should happen."

"I think it's a delayed effect. cyclin D production isn't shut down until after enough osteoblasts are produced to heal the fracture."

"All right. I'll buy it."

"You should. I'm betting it's a cure for osteosarcoma. Maybe other cancers, too."

One of the wait staff brought a basket of hot bread and their dinner salads. Mark placed his napkin in his lap. "You're funny," he said quietly.

She tilted her head. "Funny?"

"Excitement . . . innocence, enthusiasm. I don't see much of that these days."

She smiled and sipped her wine. "There are a couple of other possible explanations. I'm not going to tell you about the retinoblastoma protein and the E2F transcription complex."

"Thanks, ß-catenin and cyclin D are about all I can handle. Your theory is solid. Now, you have to test it."

"I know. I've got some ideas for experiments, but we need more drug. We're almost out."

"So? Call Roberts. Have him send it."

"I did."

Mark shrugged. "And?"

"He's not sure if they have enough."

"Why not? So far, they've given us all we need," Mark said.

"That's the problem. We're going to need a lot more. They may not be able to produce it fast enough. He wants me to talk to his lead scientist, Meera Jindal. She runs the lab."

"Do it. We have to treat Hyperion and the rest of our patients."

"I know. That's why I'm going to Panama," Claire said. "I want to see her lab and bring back as much as they'll let me have."

Mark stared at her.

The waitress brought their entrees. The steak sizzled and smelled like it came straight from the grill. "When do you leave?" Mark asked.

"Tomorrow morning."

"Be greedy. Bring back as much as you can."

"I will. Endovancin is the key," Claire said. "My flight leaves at seven."

EIGHT

THURSDAY, MARCH 23RD

Piedmont Apartments, Durham, North Carolina

ROBERT ARD WALKED through the entrance to his apartment building without noticing the custodian. His gaze was drawn to the young woman across the lobby. She was standing by the bank of mailboxes flipping through a stack of letters. She wore tight jeans and filled out the top half of her low-cut V-neck sweater.

"Watch out. Wet floor," the janitor warned just as Ard's right foot began its skid. His phone flew from his hand while his body twisted in midair like a diver. He almost landed on his hands and toes, but his arms splayed outward and he belly-flopped on the linoleum. His glasses clattered across the deck.

"Oh . . ." Ard groaned as he rolled to his back.

"I told you to watch out," the janitor said. "Can't you read the sign?" He looked down and returned to his chore, wiping the mop over the mark left by Ard's path to the floor. "Stupid kids can't walk anywhere these days without their noses stuck in a cell phone."

"Are you all right?"

Ard rubbed his eyes and stared at the blurry blonde vision kneeling beside him. She smiled and handed him his glasses. He put them on and noticed the pink ribbon at the base of her ponytail on the right side of her head. It gave her a schoolgirl look, and for a moment he forgot his embarrassment.

"I think so." He struggled to his feet as she helped him up. "I'm sorry."

"For what?" she asked. "Slipping?"

"For being so clumsy."

"Don't be ridiculous. It was his fault for mopping the entrance at this time of day. What a jerk." The woman walked back to her mailbox and locked the metal door. She bent down to pick up several large boxes.

He followed her and held out his hand. "I'm Robert Ard. Do you live here?"

The woman smiled. "Yes. Fifth floor."

"Me too. You need a hand with those?"

"You feel up to it?"

"I'm fine."

"That would be great. Thank you. I'm Eileen . . . Eileen Logan. I just moved in."

"I thought so. I live down the hall. I saw them delivering some-one's stuff yesterday."

"Really?" she asked in surprise.

"I mean, I'm not a stalker or anything like that. I couldn't help but notice. They made a lot of racket."

She laughed. "I didn't think you were stalking me."

He squatted and stacked two boxes on top of each other.

"Thanks for the help."

"Sure, no problem." He stood up and followed her to the elevator. "You live alone?"

She smiled. "At the moment. Just moved from Philly. It's just me. I work for Blue Cross and start my executive MBA next semester."

"That's great."

"What about you?" she asked.

"I'm a lab tech at the medical school but hope to start next year."

"Start medical school?"

He nodded and she noticed a trace of strain on his face. "I have a bunch of applications I'm waiting to hear from."

"That's awesome. You can put them down, you know," she said, looking at the boxes.

"Oh, no. I'm okay." They got off at the fifth floor and Ard followed her down the hall. "It's not a done deal, but I have a pretty good shot."

"Well, good luck." She opened the door to her apartment, and he placed the boxes just inside and let out a small breath. She smiled, noticing the relief. "I'm meeting some friends at The Cellar later. If you drop by I'll buy you a drink."

"You're on. What time?"

"Say eight o'clock?"

"See you then." He waved and walked down the hall. Everything was going his way.

ARD LOOKED over the pilfered data and reread Meghan's comments. He pulled out part of his shirttail and used it to clean his glasses. *No wonder Sorenson wants this information.* He smiled, pulled out the business card, and dialed the number. Sorenson answered after the fourth ring.

"Neil, it's Robert Ard."

"What can I do for you, Robert?"

"I've got something."

Sorenson paused for a second. "Really? That's excellent. I wasn't expecting a call so soon."

"I wasn't either, but there's been some developments in the lab. Stuff I think you'll be interested in."

"Yes. Go on," Sorenson said.

"The latest results."

"What are you trying to say, Robert?"

"They're impressive."

"We're talking about Endovancin, right?"

"Yes. I've also been thinking about what we talked about on Monday."

"And?" Sorenson asked.

"I think the information you're after may be worth a lot of money."

"I hope you're right. That's what we're counting on," Sorenson replied.

Ard pulled out a chair at his kitchen table and sat down. "It's worth more than the deal you proposed. The experimental results are incredible. Almost unbelievable."

"That's interesting, Robert, but how do I know this is true?"

"I have copies of the original data, photos of the lab books, and the histology slides. With these details you can reproduce the experiments, or some similar version, in Telos labs. You can claim it's your drug, file a patent, and be first to market. Your IPO price will go to the moon." Ard's voice rose as he laid out his vision.

"Robert, how much do you know about pharmaceutical patents?"

"Not much."

"I thought so. Your vision of the future is one I'd like to see happen. However, in all likelihood, Electra already has filed for the patent. We couldn't produce and market it in this country. Telos would be shut down immediately, and we'd be tied up in the courts for ages."

"Then . . . why do you want it?"

"That's not your worry, son."

Ard noted the condescension. "But the drug cures cancer, for God's sake. It's not just an antibiotic. You could bring it to market as a totally different product. You could claim Telos has been developing it as an anticancer drug. Wait until you see the data. It's incredible."

"Don't misunderstand me. We're still interested in the information. Do you have the formula?"

"No, but I know where you can get it."

"When can I see the data?" Sorenson's voice quickened. "The sooner the better."

"Not so fast, my friend. You and I both know what this means. Endovancin will be worth hundreds of millions, maybe billions. This is game-changing, career-making information. You think I'm going to just hand it over to you?"

"Robert, we have an agreement," Sorenson reminded him. "In return for the information, we help you get into medical school, and your current salary will be handsomely supplemented."

Ard laughed. "I have a better idea."

"And what might that be?"

"The other day you mentioned Thomas Jefferson as a possibility for medical school. They rejected me this year but still have my application. Maybe they made a mistake."

"Maybe they did," Sorenson agreed.

"I'll need a letter of acceptance for next year's class. I deserve it. I've earned it! No one's more qualified than me!"

"I think that can be arranged," Sorenson said. "Provided what you say is true."

"Oh, it's true, but there's more. If you're going to develop a drug worth hundreds of millions, I want a little piece to fund my education, of course."

"Naturally, a reasonable request."

"I want Robert Ard to be the recipient of the first Telos medical education scholarship. The prize being a trust set up in my name funded with four hundred thousand dollars, fifty thousand to be paid out at the beginning of each semester for the next four years. Fair enough?"

"Provided the information is what you claim."

"Trust me. It is," Ard said. "Oh, and I'll need a little extra to get me through the rest of this year. Say a hundred thousand wired to an account in the Caymans."

Sorenson laughed. "We're not handing over half a million bucks without full disclosure. Hell, the acceptance letter will cost us a million-dollar donation to the medical school endowment. Show me what you've got."

"The scholarship and donation are charitable write-offs," Ard said. "I'm not feeling too sorry for you, and I'm not being greedy. You're getting off easy. It's the best deal you'll ever make."

"Show me the data."

He thought about it for a moment. It would be best if it were a public place in the middle of the day. "A peek, but that's all. Lunch tomorrow. Same place as before. I'll bring a sample for you to look at. No pictures. You'll see what I'm talking about."

ARD LOOKED AT THE CLOCK. There was time to stop by the bank on the way back to the lab. He parked in the metered spot along the street and ran into the Mid Atlantic Bank & Trust. The assistant manager's desk was in the far corner of the lobby. A middle-aged brunette in a white blouse with a cultured pearl necklace looked up from her desk as he approached.

"May I help you?"

"I'd like to access my safety deposit box." He gave her the number, signed the register, and followed her to the vault. She took his key and used it to open the small door. She slid the metal box out and walked with it to a private room next to the vault.

"Let me know when you're finished."

"This will only take a second," he said. She shut the door and he removed the manila envelope from his backpack, folded it, and placed it in the long narrow box. *My Telos insurance policy.* He smiled then shut the lid and opened the door. "I'm ready." He watched her lock it and took his key. "Thanks."

Fifteen minutes later he was back in the histology laboratory preparing reagents for pathology specimens. He worked until five thirty and was standing in his cubicle with a backpack slung on one shoulder, ready to go home, when Meghan approached.

"Dr. Hodgson needs you to make some slides. There are five specimens she wants to take another look at." She handed him a piece of paper. "These are the numbers."

"When does she want them?"

"In the morning."

"Tomorrow?"

Meghan nodded. "Sorry, it's important."

"Damn. I've got plans," Ard said.

"It shouldn't take too long. I put the biopsies on the lab bench. All you have to do is cut the tissue and stain them."

"Easy for you to say."

"Want me to help?" Meghan asked.

Ard thought about it but realized it would go faster if he worked alone. "No, thanks. I'll do it. See you in the morning." When he finished it was almost eight o'clock. He locked the lab door and headed to his car.

He drove ten blocks and parked in the public lot across the street from The Cellar. It was crowded and noisy. Thursday was ladies' night and the promotion was working. It helped that the first round of the NCAA tournament was on the screen above the bar. The Duke game started in an hour and some of the Cameron Crazies were warming up in the back room. He made a lap around the joint but didn't see any sign of Eileen. He decided to eat dinner and stick around for the first half of the game. He sat at the end of the bar and ordered a draft and a burger. Every few minutes he'd look away from the ballgame and search for long blonde hair with a pink ribbon. *She probably took it out,* he reasoned to himself. He watched one of the teams make a run, then he ordered another beer as his dinner arrived.

Thirty minutes later, the first game was over and his plate was empty. The Blue Devils were warming up and he was looking at his empty glass. The bartender removed it and replaced it with a full one. "I didn't order another," he said.

"It's from the lady at the end of the bar." He jerked his thumb and Ard turned his head to the left. She smiled and waved as she started making her way toward him, moving in and out of the near-capacity crowd.

"There you are," Eileen said, squeezing in between the guy sitting on the stool next to him. She had to put her face a few inches from his ear in order to be heard as the tip-off occurred and the first Blue Devil basket was scored. "I've been looking for you."

"I've been here for almost an hour."

"I thought I was meeting a friend, but her boyfriend called and she bagged out on me. Sorry I'm late." She wore the same outfit, but a coat covered the low-cut sweater. He felt the pressure of her breasts press against his arm. Her makeup was flawless. He took a large sip from the new glass. He'd never been with a woman this beautiful. The amber liquid was courage.

"You're not late. It's not like we had a real date or anything," he said.

"Now that I'm not with anyone it could be, if you want," she said and flashed a perfect smile. Eileen slid onto the vacated barstool next to them as the guy stood and walked toward the bathroom. Robert took another drink and pinched his forearm. She ordered a glass of wine and leaned close to him. "Been in this town long?"

Ard proceeded to tell her the general details of his recent past, the undergraduate years and his decision to go to medical school. "I'd originally planned to get a master's degree in histology then become a pathologist but didn't want to do the experiments and write a thesis. I'm good at handling tissue and preparing slides. I decided to work as a lab tech and concentrate on the MCAT."

"The what?" she asked.

"Medical college admissions test. You need a good score or they don't even look at you, even if you have great grades."

"Did you do okay?"

"Good enough." He smiled and slid his empty glass toward the bartender and nodded for a refill. "I have a trump card."

She turned her face toward him and placed her hand on the back of his neck and moved close. Her cheek brushed against his ear as a rowdy patron bumped her stumbling past in the aisle. "Excuse me!" she said to the brute as he moved on. She looked back at Ard. "What do you mean?"

"One of the scientists I work for is doing some really great stuff. I'm part of it. Some people I know have inside connections with some med school admissions committees. It's practically a formality. Me getting in, I mean."

"That must be exciting to be involved in real medical research like that. What kind of work are they doing?" She placed her hand on his thigh. Robert felt a stirring and took another gulp of ale.

"You're in my seat," the big man said. Eileen turned around and looked at the man who had vacated the stool a few minutes ago. "I said I'd be back. You're in my seat," he practically shouted. His face was flushed. "Move or I'm going to drag your boyfriend out back and kick his scrawny ass."

Ard stood and pushed his glasses up on his nose. "It's not your seat. You got up."

The big man grabbed Ard by the shirt collar and flicked the tip of his nose with his finger. "This is going to be fun. Duke punks are always easy."

Eileen put her hands on his chest and pushed. "Back off jerk, you can have your seat. We were just leaving." She picked up her purse and pulled Ard toward the door. "What an asshole," she said as they stepped into the cool evening. On the sidewalk she turned to him. "You want to go someplace else?"

"Sure, where?"

"I've had it with the bar scene for tonight. Can we go back to your place? Mine's a wreck. Boxes all over the place."

"My car is in the parking garage," he said, pointing across the street.

The elevator doors opened and they walked down the hall. She wrapped her arm around his and leaned against him. "I have some really good Kentucky bourbon. Let me get it and we can have a night-cap," she said as he was unlocking his door. "I'll be right back."

"Hurry," he said. He walked into the apartment and hung up his jacket. He went to the bathroom then turned on the game. He watched the opposing team hit a three-pointer at the end of the half to tie it up. He heard the knock and looked up as Eileen entered. She had changed out of her jeans and wore loose-fitting sweatpants. She still wore the snug sweater but had apparently taken off her bra. Her round breasts bounced as she walked, and her nipples looked like two half-dollar-sized buttons under the material. Ard gulped.

"Kentucky's finest," she said, holding up the bottle. "I brought it back from the Derby last year. Want some?" In the other hand she held out two small brandy snifters. She placed them on the coffee table and poured a finger full into each. She handed one to him and brought the other to her nose.

"Smells great," he said and coughed after taking a sip. "Strong too."

"It gets smooth after a few sips." She sat next to him on the couch and nestled against his arm. "Now, tell me more about your work."

He felt the softness of her sweater rub against his arm. "It's not really that interesting."

"I find it fascinating. Such important work. You could be famous one day. You did all that cancer research?"

"How did you know about that?"

"You started to tell me about it in the bar."

"I did?" She nodded and he proceeded to explain the experiments he'd worked on over the last eighteen months. His words were becoming harder to speak. He needed to slow down. The beer and the bourbon were adding up.

"I'm a science geek deep down," she said again, placing her hand on his thigh. Ard took a deep breath as her hand moved up and rubbed his chest. "Show me where you do your work." She stood and pulled off her sweater. Ard blinked at her perfectly shaped breasts. She took his hand and led him toward his bedroom. She knelt and pulled his pants down. "I have something that will help you," she said holding him. "It'll make it really fun, better than Viagra." She held out two pills and placed them in his mouth. "Give that a few minutes and you'll be a tiger."

The room was spinning and it was hard to keep his eyes open. He felt so relaxed, like he was floating in warm water. "What did you say?" he asked. *Why was she asking so many questions?*

"Where is the data?" she asked. "Tell me where it is."

He reached out to touch her luscious breasts and cupped them in his hands. He tried to kiss one of her nipples.

"Where is it?"

"Phone . . . pictures," he slurred.

She let out an exasperated breath. "No, we're not taking any pictures. Where is the information? I need the data from your lab."

"Data, pictures," he mumbled almost incoherently. "These are . . . incred . . . ible." He pawed at her like a giant infant with an empty belly.

It dawned on her when she laid him on the bed and finished removing his pants. Putting her hand into the front left pocket she pulled it out and pressed the home button. It was locked. "Damn!" She looked at the sleeping body on the bed and shook him. "What's the code? The code to your phone?" she asked. He lay there unresponsive. She looked back at the phone and punched in *1 2 3 4*. Nothing. She sat on the side of the bed, and his left hand moved. She smiled and took his thumb and pressed it against the home button. Nothing. Then, she reached across the bed and held his other thumb and pressed it against the phone. A second later the screen displayed a field of icons. She opened the one containing his photos and looked at the most recent. It was a photograph of a handwritten table of numbers labeled *Yemassee Data*. The next several pictures were similar. "Jackpot," she whispered. The last few pictures were of handwritten conclusions. It didn't mean anything to her.

She dressed and found her cigarettes in her purse. She lit one and picked up her own phone and dialed. It was almost midnight. Her hands were shaking.

"How did it go?"

"I got it."

"Did he take the pills?"

"Yes. He almost passed out before getting them down," she laughed.

"That would have been a major fuck-up."

"Yeah, well, it worked."

"We needed him to swallow them. You have the patches?" asked the man.

"I ain't doing that," she replied and took another drag from her cigarette. "I got him drunk and got your information. Now, pay me."

"Do what I told you. Take the patches and peel off the back and place them on his skin where he doesn't have any hair. You're already an accessory."

"I'm not gonna do that. I won't kill him. That wasn't part of the deal," she said and blew a stream of smoke toward the ceiling.

"You're not killing him, you're sedating him. Put the patches on and send me the pictures. Leave the door unlocked. Understand?"

"I'm not doing anything until I get paid."

"You'll get paid. Now, send them or you'll be looking over your shoulder for the rest of your short life."

"You won't do that. You need me," she said.

"The money's in your Paris account. Check it. Then, put the damn patches on and send me the photos. If I don't have them in thirty minutes, someone will be at your apartment and they'll find both of your bodies lying next to each other tomorrow morning. Don't make me do that."

She went back to her apartment and opened her laptop. She logged into her AXA Banque account and found what he'd said was true. She closed the lid and stubbed out her cigarette, then went back to Ard's apartment. She rolled him on his side and placed two one-hundred-microgram fentanyl transdermal patches onto his skin and rolled him back. She stood and looked at him. "Sorry, little man, you tangled with the wrong crowd." She held his thumb and unlocked the phone and located the photographs. She forwarded them and deleted them as instructed. She placed the device back into his pants pocket and dropped them on the floor without caring if her prints were on the phone. If anyone found it, she would say he handed it to her to show pictures of his friends before he passed out, but she knew it would be an incinerated glob of metal and plastic by tomorrow morning.

MULLION MAGNIFIED the images on the computer. He read the conclusions a second time and blinked. He picked up his phone and dialed Ramon.

"You know what time it is, amigo?"

"This couldn't wait. Ever heard of Barro Colorado Island?"

NINE

Stem Cell Research and Regenerative Medicine Laboratory, Durham, North Carolina

A SEVEN-INCH INCISION angled across the front of the patient's shoulder. Mark adjusted his headlight to illuminate the surgical field. The cephalic vein lay between exposed deltoid and pectoral muscles. It was soft and spongy like a thick purple earthworm. A small pool of blood enlarged near the center of the vessel and spilled down over the tissues, obscuring anatomic details. He cauterized the leaking branch. "Suction. Sponge, please." He blotted the field and positioned retractors then opened the interval between the muscles. The red fibers parted, exposing the cut surface of what remained of the arthritic joint. The shoulder replacement was going well, and he'd just finished cutting away the diseased surface of the humeral head. Next he adjusted retractors to improve the exposure.

"It's about an eighteen by fifty," said the scrub tech, holding up the cut portion of the humeral head that resembled a slice off of the surface of a deformed cue ball. Alongside it, he held a plastic object of almost identical shape.

Mark took the piece of bone from the tech and matched it with a polyethylene spherical cap that was eighteen millimeters thick and fifty millimeters diameter. He compared it to several other sizes. "I agree, it's the best fit. We'll trial it in a few minutes." He turned his attention back to the surgical field. Kim, one of the orthopedic trauma PAs, suctioned more blood while he manipulated his index and long fingers into the incision. This created a space for a retractor. With his right hand he inserted the instrument deep into the shoulder so it would catch on the rear edge of the socket. He adjusted its position, levering it backward, pushing the remaining humeral head out of the way.

"Got it," Kim said, grasping the handle.

"Pull a little harder." She did and the surface of the glenoid appeared. "Nice," he whispered while two more retractors were inserted. The entire surface of the socket was now exposed. "Bovie and pickups." These were placed in his hands and he used the electrocautery device to clear the rim of soft tissue and excised the remnants of the biceps tendon. The arm jumped and Kim's eyes widened.

"Careful," she said.

"Why?" he asked, quizzing her.

"The axillary nerve?"

He nodded. "It's right here." He pointed into the depths of the wound. "It's giving us a warning. The cautery device was close enough to make it depolarize and cause the shoulder muscles to contract."

"You didn't hurt it?"

"No, and I'm smart enough to heed its advice to stay away. Hand me the glenoid drill guide," he said. The scrub tech had it ready. "Now, the drill." He took the instruments as his phone rang from across the room. He glanced at the circulating nurse. "Answer that, please." She grabbed the device, swiped it, and held it to her ear.

Mark paid her no attention and proceeded with the operation. He positioned the drill guide against the bone and drilled the two-millimeter-diameter stainless steel wire into the center of the socket. When he was satisfied with the wire's position, he removed the guide and looked at the nurse. "Who was it?"

"Someone named Meghan wants you to call her. She sounded upset."

"Who's that?" Kim asked while holding the retractors. Her eyebrows arched. "New girlfriend?"

Mark smiled behind the clear face shield of his surgical helmet. "No." He smoothed the surface of the socket with the glenoid reamer then drilled the four holes for the positioning pegs and press-fit the new artificial polyethylene socket in position.

"Who's Meghan?" asked Kim as everyone relaxed. "If you don't tell me, I'll ask Ryan."

"He won't tell you."

"Wanna bet?"

"She works in Claire's lab. She's her postdoctoral fellow."

"What does she want?"

"How should I know? What's up with all the questions today?"

Kim shrugged. "Just curious."

A half hour later, he had the humeral head component positioned and was repairing the subscapularis tendon. The patient's new shoulder was in place. "Do you mind closing? I want to return Meghan's call."

"No problem. Let me know what's going on," Kim replied.

Mark removed his soiled surgical garments and entered the sub-sterile hallway between ORs. He called Meghan. She answered on the second ring.

"You're not going to believe this," she said, her voice quivering.

"Try me."

"There was a fire in the lab last night. It's destroyed."

"Say again?"

"The lab was destroyed."

"Claire's lab?"

"Everything's gone. Years of work," she said sobbing.

He squatted down next to the flash sterilizer and leaned against the wall. "Was anyone hurt?"

"I don't think so. It was late and the place was deserted." There was momentary silence followed by sobs. "My postdoc research. Our work. The Endovancin results. All gone."

"I'm on my way. Does Claire know?"

"She's in Panama."

"I know, but did you call her?"

"They're at Dr. Jindal's lab on some island. I tried to call but couldn't get a connection," said Meghan.

"Let me tell her. I'll be over there in less than an hour."

"You can't get near the place. There's fire equipment everywhere. Call me when you get here, I'll be in the crowd."

He placed the phone in the back pocket of his scrubs and went to the surgery waiting area. After speaking to the family of the patient whose shoulder was just replaced he went back to talk to his trauma fellow, Dr. Ryan McIntire. He was sitting at a computer terminal outside the PACU entering post-op orders.

"Can you handle the next case?"

"I should hope so. It's a straightforward ankle fracture," Ryan said. "What's going on?"

"There's been a fire at Claire's lab. I'm heading there now to see what's left of our work."

"Oh, shit." Ryan's jaw dropped like he'd been punched in the gut. "You're serious?"

Mark nodded. "Meghan just called."

"Our research. My fellowship project."

"It could be a setback. I don't know any details yet."

"I have most of the data saved to my laptop and backed up on thumb drives," Ryan said.

"So do we, but it still may stop forward progress for a while."

———

MARK FOUND Meghan among the spectators gathered on the grounds surrounding Althouse Laboratory, where Claire's research facilities were located. The fire department secured the area and people were fifty yards back from the scene. Smoke curled from broken windows on the fourth floor. Several fire trucks were parked close to the building. A team of firemen were directing a geyser of water into one of the windows. Mark thought it was Claire's office but wasn't sure. He stood next to Meghan and placed his arm around her shoulders.

"Good Lord, you weren't exaggerating," he said, taking in the spectacle.

"They were here when I arrived. It must have started well after midnight," said Meghan. "Have you seen Robert?"

"No. Stay here." Mark walked toward one of the fire trucks and several firemen turned toward him. He held out his reserve officer police badge and approached the man with the star on his shirt collar. He waved him over.

"Dr. Thurman," he said holding out his hand. "I'm the SWAT team medical officer for the Raleigh PD. I also work with Dr. Hodgson. It was her lab that was destroyed."

"Jim Daniels," he said, shaking Mark's hand. "Helluva mess here. Sorry we have to meet like this. We have an unidentified body. It may be a while before we have an ID."

Mark nodded and replaced his wallet. "A body? I was told there weren't any injuries."

Daniels spoke into his shoulder radio. "Copy. Don't move it. The ERT guys will want to take a look." He turned back to Mark. "It looks like a male victim. Found him on the fourth floor in the back of a lab. He must have been doing some late-night work and was overcome by the smoke."

"Evidence response team? Is this a crime scene?"

"The cops want to treat it like one."

"Any idea how it happened?"

"Haven't had time to investigate, but it looks suspicious."

"Arson?"

The battalion chief shrugged. "I don't know. There is so much accelerant in those labs it's hard to tell."

"When did you guys get here?"

"The alarms came in around four this morning. We rolled in ten minutes later. Thank God for the fire safety system. It was updated a few years ago. Without it we'd still be trying to contain it. Funny thing, though."

"Yeah, what?"

"The lab was torched but so was an office down the hall on the other side. Like two separate fires. That's what's suspicious," the fire chief said. "A fire wouldn't spread like that."

"Thanks. I appreciate the information." He turned and walked back toward the crowd. He saw Meghan and noticed the trim athletic black man next to her. He was over six feet and looked the way an NFL defensive back would look if he were wearing a charcoal three-piece suit with gleaming black wingtip shoes, a white shirt, and a solid blue tie. Mark recognized his friend and quickened his pace. Detective Jackson Ingram, a member of the Raleigh homicide division and the Raleigh SWAT team commander, surveyed the scene.

"I figured you'd be here," Ingram said.

"What are you doing in Durham?"

Ingram looked over his sunglasses. "Is there some place we can talk?"

"There's a cafe near the chapel."

Ingram nodded. "Lead the way."

"Will you call me after you talk to Claire?" Meghan asked.

"Of course." Mark hugged her then gripped her shoulders. "We'll get through this. Hang in there." He and Ingram ducked through the crowd and walked toward the bell tower. The morning coffee shop crowd was sparse because of the spectacle a few hundred yards away. They purchased their drinks and sat at a small table for two.

"This isn't your jurisdiction, so why the visit?"

"The dead body. What else?" Ingram sipped his coffee. "I got a call from one of my associates on the Durham PD. We won't know until we get a positive ID, but they think the body is Robert Ard. If he's the vic then he worked here but lived in an apartment building in Raleigh. We're checking the apartment. If anything happened there, that makes it overlapping jurisdictions."

"He worked for us. A histology lab tech. He made slides for our biopsy specimens and was good at it. What makes you think he's the dead guy?"

Ingram nodded while stirring his coffee. "He worked in the lab where the fire started and he had access. The body is about his size and he'd have a reason to be there late at night, *and* he didn't show up for work."

"He's missing?"

"He was supposed to have some slides ready for a neurosurgeon. They had an eight o'clock meeting to go over them. The guy got worried when Ard didn't answer his phone, so he called his apartment building. The surgeon needed the slides today and asked the building supervisor to go into his apartment and make sure he was all right. He wasn't there but when our guys checked his apartment, his pill stash was found. He could have been using and didn't wake up. That's what makes me think he's the crispy critter."

"What are you talking about? Narcotics?"

"A couple of months' supply, maybe less depending on how much he was using. Counterfeit Oxycontin and hydrocodone."

"No way. He's a good kid. Good work ethic. Claire helped him get the job. He doesn't fit the type."

"I'm just telling you what they found."

Mark shook his head. "It was planted."

"Most don't seem like the type. You'd be surprised," Ingram said. "They found a bottle of pills next to the bed. It looks like Oxycontin. Another one was in the bedroom closet. These days with the counterfeits sometimes they're laced with fentanyl. That shit's a hundred times more potent than morphine. We see it every day. There are no economic boundaries. It's an epidemic."

"Save me the lecture. I see it every day in the ER, but I don't know about Ard. He seemed like a straight-laced guy. He's a nerd's nerd. He was doing research trying to get into medical school. Claire thought he was great. Even wrote a letter of recommendation for him last year."

"Narcotic addiction doesn't discriminate. It cuts across all class and educational barriers. Once it gets you, it's usually just a matter of time. Did he have any friends?"

"I didn't know him that well. He was a loner, an introvert, as far as I could tell. Meghan knew him better than anyone except maybe Claire. She worked with him every day. He had a desk cubicle in the lab near hers."

"Not anymore." He took another sip of coffee.

"She'll take this hard," Mark said.

"I'm sorry. It would be easy to sweep this under the table and classify it as an accidental death, but it doesn't feel right. Arson with him in the lab. It stinks. Too convenient."

"Why would someone kill him and cover it up with the fire?"

Ingram shrugged. "Drugs? Money? I don't have a motive, but I've seen it all. We're talking to his neighbors. I came over here to talk to his coworkers. Where's Claire?"

"Panama."

"Panama?"

"She flew to Panama City yesterday to visit a colleague," Mark said.

"I need her phone number."

"I tried it. She didn't answer."

"Do me a favor and try again."

Mark took out his phone and dialed her number. He let it ring until the voicemail kicked in and shook his head. "We can't get in touch with her. She's in a rain forest in Panama."

"Doing what?" Ingram asked.

"I can't tell you details. I'm bound by a nondisclosure. Let's just say she's looking for an important plant."

"Jesus, her life's work just burnt up, a coworker is probably dead, and she's in a Central American jungle looking for plants?"

"Not just any plant. It's the source of a miraculous chemical compound," Mark responded. "I'm not exaggerating."

Ingram squinted and pinched the bridge of his nose. "You're serious?"

Mark smiled. "It may cure diseases you've never heard of."

"I don't give a damn about that. I've got a homicide investigation to run. I need to talk to her."

"So do I. She's supposed to phone this afternoon. I'll have her call you."

Ingram frowned and stroked his jaw. "What is it with you two? Black clouds follow you around."

Mark shrugged. "I didn't ask for it." He watched as Ingram scooted his chair back.

"Don't forget. I want to talk to her *today*."

"What next?" Mark asked.

"I'm going to question Ms. McKenna and find out what she knows about Ard and wait for Claire to call me. In the meantime, the crime scene unit will continue turning his apartment inside out. Make sure you give her my number."

"She has it."

"Good. Send me hers. I'll call you if I have more questions. See you at the range Saturday."

"I may be in Virginia." He summarized the situation with Hyperion. When he was finished they both stood and walked toward the parking lot.

Ingram slipped on his sunglasses. "If you're in town, it's our monthly team training. We're scheduled for building clearing operations."

"If I'm not practicing veterinary medicine, I'll be there."

FOUR HOURS LATER, Mark sat in his office at Saint Matthew's Hospital twirling a pen through his fingers. His clinic schedule had been cleared for the week in order to deal with Hyperion. However, everything was falling apart. He rocked in the desk chair and cracked his knuckles. *Damn it, Claire, answer the phone. What is she doing?* He stood and walked to the window and looked down at the courtyard four stories below. He watched a nurse pushing a patient in a wheelchair rigged with an IV pole. They stopped by a bed of brilliant Scarlet Dragon azaleas. A breeze rippled through the blossoms. *Everything depends on Endovancin. Without it we're screwed. After last night we're probably screwed anyway.* His stomach made a hollow rumbling noise. The clock over the door read three. It would be an hour earlier in Panama. She and Meera should be back at the lab. He called for the seventh time. Her phone rang then clicked to voicemail. He touched her number once more and counted the rings. This time it clicked. They had a connection.

"Claire. Can you hear me?"

"Help, we're in trouble."

"Claire! Talk to me! Claire!"

The connection was breaking up. He pressed the phone to his head but only caught faint snatches of a male voice.

"Dr. Jindal . . . Hodgson . . . pleasant surprise . . . nice of you to join us . . . Endovancin files . . ." Then, silence. The connection was lost.

TEN

Panama Canal, Panama

THE SOUR ODOR of mildew tickled Claire's nose. She lay sprawled on a narrow bunk in a small dim room, a ship's cabin. The mattress was damp. It was jungle hot and the steel-plate walls dripped with condensation. Splotches of mold grew on her bare pillow like tiny black weeds. She resisted the urge to sneeze but it built inexorably until three nasal blasts erupted in an explosive chain reaction. "Bloody hell," she whispered, rubbed her eyes, and imagined being trapped in a giant petri dish.

Light from a naked bulb gave a twenty-five-watt yellow glow. *What time is it?* She remembered brown leathery hands grabbing her wrists and dragging her up and over the ship's railing. Two men pinned her arms while another grabbed at her shirt. She pulled and kicked and someone slapped her face. Pain pierced her shoulder like a punch. They threw her to the deck as her muscles weakened and vision blurred. Then a huge black cloud eclipsed the sun.

It hurt to move her right arm. Her nails were broken and palms scraped. She threw off the sheet and sat up, almost striking her head on the overhead rack. Her shirt and trousers were the same ones she'd put on this morning. The canvas jungle boots were laced and tied. The room moved, swaying with a gentle rhythm. A few inches to her left, fingers protruded from the edge of the top bunk. She touched them. They were warm but didn't move. She stood and peered at the body. *Meera, thank goodness.* Claire shook her shoulder and put her head near her face. The soft breaths were like whispers. "Meera, wake up," she whispered while placing her fingers on the side of her neck. The pulse was strong but there was no response from the unconscious woman.

Claire shuffled to the sink and looked at her reflection in the cracked mirror. She rolled up her shirtsleeve and squinted at her shoulder. The tender pink welt resembled a mosquito bite, but there was a tiny red dot in the center, a needle puncture. *Some type of sedative. Probably ketamine or Sodium Pentothal.* It would have taken a big dose to put her out in less than a minute. How long had she been asleep? She reached out and steadied herself on the corner of the basin. A door was a few feet away, and she reached for the handle. It rattled but didn't turn. Across the murky compartment a roller shade covered a porthole. Claire went to it and peeked out. The sunlight hurt her eyes. She blinked and looked away.

Their room was at least five stories above the surface of the water. Tree-covered hills on the distant shoreline were stationary, and she realized the freighter was at anchor. She tried to concentrate. *Had the ship moved?* No other vessels were visible. The sun was shining directly on her face as it descended toward the horizon. *It must be late afternoon. I'm facing west near the stern, so the bow must be that way. This has to be the starboard side, so the ship must be pointing south.* She let the shade fall and made her way back to the moldy bunks and considered the situation. *They've stolen the formula for Endovancin and kidnapped the only person who knows how to make it. But why am I here? I'm no use to them.* With that thought her spine stiffened.

Sometime later, perhaps an hour, footsteps shuffled in the passageway. They stopped. She recognized the jingle of keys as the door handle turned. A man entered carrying a tray. He placed it on the deck next to the bunks.

"Eat," he grunted and retreated, locking the door.

There were two small bowls half filled with rice and a few stinking chunks of fish, along with two halves of a cheese sandwich made with white bread and two plastic bottles of water. There were no utensils. Claire began scooping the rice into her mouth with her fingers. The food was cold and tasted salty. She took a bite of the sandwich and washed it down with water. She filled her mouth like the monkeys at feeding time on Morgan Island. While she chewed her friend stirred. Meera brushed hair from her eyes and sat up half-way, supporting herself on her elbows.

"Where are we?"

Claire swallowed then spoke. "Careful, don't hit your head. You're on the top bunk. So, don't roll off."

Meera glanced upward at the ceiling two feet above.

"We're on that freighter anchored in Lake Gatún. Probably waiting for permission to get underway."

"Kidnapped?" Meera asked.

Claire nodded and handed half of the cheese sandwich to her friend. "Eat this. It's not bad, considering."

She inspected it. "Did they get my files?"

"Probably, I don't see your backpack. That's what they were after. They know about Endovancin."

"But how could they?" Meera asked.

Claire shrugged. "A spy? Someone from your lab . . . Rafael?"

"No way, he loves me. He asked me to marry him," Meera said.

"You're not engaged . . . are you?"

Meera managed a half smile and shook her head. "No. I'm not ready."

"Still waiting on Plunkett?"

"Am I that transparent?"

"It's pretty obvious. I wouldn't wait too long. Rafael seems like a great guy. Plunkett isn't worth it." She pushed the food closer to her friend. "Eat this. Who knows when we'll get another chance. You need to keep your strength."

Meera held the bowl close to her face and fingered rice into her mouth. "After you get over the smell, this isn't bad."

"Like French cheese," said Claire.

Meera finished eating and scavenged for stray rice grains. "What are they going to do with us?"

Claire walked to the porthole. By now it was dark outside, and there were no lights on the shore. "They have your files. How difficult is it to make?"

"Endovancin? It's not too hard if you can extract the active ingredient from the leaves."

"The orchid leaves?"

Meera smiled. "They won't find that information in my files. No one knows the actual source but you, me, and maybe Rafael. Plus, there are a couple of modifications I never wrote down."

"We have that going for us. They won't kill us." Claire hesitated. "They won't kill *you* as long as you have information they need. You can't tell them. Once they're able to produce the drug, you're expendable. God, I hope Mark figures out what's going on. He called just as they were breaking into your office."

"Really?"

Claire nodded. "That's why that jerk freaked and threw my phone across the room."

"Don't get my hopes up," Meera said. "Even with a best-case scenario, by the time he gets to BCI and finds out what's happened, we'll be somewhere in the middle of the Caribbean."

"Or the Pacific, or halfway around the world." Claire sat on the bunk and put her head in her hands.

Footsteps stopped outside the door and moments later three men entered. The first wore a familiar linen sport coat and hat. Claire recognized him as the man in Meera's office. The other two had

Asian features. One reached down and picked up the tray and left. The other stood at the door.

"He's unnecessary," said the man in the sport coat. "There's nowhere for you to run. If you escaped and jumped overboard, you'd be crocodile food before you reached the shore."

"You think so?" Claire strode forward and smashed her fist into his nose. His head snapped backward. She struck again, landing a jab on his jaw. He reached up and grabbed her hands as she kicked at his groin.

"Grab her, you moron!" the man shouted as the guard reached around Claire's waist, pulling her away. Two men rushed in from the hallway. Claire's arms were locked behind her back, and she was held upright as she struggled. One guard punched her in the stomach. The blow caused her to lean forward where her chin met his fist, rocking her head upward. She went limp and the men let her drop to the floor.

"Damn it! Son of a bitch!" the man screamed through the bloody fingers he held to his face. He pulled them away and looked in the cracked mirror. "That bitch," he whispered, dabbing his bloody nose with a dirty rag that hung next to the sink.

"You all right, Dr. Sorenson?" a guard asked after they'd finished binding her wrists and ankles.

"Of course I'm all right. You dumbass. What do you think? If you did your job, she wouldn't have had the chance." He looked back at the mirror. "Idiots." He replaced the towel to his nose. "Take her to the brig when we're done." He grabbed the half-full bottle of water on the floor next to Claire and poured its contents on her face. She sputtered and shook her head.

"You little shit. Try another stunt like that and I'll let these animals have their way with you until we reach port. You understand?" He wiped a streak of blood from his upper lip.

Claire groaned and shook her head. "Who are you?"

"Shut up. I'll ask the questions."

"What do you want?" Meera asked, ignoring him.

He went back to the mirror. The bleeding had stopped. He touched his cheek and grimaced. "Damn that woman." He turned to Meera. "Surely you can guess. We want your help. We're close to developing an incredible new drug. A long-acting antibiotic and cancer drug. I think we'll call it Endovancin."

"You're insane," Meera said. Claire lay silent on the floor.

"On the contrary." The man nodded at the guard. The stocky Asian smiled, displaying small stained teeth like red Chiclets. The compact brute approached Meera and slapped her. She fell backward and put her hands to her face. The creature spit a glob of red juice on the floor.

"I can assure you I'm quite sane," said Sorenson. "However, I'm not sure about Mr. Chen. He's a man of many talents, trained by the MSS." He dabbed his lip and looked down at Claire. "The Ministry of State Security in Beijing. Besides being a betel nut connoisseur, he's an expert at extracting information. You'd better cooperate so we don't need his assistance." He squatted next to Claire and pulled a pipe from a coat pocket. From another pocket he took a pouch of tobacco and began to fill the bowl.

She lay still, following his movement as he directed his gaze to Meera.

"Since your laboratory was destroyed in the accident, we're providing you with a new one. We have special arrangements with our Colombian partners. They've built a new drug manufacturing facility. It's beautiful, state of the art. Their pharmaceutical industry is really quite advanced. It's refreshing to not have so many FDA regulations. So different from the usual narcotic trade. I'm anxious to begin work. Now, if you will excuse me. I think you'll find the accommodations austere but acceptable." He patted Claire's breasts as she recoiled.

"Don't touch me."

He laughed. "I'll do a lot more than touch you if you ever hit me again. Take her to the brig." Two guards grabbed her arms and lifted her to her feet. They untied her as he sucked on the stem and lit his pipe. A cloud of smoke trailed his head as he walked to the door and opened it. "Make yourself comfortable, Dr. Jindal. I'll be back soon. We have a lot to discuss. Come, Dr. Hodgson. I think you'll enjoy your new cell. We get underway in an hour." The sweet aroma of pipe smoke lingered as her captors pushed her out the door. They led her down a dim passageway. At the end was a series of metal stairs almost as steep as vertical ladders. "Down you go, all the way to the bottom. Don't fall." Sorenson laughed and disappeared from the stairwell. She turned around facing the stairs, held the metal railings, and descended into the bowels of the ship.

MARK SAT at his desk staring at the computer screen. He had to do something. *"Help, we're in trouble."* Those words haunted him, echoing in his head. He'd called Claire every fifteen minutes for the last hour. Each time it went directly to voicemail. Meera didn't answer her phone either. Texts went unanswered. There were no responses to emails. He'd called Jim Roberts, the CEO of Electra Pharmaceuticals, to find out if he'd heard of any problems at the BCI facility. After explaining the situation, his secretary informed him Roberts was in critical condition in an ICU. An automobile had struck the bicycle he was riding that morning. Immediately, he'd called Claire's mentor, Evelyn Heinricht, in Scotland to see if she had heard from her. She hadn't. He'd called the US Embassy in Panama City and had been referred to the State Department, who asked that he fill out some online forms. He was wasting time. He reached for his phone and looked up John Bristow's number.

"Hello," a woman answered.

He should have expected her voice. Her husband hated to answer his phone, for good reason. "Emily, it's Mark Thurman. How are you?"

"What a nice surprise. I'm fine."

"Is John around?" Mark asked.

"Actually, he is. Hold on."

"Thanks."

"Is everything all right?" she asked.

"I don't know. That's why I called."

"Here he is," she said as she handed her husband the phone.

"Doc?"

"I was worried you'd be traveling or unreachable," Mark said.

"Not now. Just farming these days. Hector's planting schedule has me worn out."

"Glad to hear he's back at it."

"He's a step slower but putting in a full day's work. What's up?"

"It's Claire . . . she's missing," Mark said as he began the story. He and John Bristow had been friends for a dozen years going back to the time when both were part of the Naval Special Warfare Development Group. Bristow had been a sniper for one of the teams and Mark was the DEVGRU orthopedic surgeon. Much of his hand-to-hand and firearms training had come from the years he'd spent there. After his medical discharge, he'd lost track of Bristow until last year, when he showed up in Saint Matthew's Emergency Department with a bullet-riddled body that Mark and Claire had helped put back together.

"You haven't talked to her since yesterday?" Bristow asked.

"She called last night after dinner, everything was fine. This morning she and a colleague were going to the laboratory where the drug is produced."

"Where, Panama City?"

"No. A couple of hours from there, in the rain forest, some island in the Canal Zone, Barro Colorado Island."

"So let me get this straight—you haven't heard from her since last night?"

"I've been trying to call since this morning. I finally got through a few hours ago, but the connection was terrible. She said, 'Help, we're in trouble.' Then we were cut off."

"What do you think was happening?"

"I don't know. I'm worried. Claire wouldn't joke around like that. Something bad was going down there."

"Is the drug worth that much?"

"I'm not exaggerating, John. It might be the pharmaceutical Holy Grail. If the early results hold true, it could generate billions in revenue in a few years. The sky's the limit. What I can't figure out is how anyone knows about it," Mark said.

"Are you sure anyone does?"

"*Someone* must know. Claire's lab was destroyed by a fire this morning."

"When were you going to tell me about that?"

"I was getting to it. That's not all. A charred body was found that we think is one of her lab techs."

"Arson?"

"And murder." Mark repeated the events of this morning.

"You think both labs were hit simultaneously?"

His face went slack-jawed.

"You still there?" Bristow asked.

"Is that possible?"

"You tell me," Bristow replied. "It would be one hell of a coincidence."

"Who could pull that off?"

"People you'd rather not know. Is your passport up to date?"

"Always."

"Hold tight. Let me call the admiral. Keep your phone close by."

"Thanks, my friend," said Mark.

"No problem. I've been looking for a way to square things. If Claire's in danger, Jaggears will move mountains to get her back. I'll call soon."

ELEVEN

FRIDAY, MARCH 24TH

Telos Pharmaceuticals Corporate Headquarters, Philadelphia

THE FOUR MEN around the boardroom conference table rose as their boss entered. Jeff Mullion's arrogant strut had been forged by his instructors at Julliard. It was a strained, upright carriage with extended neck and outward pointing toes. The gait of one trained in classical ballet. The dark Armani suit clung to his lithe five-foot-nine frame like it would on a runway model. His black hair was slicked straight back and would require a stiff breeze to displace even a single strand. He was Domenico Dolce with the personality of Gordon Gekko. "Sit down, gentlemen." He placed an insulated water bottle on the surface of the table and pulled out his chair.

The brash CEO of Telos Pharmaceuticals appeared much younger than his thirty-nine years. This was in part due to his lack of facial hair, rumored to be due to a prescription-induced hormone imbalance. This delicate appearance belied his personality. He'd been hired two years ago after the previous chief executive had been fired for malfeasance. Mullion was brought in to turn the company around when no one else wanted the job. He believed he was on the fast track in the corporate world, and the Telos board of directors thought they got a charismatic spin doctor for a bargain.

Ten years ago Mullion dropped out of Harvard's MBA program after raising enough capital to buy a small pharmaceutical company called Valence. The company's stock had risen on the news it had developed a cure for the skin disorder psoriasis. Mullion sold two hundred thousand shares of the stock a month before the FDA filed a damning report following the conclusion of phase three clinical trials. No proof of insider trading was identified, and Valence filed for Chapter 11 bankruptcy. Mullion resigned and left the company scrambling to fend off insolvency.

His next venture was the acquisition of a nutraceutical company that advertised products touted to cure everything from erectile dysfunction to arthritis. His marketing campaign worked far better than the dietary supplements, and he proceeded to make a fortune selling snake oil. A retail pharmacy giant bought the company for two and a half billion dollars. He spent the next six months traveling in Europe, making sure to schedule time to attend Paris Fashion Week before being hired by Telos. His first year hadn't started smoothly and his corporate critics were increasing. Mullion didn't care. The pieces of his puzzle were coming together. His critics would never know about the Colombian deal with Bonsantos, and they hadn't heard of Endovancin. Mullion surveyed those seated at the table and focused on the man at his left. "Where do we stand, Dr. Plunkett? Is Endovancin our next blockbuster?"

Dr. William Plunkett, MD, PhD swiveled in his chair. He thought for a moment. "Based on your purloined data, the pharmacological effects of Endovancin are real. It's not hyperbole to say it could wind up in the pantheon of drugs alongside penicillin, insulin, cortisone, and aspirin. It's phenomenal. Millions of patients would benefit from it annually."

"Can we manufacture it?" Mullion asked.

"That . . . I don't know." Plunkett removed his wire-rimmed

glasses and placed them on the table. "We don't have enough information."

"We have the formula. Can we produce it?"

"That's the problem. We don't actually *have* the formula. Jindal's files are incomplete. What you showed me isn't Endovancin. It's the formula for vancomycin. A common antibiotic that's been used for decades and has no chemotherapeutic effects."

Mullion squinted. He unfolded his arms and placed them on the shiny conference table. "The chemical structure isn't Endovancin?"

"I just told you. It's vancomycin. Found in every hospital in the US."

Mullion looked to the fifty-inch video monitor on the wall at the other end of the room. The man on the screen was seated at a table. Portholes could be seen in the background. "What on earth happened to your face, Neil?" A dark purple half ring had formed under his swollen left eye.

"I tripped going through a hatch on this tub. Hit my head."

"Be careful. It looks like you broke your nose."

"I don't think so," Sorenson replied.

"Perhaps you have an explanation for the discrepancy in the formula?"

Sorenson frowned. "You examined all the files?"

"Every one," replied Plunkett.

"I don't understand. They contained electron micrographs of the molecular structure and instructions for the purification of the compound. I saw them. They were labeled Endovancin," Sorenson said.

"Check again. You've been tricked. I've known Meera Jindal for years. She was one of the smartest PhD students I ever had," Plunkett said.

"Perhaps it's you who's been duped," Mullion said to Plunkett.

"Impossible. Meera wouldn't lie to me. I handpicked her for my program. I guided her research and made sure her project was well funded. I put together her dissertation committee. She owes her professional career to me and trusts me."

"Telos hired you because of that relationship."

"You'll get your money's worth, Mr. Mullion. You know as much about the drug as I do. I've told you everything she's reported," Plunkett said. "I've been her confidant from the beginning. She's got the formula and knows the production process. She's smart enough to keep them hidden. Don't screw this up."

Mullion leaned back in his chair, placed his hands behind his head, and smiled. "I believe you, Doctor. Your reports and the data supplied by the late Mr. Ard have convinced me." He looked back at Sorenson on the screen. "She has the information. Get it."

"Yes, sir. What about the other one?"

"Hodgson? She knows too much."

"What do you want me to do?" asked Sorenson.

"Keep her sedated. I'm sure our BACRIM colleagues will have use for her. Perhaps a gift to one of our customers in Shanghai or Beijing."

"I'm for tossing the bitch overboard," said Sorenson.

"A woman like that is valuable in many ways. We can use her for leverage. I'm sure Dr. Jindal won't want any harm to come to her dear friend. Keep her drugged and deliver her to Medellín. Let them deal with her, *after* we get the formula."

One of the men leaned forward and looked at the video screen. "Have you seen the lab in Bogotá?"

Sorenson nodded. "I made sure it was operational before executing the BCI raid. It's impressive. A fifty-thousand-square-foot state-of-the-art processing and manufacturing plant on the Bonsantos campus north of the city."

"What about transportation logistics?" Mullion asked.

Sorenson laughed. "Beautiful, isn't it?"

"A cash cow," replied the CFO. "The Bonsantos deal was brilliant. It cuts out the middlemen. The Mexicans were gouging fifty percent of profits for their distribution routes, and the Colombian police have been jamming the northern ground shipments. Air transportation eliminates both problems."

"And we may win the Triple Crown," said Mullion as he leaned back and steepled his fingers.

"Congratulations," said a board member. "Now, if we continue funneling those profits through our legitimate pharmaceutical portfolio, it keeps Telos out of debt, keeps the DEA and IRS off our back, and generates enough revenue to make the shareholders happy."

"A bulletproof balance sheet," said the chief operating officer. "Goddamn genius, Jeff. Great job."

"Gentlemen, you can keep your narcotics operation to yourselves," said Plunkett. "I want no part. I'm strictly a consultant for the pharmaceutical enterprise."

"It's all pharmaceuticals, Doctor. Just how do you think you're getting paid? The signing bonus you deposited didn't appear out of thin air. You can thank our Colombian partners for the funds to pay for your expertise. Whether you like it or not, your hands are dirty like the rest of us. I suggest you embrace it. You're going to be richer than you can imagine. Welcome to the team."

"I have a question," Plunkett said.

Mullion looked at him and turned his palms up on the table. "Go on."

"Just how do you plan to market Endovancin in the US? I have no doubt Electra has filed for the patent. They'll sue you in a heartbeat once they test it and find out it's identical to theirs."

Mullion smiled and leaned forward. "For your information, the patent rights are unclear, at the moment. But if we can't obtain them, I don't plan to market it in the US. I plan on cutting a deal with the Chinese. They don't give a rat's ass about American patent laws. They're interested in results and profits. We'll make the drug in Colombia and sell it to China. They can market and distribute it any way they want as long as Telos gets a percentage. Am I making myself clear?"

"Crystal clear," Plunkett said with a thin smile.

"Very good. Before we adjourn, Dr. Plunkett, do you have anything to report on the phase two arthritis drug trial?"

The professor leaned back and crossed his legs. He picked his wire-rimmed glasses off the table and began cleaning the lenses with a handkerchief pulled from his back pocket. "Grant is making progress. It's better than I expected. The JVC107 experiments will be completed in two weeks. He told me he was tempted to end the trials early because of the clear differences between the groups."

"It's double-blind?" asked Mullion.

"Correct, one group is getting the drug and the other saline. No one knows who is getting what. They'll decode and have the results by the end of the month," Plunkett reported.

"Sounds like he's impressed."

"As I mentioned, he almost terminated the study early."

"I'm glad he didn't," said Mullion. "No one knows for sure until we figure out which subjects got the drug."

"Nevertheless, there appears to be a clear difference between the groups. One runs like a herd of two-year-old colts, and the other can barely get to the feed trough."

"Excellent. I want the results in the hands of the FDA as soon as the report is ready. We'll start phase three trials whenever we're given permission," Mullion instructed.

The chief financial officer raised his hand to shoulder height. "Excuse me, what's JVC107?"

"Your NDA covers everything we talk about," Mullion reminded him.

"Come on," Plunkett scoffed. "You just discussed deals with the Colombian mafia and the Chinese and you're worried about a nondisclosure agreement? Give me a break."

The room was silent. Mullion pulled an emery board from his coat pocket and began filing. His gaze locked on to the professor. "I don't think you understand. I was referring to a Colombian NDA. They have unique methods of enforcement. Pray you never have the experience."

Plunkett swallowed. "JVC107, soon to be named Juvanimab, is an anti-arthritis drug."

"Marketing wants us to call it Rejuven," added Mullion.

"Apropos, if it gets FDA approval." Plunkett wiped his forehead with the handkerchief. "We still have a few hurdles to clear. It's a potent monoclonal antibody anti-TNFα derivative currently in clinical trials. We've been testing it on an equine metacarpal osteoarthritis model. A veterinarian, Dr. Warwick Grant, is the lead investigator at the Wilson Andrews Equine Research Center in Virginia."

"Quite a drug portfolio, Jeffery. Endovancin and Juvanimab, new treatments for infections, cancer, and arthritis. Shareholders are going to love you," said the CFO.

Plunkett hooked the wire rims behind his ears and adjusted his glasses. "Provided nothing goes wrong."

MARK FINISHED WORKING over the heavy bag steadied by Ingram. He threw a series of left jabs followed by a right cross. Ingram leaned into it, counteracting the force and controlling the bag's movement. His left hand lashed out three more times followed by a blistering right. Mark stepped back, planted his left foot, and ended with a roundhouse kick. The bag rocked backward and Ingram stepped away, letting it go. Mark relaxed and wiped sweat from his eyes with the back of his glove.

"Save something for the enemy," Ingram said, smiling.

"There's plenty left in the tank."

"I know you're worried. I am, too. If you don't hear from her by morning, I'll start making calls. Senator Portis is a friend and he owes me for the campaigning I did for him last year. He'd help anyway."

"Thanks, I've got the number for the embassy in Panama City. I'll call in the morning. I'm going down there tomorrow. If someone has her held captive, every hour that goes by is critical."

"We both know that, but there's not much you can do. This is in the hands of Panamanian officials. Don't ruffle their feathers. You could make things worse," Ingram said.

"I really don't give a damn. I'm going to find her."

Ingram put an arm around his shoulder. "Look, I understand. I'd do the same thing. I'm just saying be smart. We're not sure anything is wrong."

"I got a bad feeling. She's in trouble." Mark looked up at his friend. "I called Bristow."

"I thought you might," Ingram said.

"He's supposed to get back with me soon. That's all I know right now." Mark took off his gloves and foot guards and threw them in his bag. He sat cross-legged on the floor, unwinding the tape from his wrists and hands.

"Good luck and be careful."

An hour later, he was toweling off in his bathroom when the phone buzzed. He picked it off the countertop.

"All right, hotshot, get your stuff together. I'm picking you up at twenty-two hundred. We're not flying commercial. Pack your handgun and body armor. We'll have the rest."

Three hours later, Mark was ready. He'd shoved combat utilities and civilian clothes into his travel bag. His Sig Sauer nine millimeter was in its holster on his right hip. Two loaded magazines were stuck in the mag pouch on his left. In front of his holster hooked to his belt was his police department gold shield. He saw lights go by the front window then heard a vehicle in the driveway. Mark pulled the edge of the curtains back and peeked into the darkness. Bristow's new Super Duty F-250 was parked by the front walkway. Mark grabbed his gear and headed to the garage.

"Where we going?" he asked as Bristow backed out of the driveway.

"Fayetteville, where else?"

Mark nodded. "Game plan?"

"We're catching a midnight flight to Panama City. Two other guys are coming with us."

"What did the admiral say?"

"He wasn't happy. I think he's got a thing for her."

"He's not the only one," Mark said.

"I mean a father-daughter thing."

"Yeah, I know."

"It was strange. I got a call right before I talked to you. I was instructed to pick you up and be on base at midnight. That's all. I'm carrying out my orders." They sat in silence for ten minutes until they were heading east on Interstate 40. "You sure this isn't just a third-world 'kidnap for cash' situation?" Bristow asked.

"It could be. I doubt it, though. There's been no ransom demand, and that drug is a potential game-changer. Whoever brings it to market is going to make a lot of money."

"Is it worth killing for?" Bristow asked.

"I think we know the answer to that," Mark said and thought of Robert Ard.

Bristow nodded as he kept his eyes on the interstate. "I forgot about the fire. In my experience, there are too many assholes in this world who think life is cheap."

It was just before midnight when they approached the security gate. A uniformed guard with a sidearm stepped to the door. Another stood on the opposite side of the pickup ten yards away holding an M16. Bristow lowered the window.

"Good evening. State your business," said the guard.

"John Bristow and Dr. Mark Thurman reporting as instructed."

"Identification, please."

Both handed him their ID cards. The cards indicated they were employees of an executive protection firm, Trident Sentinel International. It wasn't a cover. The firm actually did executive protection jobs from time to time, but its primary directive was to carry out missions at the direction of the Homeland Security director.

"Passports," the guard requested. He returned the documents

after scanning them with a device in the guard shack. Next, he handed them a computer tablet. "Place your right hand on the screen." The device read the palm print and confirmed both identities. The guard finished processing them and spoke into a radio on his shoulder. The gate slid open. "You may proceed."

"Thanks," John said. He gave an informal salute and accelerated through the entrance. They drove on a winding road for several minutes through a dense forest of pines. They came to a second checkpoint and stopped.

"Just your TSI ID cards," said the guard. They produced them and the metal arm blocking the road swung upward.

"What do you guys have in here?" Mark asked Bristow.

"If you thought Dam Neck was special, wait until you see this," he replied. Thirty seconds later, they broke into a large clearing. A building was a hundred yards away. Mark recognized it as the facility he visited the previous year. It was where he and Claire had been read into the agency. On the other side of the building was an airplane hangar with its doors open. A corporate jet was lit up sitting on the tarmac with a fuel truck next to it. Bristow parked on the side of the main building. They grabbed their bags. The entrance door opened and they followed the guard to a conference room. A minute later, Admiral (Ret.) Zachariah Jaggears entered along with two other men. Mark smiled. *Daggers Jaggears.* Even at midnight Jaggears was dressed impeccably in a suit and tie.

"Good evening, gentlemen," the admiral said, shaking their hands. "I want to introduce you to your teammates for the next part of your mission. We're not expecting an enemy engagement, but you will be prepared. The group will function as a standard special ops fire team." He motioned to the two men behind him. "Meet Emanuel Sanchez and William Kearns. Sanchez is your communications expert and is fluent in Spanish. Kearns is your demolitions engineer. I hope you don't need his skill set."

"Neither do we," said Mark.

"You never know," said Kearns. "I'm just here to help."

"Bristow is the weapons and tactics expert and has the team lead," the admiral continued. "Thurman, your role is medical." Jaggears motioned for them to sit and clicked a remote control in the palm of his hand. A large panel opened, revealing several computer screens. The left screen displayed a satellite image of what appeared to be the Panama Canal. "After John briefed me on the situation, I called our friends at NRO." He looked at Mark. "National Reconnaissance Office. If I get into too much jargon, stop me, Doc. These are the satellite images they provided from earlier today." A picture of Panama appeared on the screen. Jaggears zoomed in until the image showed the canal from the Gatún locks on the Caribbean side to the Miraflores locks at the Pacific. Mark recognized ship traffic in the new expanded portions of the canal. "The Smithsonian research facility is on a small island in the middle of Lake Gatún." The island was a green spot on the screen that became larger as Jaggears magnified the image. The only sign of habitation was a floating dock and a half-dozen buildings rising from the hills above a cove. Two boats were sunk at their moorings alongside the dock. "This was shot just before sunset." Smoke still streamed from several buildings. "There's no fire department on Barro Colorado Island. Fortunately, the fires appear to be under control and the destruction isn't spreading." Jaggears turned on the other screen. "This is the infrared satellite feed. You can see where the fires were located." The image depicted two larger yellow areas and multiple small figures moving about the buildings. "This facility was attacked earlier today. Dr. Claire Hodgson, a member of TSI, was visiting the director of pharmacological research at the facility, Dr. Meera Jindal. Contact with them and the facility has been lost. Your mission is to rescue them and find out what happened. Do you want to add anything, Doc?"

Mark's mouth hung open. "That's what happened today? Someone attacked Meera's lab?"

Jaggears pointed to the smoking buildings with his laser. "These satellite images confirm what happened."

"It must have been going on when I called her."

"What'd she say?" Kearns asked.

"That they were in trouble and needed help. She didn't have a chance to talk before the connection was lost," Mark answered. "All I heard was a lot of commotion and unfamiliar voices." He rubbed his jaw and looked at the screen. "You were right, John. Two labs, working on the same drug, a thousand miles apart, destroyed on the same day."

"Not much of a coincidence," Jaggears said. "What can you tell us about this facility that's so important, Dr. Thurman?"

Mark briefed the group regarding Endovancin and its remarkable dual properties. He also recounted the fire at Claire's laboratory, the suspicious narcotic overdose death of Robert Ard, and the cycling accident involving the company's CEO, Jim Roberts.

"What is going on?" asked Sanchez.

"I don't know," Mark shrugged. "Your guess is as good as mine. The drug is in its infancy. Its chemotherapeutic and antibiotic properties are just now being appreciated, and outside of a small circle of people, no one knows it exists."

"Some of those people aren't good guys," Jaggears added his opinion.

"Someone's out to steal it," Mark said. "The discovery of this drug will revolutionize the treatment of cancer and infectious diseases. This can't be overstated. Whoever controls this drug is going to dominate the pharmaceutical space for years."

Jaggears looked back at the smoking buildings on the screen. "I hope I don't need to remind you that the pharmaceutical industry has the largest political lobbying organization affecting our government. They donate more money to politicians than any other lobbying or special interest group. If this drug does half of what you're claiming it can, that's a lot of political influence. It cannot fall into the hands of terrorists or drug dealers. There's too much at stake."

"Admiral, I'm really not too worried about the drug," said Bristow. "I care that these scumbags have one of our own, someone who's dear to me and this organization. TSI doesn't leave personnel behind. If you're missing, we'll find you."

"We share your sentiments, Mr. Bristow. I'm prepared to bring to bear considerable resources in order to recover those women and that drug. Let's get started. Your flight leaves in fifteen minutes."

———

MEERA WATCHED THE VIDEO SCREEN. The lighting in the cell was dim but she could make out the figure lying on the cot. She was curled on her side in the fetal position and wasn't moving.

"I can assure you she's alive and unharmed," Sorenson told her.

"Can I talk to her?"

"I'm afraid not. She'll be departing the ship as soon as we make port tomorrow morning. There is a way you can help her."

"Cooperate?"

Sorenson smiled and placed his hand on her shoulder. "That's right. Think about what you're being offered. You'll be in charge of developing the single most important drug in modern history. Your salary will be double what the CEO of the company you just left made."

"You're asking me to do something illegal?"

"Don't be ridiculous. There's nothing illegal about coming to work for us," Sorenson protested.

"I have a noncompete clause."

"Those are easily broken these days."

"I don't think so," Meera said. "Plus, it's wrong. You stole the formula."

"Not really. You have the formula. We're just trying to hire you away from Electra."

"You call this a recruiting trip?"

"Meera, we're aware of your family's financial difficulties. I can make Aaray's hospital bills go away."

Meera's eyes widened and her mouth gaped. "How do you know about that?"

Sorenson grinned. "We can also make sure Sanjay remains in the States and has the funds to complete his studies. On the other hand, I would be worried about your friend. If you don't cooperate, it will be difficult to ensure her safety."

"Is that a threat?"

"Take it how you like. We reach Cartagena tomorrow morning. You have until then to think about what we've been discussing."

TWELVE

SATURDAY, MARCH 25TH

Panama Pacífico International Airport, Panama

MARK ADJUSTED his seatback and stared into the cloudless predawn sky. Scattered specks of light dotted the ground thirty-five thousand feet below. The starboard wingtip dipped as the plane adjusted its course in preparation for approach. His watch indicated five thirty and, in spite of the early hour, he felt refreshed. The four hours of sleep during the flight had been needed.

"Morning, Doc. Rise and shine. It's another great Navy day," said Manny Sanchez, grinning from the seat across the aisle. He handed Mark a paper cup with a lid. "Coffee? It's Costa Rican."

He took a sip and nodded. "Good stuff."

"If you look out this side you can see the canal. Pedro Miguel locks and the new channel are right below."

Mark unbuckled his seatbelt and moved across the aisle. Vessels of various sizes were loaded into the chambers and moving through the canal. "Ships go through there night and day?"

"Twenty-four seven, about twenty thousand vessels a year. Commerce doesn't sleep."

Mark went back to his seat. "Where do we land?"

"The old Howard Air Force Base. Uncle Sam turned it over to the Panamanians in 1999 along with the canal. Now, it's the Panama Pacifíco International Airport. We've helped their government on several occasions. So, in return, they let TSI rent space for our Central American operations. A helicopter is waiting to take us to the site."

Mark nodded and drank from his cup. "Thanks." Sanchez leaned back in his chair and opened his laptop.

Mark closed his eyes and a vision of Claire appeared. In his imagination she was turning around, her long golden hair flowing over her shoulders. Their eyes met and she broke into laughter. The image made him think of the song by Jackson Browne, "Late for the Sky." He recited the lyrics in his head and held the vision a few moments too long until his heart ached. He pinched his nose, blinked, and peered out the window.

"Gentlemen, fasten your seatbelts. We'll be on the ground in ten minutes," the pilot informed them.

A warm tropical breeze swirled as they descended the steps onto the runway. They loaded their gear into the back of the waiting van and climbed in. Bristow rode shotgun and looked back at Mark. "This is Captain Esteban Enrico of the Panamanian National Police. He's in charge of this mission." The driver raised his hand in acknowledgment but kept his eyes ahead.

Several hundred yards in the distance a Black Hawk helicopter sat on the tarmac with its rotors turning. The van stopped next to it and the team made a rapid transfer. The side doors stayed open as the main rotors increased speed and the ground fell away below them. Enrico was seated in the crew chief seat position, and the cargo compartment was less than half full with only the four TSI men. Mark noted several empty medevac litters in the rear of the cargo hold and hoped they wouldn't be needed. He had a close-up view of the new canal expansion as they passed over ships in the Cocoli locks and the three immense water-saving basins. A few minutes later, the twin peaks of the Centennial Bridge appeared on the horizon with the rising sun in the foreground.

"The Culebra Cut is coming up," said Enrico. "In a few minutes we will be over Lake Gatún."

The thumping blades beat the air, propelling them over the rain forest, and then water. Within minutes the Black Hawk banked, making a slow turn. "Barro Colorado Island," said the voice in his helmet. "We're going to make several recon passes over the island. There's a clearing south of the compound. We should be able to land there."

It took less than a quarter of an hour to assess the situation from the air. The only buildings on the island belonged to the Smithsonian research outpost. Smoke continued to drift from several windows in two of the buildings. A handful of people came out of the structures and looked up at the circling helicopter. Several waved and began jogging to the makeshift helipad in the only flat area on the outskirts near the water. The Black Hawk descended into the clearing as a vortex of brown dirt and dust was whipped into the air. The TSI team and Captain Enrico hopped out, and the helicopter rose back into the sky.

"Where's he going?" Mark asked.

"Too vulnerable for him on the ground until we check things out," Bristow replied. "He'll make a few sweeps around the island, and once Enrico gives him the all-clear signal, he'll return and set down. If shit hits the fan, this is where we pull back for evac. Got it?"

"Check," Mark said.

"Time to Ranger up, gentlemen. Weapons check," Kearns said, handing Bristow a rifle. Mark recognized the standard SWAT weapon of choice he trained with in Raleigh. It was an MK18 CQBR decked out with a four-power ACOG and light. He accepted a similar one from Kearns.

"Brings back memories, huh?" Bristow asked as he shouldered his gun and looked through the scope.

"Yep, the suppressor is a nice upgrade," Mark replied, thinking back to the time spent with DEVGRU. He'd lost track of the number of training missions they'd been on together before his illness.

"You used to be pretty good with that," Bristow said.

"Still am," Mark said.

"Just hope you don't have to prove it."

Mark nodded, slipping on body armor and adjusting his battle belt. "Let's find Claire." He fastened the chinstrap to his helmet and slung his rifle and checked his magazine holders. He inserted a thirty-round magazine and slapped it into place. He cycled the charging handle and noted the shell being pushed into the chamber and checked the safety. He let the rifle hang from its sling and drew his handgun. He peeked into the chamber then made sure his magazine was full. He holstered the pistol then gripped the rifle. "Weapons hot."

Bristow walked over to Captain Enrico and began conversing in Spanish. A minute later he turned to face them. "Listen up. It looks like whoever raided this place bugged out last night, but we're not taking chances. They could've left people behind. There may be wounded civilians. Be ready for any developments. We're here to get information. We want to know what happened and the location of the two women scientists. We're not here to gather evidence or solve this crime. Captain Enrico and his people will do that later. We'll divide into two teams. Thurman and I will accompany the captain—that's team one. Bill, you and Manny are team two. Check out the docks and work your way up to the lab buildings. We meet back here in two hours." He paused for a second while he looked at each man. "Let's get some." They set off on a path leading to the buildings. Mark followed Bristow and Enrico up a set of concrete stairs while Kearns and Sanchez continued toward the docks.

The place was silent except for the sound of birds squawking from the rain forest and insects buzzing around their heads. He was thankful for the insect repellant Kearns had sprayed on his clothing and exposed skin. They walked for ten minutes along the jungle trail. He almost kissed a four-inch katydid on a vine at face level draped across the path. He brushed it out of the way and marched up the hill. The smell of smoke greeted them as they approached the first building. Two men stood at the top of the long steep flight of stairs leading to the entrance.

"Alto! Policía Nacional," Enrico barked as they hustled upward two steps at a time. When they reached the landing, the men were standing with their hands raised.

"Who are you?" the older one asked in English. He appeared to be in his midforties and was dressed in khaki pants and a light blue polo shirt with Electra Pharmaceuticals embroidered in yellow over the left breast. The other man was at least ten years younger and wore similar attire. Both were sweat-stained and dirty.

"We're friends. Put your hands down. We mean no harm," Enrico said. "We're here to help. I'm with the police and these men are with me. What happened here?"

"Was that your helicopter?" the young man inquired.

"Sí," Enrico answered. "Please, who did this?"

They moved out of the sun into the shade. The older man spoke. "Yesterday afternoon, around three o'clock, two boats came into the lagoon at high speed." He moved his hand across his chest parallel to the ground. "They each carried at least a dozen men."

"Banditos," the younger said, his eyes wide. "Hombres muy malo."

"They were armed." He pointed to the structure at the top of the stairs leading from the docks. "I work in a laboratory in that building and saw them approach. They got out and began shooting our boats. Then, they separated into two teams and went into the new buildings. A few minutes later the explosions started."

All heads whipped around as the sound of gunfire echoed throughout the compound.

"What the hell?" Bristow scanned the area.

"It's coming from the docks," Enrico said, pointing.

Kearns's voice came over their headsets. "Team one, we have two armed men in building five . . . small arms, AK-47, and handguns. Could use some assistance."

"Roger," Bristow replied into the microphone at the corner of his mouth. He looked at the older man. "Show us how to get to building five without being seen."

"This way." The blue-shirted men ran along the side of the building and disappeared around the corner. Team one followed. They jogged up a steep stairway leading into the rain forest. Every couple of minutes the sound of sporadic gunfire came from below them near the lagoon. The older gentleman became winded and fell behind. Mark, John, and Enrico stayed close to the younger employee as they circled above and behind the buildings. They ran in single file along a jungle trail. The vegetation was so dense the concrete walls were glimpsed only every ten or twenty yards. In the humid foliage the air was hot and still. Sweat stained their clothing and dripped from their faces. The young man stopped abruptly and knelt on one knee on the path. The patrol halted next to him and huddled together as the older man caught up.

"Down these steps," he whispered and panted, pointing to a cinder block stairway with a rusted iron pipe railing leading down into the compound. The stairway curved to the right into the jungle twenty yards below. "At the bottom, there's a clearing and two buildings. The one on the left is the back of building five. The rear doorway puts you on the second floor."

"What's your name?" Enrico asked the older gentleman.

"Rafael Alvarez, señor."

"What do you do here?" Mark asked.

"I'm the director of R & D for Electra at BCI. I'm Dr. Jindal's assistant."

Bristow reached out and grabbed a fistful of his shirtsleeve and pulled him so their faces were only a few inches apart. "Thanks for your help. Stay here. Be quiet and out of sight until I yell all clear. Comprende?"

He nodded. "Sí, señor."

"Let's move," Bristow said and started down the steps. The sound of gunfire was getting louder. "Team two, we're approaching the back of building five. What's your twenty?"

"Penned down near the docks. Receiving small-arms fire from two locations in building five."

"You're sure?" The distinctive sound of an AK-47 came from the building directly in front of them. "All right, I believe you."

"Third floor, second and fifth windows. That's my left, your right."

"Copy." Bristow signaled for verbal silence and crossed the ten-yard clearing and leaned against the wall next to the back door. He gripped the handle, turning it to the right. He pushed it open. They moved as a team. Bristow cleared the space to his right. Mark followed, checking the left. Enrico entered last, covering straight ahead. The doorway led into a stairwell. They maneuvered to clear the stairs and Bristow climbed. He stopped at the next level by the door as Mark and Enrico followed. More gunfire. Much closer. They used three-man tactics and entered the hallway, moving down the middle of the third-floor main corridor. Bristow signaled Mark and Enrico to take the second door while he proceeded to the fifth. He held up his left fist and signaled one, two, and three. Rifle fire exploded in the hallway. The door handles and locks disintegrated as bullets ripped through. The two doors flew open by the force of simultaneous kicks.

"Hands up! On the ground!" Mark shouted.

"Manos arriba!" Enrico screamed. The man dove on the floor with his hands outstretched. Gunfire came from down the hall. Mark kicked the rifle across the room. He straddled the man dressed in black fatigues and pulled his hands behind his back. He secured them with zip tie handcuffs. Then, he rolled him over and checked for weapons. He removed a semiautomatic pistol and a fixed-blade knife.

"I'll check on John." Mark gripped his rifle and left the room. He walked to the open doorway. "Bristow, clear?"

"All clear. Bring your medical gear."

Mark knelt by the mercenary sprawled on the floor. "He's losing blood fast." A large red stain was spreading over his chest. "He's got a pulse." The man's eyes widened as blood trickled from the corner of his mouth. Mark ripped open his saturated shirt. Blood pumped like a well from the hole where his left nipple used to be. A second entrance wound was just above it. He clamped his hand over the wounds. The man's breathing was raspy and shallow. His lips were oyster gray and his skin was pale. Mark looked up at John. "I can't stop this. He's bleeding out."

Bristow leaned over the wounded man's face. "Where are the two women?"

Mark turned him on his side and pulled up his shirt. Broken ribs and lung tissue extruded from a hole the size of a fist. Mark turned him back. The man coughed bloody sputum and struggled for air.

"Where are they?" Bristow yelled and pulled open his eyelids with his thumbs. The man blinked and stared at him.

"Nunca los encontrarás, amigo."

You'll never find them. Mark silently translated as he felt for a carotid pulse and shook his head. "He's dead."

"I had no choice," Bristow said, handing him his bandana. "He turned toward me with his rifle."

"The other guy's alive." Mark stood and wiped his bloody hands on the cloth. "Let's see what he can tell us."

ENRICO HAD the prisoner kneeling in the middle of the room. "Colombian." He pulled up his shirtsleeve and pointed to a tattoo on his shoulder. "Los Rastrojos Comandos Urbanos."

"Drug cartel," Bristow said.

"An older group that came out of the Cali cartel," Enrico explained. "They're now part of what is known as BACRIM. They operate out of the northern region of Colombia, Urabá Antioquia, bordering Panama where they move drugs north." Enrico kept his rifle pointed at the prisoner. "They're a paramilitary organization. The strongest remaining Colombian drug trafficking ring."

"Colombian narcos. So, what's he doing here?" Mark asked.

Enrico spoke to the prisoner in Spanish then translated for Mark. "BACRIM are involved in all sorts of criminal activities. He says they were ordered to kidnap the two women and blow up the laboratories. He and his partner were to blow up the cell tower on the roof of this building. Two security guards discovered them. They took out the tower but were delayed by the gunfight and left behind. He said they were taking the women to a ship that would take them back to Colombia. He doesn't want to go back. They will kill him."

"Why?"

"As an example of what happens when you fail."

"Kill him for being left behind?" asked Mark.

"He will be suspected of providing us with information. The BACRIM need little reason to kill. They exert their power through fear and intimidation," Enrico said.

"Ask him the name of the ship," said Mark.

"I already did. He doesn't know."

MARK CINCHED the body bag to the litter and made sure it was sealed. He sat next to Bristow. Enrico sat across from the prisoner, his right hand near his holster. There was little chance of escape. The helicopter blades began to whirl faster, and the resulting dust cloud darkened as the aircraft rose. Mark spotted Rafael in his blue shirt standing on the pathway watching the takeoff. He waved as the helicopter rotated and flew westward. They retraced the course to the base and landed a half hour later. A police van was waiting, and Enrico turned the prisoner over. He spoke with the driver for several minutes before returning.

"Our friend will be taken to a detainment center and interrogated. My men will let us know if he remembers anything that may have slipped his mind."

"Thank you, Captain. We appreciate your help and the assistance of your government," Bristow said.

"I can assure you this incident will be thoroughly investigated. Justice will be swift. My country will not tolerate this from anyone. *Especially* the Colombian BACRIM."

They began walking toward the building Mark recognized from earlier that morning. The G650 was parked on the tarmac gleaming in the early afternoon sun. "We should have the ship information by now," Bristow said.

Ten minutes later they sat around a table in a dim room. Video screens hung from the walls on three sides. Several men wearing headsets were sitting in front of computer consoles. Admiral Jaggears took up most of one screen, and a map of the area surrounding the eastern half of the canal was displayed on the other.

"Good day, gentlemen," the admiral said. "BCI is under our control. The National Police have the place secured and will be watching for anyone coming to get the men they left behind. While you were carrying out your mission, I had our organization check satellite images from yesterday and this morning. It's such an important element of global commerce that satellite data is collected at thirty-minute intervals during daylight." The large screen at the front of the room flickered and a picture appeared. "This image of Barro Colorado Island was taken around three yesterday afternoon." A cursor stopped over a small island in the middle of the screen. Jaggears zoomed in for detail. "Notice the freighter. It's anchored about two miles off the island waiting to complete its eastern transit, while the shipping traffic moves westbound during the day. Also, notice the two forty-foot vessels moored at the BCI docks." He zoomed in closer.

"They're armed," Mark said.

"Affirmative. This image was taken as the raid was beginning." He pointed out a large group of men climbing the stairs to the research facility.

"There are the two punks going into building five to knock out the cell tower," Bristow said.

The image changed. "This is an hour later," Jaggears said. Smoke was pouring from the laboratory windows. "The boats are leaving." He pointed to the vessels speeding away from the island. The image changed again. He zoomed in over the freighter. "This is thirty minutes later."

"Are they tied up to the ship?"

Jaggears magnified the image.

"I'll be damned, they are," said Bristow. "A transfer."

"This is two hours after that, six o'clock yesterday evening." Jaggears pointed to the screen with a laser.

"They're gone. Any images showing the boats leaving?" Bristow asked.

"Negative, that's it."

"Damn," John said. "We don't know where they went."

"If we assume the women were hostages on board, one of two things occurred. They either remained on the boats and are somewhere in Panama, or they were transferred to that freighter." He showed several images in quick succession. "Here is six thirty and seven o'clock."

"It got underway," Mark said.

"The ship's name is *Kapitan Kurov*. It's owned by FESCO, the Far Eastern Shipping Company, with headquarters in Moscow. You may find it interesting that five years ago, FESCO was acquired by the SUMMA Group, a private investment company."

"A private equity company in Russia? I didn't know there was such a thing," Mark said.

"Now you do. FESCO is the largest transportation company in Russia. They're involved in marine transport, rail lines, and port handling."

"What does Russia have to do with this?" Kearns asked.

"We don't know. The *Kapitan Kurov* passed through the Gatún locks at seven thirty last night," said the admiral. "Traffic typically goes in the opposite direction, but the authorities changed it last week. It will run like this for the remainder of the month."

"Where's it going?" Mark asked.

"According to the cargo manifest filed in Balboa, its destination is Cartagena, Colombia. A twenty-four-hour transit."

"They're on that ship," Mark said.

"And already over halfway there." Bristow stood up. "What are we waiting for?"

"Captain Enrico?" Jaggears asked.

"Yes."

"Would your men be so kind as to locate the other boats used in the raid? I'll bet you'll find them somewhere in the port of Colón."

"I agree, Admiral. It would be my pleasure."

"Thank you. I'll be in touch later this evening."

"If you will excuse me, I have work to do." Enrico stood and shook hands with the men around the table. "Good luck, gentlemen."

"Same to you," Manny said. Enrico left the room.

"All right," said Jaggears, "the plane is waiting. You leave for Cartagena in an hour. Before you take off, there are a few details I want to go over."

THIRTEEN

SATURDAY, MARCH 25TH

Kapitan   Kurov,   Caribbean   Sea   (10°17'35.8836"   N;   76°56'53.6712"W)

CLAIRE LAY ON HER BUNK, staring at the wall. A black spider the size of a bottle cap moved diagonally toward the ceiling. Cold air from the ceiling register moved across her face. The grill was covered with a gray dust film. She coughed and wiped her nose with the back of her hand. She listened for sounds of movement in the hallway but only heard the rumbling of her empty stomach. The gentle up-and-down oscillation of the ship might have been soothing, but not when one was locked in the brig on a freighter bound for an unknown destination.

The powerful diesel engines vibrated her mattress like magic fingers as they propelled the ship onward. For the tenth time, she thought about the situation and asked the same question. *What do they want with me?* She closed her eyes and thought of her parents in Sydney. Was Mark looking for her? How could anyone possibly find her?

The door burst open. "On your feet." A man stood pointing at her. He crossed the room and grabbed her arm. "Move." Claire yanked her arm away.

"Don't touch me," she spat out.

He grabbed a fistful of hair and yanked her to her feet. "I said move."

She swung at his face, but he held her at arm's length and her fist connected only with air. "Let go of me!"

He let go of her hair, gripped her arm with the force of a steel clamp, and pulled her toward the hallway. "Shut up."

She was shoved out of the room. Another crewman led the way down the narrow passage. She lost all sense of direction as they made turn after turn in the narrow passageways in the windowless confines of the ship. Next, they passed through a series of watertight hatches. Pipes and conduits ran above their heads. The temperature and noise level increased as they walked. The sound of the marine diesels and machinery was deafening. Through a doorway, she saw crewmen in dark blue coveralls and Mickey Mouse hearing protection checking gauges. The man behind prodded her onward. She stayed close to the lead guard as they walked along a catwalk. Two levels below a gigantic rotating two-foot-diameter propeller shaft turned one of the screws. They continued forward and went up two ladders. The temperature and noise level once again became tolerable. They stopped in front of a door marked with a red cross. The man in the lead opened it and stood aside. Claire felt a hand on her back push her inside.

"So good to see you again, Dr. Hodgson. I trust your accommodations have been satisfactory. Unfortunately, all good things must come to an end," said Sorenson.

"What do you want with me?" she asked.

"That's the problem. We don't *need* anything from you. You're no longer useful. Your work has proven that Endovancin is a miraculous drug, and that's all we needed to know."

Claire stared at him. "How could you know that?" She walked

forward. "Where did you get that information?" The guard behind her grabbed her shoulder, and she shook him off and looked back. "Keep off me."

He grabbed the back of her collar and yanked her backward. "Don't move."

Sorenson laughed. "Easy, don't hurt the merchandise. Dr. Hodgson, we know a lot of things. Our intelligence-gathering methods are of little concern to you now."

"If you're going to kill me, at least answer a few questions."

"Very well, if you insist. The data came from a lab tech, the histologist."

"Robert would never do a thing like that."

"We made him an offer he couldn't refuse."

"What kind of offer?"

"A final offer," Sorenson said. "You'll never know. Now, hold her still." The two guards grabbed her arms while Sorenson rolled up her shirtsleeve. A syringe with a hypodermic needle appeared in his hand. Claire tried to pull away. She kicked at her captors.

"Stop. Let me go."

Sorenson wiped her shoulder with a swab and injected the contents of the syringe in less than a second. "There. In a few minutes you'll settle down. Put this on her." He held out a straitjacket. "This will keep you under control." The men dressed her, picked her up, and moved her to a bunk and tied her feet. "I'm obliged to deliver you unharmed. I have to admit, the bidding was quite impressive. Your new owners will decide your fate. Rest assured it won't involve returning to the US. You'll be put to use in some imaginative ways, and when they're bored, you'll be sold to someone else on the other side of the world. Goodbye, Dr. Hodgson." He placed a hood over her head. "Put her in the box."

FOURTEEN

SATURDAY, MARCH 25TH

Wilson Andrews Equine Research Center, Roanoke, Virginia

WARWICK GRANT KNELT beside Hyperion's unbroken hind limb and felt for its pulse. He looked up at Roger Coleman. "It's stronger than usual but not what I'd call bounding."

"His insulin levels have been elevated," Coleman replied.

"That can be stress related. The hoof looks healthy, and it's not too warm."

"What's the white line look like?"

"It's intact. No separation," Grant said. "No sign of seedy toe."

"He's lucky," Coleman stated.

"He's not showing any symptoms of support-limb laminitis."

"Yet . . . it won't be much longer. Should we sling him?"

"I think we have to since surgery's been delayed," Grant said.

"Dr. Montgomery is testing her new system. Want to ask if we can try it?"

Grant stroked the three-day stubble on his face and nodded. "I'll talk to Fiona. He'll need to be moved to stall seven. That's where she has it set up."

"The engineers were installing the new pressure transducers in the hoist," Coleman said. "I saw her testing the slings yesterday. What about giving him acepromazine?"

"Since he's not having surgery for a while, go ahead. We don't have anything to lose." Grant walked beside the horse, stroking his coat. He stood in front of him and rubbed his nose. "You're a champion," he said to Hyperion. "Hang in there, we'll get you well."

"Do you actually believe that?" Coleman asked.

"Of course. Mark my words, he'll run again."

"C'mon, you can't be serious. This is a publicity stunt. I love this horse as much as anyone, but I'm a realist. This is a mortal injury." He pointed at the splint. "Look at Barbaro. How's this any different? He won the Kentucky Derby and had a good shot at the Triple Crown, and after his injury he lasted, what? A couple of months? Hyperion had promise, but he's no Barbaro. Horses are their own worst enemies. He'll break another leg trying to run after you fix him. Even if you're able to fuse his fracture and have it actually heal, he'll still be no better than a nag."

"Barbaro lived eight months after his injury. They almost had him healed. What are you saying, Roger?"

"Stop this charade and put him to rest with dignity."

"I hear you, but I don't agree. This isn't a stunt. He's got a chance if Hodgson and Thurman can do what they claim. He's not going to end up like Barbaro . . . are you boy?" Grant reached up and rubbed his nose. "We're going to show them, aren't we?" He turned back to Coleman. "I promise you. The second I believe this is hopeless, we'll put him down. Now, let's get that sling set up."

DR. FIONA MONTGOMERY finished entering data into the tablet she cradled in her arm while Coleman and Grant buckled the straps attaching the abdominal sling to the hoisting mechanism. The veterinarians double-checked the apparatus to make sure it was snug and there were no pressure points that might injure his hide.

"Looks good," Grant said. "Start whenever you're ready."

Fiona tapped the screen and the worm gears began to turn. The stainless steel cables attaching the sling to the ceiling made Hyperion look like an enormous puppet. "The injured hind limb will remain completely off-loaded. I've programed the unit to reduce the pressure on his front limbs by thirty to fifty percent in a cyclic pattern that varies over the course of an hour. His abdominal organs won't be compromised."

"I'll assign a nurse to check the sling every shift," Grant said.

"The computer records data from each transducer on a second-by-second basis and displays a graph of the weight placed on each limb. I can check it on my phone." She showed them the information displayed on her screen, then slipped the phone back into her pocket. "Pressure sores are our main worry. If his skin stays healthy and he doesn't develop any internal or respiratory problems, he can stay in the sling for weeks," said Fiona.

"If something doesn't happen soon, it'll kill him," Coleman said. "This magnificent animal wasn't meant to hang from a sling like a side of beef."

"Roger, don't be so dramatic. This is temporary," Fiona rebuked. "I've read Hodgson and Thurman's work. This shouldn't be needed for more than a couple of weeks."

"Yeah, if they can do what they claim. Where *are* they? I haven't seen any miracle cure. It's bullshit. I see nothing being done and a horse suffering," Coleman said. "You call this medicine? Humane treatment?"

"Roger, c'mon, give them a chance. They'll come through," Grant said.

"I'll believe that when I see it. This is a three-legged horse, and three-legged horses don't live long."

FIFTEEN

Puerto de Cartagena, Colombia

THE MERCEDES SPRINTER van accelerated through midmorning traffic, shifting lanes with borderline reckless skill. Mark checked his seat belt and adjusted his sunglasses. Cars moved out of their way when they saw the flashing lights. The driver had thus far kept the siren silent. The monstrous ancient Spanish fortress of Castillo San Felipe de Barajas loomed high on the Hill of Lázaro as they sped down Calle 30. It was a balmy seventy-eight degrees in Cartagena. Bristow tapped his phone and shoved it into his front pocket. Mark leaned forward from the rear of the vehicle. "What did he say?"

Bristow pulled a map from his backpack. He unfolded it until it covered his lap.

"Anytime you want to clue us in on this operation, it's all right with me," said Manny. "Where in the hell are we going?"

"Sorry, Jaggears was giving me the latest," Bristow replied. "He spoke with General Restrepo, the head of Colombia's Anti-Narcotics

Police, and is calling in some markers. Our guys have been working with them on several recent operations. The general has been generous enough to allow Colonel Medina and a detail of his men to lend us a hand." Bristow nodded to the driver.

Miguel Medina kept his eyes on the road and smiled. "We're grateful for the assistance Admiral Jaggears and your organization has provided. I'm honored to help."

Bristow looked back at his men. "We're heading to the SPRC Marine terminals on the western outskirts of the city. The *Kapitan Kurov* is scheduled to dock there in one hour."

"The official name is the Sociedad Portuaria Regional de Cartagena," said Medina. "A private company controls its operation and has transformed the shipping economy of the region. Colombians are proud of this port. Unfortunately, the cartels still exert their influence."

"Still?" Mark asked.

Medina nodded. "They're basically organized crime and almost as sophisticated as your mafia."

"So, you're saying the mob controls the port?" Manny asked.

"Not entirely, but we may meet resistance. Their tentacles are far-reaching. We're going to surprise the ship's captain. He won't be expecting us."

"Is this the same outfit our captive was a member of?" Kearns asked.

A voice cracked over the police radio. Medina reached for the handheld radio and responded in Spanish. A moment later, he replaced it on the console and glanced in the rearview mirror at the men in the back seat. "The cartels have evolved since the days of Pablo Escobar. Your prisoner was, at one time, part of Los Rastrojos Comandos Urbanos. Which was a second-generation cartel that evolved from the Medellín and Cali cartels into the Los Urbeños. Over the last decade the cartels have advanced further, and a third generation exists today. They control most of the country's organized crime. Drugs, extortion, illegal mining, prostitution, kidnapping, and human trafficking. They are known as the bandas, criminals . . . the BACRIM."

He continued to explain. "They are franchised into many dispersed cells. They run the illegal operations in a very decentralized manner much different from the Medellín or Cali cartels of the 1980s." Bristow continued to study the map as he listened to the colonel. "Those were centralized, vertically integrated organizations. The BACRIM is an amorphous organization that's much more difficult to detect and fight. Tens of thousands, perhaps hundreds of thousands, of lives have been lost during this evolution. It's a tragedy for my country. The corruption goes to the highest levels."

"They have Claire and Meera now," Mark said. "How do we get them back?"

"We have to find them first," Bristow said. "The *Kurov* is a hybrid container ship with roll-on roll-off capabilities for vehicle transportation. She's scheduled to unload her cargo over the next several days and take on another load for transportation back to Singapore next Monday."

"How are we going to find them? Can't we impound the ship and search its cargo?" Mark asked.

"It's not that simple," Medina said. "The ship is enormous. It would take a hundred men to secure it and a week to search all its spaces and containers."

"Still, our best chance is to surprise them and search the ship before the hostages are moved somewhere else," said Bristow. "We can't lose them."

"My men are waiting."

———

COLONEL MEDINA PARKED the van on the concrete pier next to two uniformed guards wearing Kevlar vests with the words DIJIN Policía stenciled in front and back. Medina opened the door and got out. The guards snapped to attention and saluted.

"Who are they?" Mark asked.

"Colombian National Police, Miguel's men. There's a whole company of them in that bus. They're going to search the *Kurov* as soon as it ties up," Bristow said.

"The Russians aren't going to like that," said Kearns.

"This isn't Russia *and* we have reasonable cause to believe kidnapping victims may be on board," Bristow said as he opened the front passenger door. Mark got out and the men walked to the other side of the vehicle. They watched the tugs push the ship into place and the line handlers secure the huge ropes to the mooring bollards along the pier. A crane maneuvered the gangway into place. When the signal was given, Colonel Medina, Bristow, Mark, and the others climbed the stairs and crossed over to the ship. The officer of the deck met them.

"Good afternoon. I am Colonel Medina with the Colombian National Police. Please inform your captain I would like to speak with him."

"Is he expecting you, sir?"

"No," said Medina.

"I will notify him. He's on the bridge. This man will take you to him."

A sailor motioned to them. "This way, sir."

Before proceeding, Medina turned to the officer. "Do not begin unloading until we have finished our inspection. Is that clear?"

"Understood, sir."

Medina turned and the group followed their escort inside the ship to a stairwell. They climbed to the bridge and the sailor opened the door. They stepped into an open room spanning the width of the ship filled with electronic equipment. A panorama of windows gave a one-hundred-eighty-degree view of the forecastle and the surrounding harbor. The bow stretched several hundred yards into the distance. The deck had cargo containers stacked almost to the bridge. The helm was in the center of the bridge with several men standing nearby. A middle-aged man dressed in a pressed white shirt with gold-striped shoulder epaulets and navy blue slacks stood talking to a civilian dressed in a sport coat. The officer turned and smiled while extending his hand to Medina. "Good day, Colonel. Welcome aboard. I'm Captain Stromstead. How can I be of assistance?"

Medina stood rigid facing the captain. "We have reason to believe two women are being held on your vessel against their will. I have orders from General Restrepo to search the ship and its cargo. With your permission we will begin."

"I'm sorry, Colonel Medina, but I must object. That is preposterous. There are no women on board this ship, crewmembers or otherwise."

"Then you have nothing to hide."

"This is highly unusual. My employers in Moscow will also object to such treatment. Unless you have proof of this outrageous claim and produce the appropriate documents allowing such a search, I will proceed with our normal off-loading procedures. I can assure you there are no women being held against their will on board this vessel." He handed him a piece of paper. Medina read it and handed it back.

"I need to make a phone call. Excuse me." Medina walked to the doorway leading outside the bridge. Mark watched him on the phone. His face became agitated and blushed several shades of crimson. He ended the call and returned. "Thank you, Captain. I apologize for the interruption. You may proceed with unloading your cargo."

"What?" Mark said. "We can't just leave. Claire and Meera are on this ship. They have to be. If we don't find them *now*, we may never find them."

"I just got off the phone with President Santos's chief of staff. My orders are to leave the vessel."

"Two world-renowned scientists are being held prisoner on this ship, and we're just walking away? What happened to cooperation?" Mark asked.

"C'mon, let's go. You heard the colonel." Bristow grabbed his arm and pulled him toward the doorway.

"This is bullshit." When they reached the bottom of the stairs, Mark walked to the edge of the ship. He gripped the railing and looked down into the water between the ship and the pier. The space was darkened by shadows. He squeezed so tight his forearms began to cramp. "She's here. I know it. We're going to lose them."

Bristow pulled his arm. "C'mon, it's time for plan B."

As they approached the quarterdeck, a man in civilian clothes holding a linen sport coat over his arm and wearing aviator sunglasses and a panama hat crossed over the gangway ahead of them. A gust of wind blew and lifted the hat from his head. He grabbed for it but missed and turned around. The hat landed at Mark's feet. He bent down and picked it up, glancing inside the crown.

"Thank you," the man said, reaching out.

"You're welcome." Mark handed him the hat.

The gentleman proceeded across the gangway and down the stairs to the pier.

"I wonder who he is?" Mark said.

"Wasn't he on the bridge? He can't be a member of the crew. They wouldn't be getting off the ship this fast. Too much work to do," Kearns said.

"He was talking to the captain when we were up there. Maybe the ship's doctor?" Manny said. "Once the ship is tied up, the doc doesn't have much to do. There's no sick call. The crew wants liberty as fast as possible."

"He was in civvies and ready to go," said Kearns.

"He might not be a member of the crew." Mark watched as the man walked along the pier and lit a cigar. Vehicles were driving out of the ship from the forward cargo hold. A panel van drove down the ramp and parked on the pier. The man with the hat opened the passenger-side door and got in. "His name is Sorenson. First initial N. At least, that was the name written in the hat." The van turned around and drove away.

"If we can't search the vessel, we'll watch them unload. I'll have my men report anything suspicious," Medina said.

"Do you have anyone watching the airport?" Bristow asked.

"Of course," the colonel replied. "That's where we're going. There's nothing else we can do here."

"Shouldn't we wait? What if your men see something?" Mark asked.

"If anything suspicious happens, they will contact me. There are over two thousand cargo containers on the *Kurov* and several hundred vehicles in her hold. If the hostages are in one of them, we cannot stop them from being removed from the ship. Although, we may be able to catch them being transported after leaving. If they are driven by motor vehicle, it will be difficult to find them. However, if they are to be moved by air, then we may be able to observe them at the airport. It's our best chance."

"Two *thousand* containers? How in the hell are we going to find them?" Manny asked.

"Say some prayers," Kearns replied. Mark touched his chest and glanced up into the sky.

THE HEAT WAS STIFLING. No light penetrated her blindfold. The straitjacket kept her arms locked around her body in a permanent self-hug. It was like wearing a parka in a steam bath. Claire felt her sweat-drenched clothes clinging to her body. Breathing through her nose was like drawing air through a towel. The gag was so tight it cut into the corners of her mouth. She forced herself to remain calm.

This is like being in a coffin. What if I'm buried in this thing? She fought back panic as her heart rate rose. *Would it be better to die in this box than to be the chattel of a drug trafficker?* Her head struck the roof of her prison if she moved even an inch forward. Her toes touched the bottom wall. *This is a coffin!* She choked back claustrophobic terror. The drugs helped. They made her feel as if she was floating, and the sensation of spreading dread slipped away as she relaxed under the effects of fentanyl and Versed. She felt the crate being lifted. Then, she heard doors close and an engine start. The sensation of motion came over her as the vehicle accelerated and nosed down a steep incline. She stopped caring about what was happening. She was floating on a soft marshmallow bank of clouds. Panic had slipped away. She felt warm and weightless. Dreams of Sydney and of being home blossomed in her mind.

SIXTEEN

SATURDAY, MARCH 25TH

Wilson Andrews Equine Research Center, Roanoke, VA

ROGER COLEMAN TAPPED on the glass window of the inpatient pharmacy. The assistant with strawberry blonde hair and freckled cheeks looked up and smiled from the other side. "Afternoon, Janice."

"Hello, Dr. Coleman. Doing a drug run?" she asked.

"I'm collecting this week's meds for Dr. Grant's arthritis trials and, if it's ready, the infusion for the new patient, Hyperion."

"Just a moment." Several minutes later she returned with a shoe-box-sized container and a liter bag of IV fluid. "The pharmacist just finished making the infusion. You may want to wait a little while for the arthritis meds to warm up. The box was in the fridge. How are the horses doing? Can you tell a difference?"

"I'm not supposed to know who gets what. It's a double-blind study," replied Coleman.

"I know, but can you tell if it's working?"

"Just between you and me," Coleman said, leaning close to the hole in the window, "about half of them are running around like a pack of stallions while the others are lame as fence posts. The difference is so dramatic, Grant is talking about stopping the study early. Telos may have a winner. I'm thinking about trying to find a way to invest."

"Telos? What's that?"

"The company that makes the drug."

"What does it do?" Janice asked.

"I just told you. It's a pharmaceutical company."

"Not the company . . . the drug," she said and smiled.

"You mean, how does it work?"

She folded her hands on the countertop and looked up at him. "Yeah, what's the mechanism?"

"What do you care?"

"Just curious. I'm applying to pharmacy school next year. I was thinking about trying to work with Dr. Grant this summer for a research project."

"If you want to impress him, read up about anti-tumor necrosis factor alpha drugs. This drug is in that class." He held up the bag with the vials in it. "This stuff affects cells with $TNF\alpha$ bound to its membrane surface. We've been injecting it into horses' arthritic joints."

She squinted. "Which one?"

"The joint above their hooves. It's where they commonly develop arthritis. Humans get it in their hips and knees. Horses get it in their MCP joints. The drug is a modified monoclonal antibody that binds to $TNF\alpha$. It's a powerful agent that shuts down inflammation. Unfortunately, it can have side effects. If too much is given, it can suppress the immune system."

"Like AIDS?"

Coleman looked behind him then turned back. The corners of his mouth turned downward as his eyes shifted from Janice to the box. "That's the one problem with this drug. They can contract all kinds of opportunistic infections. It can mimic AIDS. Learn as much as you can about the anti-TNFα family of drugs and their effects on arthritis and autoimmune diseases before you talk to Grant. Come by my office and I'll give you a reading list and some recent journal articles. You'll shine like a new penny."

"Thanks. Can I come by tomorrow afternoon after my classes?"

"If I'm not in my office, wander over to the inpatient ward. I'll be around Hyperion."

"I'd love to see him."

"I'll introduce you."

"See you then," she said as Coleman backed out of the doorway.

COLEMAN PUT the medications on the desk and double-checked the lock on his office door. He went over to the sink in the corner and slit a hole in Hyperion's IV bag and watched the infusion go down the drain. Then, he opened the bottom drawer of his filing cabinet and retrieved a full IV bag of saline and transferred the label from the empty bag. He went to his desk and opened the equine osteoarthritis study data file on his computer. The spreadsheet filled the screen.

He looked at the entries and their drug codes and opened the box of vials. He separated them into two groups based on the data results. The actual key for the treatment groups was kept in the pharmacy department locked in a filing cabinet. But Coleman was pretty certain which vials contained the arthritis medication and which contained the placebo. It was obvious from the results. After sorting the vials, he took a sixty-milliliter syringe fitted with a twenty-gauge needle and filled it with the medication from the vials in the treatment group. He figured dosing with this amount of the anti-TNFα medication three times, forty-eight hours apart, should shut down the horse's immune system beyond repair. He held up the IV bag and rubbed his thumb over the label to keep the edge from peeling up. He injected the anti-TNFα medication into the bag and mixed the solutions. Coleman refilled the vials with saline, placed them back in the box, and put the syringe in his pocket. He'd dispose of it in a sharps container in the clinic. He threw the packaging from the syringe and alcohol swabs in the trash and walked to the inpatient ward. Coleman smiled. He was on a mission of mercy.

SEVENTEEN

SATURDAY, MARCH 25TH

Rafael Núñez International Airport, Cartagena, Colombia

COLONEL MEDINA STOOD next to a tall man in a charcoal suit and starched white shirt with a perfect dimple in his red tie. Mark estimated he was in his late twenties. Perhaps thirty. Their attention was focused on a large computer screen in the airport administrative wing. The younger man, Juan Ortega, chief of airport security, leaned forward, dragging the end of the tie across the desk. He pointed to the screen. "These are this afternoon's security tapes." He clicked on one, and time ran backward through the video. Bristow and Mark stood behind Medina, letting him do the talking. Kearns and Manny looked over their shoulders. There was barely enough room for all of them. The men watched the video run in reverse until the images stopped at the ten thirty mark. Half an hour after the *Kapitan Kurov* moored at the pier.

"We'll start here," Ortega said.

"This was taken at the general aviation terminal?" Medina asked.

The security chief nodded and combed his fingers through his shock of black hair. "Yes, sir. As you requested. This was a private flight that departed for Medellín two hours ago."

"Whose jet?"

"Corporate from the US. I don't know who owns it."

"That knowledge would be helpful."

"I'll find out, sir."

"Thank you, Juan. I appreciate your assistance. This matter is of personal importance," replied Medina.

"Then it's also important to me, Colonel. Can you tell me what we are looking for?"

"These women." He showed him photographs of Claire and Meera. "We believe they were on a freighter that arrived earlier today."

Ortega's eyes widened as he examined the photographs. "They would be hard to miss. You think they were flown to Medellín?"

"It's a possibility we are considering."

"They could still be on board the *Kurov*," said Bristow.

"We believe they were taken by the BACRIM, who will use their network to move them north. We tried to search the ship when it docked, but someone at high levels of the government blocked my attempt."

"They are everywhere," Ortega said.

"Not like before. You are too young to remember when Escobar was part of the government." Medina placed both fists on the desk and leaned close to the security chief. "You can be assured I will find their mole. In the meantime, I have information a private plane from Cartagena landed in Medellín less than an hour ago. We would like to see who took the flight."

"I've reviewed the tape and those women weren't on it."

"Nevertheless, we would like to see who boarded." The security officer ran the video in fast motion. Twenty minutes elapsed. A dozen or so men and women arrived, queued up, and passed through the doorway onto the tarmac. None of them looked like Claire or Meera. Several minutes later, the final passenger stepped up to the counter.

"There. Stop it. The man with the hat," Mark said. "Sorenson."

"Well, well, well," Bristow said. "What a coincidence. I wonder what our friend from the *Kurov* is doing in Medellín? What urgent business could he have there?"

"This is the only flight to Medellín since your ship arrived," Ortega said. "The next domestic flight doesn't leave in the main terminal for another hour."

"Thank you. Please keep looking. You can keep the photographs. I have others. Distribute copies to your men." Medina stood and put his cap on. "Gentlemen." He nodded and motioned toward the doorway. "We have business elsewhere."

"Our plane is fueled and standing by," Bristow told them when they were in the hallway. "How did you know it would be Medellín and not Bogotá or Cali?"

"A compañero. One of our men posing as a lookout for the cartel. He's an ex-FARC soldier working undercover for the government. I took his call before our meeting with Ortega."

"Anything else?" Mark asked.

"An attorney and several men met the plane. The lawyer is well connected with the local BACRIM. We've been watching him for years," Medina said. "The compañero saw a casket being unloaded from the plane. It was placed in their vehicle. He followed them to a building on the northeastern outskirts of the city in Comuna 8 de Medellín . . . the eighth district. They took the coffin to a warehouse across the street from his law office. The Bonsantos Company owns the building. On the surface, it is a legitimate agricultural company, but more than food products flow through there."

"Things more profitable than coffee, fruits, and vegetables?" asked Kearns.

"Exactly. We believe much of Antioquia's coca and marijuana production used to make its way through this facility before being delivered north to the Mexican cartels."

"Used to?" Bristow asked.

"There has been a subtle change, recently. Fewer shipments have been moved through Medellín. Our sources say the product is being diverted to Bogotá."

"Why there? That's in the opposite direction and much farther from the northern supply routes through Mexico," Mark said.

"True. We don't know the reason. Perhaps a new method of transportation. The BACRIM have lost a large portion of profits from the narcotic trade with the rise of the Mexican cartels. When Pablo was running the operation, he had strong centralized control. A monopoly, and all the profits came to the Colombian cartels. Now, half of the money goes to Mexico and others. The BACRIM would like to go back to the old ways."

"How would they do that? It would require a new system for distribution."

"Sí, a new system to bypass the Mexican supply channels north," Medina stated.

"Is that possible?" Kearns questioned.

Medina held out his palms and shrugged. "Who knows? The ground routes through the jungles are slow and expensive but difficult to stop. It is very difficult to move product by air or rail. It's much easier to detect. We're investigating the situation but tonight, it's business as usual. A large shipment of cocaine, marijuana, and heroin will leave Medellín in a few hours."

"If you know so much about them, why are they allowed to operate?" Bristow asked. "Just shut down the warehouse."

Medina laughed. "This is Colombia, my friend. Things are not that simple. Bonsantos is a large company based in Cali that provides jobs for many of our people. Those jobs are important. They put food on the table of many families. Like your country, we are not allowed to barge into a place of business without good cause. It is protected and the operation is well organized. We have raided this building twice in the past three years, and each time they were warned in time to remove the contraband. I've been patient, waiting for the right opportunity. Tonight, we will revisit the Bonsantos warehouse."

"We want the women recovered . . . unharmed," Mark said.

"That is the goal," Medina said, then paused for a moment. "The word on the street is that a US company is considering a sizable investment in Bonsantos. A partnership in a new venture."

"What company?" Bristow asked.

"A pharmaceutical company. I don't recall the name. They want to build a manufacturing plant in Bogotá. Legitimate medicines produced and distributed from Colombia," the colonel replied.

"You think there's a connection?" Bristow asked.

The corners of Medina's mouth drew back in a tight smile, revealing more than his words. "I don't know. Perhaps."

"That's later. What's the plan for tonight?" Bristow asked. "I want answers. I want to know what or who was in that casket."

"We all do. My men in Medellín are preparing this evening's operation. We're expected there soon. The flight is a little over an hour."

"Hooyah!" said Manny. "Time to rock and roll."

THE PHONE VIBRATED against his thigh as he settled into the seat. He retrieved it from his pants pocket and peered at the screen in disbelief. "Warwick?"

"Mark, where are you?"

"You don't want to know, and I can't tell you."

"I tried to call Claire several times. She didn't answer. We need you back here. Hyperion has taken a turn for the worse."

"I'm sorry, but we're having our own set of problems. What's wrong? Are his other legs okay?"

"So far, there's no sign of laminitis," Grant said.

"That's good."

"We've off-loaded the support legs with a sling device. I've no idea if it will continue to work, but so far so good. That's not the reason I called. It's something else. He's developed a post-op wound infection at the biopsy site. It's getting worse and not responding to antibiotics. I have him scheduled for debridement in the morning."

"Cultures?"

"We got some this morning. They're cooking in the micro lab. The gram stain looks like mixed flora. Blood cultures are pending. I'll get a deep tissue set tomorrow during surgery."

"Mixed flora? What's up with that? Is he immunosuppressed?" asked Mark.

"No, he shouldn't be. Except for the fracture, he's healthy."

"What antibiotics?"

"Vancomycin," Grant replied.

"Anything else?"

"Cefazolin. We sure could use that new one of yours right about now."

"Things are swirling about the dunny," said Mark, using one of Claire's pet phrases when things weren't going well.

"Pardon me?"

"Nothing. Look, we're in a tight situation. The Endovancin supply is exhausted. We've been trying to get more but have run into problems. I can't go into detail, but we're working on it."

"Without you two and that drug, I might as well start digging Hyperion's grave."

"Don't start digging yet. Keep him alive. I'll call you in a day or two," Mark said.

"I'll do my best, but please hurry."

Mark ended the call and cinched his seatbelt. The plane surged forward then streaked down the runway and in minutes was leveling off at cruising altitude. Cartagena and the Caribbean disappeared into the distance below as the aircraft sped southward. Mark watched as Bristow and Medina looked over a street map. He lifted the sunshade and reclined his seat as Claire crept into his thoughts. He heard her laugh then watched her put her hair in a ponytail while sitting on the beach. For a moment, she leaned against him on his couch while he was reading on a rainy Saturday afternoon. The scent of her body filled his head. He felt the soft smoothness of her skin as they lay in bed and he ran his hand over her hip. Life without her would be hard to bear. A void so big it would suck him to the bottom.

Four years ago his mind and body were in ruins after a battle against cancer fought with an arsenal of chemotherapy and radiation. He'd gone into remission and appeared to have won the war, but life in the aftermath was a dystopian wasteland. He could never know for sure if the battle was over. The fear of a recurrence haunted him day and night. Psychologically, he was trapped like a larva in a cocoon. His existence was devoid of meaning until Claire entered his life and the metamorphosis began. He remembered her standing at the lectern the first time he'd seen the rising academic star. Her ideas were brilliant with visionary application to orthopedics. He approached her and they began working together. Without knowing it she dragged him from the abyss. Now the tables were turned. She needed him, and he was coming.

The plane pierced a cloud and the sky turned white. A hand grasped his shoulder and he looked up.

"Bristow wants to go over the game plan," Kearns said and walked up the aisle. Mark followed, took his seat, and stared at the other four men.

Medina spoke first. "We'll land in Medellín, soon. It'll be dark in a couple of hours. I've been in contact with DIRAN."

Mark raised an eyebrow and looked around. "DIRAN?"

"National Police Anti-Narcotics Directorate," Bristow explained.

Medina continued. "Also, I've spoken with several commanders in the directorate for anti-kidnapping and anti-extortion. This mission has become a top priority. Jose Valdez is the leader of this BACRIM faction. He's been poking his finger in our eyes for years. Breaking up his operations in Medellín, even if only temporary, will send a strong message."

"What's the plan?" Kearns asked.

"We'll be met at the airport and taken to a safe house. A rendezvous in the northern district of Comuna 8. The warehouse is a few miles away. The streets are narrow and steep. Multiple small vehicles will be used, including teams with motorcycles."

"Any possibility of stealth?" Bristow asked.

Medina shook his head. "This is a closely guarded facility. The neighborhood is a tight community run by the BACRIM combos. Street gangs. They have a shadow presence visible only to those who live there. Their soldiers wear civilian clothes and hit men ride on the back of motorcycles. If a hit is ordered on someone, they will ride up and shoot them with little worry about witnesses. A customer in a store could be one of their extortionists. They have their own compañeros watching to report anything out of the ordinary. Multiple vehicles entering the neighborhood after dark will be recognized immediately. They'll know we're coming."

"What's the strategy? Speed?"

"Speed and violence. A lightning strike. We will converge from all available roads, surround all entrances to the warehouse, and enter with force. Anyone there will be apprehended. We have reason to believe a large shipment of processed coca and marijuana, perhaps heroin, is there ready to be transported north into the Bajo Cauca region. Probably using the BACRIM intelligence networks into Urabá and across the Panama border and up through Central America into Mexico. They may have been holding up the shipment waiting for your women to be delivered. This is the underground highway for drugs and human trafficking. From Mexico, the drugs will find their way into the US, and the women will be sent west to Indonesia, China, or other parts of the world. The women will be in high demand and worth a lot of money to the BACRIM."

"You get your shipment and slap the BACRIM in the face, and we take the hostages. No screwups," Bristow said, reaching across the table.

"Sí, no errors tonight," said Medina.

Bristow stood. "Get changed. Combat gear."

IT WAS dusk when the plane landed at the small airport on the northeastern side of the city. Mark followed Bristow and Kearns down the stairs to the waiting vehicles. They placed their extra gear in the trunks. Medina and Manny got into the lead car. Mark unslung his rifle and placed it between his knees as he slid into the back seat of the second car. The high rises in the El Poblado section of the city sparkled as the sun set over the mountains to the west of the Aburrá Valley. The cars wound their way into the central part of the city, and Mark recognized the Parque de las Luces with its three hundred illuminated posts like a field of bare flagpoles. They continued past the stunning block-long public library named Biblioteca EPM.

"Are we taking the long way?" Bristow asked the driver.

"No, sir. This is the most inconspicuous route to our destination. Approaching from the south is best."

Mark noticed the two cars were no longer together. They had split up, taking different routes. He watched the city through the tinted windows. The sidewalks were well lit and the streets clean. Like most major metropolitan areas, Medellín had areas of impressive modern beauty. As they traveled farther from the central part of the city, the landscape began to change. Gang graffiti appeared. Trash overflowed onto the streets, and shadows became darker. Brightly colored murals and graphic memorials to fallen victims of gang violence covered the walls.

"Interesting," Bristow said, pointing upward to a network of cable cars moving across wires in the sky.

"Our mass transit system," said the driver. "The roads in these barrios are too steep, narrow, and winding for buses. The escalators and cable cars move people to their jobs and back home."

He made a series of sharp turns going up the hillside and turned into an alley, stopping halfway up the narrow passage. He pointed to a door on the left. "Colonel Medina will be inside." He put the vehicle in park and turned off the engine. The men got their gear from the trunk and approached the building. Kearns knocked. The hinges creaked and an M16 gun barrel was visible through the crack. Bristow spoke a few words in Spanish and the door opened.

"Glad you could make it. We're upstairs," said the uniformed man with DIRAN stenciled across his Kevlar vest.

"Won't the neighborhood notice all this activity?" Bristow asked Medina as he entered the upstairs room. The cinder block walls were bare, and the rickety roof was corrugated metal. The windows were boarded up from the outside. Battery-powered lanterns on the floor lighted the room. Mark counted twelve men, bringing the total to seventeen counting the TSI team and Medina.

"The police and army patrol these areas all the time, and it's possible suspicions could be raised. However, it's worth the risk. The attack will proceed with maximum speed once we leave this building. I want to make certain we are all working from the same sheet of music and on the same schedule. The warehouse is several miles from here, and it is unlikely that their compañeros will be alerted before we are at their door." He spoke for several minutes in Spanish then translated his message into English.

"Any questions?" Medina asked. No one responded. "Good. Let's go."

THE DRIVER MANEUVERED the car around the tight corners and up the winding roads. By Mark's watch, the trip took less than five minutes. They were divided into four groups. Bristow led their team. They had night vision capability but hoped to need it for only a short time. The two-story warehouse would soon be well lit. Each team was assigned one of the four street-level entrances to the building that covered half a neighborhood block.

The assault team lined up on either side of the doorway. Mark lowered his NVGs into place. He could feel his alert level shift from orange into red.

"Go!" The signal came. The driver levered the crowbar and the door gave way. Bristow kicked it open and they scrambled into darkness. Each man covered his territory and moved forward. Bristow signaled the driver and Kearns to go left. Bristow and Mark moved down the right hallway. Objects glowed green and shades of gray. They checked door handles as they went. All locked. They came to a corner, cleared it, and turned left. Gunfire erupted in another area of the building. Men were shouting. Footsteps came toward them. Bristow dropped into a kneeling position and Mark raised his rifle. They waited. The shadows of men crashed into view at the end of the hallway.

"Halt! Alto! Drop your weapons!" Bristow screamed. He fired a burst over their heads and the group skidded to a stop with their hands raised. More gunfire from several areas of the building could be heard. "Down, on the floor!" The men obeyed.

They approached the men with rifles leveled chest high. "Shoot anyone who moves," he said to Mark.

"My finger is on the trigger."

"Cover me while I cuff them." He kicked their guns away then bent down and secured their hands behind them. He searched and removed any remaining weapons.

"Building secure. All clear," came the message over their coms.

"Three banditos," Bristow reported.

"We have one down. He needs medical attention. Send Dr. Thurman."

"Did you find the women?" Bristow asked.

"Not yet. Still looking. Bring the captives to me."

They marched the three men to the central area of the warehouse. Thousands of cardboard boxes of produce were stacked on pallets waiting to be placed onto delivery trucks. The colonel and his squad were near the loading docks. Mark counted nine young men. Several wearing shorts and T-shirts looked prepubescent. *These are children,* he thought. Weapons were stacked in a pile on the ground. An older boy, maybe eighteen years old, lay on the floor in a spreading pool of blood coming from his right groin. Sweat and fear shone on his pale face as he pleaded for his life. "No me dejes morir, por favor?"

"Tell me where they've gone," Medina ordered.

"He'll be no good to us dead." Mark removed his medical pack and unzipped it. He put on his headlamp and directed it at the wound. With his trauma shears, he sliced through the boy's pants and threw them aside. A pulsatile flow of blood came from a bullet wound in the groin. "I need some help." Mark looked at Kearns, who knelt on the other side of the patient. "Hold this, press down," Mark said, placing a folded ABD bandage over the wound. "The bullet severed his femoral artery. It's retracted into his pelvis. I need to get a clamp on it or he will die."

"He's bleeding out," Kearns said.

Mark ignored the comment. He held a Kelly clamp in his right hand and clean sponge in his left. "All right. Release pressure." Blood began pumping out of the hole. Kearns eyes widened. Mark stuck the end of the clamp into the wound. The patient screamed. He closed the clamp. The flow remained steady. He placed his hand back on the wound and leaned into it. With his other hand he reached into the medical bag and retrieved a scalpel. "I have to enlarge the entry hole or I'll never find the end."

"It's going to bleed even more," Kearns said.

"Get ready." Mark cut into the flesh, pulling the blade upward. More blood flowed. He reapplied a pressure bandage and pulled a pair of retractors from the kit. He placed the instrument into the wound and spread the blades open. "Hold these." Kearns gripped them. Blood poured forth but this time he could see the vessel. It was a frightening quarter-inch hose spewing a bright red fountain of blood.

"Holy shit," Kearns whispered.

Mark reached in with the Kelly and clamped the end of the artery. Most of the flow stopped. He pulled another clamp from his bag and dabbed the wound with a sponge. He reached in and clamped another. The bleeding stopped completely. He retrieved a black silk suture from his bag. "Hold this clamp. Don't pull on it. Just hold it up," he told Kearns. He placed the suture around the tip of the hemostat and tied the vessel. He repeated this several times until he was able to remove the vessel clamps. The wound remained dry. He packed it with sponges and wrapped the thigh with Ace wraps. "We'll leave the sutures uncut so the next surgeon can find the artery if it retracts." He inserted a large bore IV catheter into his arm and hung a liter bag of LR. "He'll need another after that one. Get him to the nearest hospital with a vascular surgeon."

"Gracias, Doctór," the boy whispered.

Mark bent close to him. "Were there two women here?"

Medina repeated the question in Spanish, "Dos mujeres aqui?"

"No," he replied, shaking his head and holding up one finger. "Una mujer."

"Only one?"

"Sí, uno," he said, "es alto y tiene el pelo rubio."

"She was tall with blonde hair," Medina translated.

"Claire," said Mark. "Where is she?"

The boy remained silent.

"You owe me that much," Mark hissed. Medina repeated the words in Spanish.

After a moment he said, "Norte."

"Where?"

"Bajo Cauca, Guarumo or Piamonte."

"Which one?"

"He doesn't know," Medina answered. "But we can find out." He spoke to the patient for several more minutes. Then, he took out his phone. Two officers raised one of the warehouse doors. A police truck with flashing blue lights was parked outside. An ambulance pulled up and men rolled a stretcher into the warehouse.

Mark reached down and shook the patient's hand. "Buena suerte." He looked at Miguel. "Tell him to change his life. This is not worth dying for." The colonel repeated Mark's wish and stepped aside. The medics placed the young man onto the gurney, hung a new IV fluid bag, and lifted him into the ambulance. They drove away with lights flashing and siren blaring.

"Come with me," Medina said, motioning to Bristow and his men. They got into the police SUV. Medina told the driver where to go. The vehicle made its way down the hillside through the twisting streets and turned north on Highway 25 toward the city.

"What are we doing?" Bristow asked.

"We're going to find your colleague. The patient was quite helpful after you saved his life, Dr. Thurman. He said there was a large shipment of processed coca that left several hours before we arrived. They had been alerted a raid might occur. The woman with blonde hair was loaded onto the truck with the shipment."

"What about Meera?" Mark asked.

"He said there was only one woman. I asked him twice. He was quite specific. Only one woman was present."

"He said they were going north?" Kearns asked.

The colonel nodded. "To a BACRIM stronghold along the backwaters of the Cauca River. They operate out of two towns. Piamonte and the heavily fortified Guarumo. The BACRIM control the roads leading in and out."

"How do you plan to get them?" Bristow asked.

Medina smiled. "An air assault. I have contacted the Jungla. They're DIRAN's special operations antinarcotics jungle company trained by the British SAS and US Delta Force."

"And TSI," added Bristow.

"You're correct. Your organization has been most helpful. You will see tonight." Medina paused for a moment before he continued. "The BACRIM operate throughout Colombia but recently have focused operations primarily in the Bajo Cauca subregion. It's where the roads are nearly impassable and the region is lawless. The Jungla deserve much of the credit for our recent success in slowing the flow of drugs into Mexico. They're aware of the truck and have directed a UAV with night vision capabilities over Piamonte and Guarumo tonight.

"A drone?" asked Mark.

Medina nodded. "Unmanned aerial vehicle. There have been rumors of this shipment for many weeks. The Jungla have been on standby and are ready to deploy."

"We're going in?" Kearns asked.

"Air cavalry. If the drone detects a truck on those back roads, two Black Hawk helicopters and two Little Birds will unleash hell before dawn."

"*After* we get our girl out of there," Bristow said.

"Of course, my friend. She is like a daughter to me after what we've been through today," Medina said.

Mark leaned forward and tapped him on the shoulder. "Don't forget that."

EIGHTEEN

SATURDAY, MARCH 25TH

Wilson Andrews Equine Research Center, Roanoke, VA

FIONA STOOD NEXT TO HYPERION, rubbing his dull brittle coat while she checked the straps to his body sling. "How can a horse as magnificent as you become sick this fast?"

"He can't tell you, Dr. Montgomery."

She turned around. Roger Coleman stood at the stall gate. "His fall from grace has been stupendous, hasn't it? From Kentucky Derby favorite to the necropsy lab in a couple of days."

"He's not there yet."

"He's not far. The stench of that leg is getting worse by the hour. We can't give him a higher dose of antibiotics or it'll knock out his kidneys. His hearing is probably already half gone."

"Thank you, Roger. But I don't need to be reminded of side effects. If another dose of vancomycin will save his life, he'll get one." Fiona knelt down and unwound the bandages holding the splint in place on Hyperion's wounded limb. The smell of infected flesh hit her like a punch when the final saturated gauze was removed. She gagged and looked away. "Why hasn't Grant washed this out?"

"It's scheduled for first thing in the morning. He was hoping Thurman and Hodgson would be here to assist. Thurman hasn't been back, and I've never even seen Hodgson. Some help they are."

"If somebody doesn't do something soon, this animal *will* die," Fiona said. She walked over to a cabinet and removed dressing supplies. She gently cleansed the horse's wounded leg and reapplied clean bandages and the Kimzey Splint. "When is his next dose?"

"That's why I'm here." Coleman held up the IV bag. "Five grams of vancomycin in three liters of saline to be infused over two hours." He wiped the IV port running from Hyperion's jugular vein and hooked up the IV tubing. He hung the bag from a metal hook attached to the overhead sling system and made sure it was dripping. "If you're still here when this finishes, can you take it down? It'll save me a return trip in the middle of the night."

"I'll be here."

"Thanks. I have to assist Dr. Grant in the morning and want to get some sleep. See you then?" Coleman asked.

"I wouldn't miss it. Have the reporters left?"

"You'd think the president's the patient. The whole country wants to know how he's doing. Grant will have to give a press conference after the surgery."

"I don't envy that chore," Fiona said.

"That's the price of fame."

"I don't know how he could possibly sugarcoat Hyperion's situation. There's no way to put a positive spin on a raging osteomyelitis post-op infection," she said.

"Realistically, he's as good as dead. How do you survive that? Give the poor bastard a few more days, but if he doesn't turn the corner, Grant has to put him down. It's the humane thing to do."

"I'm not giving up. The antibiotics will start working. He'll perk up."

"I hope you're right. Good night. I'm taking off. Don't forget the

IV bag." Coleman closed the gate and walked down the hallway. Several minutes later, he opened the door to his pickup truck and slid into the driver's seat. He took the prepaid phone from the glove box and entered the number. It was answered on the fourth ring.

"How nice of you to call. I presume you have good news?"

"I guess that depends on your point of view."

"Mine, of course. Or should I say . . . ours?" The confident voice filled the cab as Coleman drove down the main road out of the Wilson Andrews Center and turned onto the highway heading to Roanoke.

"It's working. With the dose I used, the effect was brutal. His immune system is shot."

"Excellent. Hyperion must never run again."

Coleman laughed. "That's hilarious. The beast can barely stand. Juvanimab wiped out his T cell response, and I doubt if his B cells are making any antibodies. His fractured leg is never going to heal. He'll be septic in a few days . . . if his kidneys don't shut down first. He's damn near dead already."

"Outstanding."

"When do I get the rest of my money?"

"Be patient, Doctor. Once he *is* dead, you'll receive your reward."

"I better. It'd be a shame if the media got wind of this."

"Now, now, Dr. Coleman, that's not nice. You're in too deep."

"Bullshit. I can already see the headlines . . . 'Rampage Ensured of Victory by Elimination of Competition.' What do you think of that?"

"You better hope that doesn't happen."

"I'm just kidding, but remember this. I'm risking my career for you. Don't leave me hanging."

"Stop worrying. You're going to be a great addition to our team, provided you can follow instructions. Tomorrow, I want you to give our patient another dose of Dr. Grant's arthritis drug. That should about do it."

"That's a bad idea. It's too risky. Another dose isn't needed."

"Give him another dose. Consider it insurance." The voice became sharp and quick. "By the end of the week, the news media had better be telling a weeping America the situation was hopeless and their wounded four-legged darling is dead."

"I can't. It will screw up the arthritis experiment. Forget it."

"Do it!"

"Or what?"

"We can discuss that in our next conversation. Let's just say that my Colombian partners won't be happy."

"I'll take you with me. I'm not going down without a fight."

"You're in no position to threaten anyone. Finish the job."

NINETEEN

SUNDAY, MARCH 26TH

Bajo Cauca, Antioquia, Colombia

MARK FELT the familiar thumping of the Sikorsky UH-60 rotors. The Black Hawk was one of the new M models outfitted for night operations. He looked out from the open cargo bay door and watched the two AH-6M Little Birds flying in formation and squeezed the automatic rifle between his knees. It was after two in the early morning hours, and they were fifteen minutes out from their release point over an island in the Cauca River near the town of Guanumo. Enemy contact was eminent. He reached up and felt the night vision goggles attached to his helmet.

Moonlit jungle passed under the helicopters, which made Mark wonder if this was similar to what his father experienced in Vietnam. A Jungla soldier sat toward the front of the helicopter with his arm slung over the barrel of his mounted M134 Minigun looking out the open doorway. His brother-in-arms manned its twin sticking out the port side. The other Black Hawk was the MH-60L Gunship version. They were flying without lights and loaded for bear. The pilots had been trained by the US Army at Fort Campbell, Kentucky, part of the famed 160th Special Operations Aviation Regiment—the Night Stalkers. Bristow pointed out their emblem displayed on the side of the helicopter when they boarded. It depicted the grim reaper holding a red sword and riding a white-winged Pegasus. Manny had translated the Spanish words *Night Stalkers* above the image and their motto, Death Waits in the Night, written below.

"Get ready. Tighten your chinstrap. We'll be over the LZ in five minutes," the pilot's voice came through their earpieces.

Bristow elbowed him and kicked the coiled rope at his feet. Mark gave him the thumbs-up. They'd watched the drone video images of the prisoner being escorted from the panel truck into the house. Bristow, Manny, Kearns, and Mark would recover the hostage while the Jungla wreaked havoc.

"Thirty seconds."

Mark slung his rifle, pulled on his gloves, and lowered his NVGs.

"Go . . . go . . . go." Bristow shoved the massive coil of forty-millimeter-diameter rope out the door. He gripped the rope and slid out of sight. Mark silently counted to five and followed him. His gloves and ankles heated up as the rope passed between them while he controlled the descent. The wind from the rotors whipped the jungle grass like a mini-cyclone. A minute later the rope was being pulled up, and the Night Stalker moved up and away. The night was illuminated in shades of green as Mark looked around. Kearns was on his right and Manny knelt next to him. Bristow turned and signaled for them to spread out and move forward. They left the clearing and moved into the thick jungle. If they had been dropped correctly, a building should be a hundred and fifty meters due east. As they moved through the thick undergrowth, gunfire sounded in the distance. The battle was underway. The Jungla gunships swept the night sky, strafing the camps with machine-gun fire and unleashing Hellfire rockets. Explosions and the terrible screech of miniguns ripped the night.

"Hustle! We have to get there before they try to move her or use her as a shield," Bristow's voice came through their earpieces. A faint light was visible through the jungle foliage. A truck the size of a U-Haul was parked next to a house. "Mark, you and I move to the rear. Kearns, Manny, take the front door and right side. In two minutes, kick in the doors and toss your stunners."

Mark was drenched in sweat as he ran to the rear of the shack. He knelt and watched the door. His chest thumped. The windows flashed and muffled explosions sounded through the house. Automatic rifle fire came from the front porch. The back door opened and two men ran down the stairs. They were dragging a woman by her shoulders. Her body was limp and her feet bounced off the steps. The men ran toward the truck. Mark sprinted. He crossed the ground in seconds. One of the men turned and yelled. He raised a pistol. Mark hit him like a runaway bus. He rocked the thug's head with the crown of his helmet.

They fell to the ground. Mark shoulder-rolled and regained his stance. The kidnapper shook his head and stood. He reached for the pistol that lay near his feet. Mark charged. He closed the distance and grabbed for the gun. A round discharged. Mark swept the man's feet. They fell to the ground in the darkness. The man struggled to pull away, but Mark held fast to the barrel. The gun fired again. The two were locked together, each gripping the weapon with both hands. Mark rolled and straddled his opponent. Then, he looked up into the wrong end of the barrel. He jerked his head sideways as the gun spit fire. The man wrenched his torso and yanked the weapon. Mark held fast and squeezed with his knees in a death hold. His forearms cramped as he struggled to gain control of the pistol. His arms and shoulders shook. Sweat poured from his face. Then, the bandito's elbows began to bend. The gun barrel turned. The kidnapper's eyes widened. He fought the inexorable movement. The gun stopped when the barrel rested under his chin. It was fired for the last time. The kidnapper lay still. Mark rolled off onto the ground, searching for Claire.

She was on her knees facing him. Her feet were splayed behind her. She appeared stunned and limp. The other sicario stood behind her with one hand under her chin and a pistol in the other.

"Prepárate para morir, gringo." He raised the pistol. Mark reached for his holster but was too late. Time slowed. He heard the crack of a gunshot, but no flame erupted from the barrel. The sicario's head snapped sideways and he toppled to the ground in slow motion. Claire slumped forward. Mark rushed to her as Bristow sprinted toward them.

"You hit?" asked Bristow.

"I don't think so."

"You scared me. I counted four shots fired."

"I couldn't let go. The son of a bitch kept pulling the trigger."

"Forget about it. C'mon. Carry her. We have to get back to the LZ," Bristow told Mark while examining the motionless bodies on the ground.

Mark lifted Claire into his arms. She gasped and let out a whimper. Her eyes remained closed. "She's alive."

"These guys aren't. Let's move."

"My night vision is out," Mark told him as he followed. "Slow down."

"Stay with me." Bristow kept up the pace through the jungle. The battle continued in the distance. The Little Birds were making strafing runs. The sound of machine-gun fire and grenades shattered the night. The Black Hawk gunships unleashed their weaponry. A hundred yards to their right, a building erupted and a column of flame shot into the sky. A miniature apocalypse was unfolding around them.

Mark shifted Claire to a fireman's carry. They continued for another hundred yards and stopped on the edge of the clearing where they were dropped forty-five minutes ago.

Bristow keyed his radio. "Tango Alpha. This is Echo One."

"Roger, Echo One," came the response.

"Hostage recovered. Repeat. Hostage recovered. We're at the LZ awaiting extraction."

"Proceeding your way." Bristow turned and faced a noise approaching through the dense undergrowth. Mark stopped and lay Claire on the ground. He unslung his rifle and waited.

Manny and Kearns emerged from the jungle and knelt ten paces to their left, keeping guard.

TWENTY

SUNDAY, MARCH 26TH

Wilson Andrews Equine Research Center, Roanoke, VA

DR. FIONA MONTGOMERY stood by Hyperion's side double-checking the eight straps attached to the sling supporting his chest and abdomen. Each one was connected to a transducer that measured the tension and weight distribution. This information was fed into a computer programmed to keep pressure off the injured limb and prevent overstressing the others. The mechanism was working better than she hoped. At least *one* thing was working. She glanced at his right rear leg splint and frowned.

"I'm not looking forward to seeing what's under those bandages," she said to Hyperion as she rubbed his neck.

"None of us are."

Fiona turned around as the anesthesiologist opened the gate to Hyperion's stall. "His morning labs weren't encouraging. He's tachy-cardic and febrile. His blood pressure is holding steady, at least."

"It's as if his immune system quit working. I don't understand how one of the most fit equine athletes in the world could go down-hill so fast," Fiona said.

"I agree. It's strange. You'd think his white count would be through the roof, but it's going down."

"It doesn't make much sense, does it?"

"He looks septic," the anesthesiologist agreed.

"It's the equine version of AIDS," Fiona replied. "I think I'll order a T cell count. He could go into multi-organ failure."

"Let's hope not." She took a syringe from her pocket and after cleaning the IV port, she injected its contents. "The anesthesia team is ready. Let's get him to the OR and wash out that leg."

Fiona unhooked the straps, and they led the sedated patient from the stall. He limped, trying to place minimal weight on his splinted right rear leg. Fiona led him as he crept down the hallway. She reached for a garden hose near the entrance and washed Hyperion's mouth clean so that no particulate matter could be introduced into his air passages. "That's a good fella," she told the horse. "We don't want you inhaling any hay. You have enough problems."

Afterward, the anesthesiologist approached and injected the induction agent into the IV. Several of the operating room staff helped move Hyperion against the nearest padded wall and steadied him as he faded out of consciousness and slid to the floor. One of the team gingerly held his injured leg.

"Be gentle," said Grant, who knelt with him while cradling his head.

"God knows he's in enough trouble," added Coleman. They attached ropes to Hyperion's uninjured hooves and adjusted his position on the floor.

"Open those chops," said the anesthesiologist as she pried his jaws apart and inserted a large plastic device into his mouth to keep his teeth apart. "That's it, baby. Open up." She slid a breathing tube into the trachea. A few minutes later she said, "All right, we're ready. Lift him." Fiona pressed the control button operating the winch. Hyperion was lifted, hooves first, upside down into the air and moved on an overhead rail system across the room. When he was positioned over the operating room table, she gently lowered him onto the padded surface and unhooked his hooves.

"Hurry up. Let's get him rolling," the anesthesiologist said. She and four others pushed the table holding Hyperion's unconscious body into the operating room. She double-checked the anesthesia machine and adjusted the gas flow that would keep the patient asleep for the next hour. She placed lubricant onto his eyes and taped his lids closed.

"Excellent job," Dr. Grant observed. "Airway secure? Can we start?"

"Whenever you're ready."

Before beginning the surgical prep, Grant and Coleman unwrapped the splint and tossed the outer layer of soiled bandages into the trash can. Coleman recoiled, ever so slightly, at the unmistakable stink of infected flesh.

"Not good," Grant said as he peeled away the gauze dressing saturated with grayish-white ooze. He dropped it into the trash and looked at the surgical tech. "Hemostat, please," he said. She placed the instrument in his hand and Grant removed the surgical staples used to close the skin after the previous surgery. Foul gray liquid with a pink bloody tinge spewed from the wound. "Prep the leg while Dr. Coleman and I scrub." The nursing staff scrubbed the limb and draped it with sterile bandages. The surgeons returned and donned their surgical attire. Grant took his spot next to the fractured limb.

"Culture swabs and specimen cup," Grant instructed. He spread the wound edges and more pus oozed from within. He inserted the cotton-tipped culture swabs deep into the wound and gave them to the nurse. Next, he gathered samples of tissue and fluid and placed them into the specimen container. He handed them to the surgical technician.

"Pass these off and get them to the lab. Label them 'right leg wound.' I want anaerobic and aerobic cultures with a gram stain for these specimens."

"Fungus, too?" Fiona asked.

"And fungus, he's sick enough . . . anything's possible," Grant called out. "All right, Roger. Let's clean up this mess." He called for a scalpel and extended the incision a centimeter in each direction. Then, he handed Coleman the pulsatile irrigation device that resembled a large battery-powered squirt gun, who began washing the tissues with a sterile dilute Betadine solution.

"You sure you don't want to just put him down?"

Grant looked at him. "Not yet. But if Hodgson and Thurman don't show up soon, we may not have a choice."

"Look at this. It's a disaster. How are they going to help? Did you read the newspaper article I sent you? Hodgson's lab was destroyed in a fire."

"I read it," Grant replied. "They'll think of something."

"This is hopeless." Coleman fixed his gaze on the wound. "It's cruel to keep this up."

"He's *my* patient. It's *my* responsibility. *I'll* make that call when the time comes. Keep washing. I want nine liters run through the wound."

Twenty minutes later, the final bag of irrigation fluid was empty. "Pack it with beads and wrap it back up?" Coleman asked.

Grant nodded. "Put him on the OR schedule for tomorrow. We'll do it again. I'm not giving up yet."

TWENTY-ONE

SUNDAY, MARCH 26TH

Medellín, Colombia

MARK LOOKED out of the Black Hawk's cargo bay. The sun was beginning to crest over the eastern range of the Cordillera Mountains. Dawn was breaking on the City of Eternal Spring. Medellín was a jewel nestled in the verdant Aburrá Valley in the Andes Mountains. Someday, when he had more time, he would come back. Perhaps Claire would, too.

She started to stir. Opening her eyes. Trying to sit up. Mark put his hand on her shoulder. He was secured in the seat next to Claire's litter. Three straps held her down as the helicopter made its final approach to the airport. For the most part, she'd been unhurt. He'd found the Fentanyl patches and removed them. He administered Narcan to reverse the effects.

"Where am I?"

He couldn't hear her words over the noise of the helicopter but read her lips. He pointed upward and put his finger to his mouth. She understood and stopped talking. He ran the back of his fingers across her cheek and smiled then leaned over and kissed her forehead. She relaxed and closed her eyes. Twenty minutes later, they landed.

He unfastened their seatbelts then listened to her heartbeat with a stethoscope and took her vitals. "How do you feel?"

She reached up and wrapped her arms around his neck. She pulled him to her and whispered, "I'm hungry and filthy. God, I've been in these clothes for days. I need a shower."

Mark smiled. "You're beautiful, baby."

"Thank you. I knew you'd come for me."

He brushed the hair from her face. "Are you light-headed? Any pain?"

"Not really. A few nicks here and there. My wrists and ankles hurt. Is my face bruised?" She reached up and touched her left cheek.

"You have a shiner. Vision okay?"

She nodded. "Yeah. I can see fine."

"Do you remember anything?" Mark asked.

"I remember being on the ship but nothing after they put me in the box. It's like a fading dream. I'm trying."

"That's probably good." Mark steadied her while Bristow helped her out of the helicopter. Her first few steps were wobbly. She gripped Mark's arm, and her strides lengthened as they made their way to the van twenty yards away.

"Where are we going?" She looked at Mark.

"Home," Bristow answered. "Mission accomplished."

"No. It's not," she said, stopping at the vehicle. "I came to help our patients. To get enough Endovancin to treat them. We can't go back without it. And where's Meera?"

"There's been no sign of her. The Colombian police are still searching. They haven't given up," Bristow told her.

Mark touched Claire's shoulder. "I hate to tell you, but there's no Endovancin at the lab. The lab, the entire facility, was destroyed. We were there. It'll take a year to rebuild."

"Damn it. I need to talk to Meera. She can help." Claire looked at the two men. "We have to find her."

"We're trying," Bristow said. "We hoped you two would be together."

"We were at first. They separated us on the ship. They took me to a jail cell. The brig. I remember walking through a maze of passageways."

"Did anyone say anything?" Mark asked.

Claire steadied herself against the car door. "I punched him . . . in the face."

"What?" Bristow was startled.

"The guy on the ship. He was at the lab when it was raided. I punched him in the face. That asshole. Then, they grabbed me . . . and one of them called him Dr. Soren."

Mark and Bristow looked at each other. "The hat," they said in unison.

Claire looked confused.

Mark explained and described the man they saw leaving the ship in Cartagena.

"That's him," Claire said. "We have to find Meera, and I need to talk to Rafael."

"Who?" Bristow asked.

"Meera's colleague," Claire said. "Dr. Rafael Alvarez. He knows as much about the process of making Endovancin as anyone. We have to go back to Panama. I have to talk to him."

Mark turned to Bristow. "That's the guy we met on the island. One of the two who led us to the back of building five. The older one." Bristow nodded.

"We have to go back. Please," Claire begged.

"Let me clear it with the admiral." He took out his phone. A minute later he handed it to Mark. "He wants to talk to you."

After a few minutes and several exchanges of the phone, Bristow announced, "Change of plans. I need to call Captain Enrico and find out if his men have been in contact with Alvarez. We'll make a stop in Panama before going back to North Carolina. Questions?"

"How long can we stay?" Claire asked.

"Until we get some answers," Bristow replied. He followed her into the van. They drove to the TSI Gulfstream, where they transferred into the aircraft.

Bristow glanced at his watch. "Wheels up in fifteen minutes."

CLOUDS FLOATED by as the jet sped toward Panama. Mark pointed out the Bridge of the Americas as they made the approach into Panama Pacífico International Airport. "Captain Esteban Enrico of the Panamanian National Police will meet us. He was with us when we searched BCI after the raid. His men are performing the investigation."

"Has he spoken with Rafael?" Claire asked.

"We'll find out soon." He leaned over and kissed her cheek. "It's so good to have you back."

She put her arms around his neck and kissed him on the mouth. "It's good to be back. Thanks for fetching me."

He smiled and touched her cheek. "I have a confession."

"What?"

"I love you. I need you. I'd never have given up. Without you, I'm incomplete." His hand lifted her chin and they kissed.

"I love you, too, Mark."

The plane landed and taxied to the TSI building. The cabin steward opened the door, and a tropical breeze whipped their hair and clothes as they descended the stairs. Bristow led the way and walked to a Land Cruiser parked next to the building. Esteban Enrico stood by the driver's door dressed in his police uniform and waved.

"Good to see you again, amigos."

"Likewise. I didn't think it would be this soon," Bristow said, turning to Claire. "This is Captain Enrico with the Panamanian National Police. Captain, I'd like you to meet Dr. Claire Hodgson.

She was one of the two scientists taken hostage by the men who raided BCI."

"Thank you, Captain, you helped save my life."

The police officer smiled. "I played a small role in the effort. It is a pleasure to meet you, Doctor. I'm glad you are safe. Where is the other?"

"Unfortunately, she hasn't been recovered—*yet*," Bristow said. "She's probably still in Panama or Colombia. We're continuing our search."

"As will we," Enrico said.

"Were you able to get in touch with Dr. Alvarez?" Claire asked.

Enrico gave an almost imperceptible bow and smiled. "I will take you to him." He opened the Land Cruiser door. Mark and Claire climbed into the back while Bristow rode in front.

"Where is he?" Claire asked.

"Gorgas Medical Center." As they drove from Balboa, Enrico pointed to a hill in the distance. "That's our destination. Ancón Hill, the highest point in Panama City. When the hospital was originally built, it was far from downtown, but now it sits in the northern suburbs. It's named for the Surgeon General of the US Army, William Gorgas, who in the early 1900s helped eradicate yellow fever and malaria from the Canal Zone."

"It's hard to imagine that until then no one understood mosquitos were the cause," Claire said.

"The hospital is now a modern Panamanian medical facility and still houses the main offices and laboratories of the Smithsonian Tropical Research Institute," Enrico said. He exited from the highway and turned into the compound. They continued up the palm tree–lined lower slopes of Ancón Hill, and the twin towers of the iconic administration building came into view.

"The original hospital building has been here for over a century," Enrico explained. "Many wings and new buildings have been added over the years." The Cruiser wound its way up the road and turned right. They passed several laboratory buildings and stopped in front of a modern concrete and glass seven-story structure. He parked and they climbed a dozen steps to the front entrance. As they approached the information desk, a man wearing a white lab coat called out.

"Dr. Hodgson." He waved and strode toward them.

"Rafael." She hugged him and he kissed her cheeks.

"Where is Dr. Jindal?"

Claire frowned and shook her head. "I don't know. They separated us."

"What happened?" Rafael asked.

"After the raid they forced us onto their boats then transferred us onto a ship bound for Colombia. I haven't seen her since the first day."

Rafael looked at the floor. "I'm worried." He wiped his eyes then looked away.

"So am I."

"She is an amazing woman."

"You love her," Claire said so that only he could hear.

He nodded. "But she loves someone else."

"I'm sorry, Rafael," said Claire.

"Please find her."

Enrico stepped forward. "We'll do everything possible."

"Thank you, sir."

Claire leaned forward and hugged Rafael. "The Colombian police are helping. They found me and they'll find Meera."

"They must. Her work is too important."

"We'll find her. It's only a matter of time," said Bristow.

Claire stepped back and looked around. "Why are you here?"

"The Smithsonian has loaned us space while BCI is rebuilt," Rafael explained. "I'm setting up the lab."

"Rafael, was all the Endovancin lost?" Claire asked. "We need more. It's vital. We're at critical stages in several experiments. Can you manufacture more?"

"I'm sorry. I can't right now," Rafael told her. "It'll be weeks, maybe months, before that's possible." He turned and spoke to

Enrico. "If you would wait here, please. I will bring them back in a few minutes." He turned to Mark and Claire. "Please, come with me." He led them to an elevator. They got off on the third floor and walked down a long corridor. He stopped at a door marked Tropical Disease Research Laboratory.

TWENTY-TWO

SUNDAY, MARCH 26TH

Gorgas Hospital, Ancón, Panama

THE LABORATORY LOOKED like a typical modern research facility loaded with state-of-the-art equipment and glassware. At the moment, the room was deserted.

"Is this where you got the HPLC the other day?" Claire asked.

"It is," replied Rafael. "They lent it to me as part of an arrangement Dr. Jindal made with the director."

"Why are we here?" Mark asked as he inspected the room.

"Wait and I'll explain." He indicated for them to stop as he walked to the back of the room and disappeared through a doorway.

"What's this all about?" Mark asked.

"I don't know."

Mark took a seat on a lab stool and looked around. "You could use some of this stuff."

Claire wandered down the aisle, inspecting the instruments. "You're right."

Rafael came back carrying a box about the size of a carton of eggs. "Please take this and put it to good use," he said, handing it to Claire.

She took it and opened the lid. Her eyes became big and a smile appeared, dimpling her cheeks. "Is this what I think it is?"

"It's a dozen five-gram vials of the last Endovancin currently on the planet," Rafael said.

"You're a darling." Claire put her arms around his neck. "Thank you. Where did you get it?"

"It was part of the deal. The tropical medicine lab lent us an HPLC in exchange for the antibiotic. The director wants to see if it is effective against certain tropical parasitic infections."

"Malaria?" Mark asked.

Rafael nodded. "Also, dengue and Chagas infections. But those studies haven't been designed or approved yet. You have patients who need this now. I can make more when the lab is rebuilt."

"This will save lives, Rafael. You're a good man," Mark said.

"I know what you're doing." He looked at Claire. "Meera told me about its miraculous properties. It's good to know our work is helping others. Please put this to good use."

"We will, I promise." Claire gave the box to Mark and threw her arms around Rafael's neck once again. "Thank you. This is so important. Thank you, thank you."

Mark reached out and shook Rafael's hand. "If I can ever do anything to repay you, don't hesitate to ask."

"Just find Meera, please."

"We will. Soon."

"When can you start making more?" Claire asked.

"I don't know. Many weeks, at least. Much of our work was taken or destroyed. I still need to replace several important pieces of equipment. Once they arrive, I'll collect the plant source and start production."

"You've got your work cut out," said Mark.

Rafael nodded. "What a setback."

"Please keep us informed. We'll need more as soon as we can get it."

"I'll be in touch," Rafael said.

"We need to get back," Mark interrupted.

"Come. I will take you to Captain Enrico. Let me know if there is any news about Meera."

Claire grabbed his hand. "I promise I'll call as soon as we know anything."

MARK AND CLAIRE settled into the soft chamois-colored leather Gulfstream seats and leaned back as the jet began to taxi onto the runway. "We should be back in North Carolina by four o'clock."

Claire smiled. "Home in time for dinner. I want to go by the lab and drop off twenty grams of the Endovancin. Meghan can take it to Dr. Sayre tomorrow. That should be enough to treat the remaining monkeys."

"Actually, we *can't* go by the lab," Mark raked his fingers through his grimy hair.

She turned to look at him, confused. "Why not?"

"I didn't tell you."

"Tell me what?"

"I was holding off until we landed and you had a chance to get some rest. I didn't want to hit you with too much too fast."

"What are you talking about?"

"You don't *have* a lab. It was destroyed the day after you left."

"What?" Mark watched the color drain from her face. "Destroyed? What do you mean . . . destroyed?"

"There was a fire early last Friday morning. It gutted your lab and office. We were lucky the whole building didn't burn down. Detective Ingram thinks it was arson. A body was found. Possibly Robert's body."

Claire put her face into her hands and bent forward. "That's not possible."

Mark put his arms around her. "I'm sorry."

"Robert, dead? I can't believe it."

"It *could* have been an accident. But after what we've been through, with the fire happening the same day as the raid on the BCI lab, I doubt it. These are big stakes. Big enough to kidnap or kill for. They were going to sell you into sexual slavery to get you out of the picture."

Claire looked at her hands resting in her lap. Her face was ashen. "What about Hyperion?"

"We can fix him. The 3D printers are at BioFab," Mark said.

"The biopsy samples and the stem cell cultures were in the lab."

Mark nodded. "Yep. All gone. The lab was a total loss."

"If we can't make the bone graft, they'll have to euthanize him."

Mark folded his hands behind his head and leaned back into the chair. "We can make more. I'll just have to get another biopsy sample."

"Where will we culture the stem cells? I spent years setting up that lab."

"We'll think of something. It wasn't the only stem cell lab," Mark said as she leaned her head against his chest. He lowered his arm around her shoulders.

"You're right!" she said, sitting up straight. "Give me your phone."

"What is it? Who are you going to call?"

"You said it. My lab wasn't the only lab. We can do it at Stephen's."

"Of course. The Yemassee facility. How could I forget? We did it there for two years."

"You're bloody well right we did, and we'll do it again." Claire made the call as the plane began to accelerate down the runway. A few minutes later, she handed him back his phone. "We were cut off but I think we're all set. He's going to start getting things ready."

Within minutes, they were both asleep as the exhaustion of the last few days caught up to them.

Mark's eyes opened as the wheels touched down. He stretched and tried to work out the crick in his neck. A smile spread across his face when he saw the pine trees surrounding the airfield. Pollen coated everything like a fine dusting of yellow-green confectionary sugar. It was springtime in North Carolina. Claire peered out the window as the plane taxied to a stop. Zachariah Jaggears stood on the tarmac. Claire was the first off the plane and ran into his arms.

"Thank you," she said and kissed his cheek.

He stood rigid and blinked, looking uncomfortable. "You are a valuable asset to this team, Doctor. Don't ever forget that." He put his arm around her shoulder and guided her into the building. "I need to know every detail. It's debrief time."

Two hours later, Claire and Mark were on their way back to Raleigh. Claire borrowed Mark's phone again as the car left the TSI base.

"Meg? It's me."

"Oh, thank God!"

"No worries. We're safe."

"No worries? I've developed an ulcer and my hair is falling out in fistfuls. I've worried myself sick. Did you hear about Robert? It's been on TV and in the papers. The coroner identified his body."

"It's terrible. I still can't believe it. I'm sorry for him and what you've been through."

"I'm just glad you're all right."

"Where are you?"

"At my apartment."

"Meet me at my place. We have a package to take to Dr. Sayre."

"I'm going, too?"

"Yes, he needs Endovancin to save the rest of our subjects."

"You got it?" she asked in amazement.

"Not a lot, but enough for now. Mark's going to Virginia to get

new biopsies and start Hyperion on the drug. We have another job."
Claire paused.

"What?"

"We have to get the cell culture apparatus functioning," Claire
answered. "We have to get Sayre's lab operational as fast as possible."

"You haven't used it in over a year," Meghan said.

"I know, but we need a temporary facility, and it's the best option.
You're not going to be able to finish your postdoc projects in the old
one. Mark and I did our first experiments there. It's not what you're
used to. But it'll work. It *has* to work for Hyperion's sake."

"When do we leave?" Meg asked.

"I want to be in Yemassee by eight tomorrow morning," Claire
said. "There are several pieces of equipment I want to borrow from
Dr. Mile. Pack a suitcase and be at my place in time for dinner. I'm
craving pizza. We'll take off early."

"When is Dr. Thurman leaving?"

"Tonight. He and Dr. Grant will get new biopsies. Then he'll
bring them to Dr. Sayre's tomorrow. We need to get a culture hood
and incubator functioning first thing. I'll talk to you in a little while."
Claire ended the call.

"Our other bioreactor is in my office at the hospital. It's on the
way," Mark said.

IT WAS after nine o'clock when Worth Hobbs's plane touched down
at Roanoke International Airport. Mark slipped into the back seat of
the car Worth had waiting for him. The driver placed the bioreactor
and his luggage in the trunk and drove to the Wilson Andrews
Center. Hobbs had reserved one of the VIP guesthouses for his stay.
The center was designed to accommodate the wealthy owners of the
world's finest equine athletes.

"Dr. Grant will meet you in the lobby at seven tomorrow morning," the driver said.

TWENTY-THREE

MONDAY, MARCH 27TH

Wilson Andrews Equine Research Center, Roanoke, VA

WARWICK GRANT STRODE through the empty lobby of the Wilson Andrews Center and stopped in front of life-size statues of two of the four Virginia horses to have won the Kentucky Derby. Reigh Count, the 1928 winner, and the great Secretariat, Triple Crown winner in 1973. Mark Thurman was waiting for him.

Mark extended his right hand. "You think Hyperion will be joining these guys?"

"You have a strange sense of humor, Dr. Thurman."

"I'm being serious. It's possible."

Grant's beard was beginning to hide the deep creases in his face. He turned and motioned for Thurman to walk with him. "At the moment your confidence borders on the delusional. You haven't seen him. He's taken a considerable turn for the worse over the past three days. My resident, Roger Coleman, wants me to put him down. I almost agree with him."

"Don't give up. We're going to do this. Give us a chance."

"You've got your chance. I won't throw in the towel yet. But if you can't pull off some kind of miracle, I'll have no choice," Grant said as they walked down the main corridor. "He'll have to be euthanized." Their footsteps echoed down a wide hallway lined with portraits. They turned right, following the Department of Surgery sign. "He's being prepped for anesthesia. By the way, I'm sorry about the fire at your lab. It's bad luck for both of us."

"I don't believe it was an accident."

Grant stopped. "Really? Who'd do that?"

"I'd like to know. Maybe someone who doesn't want Hyperion to get well. Any ideas?"

"That's preposterous. I can't think of anyone who would want Hyperion dead. That's insane."

"You just mentioned your resident," Mark reminded him.

"That's out of a sense of mercy. Not self-interest."

"It's just a thought you may want to consider." They halted while Grant punched a code into a keypad on the wall and a door swung open, leading to the pre-op area. "What did you mean by a turn for the worse?" Mark asked.

"He looks terrible. It's like his body has given up. It's not mounting an immune response. He looks septic but his white count is low and he's afebrile."

"The equine equivalent of HIV?"

"I don't know. His CD4 count isn't back, but a mixed bacterial flora has been identified from the leg wound and his blood cultures are positive. The vancomycin and cefazolin haven't been doing much. His specimens are growing gram positive and negative organisms. We're still waiting on the sensitivities. It's only a matter of time before we're fighting fungus."

"Well, cheer up. I've brought new ammunition for the fight." Mark held up a clear vial about the size of a shot glass with white powder filling the bottom third. "This is the secret weapon. Five grams of bacterial whoop-ass. When he pulls through, this drug will be the main reason."

CLAIRE AND MEGHAN drove down the two-lane highway heading southeast toward Yemassee, South Carolina, passing pine trees and an occasional palmetto palm. They'd been on the road since well before sunrise.

"So, this is where it all started?" Meghan asked.

Claire nodded. "This is it. Three years ago, Mark and I drove down here and met Stephen Sayre."

"The guy who runs the island?"

"Morgan Island. The FDA owns it and has a long-standing contract with the company Stephen works for. He manages the place and cares for its occupants."

"Experimental animals on a remote island. Reminds me of Jurassic Park."

Claire chuckled. "Good Lord, there's nothing over three feet tall living there."

"Sounds creepy."

"Usually it's not," said Claire. "However, a couple of the veterinarians were attacked by a group of them last week."

Meghan turned toward Claire. "Were they hurt?"

"Not really, a few scratches and bites, scared them though."

"I'm not getting near those things," said Meghan.

"You shouldn't have to. Sayre will administer the medicine. We're here to set up a cell culture lab. That's our goal."

"No sweat. That I can handle. Dr. Sayre's a vet, right?" Meghan asked.

"Stephen's one of the world's leading experts on rhesus monkeys. When Mark and I were awarded NIH and US Army research grants to study accelerated fracture healing, part of the grant money included funding to work with Stephen at this facility. Proving that our methods would work in a primate model was essential prior to testing it on human subjects." She turned onto a road and drove past a sign, RESTRICTED AREA KEEP OUT. "He's compassionate, competent, and hard-working. I think you'll like him."

"This place is in the middle of the boonies," Meghan said.

"That's the idea. The FDA and CDC want it that way. Who do you think put up that sign?"

"What other kind of research goes on?"

Claire shrugged. "Vaccine studies. The military has several labs."

"*Here?* We're working at a biological warfare facility?"

Claire looked at her and smiled. "Relax. They have some restricted areas in the facility, but it's safe. Besides, this is our only option."

"Just my luck," she said as Claire pulled up to the gate. A twelve-foot-high chain-link fence surrounded the compound. Signs every thirty feet announced it was electrified and to stay away. "You're *sure* this isn't Jurassic Park?"

Claire smiled before rolling down her window and punching a button on a speaker box. "Drs. Hodgson and McKenna here to see Dr. Sayre," she said. Thirty seconds later, the gate opened.

"The place looks sterile even on the outside," Meghan said. The single-story buildings were set back several hundred feet from the entrance. The manicured emerald lawn around the facility looked like a golf course practice area in the early morning sunshine. The structures had a brick façade with small rectangular windows located at least eight feet from the ground that looked like transoms without doors. "They take security seriously around here."

"They better. No telling what's being developed back there." Claire pointed toward several detached buildings near the rear of the compound. She parked and they went up to the main entrance. As they approached a latch clicked and the door swung open. A tall man in his midfifties dressed in khakis and wearing an Australian bush hat came toward them.

"Love your Akubra, mate," said Claire.

Sayre smiled and touched the brim. "Wore it especially for you."

He gazed at her face for a second longer than usual. "You weren't kidding, you do look like Rocky Raccoon."

"Thanks," Claire said, touching her cheek. "It looks better than it did a few days ago."

"Sorry, come on in. I just got back from a run out to the island. All your subjects are accounted for."

"Good on ya." Her eyes brightened as she stepped back. "Stephen, I'd like you to meet my postdoctoral fellow, Dr. Meghan McKenna. She's awesome. You'll love her. I brought her to help set up the stem cell facility."

Sayre smiled. "Pleasure to meet you. Where'd you do your PhD?"

"University of Michigan," Meghan replied, shaking his hand.

"Excellent. I hope you'll find this place workable. It may not be up to your usual standards, but I think it will do."

"It'll be fine," replied Meghan with a warm smile. "We'll make it work."

Claire tucked a strand of hair behind her ear then adjusted her glasses. "How's the old equipment?"

"Everything should be in good shape. You were the last ones to use it. No one's touched it in over a year. C'mon, let's find out." He led the way down a white-tiled hallway with matching walls and ceilings. The corridor gleamed and had a faint bleach smell as if the floor had just been mopped. They passed windowless white doorways labeled with three-inch-tall black numbers. Sayre stopped at 18. He removed an ID badge and swiped it over the card reader next to the handle. A metallic click sounded from the door, and Sayre pushed it inward then clipped the card back onto his belt. "I'll take you by admin tomorrow and get you one of these."

"This is nice," Meghan said as she inspected the equipment. "What's in there?" She pointed to a yellow cabinet that resembled a large metal armoire.

"That contains the PPPS equipment. You'll have to try one on. Make sure it fits. Regulations, you know."

"The what?" Meghan stopped and turned to Sayre.

"Positive pressure personnel suits. Space suits. This is a BSL-3 biocontainment lab, but there's a BSL-4 lab on the premises. That's the Army facility in the rear. In the *very unlikely* case anything should happen there, you'll need to put one of these on . . . in a hurry," Sayre said.

"Jeez," said Meghan, approaching the cabinet. "You're serious?"

"That's if you want to live."

"Oh my God, you *are* serious."

"Don't freak out. I've been working here for years, and we've never had an incident. It's just a precaution. You have nothing to worry about."

Meghan gripped one of the handles on the cabinet door. "It's locked."

"In the case of an emergency, the doors automatically open," said Sayre. "I'd be more worried about getting your cell cultures going."

Claire moved about the lab and began turning on machines. "Everything we need should still be here. This is where Mark and I worked out the early methods. You can't imagine how excited we were when the bones healed so fast. Just like what you've seen with our human subjects."

"I hope it translates to horses." Meghan adjusted the controls on the incubator and looked at the dates on the chemical bottles. "I brought all new reagents."

Claire nodded approval. "Good. Let's get the boxes from the car." She pulled a clear vial from her pants pocket and gave it to Sayre. "Don't drop that. It's Endovancin. I have several more. Enough to treat our patients."

A broad grin spread across Sayre's face as he held up the vial and shook the white powder. "When we're done here, I'll give those little rascals their medicine. That should fix one problem."

Two hours later the equipment was operational and Meghan was preparing the culture medium to be used on Hyperion's biopsy samples. "I'm starting to believe we're going to pull this off. Although

I never would have thought I'd complete my fellowship in the Carolina Lowcountry."

"Sometimes you have to play the hand you're dealt," Claire said.

MARK STOOD next to Grant and Coleman, watching as the last of the Endovancin dripped from the IV bag into Hyperion, who lay anesthetized on the OR table. Grant's eyes were on the wound as he pulled the trigger on the pulsatile irrigator and began cleansing Hyperion's infected fracture. Coleman held up a blue OR towel to block saline spray from splashing on them.

"You're doing daily washouts?" Mark inquired.

"We've had to for the time being, at least. This is looking a little better," Grant said.

"Give it twenty-four hours for the Endovancin to kick in," Mark advised. "I may give him weekly doses instead of bimonthly. I'll make that decision based on his response. We're heading into uncharted waters, if you know what I mean."

"I get the picture."

"How long until we see results?" Coleman asked.

"If he's like most patients, less than twenty-four hours," Mark answered.

Above his surgical mask, Coleman's eyebrows furrowed. "That soon? By tomorrow?"

"Not healed, but we should see some significant improvement," said Mark.

Grant called for the ultra-high-speed Midas Rex Drill and stepped on the foot pedal. The carbide-tipped burr began spinning at twenty thousand rpms. Grant pressed the tip into the infected bone. A shriek pierced the room and a curl of smoke rose from the tissue with each touch as the outer infected layer was stripped away. "Equine bones are so thick and dense, this is the only thing that works."

"If the Midas won't work then nothing will. You could break into a bank vault with that thing," Mark replied. "I use it to cut steel plates and screws when I have to remove hardware from patients."

"It does the trick, but you have to be careful it doesn't get away from you." Grant took his foot off the pedal, and the high-pitched whine stopped. "I hope his immune system is competent enough to defend itself."

"I can't figure out what's going on. A young elite athlete in the peak of physical condition receiving excellent medical care should not experience multi-organ system failure because of an infected fracture. In fact his fracture shouldn't get infected in the first place. How do you explain it?" Mark questioned.

"I can't. I was hoping you might have some ideas," Grant responded. He finished the debridement and placed the burr on the surgical table. "Let's hope your drug works."

"It'll do something." Mark gripped a curette and began harvesting fresh bone marrow and placed it into a specimen cup. When he'd finished, he passed the filled specimen cup to the surgical scrub tech, who twisted on a lid to seal the container.

Mark looked at Grant and shook his gloved hand. "Good luck. If you don't mind, I'll scrub out and get this sample back to the lab."

"Where? Wasn't yours destroyed?" Coleman asked.

"We're setting up shop in South Carolina where we did the original studies."

"Oh yeah, the NIH veterinary facility. You mentioned the place in your early research papers," said Grant.

"That's right. In Yemassee, just outside Beaufort, near Hilton Head."

Coleman folded his arms and turned toward Mark. "You have another facility already set up?"

"We never dismantled it. It's been . . . hibernating for the past year."

"Is it functional?"

"It should be. I'll let you know tomorrow."

Coleman reached for a suture and forceps and began closing Hyperion's wound. "When do you think you'll be ready to implant the bone graft?"

"I'd prefer not to implant in the face of an infection. Let's give the Endovancin some time to work."

"Wednesday afternoon or Thursday morning?" Coleman continued suturing.

"Let's wait and see," said Mark.

"Call me in the morning. I'll update you on his condition," Grant said.

"Talk to you then." Mark placed the bone marrow sample into the bioreactor then ripped off his sterile surgical gown. In the surgeon's locker room, he was removing his scrub top when a text message vibrated his phone. Mark pulled the device from the rear pocket of his scrub pants. A message from John Bristow awaited his attention. He swiped the screen.

This just arrived from Miguel Medina, it was passed to him by Juan Ortega, the chief of airport security in Cartagena. The flight is departing for Bogotá. The aircraft is owned by a US company, Telos. It's the same plane that transported Claire's coffin to Medellín. Show this to her and let me know what you think. The Kapitan Kurov sailed for Singapore about an hour before this video was taken.

JB

PS BTW, how's Jaggear's girl doing?

He looked around the locker room to make sure he was alone before he tapped the screen to begin the video. It was a security clip from the airport in Cartagena. People were queuing to board. Standing at the front of the line was a woman in dark sunglasses with short raven black hair covered with a red scarf. She turned to speak to the man behind her. Mark paused the video and enlarged the image. There, in full view, was the unmistakable image of Meera Jindal. The man she was speaking to was wearing a linen sport coat, aviator sunglasses, and a panama hat . . . N. *Sorenson*. Mark called Bristow.

"What do you think?"

"It's Meera. No doubt about it, and the guy she's with looks like the dude on the *Kurov*, Sorenson," Mark said. "Claire should be able to confirm it. His nose looks swollen and I'll bet he's got a shiner under those glasses. Claire said she punched him out."

"My kinda girl. You're a lucky guy, Thurman. See if she recognizes him. The guy is definitely Neil Sorenson. We checked him out. He has a PhD in pharmacology. He's a research scientist who's been in the pharmaceutical industry for most of his career. His work has focused on antibiotics in domestic livestock. You know. Huge chicken and beef farms. He had a falling-out with his last employer. Sorenson wanted to implement a more comprehensive antibiotic program using new drugs in cattle, poultry, and pork feed. Some animal rights organizations got wind of his ideas, and he was fired about two years ago. From what we know, he works for the owner of the plane."

"Telos? Who are they?"

"A biotech-pharmaceutical start-up based out of Philly. The CEO is a guy named Jeffery Mullion. He's a hotshot young exec with a track record of building small companies into attractive acquisition targets. Then he sells them for big money. A couple of his projects have been controversial."

"What do you mean?" Mark asked.

"From what we can tell, there's been nothing illegal. Let's just say he's got a few enemies in the corporate world."

"Don't they all?"

Bristow chuckled. "Probably, but Mullion has more than his share."

"Sorenson works for him?"

"We think he works for Telos, and we know he was on the *Kurov*."

"With Claire and Meera, from Panama to Cartagena," Mark said.

"That's the way it's playing out."

"That dirtbag was part of the BCI raid."

"Destroying the lab and stealing your drug," Bristow added.

"Kidnapping Claire and Meera."

"So, why is Meera standing in line with him at the airport looking like they're going on vacation?"

"Good question. She didn't look too distressed, did she?" Mark commented.

"She didn't. Medina and the Colombian National Police are looking for them."

"If he's after the drug, he needs Meera. She's the only one who knows how to make it," Mark said. *Other than Rafael, we hope.*

"I'm starting to believe you."

"Believe what?"

"I'm starting to believe you weren't exaggerating about that drug."

"I wasn't."

"Refresh my memory."

Mark tossed the soiled scrub top he'd been holding into the hamper and sat down on the bench in front of his locker. He let out a long breath and ran his fingers through his hair. "I can't give you details, but trust me, it's important, really important. It could be a game-changer for treating certain cancers and bacterial infections. So far, the results have been shocking."

"Good shocking or bad?"

"Better than you could imagine. Meera knows the most about its production. She's the one who discovered it."

"Then, Mullion and Sorenson somehow found out."

"If they could bring it to market, it would be pay dirt. A surefire blockbuster worth untold millions. Telos isn't big enough to handle the production and distribution. But it would make them a huge target for acquisition," Mark said.

"Helluva motive for the raids."

"I think you're right. How could they have known about Claire being there? It was a spontaneous decision for her to visit Meera," Mark said.

"I don't know. Maybe someone in her lab is a mole. They could have torched her lab, too. Keep an eye on her. She may still be in danger."

"I'll be with her in a couple of hours. I may need your help keeping an eye on her. I can't be with her every minute if we're going to save this horse. She has to run the lab while I'm in Virginia."

"Let me know what you need," Bristow said.

"I'll call you tomorrow. Thanks again."

The locker room door opened and a man in a dark sport coat and slacks stepped through. "Dr. Thurman, you in here?"

"Right here."

"Mr. Hobbs asked me to check on you. The car is waiting."

"I'm sorry. I had an important call. I'll be there in two minutes." He finished changing and left the building.

"Dr. Thurman, how have you been?" Worth Hobbs asked as he slid over on the back seat.

"Fine, sir, and you?"

"I suppose I'll be better when this business is over one way or the other. Can you fill me in on what's going on with Hyperion?"

It was almost noon when the car stopped in front of the general aviation terminal at Roanoke Airport. The men exited and Mark retrieved the bioreactor. "I'll do the best I can, sir."

"That's all I can ask."

"We've been fighting an uphill battle from the beginning."

"It seems that way. Every forward step is met with two back," Worth answered.

"We have a good team and a good game plan. Our luck is due to change."

"I sure hope you're right. Have a safe flight. The plane is at your disposal."

"That's good because I don't know when we'll be ready to come back. It could be tomorrow or in a couple of days. I'll let you know." They shook hands and Mark entered the building. Ten minutes later he was on board and tightening his seatbelt.

A MUFFLED rumble penetrated the room like the violent clap of thunder. A second one followed moments later. Meghan stood up at the lab bench and looked around. "What's that?"

"Thunderstorm?" Claire asked.

"That didn't sound like thunder," said Meghan.

"Sonic booms from the air station?" Claire offered.

Red lights began flashing from warning boxes near the ceiling. Sirens blared.

"I don't think so," Meghan told her. "Lights and sirens don't go off for thunderstorms or sonic booms. Those were explosions. Oh my God!"

Sayre burst into the laboratory. "Come on. We have to get out of here. There's been a security breach in one of the labs."

"What kind of breach?" Claire asked.

"I don't know, but it's in the virology lab."

"Where's that?" Meghan asked.

"The BSL-4 lab building in the rear of the compound. Ultra-high security."

"Has there been an outbreak?" Claire asked.

"Who knows? But they're working with Marburg," Sayre said. "We have to evacuate."

"Marburg virus?" asked Meghan.

"It's related to Ebola. About eighty percent fatal if you develop hemorrhagic fever," Sayre said. "We have to get into the space suits."

"Oh, damn. Oh, shit," moaned Meghan. "Ten years without a problem and it happens now. Just my luck. Ebola." She pulled on the handle to the PPPS cabinet. "The door won't open!"

"Try to relax," Claire said and turned the handle in the opposite direction. The door opened.

"I don't want to drown in my own blood." Meghan took the suit Claire handed her.

"Stop it! Do not panic. Looks like a medium should fit."

"How do you put this thing on?"

"Watch." Claire and Stephen unzipped and stepped into their blue plastic garments. "Take your shoes off," Claire instructed.

"Be careful you don't catch the material on anything. A tear could be fatal," Sayre said.

"Thanks, Captain Obvious," Meghan snapped. The sirens were going off every several seconds, and twice a minute a recorded message played throughout the facility.

"*This is an emergency. Take precautionary measures and leave this facility immediately. This is an emergency. Take precautionary measures and leave this facility immediately.*"

"I can't get my zipper up," Meghan pulled at the front of her suit.

"You have it on backward," Claire said. "Take it off."

"Are you crazy? I'm not taking it off!"

"You have to. Your helmet will be on backward and you won't be able to see."

"I'm going to die."

"No one's going to die," Claire said. "Now, step out of the suit and turn it around."

Meghan did as instructed, and Claire zipped the suit closed from the back then helped her position the helmet. She opened the valve for her oxygen supply. The cool air hissed in front of her face. Meghan breathed deeply and began to relax.

"Listen," Sayre said. "Follow me. We have to get out of this building and make it to the decontamination area." He opened the door into the hallway that was lit by red and white flashing strobe lights. The volume of the warnings was twice what they heard in the lab. It was deafening. "C'mon."

"*Take precautionary measures and leave this facility immediately . . .*"

Two turns and several corridors later they came to a door. "This leads outside. The decon center is in the next building. Be careful." He opened the door. The bright afternoon sunlight was dazzling.

Claire heard the muffled cry and turned around. Meghan was on her hands and knees on the walkway. "What happened?"

"I tripped," Meghan said as Stephen helped her stand. Claire grabbed her hands and turned them palms up. The gloves were abraded. The skin from the heel of her right palm could be seen through a small hole. Claire held her hand to cover the puncture.

"Her suit looks intact," Sayre said after inspecting her.

Claire shook her head and pointed to the hand. "Pinhole tear."

Meghan's face was ashen within the helmet. Tears rolled down her cheeks. "I'm going to die some horrible death bleeding from every orifice. Oh God."

"Shut up. You're not going to die. Let's get moving," Claire said, holding her hand. They walked to the next building and entered the decontamination area.

An hour later, Claire and Sayre stood in an isolation chamber watching a third hazmat team enter the building on the video screen. Meghan had been isolated separately in another cell. They were each dressed in a yellow jumpsuit and wore shower flip-flops. Their personal belongings had been confiscated. Claire bent forward and wrapped her wet hair in a towel and flipped it backward so that she looked like she was wearing a turban. "When can we get out of here?"

Sayre hung up the closed-circuit phone system. "Assuming it's a false alarm and there hasn't been an actual breach, a few more hours. It'll probably be several days before we're allowed back into the facility," Sayre told them.

"What'd they say happened?"

"There were two explosions outside of the virology buildings. They're reviewing the security video. Nothing appears to have penetrated the steel-reinforced inner walls of the building. Preliminary evaluation looks promising. Nothing was breached."

"Poor Meghan," Claire said. "She almost had a heart attack."

"I would have, too, if I tore my suit. She'll be fine."

"At least you gave the monkeys their medicine," Claire said. "Where are they? Who will feed them?"

"They've been evacuated to another decontam wing. All the

animals are safe. The hazmat team will check on them and put out their food."

Claire squatted down and put her face in her hands. "Bloody hell. Someone's put the damn mockers on us."

Sayre looked at her. "Huh?"

"We're totally screwed," she translated.

They heard knocking at the door window. Mark pressed his nose against it and mouthed, "I miss you."

Claire smiled and blew him a kiss. She walked to the door and picked up the phone receiver. She held it up to the window, showing it to him. Mark picked up the unit on his side and listened to her explanation of what happened.

When she finished, Mark said, "Like *Andromeda Strain*."

Claire smiled. "Stephen says the virology silo is subterranean. Several stories below the surface, so he thinks we're safe. Plus, there's no thermonuclear device ready to detonate in case of an outbreak."

"That's a relief," he said and chuckled. "I thought that part of the book was a little extreme."

"Where are the biopsies?"

"In the bioreactor in my rental," said Mark.

"We have to find another lab."

"Why? What's wrong with this one?"

"The hazmat team has a protocol of tests they have to run before anyone is allowed back in. That takes forty-eight to seventy-two hours, depending on the results."

"What are we going to do? We have to process the biopsy samples," he questioned. "We don't have two or three days. Hyperion will die by then."

THEY WALKED through the pristine building in sterile bunny suits. "Well, what do you think of our Bogotá plant?" Sorenson asked. "Is everything here that you need? Have we forgotten anything?"

"No, it's all here. It's one of the nicest laboratories I've ever seen. Nicer than Stanford."

"Excellent," said Jeffrey Mullion, who stood with his hands clasped behind his back, admiring the facility. "We've spared no expense. Can you produce the drug using this laboratory?"

"I suppose," Meera replied.

"Dr. Jindal, we need your decision. Will you help us?" Mullion asked her.

"That depends."

Mullion laughed. "This isn't a negotiation . . . will you or won't you?"

She ignored him. "You'll do everything I asked?"

"Working for Telos will be the best decision you've ever made," said Sorenson.

"I don't have a choice, do I?"

The corners of Mullion's mouth rose in a tight grin. "Of course you do. You always have a choice."

"Not if I want to live."

"Nonsense," said Mullion.

"Then you'll hurt my friend."

"She's unharmed . . . for the time being. That could always change. Your cooperation will ensure her safety," Mullion said.

"And my family?"

"Safe and financially secure. As soon as Endovancin is being made in this facility, your brother's medical bills will disappear."

"All right. I'll help you. Although, I have other conditions, and there are a few more things we need," she said.

Mullion exhaled and folded his arms across his chest. "Dr. Jindal, I'm growing weary of your demands."

"Well then, make it yourself," she snapped.

"Don't push your luck, Doctor. You've no idea who you're dealing with. We're not in America, and we're not dealing with the FDA. Do you understand?"

"Remember Chen? Mr. Betel Nut?" Sorenson said. "He'll

convince you to cooperate, and it won't be pleasant for you *and* Dr. Hodgson."

Mullion glared. "Make your list. I expect you to start tomorrow." He turned to one of the guards. "Take her back." A guard gripped Meera's arm and led her out of the room.

When she was gone, Mullion turned to Sorenson. "I've had about enough of that attitude. Once production starts and we know how to make it, get rid of her."

Sorenson nodded.

"Hodgson? What's that about? Why mention her? She should be in China by now."

Sorenson cleared his throat. "Well, she thinks we still have her. We can use that to our advantage."

"That's not what I asked. Where is she?"

"There's been a snag."

"A snag? What is that supposed to mean?"

"Hodgson's not in China. The Jungla executed a raid on a BACRIM stronghold in the north along the Cauca River. She was rescued."

"Why am I just now hearing of this?"

"I just found out a few hours ago," Sorenson said. "What are you worried about? She can't hurt us, and she can't make the drug. We're not marketing it in the US. We're selling it to the Chinese."

"Don't be an idiot. That woman knows too much. No telling what Jindal told her. I want her eliminated."

"Then you better call Ramon," replied Sorenson.

"And I want that horse dead. That's your job. He's got more lives than a cat!"

"Yes, sir."

"And after he's dead, get rid of that vet you hired. There are too many loose ends."

TWENTY-FOUR

MONDAY, MARCH 27TH

Wilson Andrews Equine Research Center, Roanoke, VA

DR. FIONA MONTGOMERY stopped in front of the inpatient pharmacy door and waved her ID over the card reader. The latch clicked and she let herself in. It was after five and no one was around. The room was filled with rows of tall white shelves stacked with medications. She went straight to the rear and unlocked the refrigerated storage cabinet. The glass door slid open without a sound. She paused, scanning its contents. After a few moments her eyes came to rest on the empty twelve-by-six-inch space where the box should be.

What the hell? She shuffled items on the rack, looking for the container. Five minutes later, after searching each shelf, she pulled the phone from the back pocket of her jeans and called Lew Jordan, the director of pharmacy services. "Lew? It's Fiona. I'm in the pharmacy looking for Grant's arthritis study drugs. They're not in the refrigerator."

"What are you talking about? I put them there Friday. It's on the second shelf on the right-hand side."

"I'm standing in front of the refrigerator with the door open. The spot is empty," Fiona said.

"Are you sure?"

"There's no box."

"If that's true, something's wrong."

"Let's hope not. I'll check the medicine cabinet at the stable. Maybe one of the techs got ambitious and beat me to it. I wanted to get the meds ready for tomorrow's dosing. It takes a while to draw up sixty syringes."

"Let me know if they're not there. We have a big problem if they're missing. The next shipment isn't scheduled to arrive until the end of the week."

"That's going to mess up the entire protocol."

"Then Grant would have to end the study early," Jordan said. "He wouldn't have a choice."

"I don't want to be around when you tell him that."

"I'm not telling him—you tell him."

"Forget it. You're the pharmacy director."

"I don't get it; why would anyone mess with those vials?"

Fiona shifted the phone to her other ear. "I don't know, but if they're gone, someone will have to call Sorenson and tell him what's happened. He won't be happy either."

"It makes us look bad," said the pharmacist. "Like a bunch of amateurs."

"Maybe he can express ship the next dose. I'll check the stables and call you if I can't find them." Fiona ended the call and left the pharmacy.

She walked down the hospital corridors and out the rear door. She climbed into an electric golf cart and drove the quarter mile to the stable where the Thoroughbred experimental subjects were housed. It was known as the arthritis barn around the facility. The cart came to a silent stop, and she entered the side door. The building was as quiet as a mausoleum at this time of day except for the tweets of sparrows flitting around the rafters. Several stable hands were spreading hay in empty stalls as she walked to the research office and opened the clinic refrigerator.

The box was on the middle shelf. The clear tape seals had been divided. The lid opened with the ease of an egg carton. All sixty vials were in their designated spaces, but the aluminum seals on some had been broken. She counted ten vials with rubber diaphragms exposed where the protective metal covering had been removed. Each rubber diaphragm had two small needle punctures. She searched the shelves of the refrigerator for syringes. None were present. *Why would anyone mess with Grant's experiment?* She examined the vials and noted the fluid level was similar to vials that did not appear to have been tampered with. She reached for her phone and called the pharmacist.

"I found the box. It was in the barn fridge."

"Good," said Jordan.

"But something's not right. Ten of the vials have been opened. Who would do that?"

"That makes no sense. Look, write down the vial numbers. We'll keep track of it. Not much more we can do."

"I already did. I'm sending you a picture of the box and several of the vials."

"I'll store the next shipment in the narcotic safe until we figure out what's going on."

"Good idea. I'll let you know if the horses have any unusual symptoms after tomorrow's treatment," Fiona said. She closed the office door and went to round on Hyperion.

FOUR HOURS AFTER THE EXPLOSIONS, the researchers were released from quarantine once the integrity of the virology lab had been confirmed. They were reunited with Mark and escorted off the premises by CDC officials. They regrouped in Sayre's home on

Fripp Island. Claire looked up from the living room chair and summed up the situation. "We're screwed."

"You already said that," Sayre replied.

"Well, it's true."

"Maybe not. But there's no chance of us getting back into the labs for at least three days. The head CDC guy told me one of the blasts damaged the biohazard security system. It has to be repaired and tested before they will let us return."

"My phone and purse are in there," said Meghan.

"Mine, too," added Claire.

"Sorry, we can get them back but we can't get in there. They have armed guards walking the perimeter around the clock. The place is on lockdown," Sayre said. "Four platoons of Marines from the Beaufort Marine Corps Air Station have been assigned to guard the place."

"They're treating this like a terrorist attack," said Mark.

Sayre nodded. "It's a possibility. I spoke with the duty officer. He said the security cameras caught three men breaking into the building."

"The virology lab?" asked Mark.

"They disabled the perimeter fence and blew open the outside door. These aren't amateurs. It takes knowledge and skill to use breaching charges and penetrate a sophisticated security system."

"What do you think?" Mark asked, looking at Sayre.

"The video shows three hooded men entering the building and leaving a few minutes later. They planted another device next to a laboratory door inside the building, but it didn't detonate. They must have panicked."

"Men like that don't panic in the middle of an operation," Mark said.

"If they knew what they were breaking into, they might," Sayre said. "Thoughts of drowning in your own blood might trigger a bit of anxiety. The Marines brought in one of their robotic EOD teams to handle the bomb that didn't detonate."

"What's an EOD team?" Meghan asked.

"Explosive ordnance disposal. These days the military uses robots to dispose of IEDs."

"Improvised explosive device," Mark added, glancing at Meghan. "We're lucky they had a team attached to the Marine Corp Air Station."

"I don't want to think about what would have happened if it had gone off," Claire said. "Do you think this was a planned terrorist attack?"

"What else could it be?" Sayre asked. "It's pretty obvious, isn't it?"

"I don't know. What if they were trying to stop us?" she asked.

"Are you serious?"

"It's possible. The stakes are high enough."

"What stakes? We're treating sick monkeys and culturing horse cells."

Claire stood and walked to the window overlooking the salt-marsh. "The stakes are much higher."

"Then why not just blow up my lab?" Sayre asked.

"Maybe they thought they were. Or maybe they didn't know which one was yours," said Mark.

"That's crazy. We're just trying to save a horse," said Meghan.

"If that happens, it will prove Endovancin works," Mark said. "Someone doesn't want that information known. They don't want anyone to even know of the drug. They want to eliminate all knowledge of its existence."

"So they can steal it and claim it as their discovery," Claire finished his thought.

"Isn't it too late for that?" Sayre asked. "Don't people already know about it? Aren't there reports of its results?"

"Not necessarily," Mark said. "Only one or two abstracts have been published reporting the drug's antibiotic effects, and these were in obscure journals. Electra has been trying to keep a lid on it. They've allowed these early results to be published to help raise capital. We were permitted only to mention its use in the methods section of our papers without discussion of its effects."

"And no one has any idea about its anticancer properties," said Meghan. "We just discovered that a week ago."

"I think you've nailed it," said Mark.

"What now?" Meghan asked. "We need a laboratory."

"We're refugees," Claire added. "We're forced to sit here and wait while Hyperion is fighting to stay alive." She walked to the other side of the room and cursed the wall.

TWENTY-FIVE

MONDAY, MARCH 27TH

Wilson Andrews Equine Research Center, Roanoke, VA

FIONA ENTERED the stall on her afternoon post-op rounds. Hyperion tried to hobble away as she knelt by his injured hoof. She unwrapped it as though it were a delicate piece of china. The bandages fell into a neat pile in the straw and cedar shavings on the floor. The wound continued to drain but didn't appear any worse. She cleaned the site then smeared it with Silvadene and reapplied his dressing.

"C'mon, ol' boy. You can do it." She tried to comfort the young stallion as she inspected his other legs. The palmar digital pulse was noticeably stronger in his forelimbs, and she thought they felt warm. "Does this one hurt?" She asked, looking up at the horse. Hyperion turned his head downward to watch her manipulate his leg. He let out a short weak snort and tried to shake his mane. She stood and brushed his forelock out of his eyes. He took a mint from the palm of her hand as she rubbed his face.

"How's he doing?" Coleman asked as he entered the stall.

"I'm worried about his left front limb."

"Why?"

"The digital pulse is stronger and it feels warmer. I'm going to reprogram some adjustments to the sling and give him more acepromazine."

"You don't see any bleeding or separation, do you?" Coleman knelt and inspected the hoof.

"No, it's too early for that," Fiona said.

"Well, when that happens, it's time to put him down."

"Don't say that."

"You're delusional."

Fiona glared back. "Shut up, Roger."

"When have you ever seen a horse survive an injury like this?" Coleman answered his own question. "Never. You don't see injuries like this because no one is heartless enough to make the animal suffer. They put them down."

"If that's what you believe, then take yourself off the treatment team. You act like you don't want him to live."

"I want him to live with a decent quality of life. A lame horse, no . . . a crippled horse doesn't have *any* quality of life. You're trying to keep him alive for breeding purposes and media attention."

"You're crazy. Have you read Hodgson and Thurman's papers? There *is* hope. He could make a full recovery."

"Please! Don't kid yourself."

"I'm not. You are."

"You're wrong, Fiona. This is nonsense. Even if the surgery is successful, he'll end up with support-limb laminitis. Grant will put him down in a few months. History will repeat itself."

"He's not Barbaro. That *won't* happen!"

"We'll see." Coleman hung the IV bag and started the drip. "I don't see these infusions doing a damn thing."

"Stick to the protocol."

"Take off your rose-colored glasses, Pollyanna." Coleman turned to leave.

"Did you put Dr. Grant's arthritis treatment vials in the barn refrigerator?"

He stopped and turned around. "I thought I'd save you a trip to the pharmacy when I went and picked up the last infusion bag. Why?"

"It looks like they've been tampered with."

"Why would someone do that?"

"It wasn't you?"

"Don't be ridiculous. I simply brought them here to help you out. Show me."

Fiona shut the gate to Hyperion's stall and retraced her steps to the research offices near the front of the barn. She entered the room and opened the refrigerated pharmacy cabinet. Coleman shut the door to the hallway. Fiona placed the box of vials on the countertop and removed the lid.

"They've been tampered with." They looked at the sixty vials neatly arranged in ten by six rows. She looked again and began counting the number of vials with rubber seals exposed. She looked at Coleman. "Ten more have been opened."

"What are you talking about?" Coleman asked.

"I looked at these less than an hour ago. Only ten had the aluminum cover removed. Now there's twenty." She looked up at him. "What did you do?"

"Now, hold on, I haven't done anything. I just got here. Are you accusing me?" Coleman protested, raising his hands and stepping away from her.

"These vials didn't open themselves. You and I are the only ones here, other than a couple of stable hands. And they don't have access to this room. If it wasn't you, then who?"

"It wasn't me. I've been treating a sick bull twenty miles from here. I just parked the mobile vet truck and was about to restock it. I didn't do anything. I may think it's a lost cause, but I've been trying to save this horse. I can't believe you'd even think that."

Fiona turned to leave. Coleman reached and grabbed her wrist. "Hold on."

She yanked her arm away. "Let go of me."

"C'mon, Fiona, settle down. You're making a big accusation. How would anyone know which vials are treatments and which are saline? It's a double-blind study. Let's talk to Grant. He needs to know what you think is going on."

"I'll call him." She took out her phone. Twenty seconds later, she placed the phone back in her pocket. "Voicemail."

"He's at home. I talked to him earlier. He's probably working on a paper and has his phone shut off. Let's go, I'll drive."

"I'll drive myself. You can take your own car."

"Seriously?"

"Yes. I've got things to do and I'm not driving you back here."

"All right. I'll follow you," he said.

Twenty minutes later, they were driving through rolling Virginia farmland ten miles from Grant's ranch. The fields on either side of the road had recently been tilled. Rows and rows of black earth spread out in all directions. As she passed a dilapidated barn, her phone rang. Coleman's face appeared on the screen. She pressed the button. "What is it?"

"Pull over, my check-engine light just came on."

She pulled off the road and got out as Coleman pulled in behind her. "What's wrong?"

He'd exited the cab and was holding a flashlight. "I don't know, but it was making funny noises. I probably shouldn't drive it."

"Did you call for help?"

He raised the hood and inspected the engine compartment. "Triple A."

"What are we supposed to do, wait here?"

"They said it would be a half hour. Do you mind? We can go to Grant's in your car after they tow mine."

"How about if we forget going to Grant's? I'll give you a ride home. I can call him later." She exhaled and looked up and down the deserted road. "What a day. Just when you think things can't get much worse."

"Sorry, Fiona."

"It's not your fault. I'm not going to leave you stranded. Get in, we'll wait in the car." She turned and reached for the handle. Gravel crunched behind her. "Roger . . . ?" A blinding light flashed and pain shot through her head. She crumpled to the ground and felt tape being placed over her mouth. She tried to move, but he straddled her and pulled her arms behind her back like he was roping a calf. She felt bindings tightening around her wrists. Pain pierced her ankles as they were lashed. He picked her up and carried her to the back of his pickup and opened the tonneau cover and tailgate. She was engulfed in darkness as he sealed her in the truck bed.

TWENTY-SIX

MONDAY, MARCH 27TH

Beaufort, South Carolina

MARK LEANED on the railing counting the boats in the marina across from the Anchorage Inn. The briny aroma of saltwater was like incense carried on a gentle breeze. Halyards clinked against masts like nautical wind chimes. Grey and white gulls squawked and flew about scavenging food. "Twenty-four sailboats," he said to no one. "Look at that ketch. I'd like to hop on board and take it all the way to St. John's." The afternoon sunlight glinted off the ripples on the Beaufort River. On the opposite bank, seagrasses waved. In the distance, he could just make out an occasional vehicle as it moved across the Lady's Island bridge. Traffic was light. Claire came up next to him and slipped her hand into his. Meghan leaned over the railing, peering down at the barnacles on the seawall.

"It's beautiful," Meghan said. "I think I'll stay here awhile. Maybe a week or two until I figure out what's next. I feel like a graduate student refugee fleeing a war zone. Maybe Dr. Heinricht will take me in. Would you mind asking her?"

"She's in Edinburgh," Mark said. "I spoke with her a few days ago."

Claire turned and looked at him. "What did you say?"

"She's in Europe, on her sabbatical, remember?"

"Yes! That's it," Claire said, punching Mark's shoulder.

"What is?" Meghan asked.

Mark rubbed his shoulder and looked at her. "What are you talking about?"

"*Evelyn.* She's in Scotland for another three months. She took her fellow with her. I don't think anyone is using her lab. Gimme your phone." She walked up and down the riverwalk with the phone to her ear. Mark and Meghan watched her march like she was working off demerits. Twenty minutes later, she ended the call.

"Meghan, you're not staying here." She looked at Mark. "Call Worth and have the plane pick us up. We're going to Winston-Salem."

THE CAR LET them off in front of the Richard H. Dean Biomedical Research Building. Mark pulled the bioreactor from the trunk. Claire presented an old identification card they'd retrieved from her apartment to the security guard.

"Dr. Hodgson, what's up?" the guard asked.

"Hello, Sam. Good to see you again. We have some samples to process in Dr. Heinricht's lab."

"She called a couple of hours ago and said you'd be arriving. Sorry to hear about the accident."

Claire looked up at him. "Thanks. It was tragic."

"It was all over the news. I feel bad for that boy and his family," Sam said as the elevator door opened.

"I appreciate your concern. We'll be working late. I may have pizza delivered. You want some?"

"Thank you, but I already had dinner. I'll let you know when they get here." The door closed.

"Sam's been working the night shift at that desk since before I did my postdoc fellowship," Claire explained. The door opened on the fifth floor and they exited into the Wake Forest Institute for Regenerative Medicine. Claire's ID card opened Dr. Heinricht's lab and she flipped on the lights. A smile spread across her face. "I can't believe I didn't think of this earlier." She walked to the back of the lab and turned on the cell culture apparatus. Mark placed the bioreactor on a lab bench.

"Show me where the reagents are and I'll start making culture medium," Meghan said.

By ten thirty that evening, Hyperion's biopsy samples had been prepared and the stem cell line was in the incubator. "They should be ready for expansion in the morning," Claire said. "Let's get some sleep."

"I'm staying here," said Meghan. "There's a sofa in the office. I can sleep there."

"Nonsense. Worth sent me a text. He made reservations for all of us at the Marriott downtown. I'll call for a car."

"WOW, he didn't have to do this. We're only going to be here one night," Claire said as she walked around the suite.

Mark stood at the window on the top floor. The mass of red tail-lights resembled a glowing lava flow as stoplights turned green on Fifth Street. "Hell of a view of the city." They watched the traffic for a minute. Then, he pulled the cord and the curtains closed. They faced each other. "Can I hold you?"

"Tight, please. When they took me, I was afraid."

"I know. I was, too." He placed his arms around her and kissed her neck. Then his lips touched the bruise on her cheek. "I'd have never stopped."

"Stopped?"

"Searching for you."

She looked up, arching her slender neck. "I had no doubt."

"Nothing would have stopped me. There is no force on earth that could have kept me from finding you."

"Thank you, darling."

"It would be hard to live without you. Is that selfish?"

"No. I don't think so. I knew you'd come." She caressed his face. Then she kissed his mouth. Her lips parted.

"You're like oxygen . . . and food. I need you." They kissed again. The pressure of their embrace increased. "It seems like ages since we've been alone."

"It has been."

Mark pulled her T-shirt over her head. She pulled on his belt and released the waist button of his trousers. They fell to his ankles and she smiled as she removed his shorts.

"I'm glad you've missed me, Dr. Thurman." She ran her hands over his arms and chest. He tensed. She crinkled her nose. "Now, it's into the shower, you filthy animal."

"Now?"

"Yes, right now." She led him to the bathroom and turned on the water. She turned and stripped. He gathered her into his arms.

"You don't smell so bad," he said.

"But you do."

"We can fix that," he said while looking at their reflection. "You're beautiful. I love looking at you."

She turned, facing the mirror. The corners of her mouth curled upward as she pulled her hair over her shoulder.

He crossed his arms. "You're a shameless flaunt."

She bit her lower lip and turned for an oblique view, cupping her breasts. "Are you complaining?"

He stood speechless, staring.

"You can look all you want, *after* you get cleaned up." She pushed the glass door open and felt the temperature. "In you go." She pulled him into the stream of warm water. They clung to each other like vines. After a few minutes, she reached for a washcloth and began washing the memories of the last few days from her mind and body. When they were dry Mark carried her and placed her on the bed. She wiggled under the sheets as he joined her. She crawled on top of him and kissed his face.

"Thank you for saving me," she whispered. Then, she clenched and began to move. A soft moan escaped as they became lost in the building rhythm. Afterward, as they lay entwined she whispered, "You're a fine man, Mark Thurman."

He smiled and brushed damp strands of hair from her flushed face, kissing the droplets of perspiration from her upper lip.

"How can I ever repay you?" she asked.

"Just love me."

"I do," she replied. "Hold me tight."

"I won't let you go. Ever."

FROM HIS TENTH-FLOOR HOTEL ROOM, the nighttime panorama of Bogotá spread out before Jeffery Mullion. It was a dazzling display with fingers of lightning touching the horizon from the black sky. The rain had not yet started. "Where are they, Neil?" he asked.

"I don't know. The plane left Beaufort late this afternoon," Sorenson replied.

"Well, what did the flight plan say?"

"It's incomplete. We're not sure if Hodgson and Thurman were on it."

"How's that?"

"Flight plans don't list passengers, just the pilot. The plane landed in Atlanta a few hours ago."

"Atlanta? What the hell?"

"They're not in Atlanta," Sorenson said. "The pilot and crew were the only ones who exited the plane. We don't know where they are."

"Check if it stopped in Raleigh or Roanoke. We have to find them."

"Let Ramon find them." Sorenson removed his glasses and pointed them at his boss. "You called him, right?"

"Of course. A salvage team is on the way," Mullion said.

"And they can find them." Sorenson pulled a pack of cigarettes from his inside jacket pocket. "That should take care of the problem."

Mullion scowled. "Don't smoke in here. Do that somewhere else. You better hope it takes care of the problem. I want them out of the picture. Am I clear?"

"Perfectly." Sorenson stood and walked to the door.

"Where in the hell do you think you're going?"

He waved an unlit cigarette in his left fist. "I need this. Call me if anything happens."

LIGHT SHONE around the edges of the curtains when Mark opened his eyes. His phone was vibrating on the nightstand. "We have to get a replacement for yours," Mark said to Claire as he swiped the screen. "It's Meghan. I can guarantee she doesn't want to talk to me." Claire's head lay against his shoulder. Her hair was strewn across his neck and chest like a golden silk scarf. "Good morning, McKenna. What can I do for you?" He listened as Claire sat up and rubbed her eyes. "I'm putting you on speaker. Say it again."

"I'm heading over to BioFab to get the printers up and running. Hyperion's updated CT data arrived."

"Mark and I will check the stem cell cultures," Claire told her.

"I can have the 3D printer ready by this afternoon," Meghan said.

Claire leaned closer to the phone. "I doubt if the cells will be ready by then. Let's shoot for a print run at seven o'clock tomorrow morning."

"The graft shouldn't take more than an hour and a half. Maybe two hours to print," Meghan said.

"I'll notify Hobbs and Grant. We should be able to implant on Thursday," Mark said.

"All right, then. We meet at BioFab at six tomorrow. See you then." Claire touched the screen, ending the call. She stood at the doorway. Her body was silhouetted against the bright bathroom lights. She turned and beckoned to him. "When we're finished, I'll get a new phone."

FIONA HEARD Coleman's truck bouncing over the ruts in the washed-out dirt road. It stopped and the door slammed. A few seconds later, she heard footsteps and felt the breeze as the front door opened. She felt his approach as boot heels struck the wooden floor. The scent of horses and Copenhagen dipping tobacco clung to his physical presence as he bent down close to her hooded face. "Fiona, why did you poke your nose where it didn't belong? You leave me no choice now. It was my job to set up the syringes. Not yours. Why did you take it upon yourself to meddle with the treatment medications? Were you trying to score points with Grant? Trying to make me look bad?"

She grunted and shook her head. He removed her hood and peeled the tape from her mouth. She breathed in through her mouth until her lungs were full then exhaled like a bellows. "I could hardly breath. Where are we?"

"Somewhere no one will find you."

"Were we at your house last night?"

He smirked and let out a chuckle. "Astute, Dr. Montgomery, but that quick-witted brain will do you no good out here."

"Out where? Where are we?"

"Why do you want to know? We're not going to be here much longer."

"Roger, what is going on? What are you doing?"

"I'm sorry, Fiona. You know too much." He placed the tape back over her mouth then placed the hood back over her head. "You shouldn't have messed with those drugs." His footsteps receded and a door opened.

She tried to sort it out. At the moment she was sitting upright lashed to a wooden chair, blindfolded and gagged. She'd lost count of the hours and her hands and feet were numb. At first, he must have taken her to his house, where she'd spent the night bound on his basement floor. Before dawn he'd blindfolded her and brought her to this place somewhere in the mountains. She wasn't sure how far from town but thought it was less than an hour drive. Her head ached from where he'd hit her. The room was damp and smelled dank and musty like a root cellar. Her body ached and the seat was wet from when she'd voided her bladder twice. The tape covering her mouth was wrapped around her head and pulled her hair whenever she tried to rotate her neck. The hood covering her head felt like a black shroud. She tried to scream.

"Scream as much as you like. No one can hear you. We're miles from anywhere. You've made a mess of things, Dr. Montgomery. If you'd minded your business, we wouldn't be here. But no . . . you had to try and save the world. Well, it's not going to work. I'm putting an end to it. There won't be any heroics. Hodgson and Thurman aren't going to make any new bone for Hyperion. They don't have a lab to make it in. I took care of that with a couple of phone calls," Coleman said. "No more surgeries. Hyperion will be put out of his misery. But now I'm left with you. What to do?" He continued walking around the chair. "Have you ever been to Montana? Maybe Idaho or North Dakota? How about a spring hunting trip for elk in Wyoming? That's big country out there. It would be easy to get lost in those mountains and wind up as bear food. The body might never be found. What an excellent idea. You'll come with me on a hunting trip. In the pickup bed, of course."

She let out another muffled scream and thrashed in her chair until it toppled over. She felt him pull the hood firmly down over her head then lift the chair into an upright position. He checked her bindings.

"That's pointless, Fiona. Stop it. I have to get back to work. Hyperion needs me. Oh, and don't worry about your car. I've taken care of that. No one will find it."

MEERA GAZED at the palatial grounds from the window of her second-story suite. Based on the direction they'd driven from the El Dorado airport, she surmised the ranch was at least thirty miles northeast of the city. She could no longer see any signs of Bogotá. Her bedroom window faced the Cordillera Oriental range, whose peaks were shrouded in dark clouds a few miles in the distance.

She considered her predicament and wondered how long they would keep her there. She wanted to go home, her real home in Palo Alto. *Where is Claire? What was happening to her? He promised she would be safe. That was part of the agreement.* She wanted to speak with her parents but knew this was impossible. *Would Papa understand?* The offer to work for Telos was like a Gordian knot. If she accepted, it might prove to be inextricable. *What has happened to my life?* She sat on the side of the bed and placed her face in her hands. Tears welled up and wet her palms. There was a knock at the door and she turned toward the sound.

A handsome man with slicked-back jet-black hair dressed in a dark suit opened the bedroom door. "Good evening, Dr. Jindal, it's time." He took two steps closer. "Are those tears?"

She wiped her cheeks dry as she stood by the bed and smoothed her blouse. "Who are you?"

"I'm your escort. *Who* I am is of no concern. Clean yourself up and come with me. I'll be in the other room." The man began to close the door then paused. "Hurry up, it's not a good idea to keep Ramon Bonsantos waiting."

TWENTY-SEVEN

WEDNESDAY, MARCH 29TH

BioFab Facility, Research Triangle Park, North Carolina

THEY WATCHED the CT images rotating on the computer screen. Three-dimensional bones spun on their axes orchestrated by Mark, with Claire and Meghan standing at his shoulders.

"The horse's hind limb structure is like an elongated human leg. What you would intuitively think is the horse's knee is actually its ankle," Mark said. "That bony prominence isn't his kneecap. It's his heel. The os calcis, or what we would call the calcaneus."

"Since when did you become a veterinarian?" Claire asked.

"I'm a surgeon. We know anatomy."

"This is one of the bones Hyperion broke, right?" Meghan pointed to the CT image.

"Affirmative. This large leg bone isn't his tibia but a fused form of metatarsal bones. In a horse, this is called the canon bone. It makes up part of the next joint, which is not the ankle but is called the fetlock." Mark pointed to what would be the equivalent of the joint where a human bunion forms, anatomically known as the metatarsal-phalangeal joint. "It's the joint between the midfoot and toes. In a horse, all of the proximal phalanges are combined into one big bone called the long pastern. Hyperion broke his canon and long pastern bones."

"And that other one?" Meghan asked.

Mark nodded. "The sesamoid."

"So he broke his toe?"

Mark scratched his head. "In a way, yes."

"That seems ridiculous," Claire said. "How can anything die from breaking its toe?"

Mark looked at Meghan and pointed to the screen. "Your boss is oversimplifying. The fetlock is the single most important mechanical link in a horse's limbs. Most severe horse athletic injuries involve these joints. It makes sense if you understand comparative anatomy." Mark brought up x-ray images of the original injury. "Look here. Hyperion shattered his right rear fetlock joint where the canon and long pastern bones meet. This is almost the exact injury Barbaro had."

"Who?" Meghan asked.

"Barbaro, one of the greatest Thoroughbreds since Secretariat. He shattered his leg at the start of the 2006 Preakness two weeks after winning the Kentucky Derby. Hyperion broke the same leg . . . the same joint," Mark explained. "The fracture patterns are remarkably similar. Look, you can Google his x-rays." He took out his phone and a moment later showed it to Meghan.

She took it and enlarged the image. "They're almost identical."

"Let's hope the results aren't," Claire said.

Meghan looked back and forth between her mentors. "What are you talking about?"

"Barbaro died after undergoing surgery to repair his fractures. He developed complications and had to be euthanized," Claire said.

"He developed laminitis, a condition where a horse's hooves separate from his limbs. It becomes so painful the horse can't stand or walk. That's why we can't delay. We've already waited too long." He switched back to the current CT images of the injured bones. "Hyperion's luckier than Barbaro. The surface of the fetlock joint has only one fracture line that's minimally displaced. Barbaro's was shattered. There are two large chunks of bone we have to replace." He pointed to a long oblique fragment in the canon bone and a shattered portion of the long pastern. "Grant debrided the infected portion of the pastern, and we're left with this trapezoidal-shaped fragment. The other piece is this long triangular-shaped butterfly fragment."

"That's going to be at least five inches long," Meghan said.

"His bones are huge. Look how thick these are." Mark pointed to the CT images. "It'll be hard to drill screw holes. The bits better have carbide tips."

The two women looked at him. Claire raised an eyebrow and tilted her head. "Save the technical orthopedic questions for Grant. Are we set, Meghan?"

She nodded. "The stem cells are loaded in the print cartridges. I've set the density to eleven times normal. According to reports in the veterinary literature, this should result in an osteoblast population five times embryonic equine bone."

"That should accelerate fracture healing so that he can weight-bear in a few days," Mark said.

Claire pinched her upper lip. "If he heals like human subjects."

"It's time to get the ball rolling."

"The chamber conditions are perfect. Anytime you're ready, I can start," said Meghan.

"Do it," Mark said. They walked into the adjoining room and looked through the window at the state-of-the-art 3D biological tissue printer. Meghan sat at a computer terminal and logged on. Several keystrokes later the print heads began to sweep back and forth. Within three minutes the first layer of new bone began to take shape.

"Anyone for coffee?" Meghan asked.

MARK GRIPPED the handle of the bioreactor like it was a fast-rope and descended the stairs. Claire walked ten feet ahead of him on the tarmac, waving at Worth Hobbs, who was standing at the doorway of the terminal.

"Welcome back," he said to Claire as they shook hands. He looked at the green-and-purple shadow under her left eye, still noticeable through the makeup. "Mark told me what happened. I'm so sorry and happy you're safe."

She smiled and tossed her hair back. "Thanks to him and a few friends. It's good to be here. I'm ready to finally finish this job."

"My driver will get your bags. Come along. Dr. Grant wants to have everything ready for Hyperion's surgery in the morning."

"How's he doing?" Claire asked.

"Not well, I'm afraid. Warwick will explain."

They walked from the terminal. Their driver placed the luggage in the trunk then held the door for Hobbs. Claire slid in beside him while Mark got into the front passenger seat. He placed the bioreactor at his feet and fastened the seatbelt. His Sig Sauer P226 pistol pressed into the small of his back as he adjusted his position in the overstuffed front seat. From this point on he was not taking any chances.

"We're still on for tomorrow morning? Correct?" Mark asked.

"As far as I know," responded Hobbs. "I received a call from Warwick just before you landed. He can't locate Fiona Montgomery and now Coleman's disappeared. They're critical for the surgery."

"Why? Just get another scrub tech," said Mark. "Grant and I can do it."

"I don't understand, either, but he seemed upset."

Claire crossed her legs. "We have everything covered from our end. The bone grafts are ready for implantation. Hyperion has been started on the Bethesda infusions and Endovancin. I have his next dose." She patted her purse.

"It's about time things started going in his favor," sighed Hobbs.

THEY ARRIVED at the research center and entered the main administration building. Hobbs led the way and knocked on the office door.

"Director of Equine Research," Mark said, reading the sign.

The door opened and Grant stood before them. "Good to see you folks. Come in. We've got a small problem."

"That's good," Mark said.

"Good?" Grant replied.

"The way things have been going, a small problem is a move in the right direction."

"You have a point. Two of my most important personnel are missing."

"I mentioned that," said Hobbs.

Mark walked to the bookcase. "Montgomery and Coleman?"

Grant nodded. "No one's heard from Fiona since Monday morning, and Roger hasn't shown up today. Neither of them have ever missed a day of work. Fiona was running the support-limb laminitis project. She's the one who developed the improved sling technology."

"Things don't come to a halt because of that, do they?" asked Claire.

"There's more to it. I had a call from the head of pharmacy services on Monday. He said Fiona had called him asking about the TNFα inhibitor I'm using in an experimental trial." Mark and Claire exchanged glances.

"What's that have to do with us?" Claire asked.

"The trial is a study evaluating a new osteoarthritis medicine. Fiona was concerned someone had been tampering with the treatment drugs. Coleman took the medicine vials from the main pharmacy."

"Was he involved in the study?"

Grant nodded. "He told the pharmacy tech he was taking them to the stable."

"So?" Mark said.

"It wasn't something he would normally do. There was no reason for him to pick up the medication. It should have stayed in the pharmacy. When Fiona went to pick it up, it wasn't there."

"I still don't get how that affects Hyperion and our surgery," Claire said.

"I don't know, either. Maybe he was just helping out but, I haven't heard from either of them since yesterday. Roger is my primary surgical assistant for cases like these. He knows all the instrumentation and my preferences."

"I'll be your scrub tech," Mark said.

Grant smiled. "You may have to."

"So where can I put these?" Mark held up the bioreactor.

"Surgery is scheduled for tomorrow morning. First case. You can leave the bone grafts with me."

"They need to go into an incubator."

"I'll store them in Phil Weinstein's lab. It has state-of-the-art equipment. He's our equine microbiology expert."

"Will they be safe?"

"If not, we have bigger problems than we think." Grant stood and reached for his cap resting on a filing cabinet near the door. It had the Wilson Andrews logo embroidered on its crown. "C'mon, his lab is over in the east wing. Then we can see our patient."

HYPERION STOOD in the stall like a giant equine marionette. Straps from the sling system hung from winches suspended above. He looked resigned to a dismal fate with his head hung low.

"He's looks more like Eeyore than a racehorse. Is he clinically depressed?" Claire asked.

"Can you blame him?" Mark replied.

"If we don't get him out of that contraption soon, he'll be broken."

"Psychologically?" Claire asked.

"It's killing his spirit. If that happens then it would be more humane to put him down," said Grant.

"He doesn't look good," Hobbs commented.

Grant looked at an empty IV bag hanging from a hook on the wall. "Coleman *must* be around. He gave Hyperion his noon infusion. I'd try to call him but I've misplaced my damn phone."

Mark took the bag and inspected it. "It's labeled correctly, but this doesn't look like the Bethesda infusion. There's a residue in the bag. I'd like to talk to the pharmacist who is preparing these."

"I'll take you by there tomorrow after the surgery."

"No. Let's go now. Something's not right with this," Mark answered.

"Fair enough," Grant said.

Hyperion lifted his head as Claire approached. "Hey, boy, how are you? Remember me? Don't give up. We're going to fix you. You're going to run again." She rubbed his nose and he licked her fingers. The great animal's snout rubbed against her cheek and neck. "Good boy."

"He likes you," Grant said. "I haven't seen him react to anyone like that. Stick around."

"I'm not going anywhere. We have too much riding on this."

Grant rubbed his mane. "We'll come back and check on him after dinner. Come on. We'll stop by the pharmacy and go to my house. You're staying with me this time. Mr. Hobbs's driver transferred your bags to my truck. We can swing by Coleman's house on the way to my place. Maybe he's sick."

"But he's been in to give Hyperion his meds," said Mark.

Grant shrugged. "We'll stop by his house anyway. If he's there, I have a few questions for him."

The pharmacist held up the IV bag. "This is his next dose."

Mark took it and held it up to the light. "That looks like the right stuff. There's no sediment in that bag."

"And the label isn't peeling," added Claire.

"I want to talk to Coleman," Mark said as he handed the IV medication back to the pharmacist.

THE TRUCK PULLED into the empty driveway and drove up the steep incline. Mark looked at the dashboard clock. It was almost three thirty.

"Should we be doing this?" Claire asked as they made their way up the driveway.

"He won't mind," Grant said. He parked the pickup in front of the garage door.

"Doesn't look like anyone's home," Claire remarked.

Grant got out. "Let's check." Mark and Claire followed him to the front door. Coleman's house was the third one on a long residential street. The houses in the neighborhood would have been new in the seventies. They were mostly brick and vinyl-siding ranch homes. Mark and Claire looked through the front porch windows while Grant rang the doorbell a second time. He tried the front door then stepped off the porch and began walking around the corner. "Let's check the back. Maybe it's unlocked." They went around to the rear of the house, and Grant turned the handle to the rear door and pushed it open. He looked back at Mark and Claire. "Come on."

"Isn't this illegal?" Claire asked.

"Not if you're the landlord," replied Grant.

"You own this place?"

"Bought it in seventy-six. Lived here for twenty years. Been leasing it to students since then. You don't have to come in if you're uncomfortable."

"Who's going to keep an eye on you?" Mark said, following.

Grant walked into the kitchen and yelled, "Roger? Anyone here?" No answer. The house looked reasonably neat. Several dirty dishes were piled in the sink, and a two-day-old copy of the *Roanoke Times* lay unread on the kitchen table along with several full bottles of medications. Mark picked them up and read the labels. "Lithobid, Depakene, and Zyprexa. It looks like Coleman is being treated for a mental illness."

"Bipolar disorder," Grant said. "He was diagnosed as an adolescent. When he takes his medications you'd never know."

"Then how do you?" Claire asked.

Grant stopped and turned around. He removed his hat and wiped his forehead with his sleeve. "He's my stepson."

Her head turned as she met Mark's gaze.

"Roger is my stepson."

Mark cleared his throat. "I'm a little concerned, Warwick. These bottles are almost full. A manic episode can be intoxicating. You understand the desire to maintain that high?"

"I do. He knows the consequences of stopping his medicines. We've been through it before. He's been on them for years."

"The prescription date on the bottles is two months old, and they're nearly full."

"He wouldn't do that. I'm sure of it."

"He's off his meds *and* he's missing?" Mark questioned. "We have a problem."

They proceeded into the family room and looked in the bedrooms. Nothing seemed out of the ordinary. "Let's check the basement." He led them to the stairs and they descended. Grant fumbled for the light switch at the bottom. He found it and the large open area was flooded with light. The basement was filled with boxes and unused furniture. "Some of this stuff has been around since Roger was a boy," Grant said. An old wooden rocking horse sat on a box against the wall.

"A rocking-horse winner," Mark said.

"What are you doing?" Claire asked.

Mark placed the rocking horse on the floor and began rocking.

"Get off, before you break it," Claire said.

Mark ignored her and rocked faster then held up one hand and said, "Hyperion by a length." He stood up and replaced the toy where he found it.

Claire shook her head. "I'm not even going to ask what that was about."

A workbench stood in a corner. Pegboard was fixed to the wall filled with tools suspended from metal hooks. Storage shelving was loaded with boxes and old paint cans. Equipment for reloading shotgun shells was set up on a table next to the workbench. Several plastic bottles of gunpowder were next to the reloader along with a box of plastic empty shells. The wads, primers, and shot were on the workbench. Mark walked over to an antique gun cabinet.

"Coleman's a gun enthusiast?"

"Yes, he's hunted all his life," Grant said.

"It's concerning."

"Why?" asked Grant.

"He has a mental disorder and a rifle is missing from this cabinet," Mark answered.

Grant inspected the contents. "It's a shotgun. His prized Benelli Super Black Eagle 12-gauge auto. It's not here."

"What would he be doing with it?"

Grant shrugged. "Spring turkey season opens in a week. Maybe he's scouting?"

He wouldn't need a shotgun if he were scouting, Mark almost said.

"What's this?" Claire asked, bending down behind a wooden straight-backed chair in the corner. She stood up holding a plastic two-by-three-inch card.

TWENTY-EIGHT

WEDNESDAY, MARCH 29TH

Jefferson National Forest, Giles County, Virginia

A FAINT SQUEAK of hinges opening and floorboards creaking aroused Fiona. Footsteps approached. The wind of decay floated into the room. Her eyelids fluttered and she coughed as the hood was ripped from her head. "Roger, have you lost your mind?" Fiona asked as he pulled the tape from her mouth.

"Drink this and be quiet," he said, holding the plastic bottle to her lips.

"You'll be arrested," she rasped. "Kidnapping is a federal crime."

"I said shut up. You ruined my plans. It was working out perfectly until you started poking your nose into things."

"Working out? Is that how you work things out? By murdering your patient?"

"You don't know anything. He was dead the second his leg snapped. Don't act so self-righteous. You and Grant were the inhumane egomaniacs prolonging the inevitable. Torturing him for publicity to promote the center."

"That's not true. If you'd stop sabotaging things, we'd have a chance to save him. Untie me. Let me go!"

Coleman placed his hands on his knees and bent over. Sweat beaded on his forehead. His bottom lip bulged, and the black edge of his Copenhagen plug covered the tops of several teeth. He looked straight into her eyes. "Monumental senseless medical heroics. For what? Your only hope was to salvage him for breeding. There's no chance he'll run. Hell, he won't *walk*. You want him to limp and stumble around lame for the rest of his life? That's one of the greatest horses to ever walk this planet. All of you want to disgrace and humiliate him for his seed? You're evil."

"Roger. Stop this. He's going to get well. He'll run. Give us a chance."

He stood and walked across the room. "I'm sick of chances. I've watched you and Grant torture him for too long. They should've never brought him here. There's no recovery from that injury. He should've been put down on the track. You make me sick. I have heard the message. Justice will be served!"

She shook strands of hair from in front of her face. "You have to let me go. I'll talk to Grant. He'll understand you're right. We can do the right thing."

"No. It's too late. You have to go away."

"What does that mean?"

"It means you're going away. With me, far from here. *I am* the instrument of his justice."

"What are you talking about?" She scooted the chair to see out a window. Tree branches were yards from the cabin. They were in a forest. The shadows were elongated as the afternoon sunlight began to fade. "Roger, it's not too late. We can go back."

"I can. But you can't." He turned and smiled. "I have a job to finish. Then, I'm leaving for Philadelphia. Free from the *great* Warwick Grant . . . forever."

"Why do you say that? He's helped you."

"No, Fiona. You don't know him. Not like I do."

She tilted her head. "What?"

"Yes. I know him. I've known him most of my life."

She stared at him and blinked. "Most of your life?"

"He's my stepfather. Mother's husband. A cold, heartless, narcissistic son of a bitch. I watched his ambition starve her of affection until she gave up. She killed herself because of him."

"I'm sorry, Roger. I'm sorry that happened to you, to your mother, but hurting me will only make things worse. Untie me. Let's go home."

Coleman didn't seem to hear her plea and continued, "That was twenty long years ago. Now, it's my turn. Let him save his precious professional reputation after Hyperion's pathetic death. Then, I'll leave and never come back. There are people who appreciate what I'm capable of. Wilson Andrews isn't the only place to work."

"Roger! Untie me. I have to go to the bathroom."

He chuckled. "I ought to make you sit there. It doesn't really matter, but it'd be messy. There's nowhere to run. We're ten miles from the nearest paved road." He came over to her and began to loosen the ropes. "Don't try anything."

He gripped her arm and Fiona winced. "You're hurting me." He laughed and stood by the door as she entered. She turned and pulled on her belt. "Do you mind?"

"Make it quick. Don't make me do something you'll regret." He shut the door and walked toward the front of the open room. He picked up the shotgun leaning against the table and clicked the safety off. As he glanced upward a movement outside of the window caught his eye. He opened the front door and listened. The sound of a vehicle filtered through the trees. It was getting louder. "What the . . .?" he whispered and shut the front door.

Fiona was washing her hands when the bathroom door slammed open. "In the back room. Now," Coleman growled as he pulled her into the hallway and shoved her into the back bedroom. "On the floor." She stood facing him and he struck her in the sternum with the butt of the shotgun. She stumbled backward, clutching her chest. "Now," he said.

She lay face down while Coleman cinched her bonds. Then, he stuffed a rag in her mouth and wrapped her head with duct tape. He knelt close to her ear and said, "We may have company coming. If you make any noise, I start shooting."

TWENTY-NINE

WEDNESDAY, MARCH 29TH

Salem, Virginia

CLAIRE HELD it up to the light. "Well, what is it?" Mark asked.

"It's an ID card." Claire flipped the credit-card-sized piece of plastic. "Wilson Andrews Equine Research Center, Fiona Montgomery, DVM."

Grant reached for it. "May I see?" Claire handed it over. "It's dated this academic year. Were they seeing each other?"

"I doubt it, but I don't keep up with the details of Roger's personal life. It would be surprising though. He's pretty much a loner."

"This could explain where Fiona is," Claire said. "Could they be together?"

Grant shrugged. "I doubt it."

Claire moved toward him. "Is he's capable of abducting her?"

Grant slipped the ID card in his shirt pocket and rubbed his chin. "If he's slipped into mania, anything is possible."

Mark walked to a door under the stairway. The doorknob didn't turn. "What's in here?"

"Storage room?" said Grant, shrugging his shoulders.

"It's locked."

"Not for long." Grant reached for a pry bar hanging on a peg over the workbench. The wooden frame cracked like a dead tree branch. He pulled the handle and turned on the light switch.

"Oh my God," Claire whispered. "He hasn't been taking his medicines for a while."

The door led to a space with a sloped roof matching the pitch of the stairs above. To the right, the storage area opened into a room that had been extended from the original basement. The floor was concrete and the walls were finished with unpainted drywall. Fluorescent lighting hung from the ceiling. The surface of the far wall was covered, floor to ceiling, with newspaper clippings and computer printouts of articles, blog posts, and photographs.

"He has several pictures of Fiona," Mark said, gazing at the collage. "Good Lord, what's been going on in his head?"

"There must be ten articles and twice as many photos of Barbaro," Claire said. "He chronicled his life."

"Check this out," Mark pointed to several photos of a modern glassed office building. In the top right corner of the photo, bold blue letters spelled the name of the business occupying the building. *Telos Pharmaceuticals.*

"What do they have to do with Roger? Here are a couple of articles about their CEO. Some guy named Mullion."

"Roger is going to work for them after he finishes this academic year. That's the company funding our arthritis clinical trials. They make Juvanimab."

"They do more than that." Mark removed his phone and took several photographs of the collage."

"Oh no," Claire said as she looked around the corner. Firearms were displayed hanging from hooks attached to the wall. "What's he doing with all this?"

"He likes to hunt," Grant responded.

"AR-15s, an AK-47, he's got several sniper rifles. Look at this, an HK417." Mark lifted the rifle from the wall rack. "Fully rigged. He knows a lot about guns."

"He's an expert," Grant said.

Claire turned to face him. "He's got a mental disorder, for heaven's sake."

"It's not against the law."

"How can it not be?" Claire shook her head.

Grant scanned the wall. "They all seem to be here; I don't see any empty racks."

"Except for the shotgun," Mark reminded him.

"Like I said, he's probably scouting turkeys. This is the time of day they start to roost."

"You don't hunt with these." Mark replaced the HK and studied the variety of handguns displayed.

"He's not hunting with them. They're all there. Every hook has a gun hanging on it."

"He could have more," Claire pointed out.

"He may have bipolar disorder. That doesn't make him a killer. He's a kind and gentle person who wants to be a great equine veterinarian. I've known him since he was a boy, and I think I know where they are." He turned toward the stairs. "I'll be back soon."

"Hold on," Mark said. "Where are you going?"

"A place he probably thinks I've forgotten about."

"You're not going alone."

"I'm not staying here by myself." Claire stepped in front of Grant. "I've had enough of that."

Grant smiled. "All right, suit yourselves." He turned and they followed him to the truck. "Roger's biological father owned a cabin on property adjacent to the national forest. He'd take Roger hunting there when he was a boy. Marion inherited it when he died. She passed it to Roger after her death. I haven't been there since before he was a teenager. It's about thirty miles from here. If we hustle, we can make it there before dark."

"Shouldn't we let the police in on this?" Mark asked.

"I hope not," Grant said. "Look, I'd rather this not turn into front-page news, if you get my drift. He's a fine son with a promising future."

Mark nodded. "Understood."

They rode in silence for the first few minutes. The hazy peaks of the Blue Ridge Mountains surrounded them. They drove parallel to the mountains in the valley between two ridges. "There are a few things you two should probably know," Grant said as they sped southwest on Interstate 81. "Roger's mental illness runs in his family. I married his mother when he was seven. It was about a year after his dad died. Around that time my career was starting to take off. I was consumed with ambition. At first, I didn't understand what was happening. I thought I was doing what every good husband and father should be doing—providing for his family. I'd finished my residency and spent most of my time caring for patients, writing grants and doing research. I was eaten up with it. I practically lived in the lab and the hospital and neglected Marion and Roger."

"You shouldn't beat yourself up. I see it all the time," Mark said.

"I should've seen the signs. I didn't. I was too self-absorbed. Marion had her first serious depressive episode when Roger was nine. A psychotic break occurred a year later." He paused for a moment. "She committed suicide when he was eleven. I raised him the best I could."

"I'm sorry," Claire said. No one spoke for several minutes.

"Why is he doing this?" Mark asked.

Grant shook his head as he sped on the interstate. "Like I said before, I hope they're scouting turkeys."

"You really think so?" Mark asked.

"I don't know what to think. I hope he hasn't gotten himself in trouble."

"How much farther?" Claire asked.

"Ten, fifteen minutes. Our exit should be a couple of miles on the right."

They turned north off the interstate and drove up into the mountains. A brown road sign announced they would be entering the Jefferson National Forest in a few miles. From the back seat, Mark glanced over Grant's shoulder at the odometer. They'd driven twenty-eight miles. The dashboard clock read half past four, and the sun was almost touching the mountain peaks in the distance. Grant turned right on Forest Road 5051 and headed into the national forest.

"I think this is right," Grant said as he turned onto an unpaved firebreak. "It's changed a lot." The road was filled with ruts from sluices created by spring rains. The dirt lane switched back and forth as it wound through the forest. Dogwoods flowered along the side of the road. Most of the hardwood tree limbs were bare except for fat emerald buds waiting to leaf. They gave a hint of green to the silver and gray branches.

"Where are we going?" Claire asked.

"Hang on," Grant shifted into four-wheel drive and slowed as they maneuvered over a deep cleft in the road. The pickup crossed over a series of hills and climbed several hundred feet. Suddenly, the road turned down into a valley that ran between two ridges for about a half mile. The forest was thick with bare trees and underbrush. An occasional redbud displayed pink blossoms. "He'll be able to see us coming. The cabin sits near the top of that ridge."

"Is this a road?" Claire asked.

"It's a fire lane used by the National Park Service. Look for an opening in the trees on the right. The driveway should be coming soon. The house sits back thirty or forty yards."

"Stop, I saw a truck. We just passed it. Back up," Mark said.

SOMETHING about the cabin looked familiar to Mark as they

approached. The trees were bigger, but the building was the same. "This is where the picture in your office was taken. The one with you and your son and the big buck."

The side mirrors almost clipped tree trunks as they drove up the dirt road into the clearing in front of the cabin. Grant smiled. "The boy was Roger. Those were good memories. It was probably the last time I was here. He was about thirteen years old when he began showing signs of his illness." Grant parked the pickup as the adult son, Roger Coleman, opened the front door and walked out onto the porch, holding the Benelli.

"What are you doing here?"

"Looking for you," Grant replied as he got out. Claire remained in the passenger seat.

Mark opened the rear door of the crew cab and stepped out. He noted Coleman's truck parked on the side of the cabin facing them. "Hello, Roger. Nice place you've got."

"Thanks. It's been in the family for generations."

"What have you been doing?" Grant asked. "We need you back at the hospital."

"I needed a break. Turkey season starts next week. I wanted to see if they were roosting in the trees down by the stream."

"I know. I want to go with you if that's okay," Grant said. "Like we used to."

"Sure," Coleman replied. "That'd be great."

"Mind if we come in? I'd love to see your place. My dad used to take me hunting in a cabin like this in North Carolina," Mark said.

"Maybe some other time. It's getting dark. We should be heading back."

"Nonsense. It'll only take a minute. They may never get a chance to come back," Grant said, stepping toward the porch. He turned to Mark. "Come on. I'll show you around."

Coleman stepped in front of the door, still holding the shotgun. "Just for a minute."

"Thanks, I appreciate it." Mark turned and motioned for Claire to stay in the truck. He and Grant followed Coleman into the cabin.

The large front room was in shadows. A stone fireplace stood in one corner. A potbelly stove was situated on stone blocks in the kitchen area. The smell of mildew clung to the surroundings. A damp, musty wave of cold air with a hint of stale wood smoke wafted across Mark's face as he entered. Antique wooden furniture hewn from logs and tree branches was scattered about. The place looked like it was straight out of a documentary on early nineteenth-century Appalachia.

"Authentic," Mark said, looking around. "It looks like a museum."

"It is authentic. Looks the same as it did when my grandfather built it."

"Must've been a long time ago," Mark said.

"Nineteen twenty-one."

"What's back here?" Mark asked as he jiggled the knob of a door in the back hallway.

"Nothing. Just a bedroom."

"Why is it locked?"

"It's not supposed to be. Something's wrong with the mechanism, and I don't have the key."

"Do you have a bathroom?" Mark asked.

"Of course. We've got a septic tank." Roger opened a door in the hallway and turned on the light. "We tore down the outhouse a couple of decades ago. Hurry up. It's getting dark."

Mark stepped into the bathroom and closed the door. There was a small pedestal sink with a grime-streaked sliver of soap lying next to the faucet. A dirty worn towel hung on a rack nearby. He lifted the toilet seat and glanced down. There was a brown ring circling the bowl, and the water had a rose color. He froze. There were two drops of blood on the bowl an inch above the waterline. It was fresh red blood. He turned and walked back into the room.

"Didn't your mother teach you manners?" Coleman asked. "Flush the toilet."

"Oh, sorry. Did you cut yourself?" Mark asked.

Coleman looked at him and looked at his hands. "No. Why?"

"There's blood in the toilet bowl."

"Maybe I scratched my ass in the woods and didn't notice it." Coleman laughed. He went into the bathroom. A moment later the toilet flushed and he emerged. "Let's go."

"Not yet," replied Mark.

"It's time," Coleman said, lowering the shotgun.

Grant and Mark turned their heads. A *thump, thump* came from the back room. Mark looked at Coleman. "You alone?"

Coleman nodded. "Must be a tree branch hitting the cabin. I've been meaning to trim them."

"Roger, why don't you put the gun down?" Grant said. "Let's go home."

"Get out of here," Coleman said, pointing the shotgun at his stepfather.

Thump. Thump. Thump.

"That doesn't sound like a tree branch," Mark said.

Grant lunged at Coleman. He grabbed the weapon with both hands. Coleman pulled back. Grant twisted. The barrel turned downward. Mark rushed forward. The discharge was deafening. The smell of gunpowder erupted into the air. Two more blasts ripped through the cabin. Grant fell to the ground screaming. Mark dove at Coleman. He twisted, raising the butt of the shotgun. They crashed together. The stock struck Mark's jaw. His fist rocked Coleman's head. They rolled on the floor as the gun hit the ground. Coleman crawled toward it as Mark grabbed his leg. He pulled free and stood. Mark tried to stand but Coleman kicked him in the chin. He fell to the floor. Coleman bent down and picked up the shotgun. He turned and raised the barrel.

"Roger, stop! What are you doing?" Grant called out as he lay on the floor, holding his bleeding foot.

"Drop the gun," Mark said as he slipped his finger inside the trigger guard.

Coleman froze. His eyes focused on the pistol pointed at his chest. Mark sat up, keeping the Sig Sauer aimed at Coleman. "Raise that another inch and I pull this trigger."

"Don't do that," he said, lowering the barrel.

"You put the gun on the floor and step away," Mark said. "Nice and slow."

Coleman lowered the shotgun to the floor. He released it an inch above the surface. The sound of it clattering on the wood was like an electric shock. Everyone flinched. Coleman bolted to the door and tore it open. He disappeared and the sound of his footsteps faded on the stairs. He rounded the corner and grabbed for the door handle to his truck. He almost had it open when the force of another body slammed into him. He was stunned. As he turned Claire's punch landed square on his nose. Followed by a left jab and right cross. One, two, three. She stepped into the right. His head snapped back.

"Stop," Mark said as he rounded the corner of the cabin with his pistol raised.

Claire stood shaking her right hand. "I think I broke my knuckle."

"Get back." He motioned for her to step away as he kept the Sig pointed at Coleman, who knelt on the ground. In the receding light he could see his right eye was half closed and blood dripped from his split lower lip and bent nose.

"You busted his nose," Mark said. "I'll check your hand later."

He grabbed Coleman by his shirt collar and pulled him to his feet. Daylight was disappearing and the forest was in shadows. He removed the knife clipped in his front pocket and shoved him toward the front of the cabin. He turned to Claire.

"Grant was shot. He's bleeding. I don't know where he was hit. Check on him and see if you can find some light in there. It's going to be dark soon."

Claire glanced at the roof line. "No electrical wires."

Coleman spit blood on the ground. "In my truck."

"What?' asked Mark.

"There's a lantern and flashlight in the cab."

Claire walked to Coleman's pickup and opened the passenger door. She emerged holding a battery powered lantern and flashlight.

Mark led the captive toward Grant's truck and opened the rear door. The dome light came on and he spotted a coiled lariat on the backseat.

Claire went inside. Grant lay sprawled on the floor and the noise from the back room persisted. It was a thumping sound like a big dog's tail whacking a wall.

"Better check out the back room, they're making a hell of a racket," said Grant, who sat up. Claire turned on the lantern and placed it on the floor. He looked at his foot and grimaced. "I may need a tourniquet."

"I'll help you in a minute." Claire grasped the doorknob and twisted, her hand slipped over the cold metal surface. Locked. She took two steps back and kicked. The jam cracked and on the second foot strike, the ancient door burst open. She flicked on the flashlight.

"Fiona!" Claire darted to her side and peeled gently at the tape wrapped around her face. Fiona spit the rag from her mouth and inhaled like it was her first breath.

"Thank God you're here," she gasped. "That maniac was going to kill me."

"Are you all right?"

Fiona nodded. "Stiff and sore." She rubbed her wrists. "I'm thirsty and starving."

"I don't have anything to eat, but we'll find something." Claire finished untying her and helped her to her feet. "Let's get you out of here. There's a bottle of water in the car." Fiona stumbled as she stood. Claire gripped her arm, pulling her close as they walked toward the front.

Mark led Coleman back to the cabin with his arms cinched behind his back. As he nudged him across the porch, he heard a rustling sound behind him in the direction of the road. He turned and stared into the woods. It was dark and hard to make out shapes. *Must be deer after acorns.* The wind was still. A moment later, there were more sounds of leaves and branches. Then . . . silence.

"Ain't nothin' out there but squirrels and deer," said Coleman.

Mark peered into the deepening shadows then turned and opened the front door.

"Look who I found," Claire exclaimed as she helped Fiona to the couch. "Grant's been shot in the foot. It's a mess." Claire sat on the floor next to Grant and removed the laces then tugged at the bloody boot.

"Son of a bitch!" he yelped.

"Sorry, but you're bleeding, it's got to go."

"Leave my foot on!"

Claire tumbled backward as the bloody boot came off in her hands. Grant lay back with his hands to his face and screamed. His mangled big toe toppled out of the boot into Claire's lap.

"Disgusting," Fiona said.

Claire held it up with her index finger and thumb. "Can this be reattached?"

Mark glanced at her and shook his head. "Crab bait." He finished tying Coleman to the iron potbelly stove and brandished the pistol. "Don't try anything."

Fiona slid from the couch and crawled to Grant while tears dripped from her chin onto the filthy floor. "Thank you." She wiped her cheeks with the palms of her hands. "You saved my life."

He pulled her to him and put an arm around her shoulders. "You would have done the same for me."

"I don't have that much courage." She sniffled and dried her nose with her sleeve. "I heard the gunshots. What happened?"

Mark squatted beside them. "He and Coleman wrestled for the shotgun." He examined the wound. "What was that load?"

"Three-inch turkey, probably number three or four."

"Lead?"

"Steel, I think." Grant groaned. "Hurts like hell." Small jets of blood were pulsing from the great toe stump. The second toe dangled like a pendulum from a small skin bridge.

Mark put his finger over the streaming blood. "See if there is a towel in a kitchen cabinet." Claire returned with a soiled dishtowel.

Mark frowned as he held it up. "Probably better than the stuff that was blown into his foot." He tore it into strips and wrapped the stump of Grant's foot. "That'll have to do for now."

"Thanks," Grant winced.

"We need to get you to a hospital. That shotgun blast blew pellets, wadding, sweaty sock, and pieces of your boot into your foot. This wound needs to be cleaned up in an operating room. Claire's got what's left of your big toe, and you'll probably lose the second."

"Hell's bells, you're just full of good news."

Mark put his hand under his arm. "Can you stand?"

"I think so."

Mark reached behind his back, withdrew the pistol, and gave it to Claire. "Watch him," he said, pointing to Coleman. "Don't shoot him unless he tries to get away." He looked at Coleman. "Stay there and don't move. Don't think for a second she won't pull the trigger if you try anything." Mark helped Grant stand and assisted him onto the front porch. The sun had set, and darkness surrounded the cabin. "Can you make it to the truck?"

"With a little help," said Grant. "Let me use the shotgun as a crutch." With his left arm around Mark's shoulder and his right holding the Benelli, he hopped down the steps on his good leg and over to the passenger side doors of his pickup.

"You go in the front seat," he said to Grant. "I'll put Coleman in the back with me. Fiona will have to drive Coleman's truck. Claire will drive and get us to the nearest hospital."

"Roanoke Memorial," said Grant. "It's a level one trauma center."

"I'll have the police meet us there." Mark stepped up onto the porch and reentered the cabin. He looked at Claire. "I'm going to untie him from the stove. Cover me, and don't shoot."

"No worries."

A few minutes later, Mark and Coleman had reached the pickup near the driver's side door. Claire stood on the other side near the tailgate with the pistol. Mark peeked in from the driver's window and checked on Grant. "You doing all right?"

He still cradled the shotgun while lying almost flat on the front seat. "I'll make it," he said and grimaced.

"Hang in there for a little while longer." He took the knife he'd confiscated from Coleman and cut another piece from the lariat. "Sorry about your rope."

"I have others," Grant replied, examining the shotgun. "He must have taken the plug out, there're two more shells in this thing."

"Good, keep him covered."

Mark squatted to tie his legs when he heard a muffled report, then Coleman jerked. *Seizure?* Coleman's limp body fell onto him and they rolled on the ground. He scrambled to his knees and saw Coleman's limp form. Blood spurted from a three-inch hole his neck. Mark yelled to Claire. "Get down! Everyone on the ground!"

She hit the dirt and rolled under the truck.

Pop. Pop. Pop. The sound of suppressed gunfire and bullets hitting the pickup shattered the evening air.

"What's happening?" Claire said.

Fiona screamed.

"Someone's shooting at us. Get into the woods," Mark said. "Stay low and get behind the biggest tree trunk you can find." He nodded at the pistol in her hand. "You know how to use that thing. Shoot anyone who comes near. Fiona, go with her. The shots are coming from the fire road. Go that way," he said, pointing behind the cabin. "Go!"

He watched the two women disappear into the darkness of the trees. A round shattered the driver's side window. Glass shards rained down on his head. He sprinted to his right into the forest. Two more shots ripped through the brush behind him. *They must have night vision.* He dove to the ground and crawled onward. After a few moments objects became easier to see in the shadows. He made his way away from the cabin and his eyes adjusted. The sound of running water reached his ears. He realized he must be close to the stream Coleman mentioned where the turkeys liked to roost. He found it and rolled down into the streambed and followed it toward the dirt road. The spring rains and the last remnants of snowmelt had the stream running hard, and its sound covered the noise of his movements. The water was ice cold and his hands and feet were going numb. After he had crawled about fifty yards, he peeked over the ledge. The shadows and darkness made it almost impossible to see anything.

Who are these guys? If they were smart, they'd sit tight and wait for us to come back to the vehicles to try and make a run for it. Then, he saw something about twenty feet away. A small round flash like someone checking the time on his watch. *Got you.* He pulled Coleman's knife from his pocket and unfolded the three-inch blade. He crawled out of the stream with the knife clenched between his teeth. The ground was soft and covered with moss. His hands and knees pressed into the earth as he moved forward. Inch by inch, he felt his way forward. He paused and searched into the darkness. There. Straight ahead. Kneeling by a tree trunk. He could make out the crouched form of a man holding a rifle.

The assassin faced the cabin. Mark closed to within three yards. He breathed slowly and inched forward. A twig snapped. The man turned. Mark pounced. The gun barrel smashed against his arm. They crashed together. Mark shoved the man's chin upward with the heel of his left hand and thrust with the knife. The point stopped when it hit the bone of a cervical vertebra. He slashed the blade sideways. The assassin fell backward and began twitching. A sucking sound came from the wound, but no cry escaped his mouth.

Mark cut the sling and hefted the automatic rifle. He couldn't tell the make in the darkness, but he could see the suppressor and forward grip. *What the hell?* He shouldered the M4 and scanned the terrain. The forest was lit up in black and white. The riflescope was fitted with white phosphorous night vision optics. There was no green glow. It was a new technology he'd only seen a couple of times. The Raleigh SWAT team couldn't afford the upgrade. Even with night vision, it took him a couple of minutes to spot the next assassin a hundred feet to his right. The camouflaged humanoid form sat cross-legged with his elbows on his knees, aiming his rifle like a sniper.

Mark looked back at the cabin and saw what he was aiming at. Claire's head peeked around the corner of the cabin. He shouted, "Claire!" She disappeared. A moment later the sniper's gun fired. A chunk of log blew apart where she'd been. She scrambled back into the woods. The sniper rose and Mark squeezed his trigger. Multiple rounds ripped into the assassin's chest and midsection. He staggered backward and fell.

Gunfire slammed into the trees near Mark. He dove for the ground and crawled behind a huge oak. A third man sprinted across the clearing toward the pickup truck in front of the cabin. He sprayed gunfire into the woods in Mark's direction. He reached the truck and yanked open the driver's side door. Two explosions blew him backward five feet, and he lay still on the ground.

"Take that, you son of a bitch," Grant's voice carried through the woods. Mark stayed perfectly still and scanned the woods for ten minutes. Then, he approached the sniper he'd shot and felt his pulse. Nothing. He checked the body of the first hitman and confirmed the kill. Two large holes marked the torso of the third Grant had blasted with the shotgun. Coleman lay motionless. Face down in a large pool of blood. He had no pulse.

"Is anyone hurt?" Mark asked, looking around for Fiona and Claire.

"What the hell just happened?" Grant asked. "Where's Roger?"

"I'm sorry, Warwick. He's dead. They shot him."

Grant put his hands to his face.

"These were probably cartel," said Mark. "They were pros with sophisticated equipment. I'll call the cops on the way to the hospital."

"He didn't deserve this," Grant hung his head.

"I know."

"Is it safe?" Fiona yelled from the woods.

"All clear," Mark called out.

Claire walked from behind the cabin, gripping the pistol with both hands and scanning the terrain like she expected another threat. "Who were they?"

"My guess . . . sicario, drug cartel hitmen."

"That's insane! What have we done?" Fiona asked as she walked out of the trees. She began crying again as she knelt over Roger's body and crossed herself.

"Whoever hired them thinks we know too much," Mark said.

"Let me see him. I want to see my stepson." Grant struggled from the truck. He knelt beside him and kissed his forehead.

"We need to get you to a hospital, Dr. Grant," Mark helped him up.

MARK AND CLAIRE stood as the surgeon approached, "Dr. Grant is lucky. He's doing well and resting comfortably in the PACU. I want to keep him on IV antibiotics for at least a week. I'm happy with the debridement, but as you know, shotgun-blast injuries are filthy. A lot of material can be drawn into the wound and embedded into the tissues. I didn't see any shotgun wadding. It's a good thing he had on those heavy boots. They probably prevented worse contamination. However, I picked out a bunch of cotton fibers from his socks and multiple pellets."

"Are you worried about a pseudomonas infection?"

The surgeon nodded. "Always with a foot wound."

"Were you able to close the stumps?" Mark asked.

"I didn't feel comfortable doing it tonight. I picked out too much foreign debris from the wound. I left it open and placed a wound VAC. I'll bring him back to the OR for a second washout on Friday. If the wounds look good, I'll close them."

"That's what I'd do," Mark agreed.

"Where'd all the cops go?" he asked, looking around the room.

"They took Dr. Montgomery to the station for a formal report. They let us stay to talk to you. I'm part of the Raleigh PD, their SWAT medical officer." He showed the surgeon his departmental shield. "I gave them a short version of my story. Dr. Hodgson and I will go by the station when we're done and give them details."

"When can he leave the hospital?" Claire asked.

"Not for a few days. Maybe Saturday. It depends. I want him on antibiotics and we have to get the skin closed. I don't want him walking around barnyards with those open wounds. In fact, don't let him near a barn or stables until his foot heals," the surgeon instructed. "Here's my cell number if you have any questions. I'll round on him in the morning."

Mark photographed the business card, placed it in his wallet, and shook hands with his colleague. "Thanks. I hope the rest of your night is quiet."

"Not likely around here," he answered over his shoulder as he walked from the waiting room back into the surgery area.

"What are we going to do?" Claire asked.

"How about some food? Then, we have to talk to the cops."

"I mean about Hyperion? How is he going to get fixed with Grant in the hospital? Fiona says he won't tolerate the sling much longer. We can't postpone this while we sit around and wait another week or two for Grant.""You're right," Mark agreed. "We have to move ahead with the surgery. Fiona and I can do the operation. If she can make the surgical approach and close the wound, I can fix the fractures."

THIRTY

THURSDAY, MARCH 30TH

Wilson Andrews Equine Research Center, Roanoke, VA

MARK OPENED the heavy wooden door and followed Claire into the conference room. It looked more like a corporate boardroom with a table long enough for a dozen well-padded desk chairs on each side. He pulled one and held it for Claire as she sat down. Through floor-to-ceiling windows he looked upon emerald-green pastures that ran a half mile to a dense line of trees. Beyond the forest the Blue Ridge Mountains stretched until they met the horizon. In a nearby corral, a dam stood watching two foals romp along a section of white picket fence.

"Hey, sit down," Claire told him. "You're making me nervous."

He stood for a moment longer, taking in the view, and thought, *What beautiful country.*

Fiona and Worth Hobbs were already seated. Mark reached for the aluminum coffeepot and filled his cup. Then, he complied with Claire's request.

"I think I've figured out what's been going on," he said.

Hobbs interlocked his fingers and leaned forward. "Please, tell us."

"I pieced it together after speaking with Grant, Fiona, and Lew Jordan."

"Lew's the director of pharmacy services," Fiona clarified.

Hobbs removed his glasses and smiled. "Yes, thank you."

Claire turned to Mark. "Come on, let's hear it."

He ignored the remark and sipped his coffee. "For some reason, Coleman was spiking the Bethesda infusions with Grant's experimental arthritis drug."

Fiona again looked toward Hobbs. "It's called Juvanimab."

"Juvani-what?"

"Ju-va-ni-mab," enunciated Mark. "According to Jordan, it's being tested by Grant as an anti-arthritis drug in phase two clinical trials. It's a monoclonal antibody that inhibits the inflammatory response in arthritic joints. In high doses, it has potent immunosuppressive actions. It's so powerful it can almost eliminate the body's immune response, mimicking AIDS. I think that's why Hyperion got infected after the first surgery *and* . . . why he's been unable to fight it."

"For God's sake, why would he do that?" Hobbs exclaimed.

"I don't claim to understand his motives. I'm not sure anyone does, or ever will. I'll give you what I know. Coleman suffered from bipolar disorder. He's never been officially diagnosed with psychosis, although he had traits of paranoid disorder. This has been known since he was a teenager. But it's been well controlled on medications. His last episode requiring hospitalization was decades ago when he was in his teens."

"By all accounts, the young man was brilliant," Hobbs said.

"There's a fine line between genius and insanity. He may have been brilliant, but when he stopped taking his medications, he crossed over the line. And from what I can tell, he'd been off them for weeks, maybe longer. This had profound psychological effects. He slowly spiraled into deeper and deeper mania. According to Fiona, he made repeated statements that were increasingly outlandish."

"He said we were inhumane in attempting to save Hyperion. He thought it was pointless and cruel—even after reading the results of your fracture experiments," Fiona added.

"That's insane. I'd never allow such a thing. If I wasn't convinced we were doing the right thing, I'd have put him down myself," Hobbs said.

Mark continued. "I don't think he believed we were being cruel. He knew we were doing the right thing. His goal was to sabotage our efforts so that Hyperion would have to be euthanized."

Hobbs stared at him. "What did you say?"

"Coleman wanted Grant to euthanize Hyperion."

"Explain."

"This is just my theory. We'll never know for sure. From what I can tell, he was able to look at the preliminary arthritis data and correctly deduce which subjects were receiving the Juvanimab treatment samples. The results were so strikingly good, it was easy to tell which samples were placebo and which were the drug."

"He cracked the double-blind treatment code?" Claire asked.

Mark nodded. "Yep. He'd empty at least ten or so vials and refill them with saline. Then, he'd inject the drug into the Bethesda infusions."

"I take it that's not the normal dose?" Hobbs questioned.

"Ten times the normal amount for a horse his weight."

"How long did he do this?" Hobbs barked, slamming his palms on the table.

"Since we started the project?" Mark replied. "At least a week. Enough time to wreak havoc on Hyperion's immune system."

"Good heavens," Hobbs said, putting his face in his hands.

"There is *some* good news," Mark said. "I've administered additional doses of Endovancin, and it seems to be working. Hyperion's neutrophil count is increasing. He's been able to start fighting the infection. We've given him several normal infusions of the Bethesda treatment with the expected response. If this keeps up, he could be ready for surgery soon."

"When?" Hobbs asked.

Mark shrugged and turned his palms up. "I don't know. I don't think anyone knows. We'll have to make our best guess. One thing I do know . . . he's getting stronger with each infusion."

"He's gaining weight," Claire pointed out.

"That's probably the best clinical sign we've had since he's been here. He's getting better with every hour. I recommend we operate tomorrow. What do you think, Fiona?"

"This is uncharted waters for me. I'm ready to help whenever. Just say the word."

"Then let's plan for Friday," Mark stated.

Fiona picked up her phone and began entering a note. "I'll make the preparations. First case tomorrow morning."

"All right, we're all in agreement, let's do it." Mark clenched his fists. "Hyperion has suffered enough."

CLAIRE AND MARK walked toward the horse barns. "You didn't tell them about Coleman's job offer and plans for leaving."

"I didn't want to cloud the issues. I still don't have that figured out."

"Have you talked to John?"

"Bristow?" Mark looked at her.

Claire nodded. "I was wondering if there had been any word about Meera."

"I spoke with him yesterday after the attack. He said TSI and the DEA are working different angles of the case. I talked to a special agent this morning. He said they found GPS tracking devices on both pickup trucks, Grant's and Coleman's. That's how the cartel found us. He wants to talk to you too."

"No one's called," Claire declared.

"Don't be surprised when they do. He mentioned Meera was spotted in Bogotá a couple of days ago at a large ranch belonging to the Bonsantos family. She was seen walking the grounds and appeared to be in good health."

"In Bogotá? What's she doing there? Why didn't you tell me?"

"I'm sorry, between the grilling by the FBI and the Roanoke PD it slipped my mind."

"She's still a hostage? Why don't they rescue her?"

Mark shook his head. "I asked . . . Bristow wouldn't say."

THIRTY-ONE

THURSDAY, MARCH 30TH

Riverside Towers, Philadelphia, PA

JEFFREY MULLION STOOD at the patio railing of his penthouse apartment, sipping coffee and gazing at the city beyond the dark waters of the Schuylkill. It was a clear, crisp spring morning. The campus of the University of Pennsylvania lay directly across the river. He looked to his left at a ten-story modern building in the distance, the corporate headquarters of Telos Pharmaceuticals. A feeling of satisfaction came over him.

A gust whipped over the rooftop, threatening to muss his hair. He turned to face into it then glanced at his Louis Moinet wristwatch and calculated he had half an hour to put the finishing touches on the notes for this morning's board meeting. He turned around at the sound of the sliding glass door. An Asian man, no more than five and a half feet tall, hurried toward him. He was dressed in black slacks, a white shirt, and a black vest. Before he could cross the tiled deck, another man appeared behind him in the doorway.

"Jeffery," the man said.

The manservant came over to Mullion and gave a quarter bow. "My apologies, sir. He insisted."

Mullion looked over the shoulder of his butler. "This had better be good."

"Would I be here if it weren't?"

"It's all right, Lopsang. Leave us for a few minutes," Mullion said. The butler gave a slight bow and marched into the apartment.

"Really, Jeff. You need to train your staff better."

"He's the Taiwanese Muay Thai champion, you fool. You're lucky he didn't incapacitate you. Don't try that again. Call me first."

"This is important. Too important for phones."

"So? Get on with it," Mullion said, motioning them to sit down.

"There's been a problem . . ." For five minutes Sorenson spoke while Mullion remained silent and sipped his coffee. When he finished, Mullion leaned forward.

"What do you propose?"

"Nothing right now. The damage is done. There's no way that horse will ever walk, much less run. He's in critical condition."

"You said their methods are revolutionary. Could he recover?"

"Not without a miracle and Endovancin," Sorenson said.

"You're sure none is available?"

"That's what Ard said."

"Yeah, well. He's dead."

"It was verified by Jindal. She said they were setting up for a production run but didn't have any in stock. Hodgson and Thurman used all of the existing supply in their earlier experiments. They're desperate. There's no more Endovancin and they can't make anymore. I made sure of it." Sorenson lit a cigarette and leaned back in the overstuffed deck chair and exhaled a stream of smoke from his nostrils.

"How in the hell did she get away?" Mullion asked.

"The CNP got lucky."

"Don't tell me the Colombian National Police just happened to execute a perfectly timed raid on BACRIM headquarters in the

Colombian rain forest just when she's delivered. That's no coincidence," Mullion retorted.

"The Jungla have been watching the Baja Cauca for months."

"That's our bad luck."

"Stop worrying. Who cares about her? She can't do anything to hurt us."

"She can identify you."

"So, have Ramon take care of her later."

"What about the shipment? That was a two-month supply with a street value in the millions."

Sorenson drew on his cigarette. "A temporary setback. Look, we don't need the northern supply routes. We have air transportation. There's nothing left of the BCI lab. We have the formula and we have the only person who knows how to make it. Re-fucking-lax." Sorenson took another drag and flicked ash onto the deck.

"I'll relax after Rampage is wearing a blanket of roses and we're marketing Endovancin under a different name."

"You won't have to wait long, a couple of months at max. There's one other item," Sorenson continued.

Mullion stood and walked back to the railing. He looked down at the river. "Go on."

"That vet who was taking care of the horse for us, the one we were going to hire if he pulled it off."

"Coleman, what about him?"

"He won't be working for anyone. He's dead."

Mullion clinched his jaw while Sorenson recounted what he knew. His face grew redder as Sorenson spoke. "Those idiots! Now, the FBI will be crawling up everyone's ass."

"Calm down, for Christ's sake. It had to happen. Coleman was too erratic and knew too much. You told me to get rid of him."

Mullion stood rigid looking out over the Philadelphia skyline. "I meant something a little more sophisticated than that! A cartel hit on US soil? Are you out of your mind?"

"C'mon, Jeff. It's under control. They're dead, all of them.

Nothing can be tied to us. They were BACRIM. The Feds will think it has to do with the Jungla raid—payback. So chill, take a deep breath."

"Shut up. How can I relax when I have to deal with imbeciles?" Mullion slammed his hand down on the railing. "They cannot succeed. That horse better not recover."

"He won't. I have fallback plans."

"Do I need to remind you of the stakes?"

"No need. Has Jindal given you her reply?"

"That's the one piece of good news I've received lately."

Sorenson got up and stood next to Mullion. He took a final drag and flicked his cigarette butt over the railing. "Stop worrying. It's not good for your health. You're gonna stroke. I'd be happy if I were you. The Triple Crown and a multibillion-dollar cure for cancer?" Sorenson watched the cigarette float through the air until it disappeared from view. "That's worth celebrating."

They turned, facing each other. Mullion spoke. "We'll celebrate after Derby Week. Screw this up and our stock options are worthless."

Sorenson stuck out a middle finger. "Gimme a break."

Mullion flinched. Once again, he glanced at his watch then turned around. Sorenson grabbed his hat and followed him across the patio to the sliding glass door. Lopsang opened it and led them through the elegantly appointed penthouse to the private elevator.

THIRTY-TWO

FRIDAY, MARCH 31ST

Wilson Andrews Equine Research Center, Roanoke, VA

MARK TIED the surgical mask behind his head and he tore open the packaging of the scrub brush. He pulled the light blue plastic pick imbedded in the chlorhexidine-soaked sponge and ran its pointed tip under his fingernails. He used the sponge to individually wash each finger before moving on to the palms and back of his hands then up the forearms. He stopped at his elbows and after several minutes, he chucked the sponge then dunked his hands and forearms under the running water at the scrub sink. He kept his fingers pointing upward, allowing the water to drip from the elbows as he backed into the operating room. A scrub tech handed him a towel. When he'd finished drying, he was assisted into his surgical gown and gloves.

"Are you ready?" Fiona asked. She stood next to him dressed in a similar manner, with her hair tucked under a surgical bonnet and her face covered from cheeks to chin with a mask. Protective glasses shielded her eyes.

"I'm always ready," Mark replied.

"Take a look at the back table and make sure you have everything you need."

Mark turned to his left and inspected the display of orthopedic instruments. "Look at this thing, it's Goliath-sized," he said, picking up a gleaming stainless steel fracture plate from its tray. It was about ten inches long, three-quarters of an inch wide, and three-eighths of an inch thick with screw holes placed at half-inch intervals. The device was designed to lie on the surface of a broken bone oriented over the fracture site and attached with screws, thus acting as a rigid internal brace. "This is what I'd call the extra-large bone-fragment set."

He inspected the rest of the surgical equipment. Most of it was familiar. The battery-powered drills and screwdrivers were the same as those used in human fracture surgery. The strangest thing was the patient. At eleven hundred pounds, he was five times the average weight of Mark's standard patients. On the other hand, the slender limb prepped and draped for surgery was pitifully devoid of muscle. It was skin, tendons, ligaments, and bone. Mark examined the leg.

"We could use some muscle to cover the plate after the fracture is fixed. This leg is basically a giant stick covered with hide."

Fiona shrugged. "It's one of the problems we deal with. The lack of soft tissue under the skin makes the surgical wound susceptible to infection."

"That. Plus walking around in a barnyard," Mark said, glancing at the draped-out hoof six inches from the fracture site.

"A sabotaged immune system makes it even worse," Fiona said.

"That's being corrected. His wound looks good. A lot better than last week."

"Where's the graft?"

He nodded toward the back of the operating room outside the surgical field. Claire lifted the bioreactor to her waist and waved with her free hand. "I've got it," she said from behind her mask.

"The contents of the container are sterile. When we're ready, Claire will open the lid and I'll retrieve the graft material."

"Got it," Fiona said. "Let's get started. Scalpel, please." She cut through the previous incision and extended it several inches in each direction. Using the forceps in her left hand, she delicately dissected the skin flaps away from the bone, avoiding damage to neurovascular structures in the area.

"Nice exposure," Mark commented as he retracted the soft tissue flaps out of the way. The trick to successful fracture surgery was obtaining adequate visualization of the fracture fragments without disrupting the blood supply to the injured bones.

"Gelpi retractor," Fiona said. The scrub tech took the scalpel and forceps and handed her the retractor. Fiona manipulated the sharp pointed ends of the device into position. Next, she squeezed the handle, spreading the retractor prongs.

"We have a little work to do," Mark said, observing the fracture site.

"Irrigation, please," Fiona said. She accepted the device that resembled a large turkey baster filled with a diluted iodine-saline solution. Mark held a basin under the limb and suctioned while Fiona irrigated the fracture site with several liters of the solution.

"Much better," Mark said ten minutes later as he poked at the fragments with a Freer Elevator. "Grant debrided this well. I don't see any devitalized tissue. The 3D bone graft should fit in this space perfectly, if we've done our job. Which do you want to fix first?"

"I think we should start with the long pastern. It's not as comminuted as I expected and should come together with a couple of plates. Once that's fixed, the canon bone can be reconstructed with the 3D graft. Then we can repair the suspensory apparatus by extending the fetlock and placing several screws across the sesamoid."

"That's like fixing a broken human kneecap. I'd like to use cannulated screws and a titanium cable. We call it a tension-wire technique. Is that stuff available?"

Fiona turned toward a man who looked to be in his early thirties standing next to Claire. "Joey is our Synthes equipment rep." She looked directly at him. "Do we have the cables and screws in the room?"

"All set, Dr. Montgomery. Let me know when you're ready and I'll open a cable. I've got the cannulated screw set on the cart outside the door. It's wrapped and sterilized."

"Claire, can you pass some of the stem cell cancellous bone graft onto the field?" She approached the surgical field and opened the bioreactor. Mark reached in, careful not to touch the sides, and removed a round cylinder container about the size of a shot glass. "When I'm finished with this, hand me some large bone clamps," Mark said to the tech. He then pried open the fracture and proceeded to smear the bone graft material onto the surface of the broken bones, filling any voids and the intramedullary canal with the material. "This primes the fracture with a mixture of Hyperion's cultured stem cells. Dr. Grant and I harvested the specimens last week. In a day or two, these cells should mature into osteoblasts that produce new bone healing the fracture." The wide-eyed surgical tech took the container and handed him two clamps, one with serrated jaws and the other with pointed tips. "Fiona, if you would get an Army-Navy, it would help." She placed the retractor in the wound while Mark adjusted the position of the fracture alignment with the clamps. Several minutes later, he glanced at the scrub tech. "Got another pointed clamp?" She handed it to him and he went back to work.

"Nice reduction," Fiona commented.

"Thanks, can you hand me the drill?" He checked the bit to make sure it was the correct size. Then he began drilling a hole perpendicular to the main fracture line. "Damn, this is hard bone," he said as smoke began drifting from the drill site.

"This will help." Fiona grabbed the bulb irrigator and squirted saline, cooling the bone and drill bit.

"Thanks," he said. Once a hole had been drilled across the fracture site, he measured its depth and called for a screw the same length. "Put it on power." The scrub tech fastened a screwdriver into the drill chuck and handed it to him with the proper length screw. Mark powered the screw into the bone, stopping just before it was seated. "Hand screwdriver," he said, giving the drill back to the tech. He did the final tightening with the handheld screwdriver. "Don't want to strip it," he said.

"Nice compression," Fiona commented.

Mark put in several more interfragmentary screws and applied two stainless steel plates. A half hour later they were directing their attention to the canon bone. Mark pointed to the surface of the fetlock joint. "Look at that."

"The joint surface is cracked," Fiona said.

"Better place a couple of screws. If he were to walk without them, the joint surface could split apart." He placed two screws a centimeter above and parallel to the joint surface. Above this, a three-inch gap in the bone looked like a large divot carved out by a sand wedge. "It's time to see if the CT scans were accurate." Mark turned and looked at Claire. He held out his hands. Once again, she approached and opened the bioreactor lid. This time Mark passed a five-inch square container to the scrub tech, who gingerly placed it on the back table.

Mark played with the retractors, adjusting his exposure. "You may have to pull some traction in order for me to get it to drop in."

"No problem," Fiona said.

"Hand me the specimen." Mark peeled the lid off. He held the bone graft with both hands and inspected it. "Perfect. It's like the actual piece of missing bone." He pried the long vertical fracture line open a few millimeters and attempted to get the piece to key in. "Fiona, pull some traction, please."

She grasped the hoof covered in sterile drapes and pulled. "Need more?"

"No, that's good." He used a bone hook to distract the fragments several more millimeters, and the piece clicked into place. "Beautiful," was all he said and stepped away.

"My goodness, I would've never believed it," Fiona said.

He applied a bone clamp to keep the graft from displacing. "Let me see those plates." The tech handed him several options and Mark gave her two back, keeping the one he wanted. "Drill." Twenty minutes later he was spreading the stem-cell-Wnt-protein concoction over the surface of the bone. "Voilà. Anatomic reduction."

"If he's ever going to run again, the sesamoid has to be perfect, too."

"Extend the joint," Mark said.

Fiona again grasped Hyperion's hoof and straightened the fetlock joint. This took tension off the suspensory apparatus and allowed Mark to bring the two halves of the sesamoid bone together. "Pointed bone clamp," he said, glancing at the surgical tech. She handed him the instrument. "Now for the magic." He reached for the container with the stem cell graft and spread it onto the fractured surfaces of the sesamoid bone. "We're lucky the jockey stopped him from walking after the injury. This could have been a lot worse. Once the sesamoid breaks, the suspensory ligament goes and the canon bone drives down onto the long pastern like a piston."

"Or a log splitter," Fiona added.

"The medical staff had him in a Kimzey Splint on the track," Claire said.

Mark applied the clamp across the sesamoid, pinching the fracture fragments together. The two halves keyed into place like puzzle pieces. "Keep the fetlock extended," he said. "If the joint flexes, it'll pull the fragments apart." Fiona nodded. "Give me a guide pin for a cannulated screw." The tech handed him the loaded drill. He advanced it through the bone perpendicular to the fracture so that just the tip and first couple of threads protruded through the other side. He then repeated the process, placing a second guide pin one inch apart and parallel to the first.

"Measuring device." He inserted the device over the first pin and measured the portion of the wire buried in the bone. "Fifty-four-millimeter screw. I'll take the cannulated drill." Fiona steadied the pin while he inserted the drill bit over the wire. He applied pressure and pulled the trigger, creating a path for the hollow stainless steel screw. With the wire in place, he inserted the hollow screw over it and began turning. Each turn of the screwdriver came with the distinct squawk of metal twisting into hard bone. Mark gripped the clamp to counteract the torque as the screw was advanced. He took a break and shook his hand. "It's like marble. They need to redesign these screwdrivers with bigger grips."

"Don't strip the head," Fiona said.

Mark smiled behind his mask. "Thanks."

"Sorry, but I had to remind you," said Fiona.

"I understand." When both screws were in place, he called for the titanium cable. This was threaded through the screws in a figure-eight pattern, crossing over the top of the bone. A tensioning instrument was used to tighten the cable, and the two ends were securely fastened with a titanium crimp. Mark then threaded the excess cable through a cutting device and squeezed the handle. He handed the cut piece of cable to the surgical tech then looked at Fiona. "Gently let the joint flex." No one breathed as the fetlock was taken through a partial range of motion. It held. Mark held out his gloved hand and Fiona shook it. "Congratulations."

"Now comes the hard part, waking him safely," she responded. Mark spread the rest of the stem cell preparation around the tissues and helped Fiona close the wound. Once the bandages were on, they reapplied the Kimzey Splint that held the fetlock joint immobile in extension.

"We can use the 3D printers to make a custom splint in a few days," Mark said as he tore the paper surgical gown from his body. The surgical team began to prepare the patient for the pool recovery system.

"Beautiful work," Claire said, coming to his side.

"Wouldn't have been possible without you," he said and held out his hand.

She shook it then pulled him close and put her arm around his waist. "Translational medicine at its finest."

The electric hoist hummed as Hyperion was lifted into the air. This time a team of four carried the rubber raft and placed Hyperion's legs into the sleeves and fastened it to the sling. Next, the horse and raft were moved over the water and gently lowered until Hyperion was floating and his head lay supported on the inflated rubber pillow.

"I'm not sure I want to watch this," Mark said.

"Why?"

"If he goes crazy coming out of anesthesia, he could tear up everything we just did."

"You're serious?" Claire asked.

Fiona, who stood in front of them, turned around. "I've seen horses ruin themselves waking up from general anesthesia. They can break other limbs and destroy successful surgeries. This worries me more than the operation."

"Can't you give them something to keep them calm?" Claire asked.

"The pool recovery is the key. A horse coming out of anesthesia is like a foal coming out of a womb. It wants to breathe on its own and thrashes about trying to stand up. With this system the water keeps him safe until he regains his wits."

Several minutes later Hyperion shook his head and thrashed in the water. Underwater cameras allowed them to view his legs during the wake-up procedure. There was no contact, and over the next half hour, he settled down.

"I think he's out of the woods," Fiona said as the winches began hoisting Hyperion from the pool. "I'll change his bandages tomorrow and give you an update on his condition. When do you think he can put weight on it?"

"If he responds like our other patients, I'd say it would be safe in two or three days as long as he's in the splint," Mark replied.

HOBBS WAS WAITING NEXT to the statue of Secretariat. He smiled and walked toward Mark and Claire, both in street clothes now. "I spoke with Dr. Montgomery. She said the operation was a success."

"It went as well as could be expected," Mark replied.

"Don't be such a pessimist. It went bloody fantastic," Claire said as she shook Hobbs's hand.

"I have your bags in the car, and the plane is waiting to take you home. What will you do now?"

"I have an orthopedic practice I need to get back to."

Claire remained silent and Hobbs looked at her. "What about you, my dear? What will you do?"

"I'm not sure. My lab will have to be rebuilt. That'll take at least six months, maybe a year. There's a ton of work to do on Endovancin. I can't wait that long. Know anyone with an unused cell biology lab?"

Hobbs chuckled as he held the car door for her. "I wish I did. I'll build you one right here if you want."

"Thank you, but I have a few options I'm considering."

THIRTY-THREE

SATURDAY, APRIL 15TH

Wilson Andrews Equine Research Center, Roanoke, VA

A WARM SPRING breeze tugged at Claire's long hair as she leaned against the chest-high railing that circled the half-mile dirt racetrack. She and Mark stood next to Hobbs and Grant watching the spectacle before them. Grant's foot was in a protective boot and he stood supported by two crutches. Fiona wore knee-high riding boots and a helmet and led a bay stallion with a white diamond patch on his forehead toward them. Hyperion. His legs were wrapped, but there was no trace of lameness.

"I'm not believing this," said Grant.

"Believe it," replied Hobbs. "He's made a lot of progress during your hospitalization."

"The muscle-priming infusions are working better than I expected," Mark said as Fiona stopped in front of them. "This is astounding." The majestic animal snorted and shook his head. His black mane flopped back and forth and he swished his tail. Claire held out a peppermint and he gobbled it from her hand as she rubbed his forehead.

"He's put on about fifty pounds since you saw him," Fiona said.

"Wow, in just two weeks," Mark responded.

"That sounds like a lot, but it's only about one and a half percent of his body weight."

"It's a start," said Claire.

"The effects of Juvanimab are gone. His infection disappeared a few days after starting Endovancin," Fiona told them.

"How long have you been walking him?" Claire asked.

"I took Mark's recommendation and started letting him put weight on it three days after the surgery. The next day, I removed the sling and let him stand in his stall. From there, we started walking a couple of times a day. Short distances at first. Gradually increasing up to a mile. He wanted more. I felt like I was holding him back."

"It's hard to believe, but judging from his latest x-rays, he *is* healed. What's your plan with the Bethesda treatments?" Mark inquired.

"Twice a day," Fiona said.

"I think he means what's your endpoint?" Claire asked.

"I'll stop them when he returns to his preinjury weight."

"How much does he have to go?" Mark asked.

"Another fifty pounds."

"How have you been training him?" Grant questioned.

"Last week, I put him in a ring with a rope attached to his bridle and let him trot in circles. I've increased that to a cantor, and he seems to be fine. I saddled him on Monday and we've been out on the track every morning since."

"I still can't believe what I'm seeing," Grant said as he reached for Hyperion's bridle and rubbed his face. "I would have bet my life this horse was doomed."

"He was close," said Claire.

Fiona led Hyperion over to the mounting block and checked the tension of the cinch and the stirrups a final time. She mounted with the grace of an expert equestrian. Mark pulled the block away as she gripped the reins and settled into the saddle. "Come on, boy. Let's show them what you can do." She made several clicking sounds with her mouth and touched her heels to Hyperion's sides. He responded with vigor and began to trot around the track in a slow two-beat gait.

"The opposite front and back legs are off the ground at the same time," Hobbs pointed out to Claire. "He's trotting."

Fiona posted in the saddle in perfect rhythm. They made several laps before she upped the tempo to a canter and Hyperion extended his limbs.

"She's got him on a nice left lead," Grant commented. "He looks fantastic. Is this the same horse that ran in the Rebel Stakes?"

"You should know. You've played a big role in this," Hobbs said and let out a laugh. "My phone hasn't stopped ringing since the *Sports Illustrated* piece came out. I had to shut it off."

"It's a lot more attention than we're used to," Mark said.

Grant shifted on his crutches. "You two deserve most of the credit."

Claire placed her hands on her hips and smiled. She watched Hobbs video the horse and rider with his phone. "What are you thinking?"

"How to contain my optimism," he said, stepping back from the railing. He touched the screen to zoom in as they headed into the final turn. "If he continues on this schedule, he'll be galloping in a day or two. That's when we'll get an idea of what he's capable of."

"Surely you're not thinking of . . ." Claire said.

"Letting him run?"

"I was going to say race."

"That's *exactly* what I plan to do. A Derby rematch with Rampage, provided he doesn't have any setbacks."

"It's possible," Mark said. "He's showing remarkable progress."

"Unbelievable progress," Grant added.

"What's the rush?" Claire asked. "Why risk a setback?"

Hobbs slipped the phone into his pocket and turned to her.

"Because, my dear, we have to. The Kentucky Derby is for *three-year-old* Thoroughbreds. Every year over forty thousand Thoroughbreds are born and registered. Only twenty will get a chance to run in the Derby three years later. It's his one and only chance. Next year, he'll be too old. It's now or never."

"But don't horses have to qualify? Isn't that why he was in Hot Springs?" Claire asked.

"He's already qualified," Hobbs explained. "Qualifying started last year. Hyperion won Derby Prep races in September and October. His victory in the BC Juvenile last November gave him enough points to get into the field."

Claire tilted her head and raised an eyebrow. "BC?"

"Breeder's Cup," Hobbs said. "He's earned forty points, which should put him in the top twenty."

Fiona slowed Hyperion to a trot and two laps later walked him over to the group of spectators. "Simply magnificent. He is a champion." Sweat foamed from under his saddle blanket and from around his bridle.

"I want new x-rays," Mark said.

"Why? You just watched him run. What's an x-ray going to tell you that this didn't?" Fiona asked.

"Because he can't talk to me. He can't tell me how he feels. Clinically, he looks fine. I want to double-check how the fractures are healing."

MARK ENLARGED the image once more, looking for any signs of dark areas around the screw threads. "Well, are you satisfied?" Fiona asked. They stood crowded around the x-ray monitor, inspecting the images just acquired using the portable digital machine.

Grant stepped back from the viewing screen. "There're no signs of any lucency. If it weren't for the hardware in his leg, you'd have a tough time convincing me there'd been a fracture."

Mark pointed to the radiograph. "Except for that. Look at the cortical bone. It's twice as dense as before."

"He's not on any pain meds, is he?" Claire asked.

"Not a chance, not even bute. Hyperion is totally clean. I would never put him at risk like that," Fiona said.

"Nor would I," Grant said. "That's a surefire way to kill a horse. If you mask their pain with drugs, they'll destroy themselves running, even with broken limbs."

"He still has a problem," Fiona said. The others looked at her. "It's nothing major, but I think the sesamoid cable is bothering him."

"Why do you say that?" Grant asked.

"Because when I rub him down, he doesn't like it when I touch the back of his fetlock. It's sensitive. You can feel the wire and crimp under his skin."

"Humans have the same problem," Mark said. "When I fix a broken patella or elbow, the bones are directly under the skin. There's no muscle padding, so the hardware irritates the tissues."

"Can we take it out?" Fiona asked. "I think it's slowing him down."

Mark drummed his fingers on the table for a moment. "Normally, I wouldn't take it out for months, but we're charting new ground. From what I see on these x-rays, he's healed enough. Take the cable out but leave the screws."

"Let's do it toward the end of next week. I'd feel better about that," Grant said.

"That doesn't give us much time before he leaves for Churchill Downs." Hobbs stood and walked toward the door. "If he's going to run, I want him there by Tuesday of race week at the latest."

"We can do it with local anesthetic and IV sedation and a couple of small incisions," Fiona said.

Grant glanced at her and smiled. "Then do it."

———————

MULLION SLAPPED the folded magazine against his knee. "Have you read this?" He opened the racing monthly and pointed to the cover. "They're making it out to be a miracle. He may run in the Derby."

"It *is* a miracle," Sorenson said.

"No, it isn't. It's a total disaster. How is that beast still alive? He should've been put down on the track."

Sorenson remained seated in the deserted grandstand overlooking the vacant track. "You're incredible. Rampage just won the Arkansas Derby in record time and you collected a six-hundred-thousand-dollar purse less than an hour ago. I thought you'd be in a better mood."

"I don't give a damn about that. Today's race was a stepping-stone. It means nothing if we don't win the Derby. If Hyperion makes an appearance at Churchill Downs in three weeks, even if he doesn't race, we'll be upstaged. He'll have the spotlight. This is not possible. I saw the x-rays after his injury. Hyperion should be dead."

"He's not and so what? Who cares? Rampage will throttle him. He's pathetic and half lame. No one gives a crap about a broke-down nag. It's publicity for Hobbs so he can say 'what if?' and jack his stud fees."

"He'll steal *my* horse's glory."

"Win the Triple Crown and you'll have all the glory you need."

"What if he's actually well enough to win? What if he wins the Preakness or the Belmont? There goes the Triple Crown," Mullion said.

"You're one paranoid son of a bitch."

"And you're paid to prevent it."

"No one can do that." Sorenson took another drag from his cigarette and flicked the ashes on the stadium floor.

"Look, we don't need any additional attention. The media will be on this like Seabiscuit and War Admiral."

"That's good. You'll have your fifteen minutes of fame," Sorenson said.

"I don't want attention. Especially from the media. They'll start dredging up stuff that needs to stay buried. Stuff that'll bring unwanted attention. Hyperion will *not* run in the Derby. Make sure he doesn't. Finish the job Coleman couldn't."

"How am I supposed to do that?"

"You're the doctor. You figure it out." Mullion stood and tossed the magazine into Sorenson's lap. "I suggest you read this. Grant and those other two are magicians."

"You worry about the shipment and I'll take care of the horse."

"I'm not concerned about the shipment," Mullion said. "I'm worried about Hyperion winning the damn Kentucky Derby."

"Not worried? You think you can snap your fingers and a thousand kilos of opium product is going to appear? We need that money if you want this operation to continue."

"I don't need a lecture on our capital situation. Especially from R & D."

"Well, I didn't sign up to be the chief research officer of a black-market opioid manufacturer. I came on board to develop potential blockbuster drugs like Juvanimab and Endovancin."

"Which is what you're doing. It takes money to develop a pharmaceutical portfolio like that. A lot of money. I've raised as much capital as I can. Something has to fund the development of power-house drugs. We can only take on so much debt. And we're not going to be acquired by Pfizer or Merck or some other giant. This is *my* operation and I'm going to grow it. Be grateful there's a huge market for oxycodone and fentanyl. We will continue to grow that market. Be thankful we have an invisible plant that can make them, and get on your knees and bow your head because we've created the greatest drug-smuggling and distribution operation since Pablo Escobar ran the Medellín cartel."

Sorenson smiled. "You made your point."

"Don't worry about the shipment. It'll arrive, and the Run for the Roses will provide the perfect cover."

THIRTY-FOUR

FRIDAY, MAY 5TH

Churchill Downs, Louisville, Kentucky

THE EASTERN SKY turned a lighter shade of purple as dawn broke over the racetrack that had hosted the Kentucky Derby since the first race in 1875. Temperatures reached into the fifties about the time the sun announced its arrival on the horizon. Mark and Claire strode over the asphalt that led from the Fourth Street entrance gate to the barns on the backside of the track. The ancient earthy scent of hay, manure, and horses drifted in the air. Hooves clopped in the alleyways as stable hands moved about the sprawling complex, leading horses to and from the track. Workers hosed down their steeds after morning workouts while others mucked out stalls. This was the sunrise routine at Churchill Downs. Horses and riders had been exercising since well before dawn on a track illuminated by high-intensity LED lights. As with every morning of race season, trainers leaned against the railing gauging their athletes and snapping stopwatches.

Mark jammed his hands into his jeans pockets and glanced

around. "Check this place out. There's a school, a church, and at least thirty separate barns. Inside the fence, it's like a small city."

"Sort of a step back in time, almost medieval, and there's the castle," Claire said, pointing across the track at the grandstand with the famous twin spires. They walked down a paved road between rows of stables.

"There it is." Mark pointed to the barn with the plaque D. Wayne Lukas Racing Stables. "Worth said he was lucky one of Mr. Lukas's horses was sold last week. He offered the empty stall to Hyperion."

"That was a nice gesture from a competitor."

"They've been friends for a long time. I think Worth helped him when he was just starting in the business."

Claire's ponytail whipped around as she turned. "There's your proof. It pays to be nice."

"I never doubted that."

She stood on tiptoes and kissed his cheek. "I know."

The barns were almost identical single-story buildings about one hundred by fifty feet. A small office or storage area was located at each end. Stalls occupied the middle of the structure, ten per side, most with horses munching on alfalfa that hung from baskets next to the Dutch doors. Each structure had a green-shingled roof that extended over the front and back, creating a ten-foot-wide covered walkway around the stalls. It was on this path that stable hands led horses, circling the barn, cooling them down after their morning workout. As Mark and Claire approached the Lukas stable, they saw the green sign that read HYPERION in white letters attached above his stall.

"There's Fiona," Claire said, pointing out a woman wearing a red riding vest. She waved as she and Mark covered the remaining twenty yards at a brisk pace. Fiona smiled and embraced them both.

"Welcome. Any trouble finding us?" she asked.

"No problems," Claire said.

"We took a cab from the hotel but almost didn't make it through the gate. I thought the cops were going to frisk us," Mark said.

Fiona chuckled. "Security has to be tight. These horses are too valuable."

Hyperion looked out from the stall. "How's he been?" Claire reached up and rubbed his face. He whinnied and nuzzled her hand. "That's a good boy."

"His leg has been perfect. The track vets have x-rayed it and examined him every day. There's no sign of lameness. I'm more worried about his conditioning. A mile and an eighth is a long way."

"Is this his last training session?" Claire asked.

"I haven't decided. We're scheduled for eight twenty this morning. We'll see how he does."

"Would you train him on race day?"

Fiona slipped on his bridle. "It won't affect his conditioning, but he likes this routine. I'll probably get him on the track early."

Mark reached up and rubbed Hyperion's massive jaw. "Has his performance plateaued? Or have you seen improvement?"

Fiona smiled. "He keeps getting better. It's a little freaky. His times are decreasing daily, and I haven't really turned him loose yet."

"That's great. Still giving him the infusions?"

Fiona frowned and shook her head. "We stopped them last week. They wouldn't let us continue giving them."

Mark knelt and examined Hyperion's right rear leg. The horse stood motionless as he ran his hand over the reconstructed limb. "Any problems when you removed the sesamoid cable? I didn't hear from you, so I take it everything went well."

Fiona held the bridle tight and stepped close to the horse. "It went perfect. A little xylazine, ketorolac, and ketamine followed by lidocaine and Valium. That little cocktail works wonders. No need for a general anesthetic. After he was sedated, I made a two-centimeter incision and had the cable out in five minutes. We dosed him with Endovancin a half hour before we started."

Mark stood up. "It doesn't look like you had any wound healing problems."

"I took the sutures out Monday."

"It looks great."

"Where is Grant?" Claire asked.

"He and Worth should be here in a few minutes. They want to watch today's session."

HOBBS, Grant, Claire, and Mark leaned on the aluminum railing at the track's edge along the backstretch. Hobbs had binoculars trained on Hyperion and Fiona as they made it through the clubhouse turn. The sun was shining and the track lights were off.

"Did you see that?" Hobbs asked, still holding the glasses to his eyes. "It was a perfect lead switch as he came out of the turn. Fiona has him in top form."

Claire turned to face Hobbs as he lowered the binoculars. "What happened to his old trainer?"

"Travis?" Hobbs said. "The gentleman you met in Hot Springs?"

Claire nodded. "Why isn't he here?"

"After the accident, he asked to be released from his contract. There was no need to keep him on. He's a high-profile trainer. His services are in demand. Everyone thought Hyperion was done, so I let him go. Another owner hired him. You'll probably see him around the track. One of their horses is in the field."

"Then, who is training Hyperion?" Mark asked. He took the glasses as Hobbs laughed.

"Fiona, of course. After what he's been through, I doubt there's anyone more qualified, *and* she's doing a great job," Hobbs said. "I've had to answer a few questions about my choice but have no regrets."

"It's nice when your trainer is also your vet. Especially in Hyperion's case," Claire commented.

"She's not going to ride him, is she?" asked the young man who was walking toward them. The group turned to look at the man. "Brandon Rabon. *Sports Illustrated.* Can I ask you a few questions, Mr. Hobbs?" He extended his right hand and held out his press credentials with the left.

"Off the record?" Mark asked.

"Come on. A guy's got to earn a living." Rabon was dressed in khaki slacks with a long-sleeve button-down shirt and sweater unzipped at the neck.

Claire moved in front of Mark, separating him from the reporter. Grant turned and took the binoculars from him and trained them on the horse and rider, who were now moving into the final turn.

"It's okay. I'm happy to discuss our team with you, Mr. Rabon."

"Thank you, sir. Can I get everyone's names?" He took out a notepad and pen and began to scribble while Hobbs made the introductions.

"Edgar Contreras, his jockey, arrives later today from California. After Hyperion was injured, he naturally sought employment elsewhere. He has had other obligations until this morning. Contreras is one of the most experienced professional jockeys in the business and knows this horse well. Dr. Montgomery's been doing a fine job in his absence."

"Contreras . . . last year's Belmont winner?"

"That's right. Edgar's ridden Hyperion many times."

Rabon watched the horse and rider on the backstretch. "They look good out there, but why risk it? This could backfire on you."

"What do you mean?"

"Many of my readers think there's a black cloud hanging over the horse racing industry. That the animals are treated without regard to their well-being. They're being used as pawns in the gambling industry to make a buck and keep racetracks profitable. They're drugged to mask pain and injury so they'll run until they break down. Then, they're euthanized. Is that what's happening here? You'd risk Hyperion's life for this race? What if something happens to him? Right now, you've got the admiration of the horse racing industry. Maybe even the nation. You might flush that down the toilet."

Hobbs bristled. "You have a point, Mr. Rabon. You could make a similar argument for several other professional sports where athletes, while not euthanized, sustain permanent physical and mental damage. All great endeavors involve risk. I believe Theodore Roosevelt said it best in his "Man in the Arena" speech. If you're unfamiliar with it, I urge you to look it up. However, I have no intention of flushing anything. It seems like once or twice a year, some high-profile media outlet runs a piece on the dangers and cruelty of the horse racing industry. They highlight the number of horses killed or maimed. That's a spotlight that needs to shine on cruel and unethical individuals. It's the noble calling of your profession to expose that sort of thing. I can assure you it is *not* the case here. Every horse is tested for banned substances multiple times before and after every race. Hyperion has received the best medical care in the world. Better than many humans. He's out here running because he's medically sound. He's received treatment under the supervision of two equine veterinarians, an orthopedic surgeon, and the world's leading expert on the anatomy and physiology of bone. How could I give him any better care?"

"I'm not questioning your team's credentials. I want to know if he's ready to race, or are we going to witness another Eight Belles or Prairie Bayou on Saturday?" Rabon asked.

"God forbid," Hobbs said, taking a deep breath and sitting down on a nearby bench.

"That's *not* going to happen," Mark said, stepping forward with clenched fists.

"How do you know? Can you guarantee it?" the reporter questioned.

Mark's jaw tightened. "I can't guarantee anything, but the chances of Hyperion refracturing his leg are minuscule. He may not win. Another freak accident could happen, but it won't be because of his right rear leg."

"Mr. Rabon," Hobbs continued, "the treatment Hyperion received someday may save hundreds or thousands of horses each year. You're witnessing a miracle."

Claire interrupted. "Sit down and let me give you some background on our research." Fifteen minutes later, the reporter was still scribbling notes and intermittently shaking his pen. "Any more questions?" she asked him.

Rabon shook his head and finished writing. "That's enough for now. Can I call you later if I think of anything?"

"Of course. Here's my card." Claire handed him a business card and Rabon placed it in his wallet. When he looked up, a broad grin spread across his face. "He could just pull this off."

"We sure hope so," Claire said as she uncrossed her legs and stood up. "We wouldn't be here otherwise."

"Can you send me pictures of the broken leg before and after the surgery?"

"That's up to Mr. Hobbs. He's the patient's owner and guardian of his medical information."

"Of course. It would be my pleasure. Give Dr. Hodgson your number," said Hobbs. "She can text them to you later. You don't mind, do you?"

"Not at all," Claire said.

Grant let the binoculars hang from his neck as Fiona and Hyperion slowed to a walk and stopped in front of them. Sweat foamed from around the edges of the saddle and the corners of his mouth like shaving cream. He took baby steps backward and sideways as Fiona held his reins tight. His chest expanded and deflated like huge bellows moving great volumes of air in and out of his lungs. "Excellent workout. He's starting to look like a Derby champion again," Grant said.

"*Starting?*" Fiona said as she dismounted. "He'll always be a champion. I'm going to give him a bath and walk him for a while. Anyone want to join us?"

"We will," Claire said as she took Mark's hand.

"Dr. Grant, can I ask you a few questions?" Rabon said.

Grant sat on the bench and put his fracture boot up on the rail. "Make it fast, son. My foot is starting to hurt."

Before Rabon could begin the interview, they became aware of thumping hoofbeats growing louder. Hyperion threw his head, neighed, and tugged at his reins. Talking ceased as the commotion escalated and the ground vibrated. They turned toward the track as a huge raven horse ridden by a jockey clothed in black thundered past. His flying tail and muscular haunches were all that could be seen above the dirt cloud as he streaked down the back straightaway.

"Did you see that?" Hobbs said.

"Hard to miss," Fiona replied.

"That beast is enormous."

"And fast," Rabon said. "Did you feel the ground? My teeth chattered. There's no doubt about his bloodline."

Mark raised an eyebrow while looking at Rabon.

"He's a direct descendant of Man o' War."

Fiona reached up and scratched Hyperion's ear and patted his jaw. "Settle down. We're not scared of him. You're our Seabiscuit."

Hyperion shook his head, flinging lather into the air.

"About the same size, too," Rabon said. "What is he, about fifteen hands?"

"Fifteen and a half," Hobbs replied.

"Rampage is over seventeen," Rabon said as the black horse and rider entered the backstretch on the far side of the track. "He looks like the Grim Reaper."

"Talk it up. It'll make your story better," Mark said. "Come on, Fiona. Let's cool him down. We can both use a nice walk back to the stables."

Half an hour later, they were standing on a cement slab near Hyperion's barn. Steam radiated from his coat as Fiona, Mark, and Claire sponged him with warm soapy water and rinsed him clean. Hyperion stood still. Fiona squeegeed the excess water from his body with the sweat scraper. He whipped his tail several times. Water drops flew like rain.

"Settle down, boy," Claire said, rubbing the spray from her eye. "Hand me the hose." Mark laughed. She dipped her face in the stream and wiped the water from her eyes. "Like I needed a shower." She and Fiona joined in the laughter.

Mark walked to the front of the horse and began scraping Hyperion's neck and shoulders. He watched water spill off the plastic tool and onto the ground. Then, he looked up and stopped smiling. He stood straight and stared past Hyperion at the barn on the other side of an eight-foot-high chain-link fence. A sign hung at the end of the barn that read BONSANTOS STABLES. The name struck a chord in his memory. The movement of two men in the barn had captured his attention. A short Asian man walked from a screened doorway at the far end of the barn. He looked like a jockey. He was following a man wearing a sport coat and a fedora. A breeze caught the hat and it toppled from his semibald pate. The Asian man bent over and plucked it from the ground as it began to tumble. He brushed the brim and handed it back to the other, who replaced it on his head. They turned and walked away before Mark could see their faces.

"What's over there?"

Fiona looked up. "Those are the quarantine barns for international entries. Horses from other countries are kept there until medically cleared to compete. They've been here for three weeks and have all passed. That's where Rampage is stabled."

THIRTY-FIVE

FRIDAY, MAY 5TH

Louisville, Kentucky

SORENSON REMOVED his hat as he entered the foyer of the presidential suite of the Greenwood Hotel. Lopsang made a respectful bow and closed the door. Sorenson strode across the marble entrance into the living room and halted in front of the coffee table. He smiled down at Jeffery Mullion, who reclined on an antique Victorian sofa. "I take it the package arrived."

"Hello, Neil." Mullion grimaced as he adjusted his position. "For what they're charging for this place, you'd think they'd have furniture that doesn't cause back spasms." He motioned with his glass, half filled with ice cubes and Kentucky bourbon. "It's in the coat closet. Keep it away from me."

Sorenson crossed the room and pulled open the closet door. He paused, stunned by the assortment of women's clothes. "I didn't know you had a girlfriend." He leafed through a row of dresses covered in clear plastic as if they had just been delivered from the dry cleaners.

"What?"

Sorenson looked over his shoulder and smiled. "Jeff, you're full of surprises. I had no idea. Where's your friend? Her entire wardrobe's hanging in here."

"Don't worry about that, you haven't met her."

"Where's the box?" Sorenson asked as he continued rifling through the clothes.

"Lopsang put it in there. I saw him." Mullion placed his empty glass on the coffee table and rose from the couch. "Be careful, don't wrinkle them."

"Is it serious? How long have you been seeing her?"

"We met in Paris, so mind your business." He nudged Sorenson out of the way. "It's in the corner." He bent over, moved several pairs of high heels, and picked up a four-inch square brown box.

"Excellent," Sorenson said, cradling the container.

"You're sure it'll work?" Mullion asked, taking a new drink from his butler.

Sorenson took out a pocketknife, flipped open the blade, and slit the edges. He tossed Styrofoam peanuts onto the floor and plucked a small vial of liquid from the box. "Ah, very nice," he said, twirling the bottle. "It'll work. Fifty micrograms of this stuff would incapacitate a rhino."

"I don't want him dead," Mullion said.

"I thought you wanted him euthanized?"

"I did right after his injury, but not now. What is that stuff, anyway?"

Sorenson's mouth tightened into a grin. "A developmental project of mine. One of our scientists is working on a long-acting local anesthetic."

Mullion raised his eyebrows. "A numbing agent?"

"Exactly, like Marcaine or lidocaine. Except the one he's working on lasts four to five days, not a couple of hours," Sorenson explained. "It's designed to reduce the need for narcotics after surgery or trauma."

"That's the last thing I want. Nothing should interfere with our opioids." He raised his glass and took a sip.

"Relax. This drug, if it passes clinical trials, will be another goose laying golden eggs. Every surgeon and ER doc in the country will be begging for it. It will add to the portfolio of our legitimate products. Your Colombian pipeline isn't going away. Addicts will always need their fix. Don't worry. This drug will have no effect on street sales. Plus, we want to play both sides of the fence."

"You better hope so," Mullion said and was silent for a few moments. He stirred his drink with the tip of his index finger. "So, how's a numbing agent going to incapacitate a horse?"

"This isn't the numbing agent. It's the precursor material. The active ingredient is brevetoxin PbTx-2."

"What the hell is that?"

"It opens sodium ion channels."

"English, please," said Mullion.

"It causes a short circuit in the digestive system," he answered, pulling a cigarette from his silver case and letting it dangle from the corner of his mouth. "A massive disruption of cell function resulting in nausea, vomiting, blurred vision, muscle weakness, and cardiac arrhythmias. It mimics a condition in horses called hyperkalemic periodic paralysis, or HYPP."

"Put that thing away. There's no smoking in this hotel." Mullion flicked his wrist, clinking the ice in his glass. He smiled as he watched the liquid swirl. "HYPP for Hyperion. Look, I don't care about the details. I don't want to *know* the details. I want that nag so sick he has trouble standing in his stall, but don't kill him."

"What do you care if he dies?"

"I don't. But if he dies, it will generate public sympathy. I don't want anything detracting from Rampage's victory."

Sorenson shook his head and lit the cigarette. He blew a plume of smoke toward Mullion. "He won't die. I'm not giving him a lethal dose. It's more like the illness you get from eating a bad oyster. He'll be losing it from both ends. Done in by diarrhea."

Mullion waved his hand, fanning the smoke away from his face. "Disgusting."

"It'll make him so weak and dehydrated, he won't be able to do anything."

Mullion coughed. "Do it, and put that thing out."

"You can afford the fine."

"I'd better not see him on the track in the morning. Hyperion has done his last training session at Churchill Downs. Do you have your veterinary staff credentials?"

"Of course," Sorenson said as he stubbed out his cigarette in an empty glass on the bar.

"Lopsang will go with you, in case someone gets nosy." Mullion drained his glass.

"I can do it," said Sorenson. "You don't trust me?"

Mullion shook his head. "Lopsang makes Bruce Lee look like an amateur . . . and yes, I don't trust you."

Sorenson snorted. "Then you do it."

"Relax, I'm joking. He's insurance. Incapacitate Hyperion and get back here.

"Don't worry, by tomorrow afternoon he'll be too sick to saddle."

"I'm already looking forward to the post parade without that gnome, Hobbs."

FIONA STOOD in the stall next to Hyperion, brushing his mahogany coat. Every muscle rippled under his skin. All four lower limbs were wrapped from fetlocks to hooves with bandages. They looked like white socks and matched the white star on his forehead. His big brown eyes blinked, and he shook his proud head. Thurman squatted to inspect his right rear leg once again. There was no sign of tenderness when he rubbed the limb. The incisions were healed, and his pelage had regrown where it had been shorn for surgery. If Thurman looked hard, he could just make out the top of a scar above the wrapping. Mark grabbed two fists of fresh straw, rubbed them together, and held it close to his face. The odor of hay and horses evoked primal emotions. It was an earthy smell, natural and reminiscent of outdoors, the polar opposite of his usual world of sterile operating rooms and research labs. Mark rubbed the healed fetlock joint, and Hyperion paid no attention to him.

"He has more muscle definition than Arnold in his prime," Mark said.

"They have the same motto," Fiona replied.

He looked at her with brows knit then smiled. "I'll be back," they said in unison and laughed.

"He's still about two stones down," Fiona replied.

Mark stroked the healed leg. "What's that? Twenty pounds?"

"Almost thirty."

"Will that hurt him?"

"I don't know. It's a fraction less than his preinjury weight. It may help. He's leaner and quicker."

"I hope you're right."

"Your training is almost over, big guy," she said to the horse. "Tomorrow, we'll see what you can do."

"Think he's ready?" asked Dusty Rhodes, who walked up with Laura and Claire and leaned on the door to the stall. The couple had flown from Little Rock and arrived that afternoon.

"Hey, glad you made it," said Mark, rising.

"Good to see you." Fiona hugged Laura then Dusty. "He's as ready as we can make him. It's all about this, now." She tapped her fist to her chest several times. "He has more heart than any of them."

"That's untrainable," Dusty said. "The mark of a champion."

Claire reached over the stall door and rubbed his nose. "He's got it. You can see it in his eyes."

"How was the trip from Little Rock?" Mark asked.

"Easy flight. No problems." For the next half hour, they talked about Hyperion and speculated about his chances of winning. After a pause Dusty looked at his watch. "It's almost five. I don't know about any of you, but I missed lunch. Let's meet in our room at the hotel for cocktails. I have seven o'clock dinner reservations at Jack Fry's. You're all invited."

Laura looked at Claire. "He makes a mean mint julep."

"Thanks. We'll take you up on that."

"You guys go on. I'm staying here," Fiona said. "I'm putting a cot in the office." She pointed to the end of the barn. "Nothing's going to happen to him from now on."

"Come with us to dinner," Laura said. "Warwick is going to meet us there."

Fiona brushed his mane. "Thanks, but I'll be playing nurse. We've come too far for anything to go wrong."

"We'll bring you something," Claire said, closing the gate after Mark exited the stall.

"I'd appreciate that."

Two hours later, the couples took Mark's rental and drove to the famous restaurant in the Highlands area of Louisville.

"I hope this place lives up to its reputation," Mark said, taking Claire's hand.

The maître d′ led them through a tight maze of tables and stopped at one in the center of the room. Next to the bar, a man sat at a vintage upright piano pounding out ragtime tunes. The dining area was crowded and boisterous on the busiest weekend of the year. Their waitress handed out menus and spoke to Dusty. She returned a few minutes later with a magnum of Schramsberg Blanc de Blancs and champagne flutes. She untwisted the wire and the cork popped into her hand.

"Shouldn't we be saving this for tomorrow?" asked Claire.

"Nonsense. We're celebrating your success," Dusty said, raising his glass toward Claire, Mark, and Grant. "A toast to a monumental veterinary achievement. Without your work and perseverance, we wouldn't be here. Congratulations and thank you."

"I'm honored but have a confession to make." Mark raised his glass toward Claire. "She deserves most of the credit. At the beginning I was against trying to save him. I thought it was too risky. I was wrong. Here's to a woman of true vision and courage."

"Here, here," said Dusty, raising his glass.

Claire smiled and touched their glasses with hers. "Thank you, but as I recall it didn't take too much arm twisting, and we couldn't have done any of it without Warwick."

"I'll be expecting Dom Pérignon tomorrow night. Here's to victory," Grant said as he raised his glass once more.

"To victory," echoed Laura. "Do you really think it could happen?"

"After all he's been through, it's a miracle he's alive and walking," Dusty said. "How could he possibly stand a chance against a horse like Rampage?"

Grant tapped the rim of his glass with the edge of his knife. "First off, let me say that he's won a victory by just getting here. No matter what happens tomorrow. Having said that, I admit I'm no expert when it comes to horse racing." He drained the last of his champagne and put the glass on the table. "But according to Fiona, Hyperion's not any slower on the track than he was before the accident. His conditioning isn't quite what it was preinjury, but I wouldn't count him out. He'll run through the hedges to win."

"You're serious?" Dusty asked.

"Damn serious. I'm putting money on him . . . to win." Grant reached for the bottle and refilled his glass.

"If you're right, then get ready for a circus. You'll all be the headline of every major sports news outlet. It'll be a tidal wave of media attention."

"Keep me out of it," Mark said. "Let Warwick have the spotlight."

"I won't take it all. You two deserve most of the credit."

"Fifteen minutes of fame is more than I want," Claire said. "Just keep the research grant money coming in, that's all I ask."

"If he wins, I doubt if you'll ever have to worry about grant funding again," quipped Dusty.

HE STOOD on the quarterdeck watching the longshoremen start to unload cargo. A man wearing a panama hat crossed the gangway ahead of them as a tropical breeze danced across the harbor. It lifted the straw hat from his head. He swiped for it but missed. The hat tumbled to the deck and landed at his feet. He bent down and grabbed it. The man said "thank you" as he read the name written in black ink on the inside label.

Mark bolted upright in bed, bug-eyed. It was pitch dark and the sound of a siren penetrated the hotel room from the streets below. His watch read ten after two.

"What is it?" Claire asked as she turned over.

"He's here," Mark whispered.

"Who's here?"

"N. Sorenson." Mark threw off the sheet and stood up. He reached for his jeans then slipped on his T-shirt.

"What are you doing?" Claire whispered.

"I'm going to check on Hyperion and Fiona."

FIONA ARRANGED her cot against the wall next to the door in the tiny office in the Lukas Stables barn. She'd wanted to set it up next to Hyperion but had been told by the security guard she couldn't sleep in the stables. He was called to another building before she'd finished gathering her stuff. When he left, she moved the makeshift bed into the trainer's office at the east end of the stable, farther away than she wanted. There, she would be invisible to the guard when he returned but would be able to keep watch during the night. Dim lights cast the barn into shadows as she made her way to Hyperion's stall.

"Good night," she whispered. The horse leaned his head down and nuzzled her face. "Go to sleep." She wondered when he did. Horses had no regular schedule like humans. They closed their eyes whenever it suited them and slept standing. She glanced at her watch. All was quiet. The stable hands would be arriving in four hours. "Get some rest. It won't be long now." Fiona walked back to the office, crawled into her cot with her boots on, and pulled the blanket over her shoulders. She fell asleep within minutes.

A steady noise registered in her consciousness. Her eyelids fluttered and she glanced at her wrist. It was less than an hour since she last looked at her watch, half past two. Then she heard the noise again. It was the sound of footsteps shuffling on the gravel outside.

A hushed voiced carried through the thin walls. "Check the other side. Let me know if you see anyone. This won't take long." The footsteps disappeared. A horse snorted and a doorknob rattled. Fiona sat up and remained silent. *Had the guard returned?*

She rose and opened the door. The stable lights were out, and she wondered if they were on a timer. She stepped into the hallway and listened. She poked her head around the corner and saw his silhouette. A man opening the door to Hyperion's stall holding something in his hands. It wasn't a guard. The beam from his flashlight snapped on and Fiona saw the syringe.

"Who are you?" she demanded. Her voice was strong and clear.

The man pivoted and the halogen beam pierced her eyes, blinding her. She brought her arm up to shield them as she approached.

"Stop! What are you doing? Help!" Fiona screamed.

He punched her and she slumped to the floor. He stood over her and struck her in the face a second time. "Shut up."

The horse whinnied and backed away. The man pointed the light on him. "Settle down, boy. I'll be gone in a second." He uncapped the syringe and moved closer, reaching for the horse's neck and then feeling for the garden-hose-sized jugular.

Fiona pushed her hair out of her face and looked up. The flashlight beam glinted off the needle. Her right hand brushed against the handle of the shovel leaning against the wall. In the shadows, she got to her knees as he held the syringe up to the light, expelling air bubbles. He steadied his hand and felt for Hyperion's jugular.

"Stop!" She took aim and then whipped the shovel downward like a lumberjack wielding an axe.

MARK DUG his hands into his jeans pockets as he made his way to the Lukas stable. It was between two and three in the morning, what he called the witching hour. He hated it. It was when evil lurked for opportunities. If he were on call at the hospital, a page from the emergency room would leave him sleepless and ruin the next day. Not many good things happened at this hour of night.

As he approached the building, he noticed an overturned chair under the streetlight near the stable. The Louisville police officer assigned to this shift must be making rounds. He set the chair upright and glanced about. A coiled water hose lay undisturbed under the faucet, but the bucket next to it was overturned and the ground surrounding it was mud. He listened to the silence for several seconds then walked toward the barn.

Hyperion's stall was on the other side of the building closest to the track. He turned into the shadows and located the hallway to the far side of the building. The horses were quiet. He came to the corner and paused. A light breeze stirred in the alleyway between the office and stalls. He moved forward then stumbled and almost fell over a large heavy object hidden in the shadows. The security guard lay motionless on the ground. Mark knelt and put his ear near the man's head, detecting stridorous shallow breaths. Warm sticky fluid matted the man's hair. He searched the body and noted the radio was absent from his belt pouch. His carotid pulse was thready. Mark wiped his hands on the ground and stood up. This man needed medical treatment fast.

A dim light escaped from around the edges of the trainer's office door. He approached and turned the door handle. "Fiona?" he whispered. No answer. Then, he heard her voice from the other side of the barn.

"Stop! What are you doing? Help!"

He bolted toward Hyperion's stall. "Fiona!"

"Help! Guards! Help!" Fiona yelled.

He dashed around the corner. Something caught between his legs. He tripped. As he fell, he glimpsed the shadow of a man. Mark twisted his body in midair as the silhouette kicked. The foot missed his head but struck his shoulder. His arm went limp. He thought his collarbone was broken. The force of the blow spun him around. He rolled with it. Pain shot through the right side of his neck and arm as he tried to stand. Another kick knocked the wind from his chest. His assailant sprang forward and struck again.

The kick glanced off his elbow that was shielding his face, and he rolled away. The small man leapt onto his back. Mark felt a forearm slide under his chin. He rolled and the man flipped over his body. The next blow cracked against his head, deafening his right ear. It was hard to focus. The figure in the shadows sprang forward.

Another head strike. Mark rolled and gripped the handle of a tool on the ground, used for mucking out stalls. It was the object the man had tripped him with. He lifted it, pointing it toward his attacker to deflect the next blow. The dark figure sprang toward him leading with a front kick. His foot struck the tool. It was almost knocked from Mark's grasp until the handle wedged against the wall. The tool twisted from his hands, and the attacker fell to the ground. Then he screamed and tried to scurry away.

Mark scrambled to his hands and knees and tried to focus his vision. The small man struggled to get to his feet. Mark reached out and grabbed the handle. His attacker screamed again. He lifted the object and saw the tines of the pitchfork protruding three inches out of the top of the man's shoe. The man tried to pull his skewered foot away, but the spikes held fast. Mark stood and stomped him senseless.

"Help!" Fiona's voice came from the other end of the stable.

He ran toward the sound of her voice and almost collided with a man cradling his forearm.

"Stop him!" she cried.

"Move out of my way," the man screamed. Mark grabbed his shirt.

"Who are you?"

"I'm a veterinarian doing my rounds. That crazy woman struck me."

"He tried to inject Hyperion with something," Fiona said, running toward them.

"Let go of me." The man jerked away and turned. The lights came on. "I'll have you arrested."

Mark's fist crashed into his jaw and he crumpled to the floor. "That's for Claire."

"Thank God you're here. He tried to drug him," Fiona said. Sorenson groaned as he began to regain consciousness. Mark saw the bloody forearm and hand angled awkwardly.

"What happened?" Before she could answer he smelled the smoke. They turned. Flames flickered from a doorway near the end of the barn. Mark turned and ran to the smoldering hay locker. The bloody pitchfork lay on the ground. His assailant was gone.

"Damn!" The smell of burning wood and straw grew stronger. The flames danced from the storage room up into the rafters. The wooden structure was ablaze.

"Fire! Fire! Get the horses out of here," Fiona screamed. They began opening stalls and leading the horses out of the building. Fiona ran to the fire alarm and pulled the lever. The building was filling with smoke as the orange flames climbed higher. The stable was becoming a raging inferno as the conflagration reached the roof.

"Hurry, we have to get them to safety," Fiona shouted as she led Hyperion out of his stall. Other people began arriving and rushed into the barn. Mark went from stall to stall opening the gates and leading the frightened animals into the road. He ran to the other end of the building toward the flames. Sirens blared in the distance and were getting louder. The heat intensified. Mark made his way into the smoke and fire. He heard the neighing of a horse to his left and squinted through the haze. He covered his face with his arm and pressed forward. The sound came again and he heard a gate rattle. The brown head of a horse appeared.

"Come on, boy, let's get out of here." He reached for the door handle. It was stuck.

The animal shook his head and began turning in the enclosed space. He stomped his front hooves. The neighing became more panicked. He kicked at the walls and reared up. Smoke billowed up throughout the rafters. The noxious haze was thickening. Mark began to cough. It was hard to breathe. His eyes burned and began tearing.

His fingers probed and found the handle. It was jammed. He twisted. It didn't move.

Think.

He stepped back and kicked. Pain shot through his heel. The gate didn't move. He moved back farther and tripped. Burning embers began to rain down. A flaming board crashed in front of him. He pushed it away as pain seared his arm. He tried to stand and felt an object leaning against the wall. He gripped the handle of a manure shovel and crawled toward the gate. The smoke was suffocating. His eyes watered. The horse reared and screamed. Mark raised the shovel and hacked at the doorknob. The flames were consuming the structure. His vision was blurred. Every breath hurt. He hacked again. The handle snapped. Again and again he struck. The knob fell to the ground.

He yanked the gate and it gave way. "Easy, boy. Settle down." He felt the animal's panic and reached out. The horse bolted, knocking him to the ground. He knelt and crawled along the path to the exit. He followed the trail of smoke pouring from the building. He felt faint and fell to the ground. Then someone grabbed his arm and pulled.

VOICES AND NOISE were all around. He opened his eyes and saw the dark blue predawn sky. A full moon beamed like a silver beacon directly overhead. He realized he was lying on a gurney next to an ambulance. Claire knelt beside him, looking away. He tried to speak. "Hey."

She turned and her ponytail spilled over his chest. She looked down at him and touched his cheek. "Don't try to talk," she said. "That's an oxygen mask. You're being treated for smoke inhalation."

He blinked then reached up and pulled the mask away from his face. "Did he get out?" He turned his head. Lights from fire trucks lit up the smoldering barn fifty yards away.

She tugged his hand and placed it by his side then adjusted his mask. "Yes, you saved him."

"Hyperion? Is he okay?"

"He's fine. Fiona got him out." He raised his hand with his thumb extended. She bent over and kissed his forehead. "Don't ever do that again. You could've been killed."

He smiled beneath the mask. "I had to." Fire trucks surrounded them. He turned his head and noticed the ambulance. His arm hurt. He looked at the bandages.

"Your arm was burned. They're taking you to the hospital." Two EMS providers approached and lifted the gurney. The wheels extended and they rolled him to the rear of the truck.

"Wait. What about the two men, Sorenson and the other guy? Do the police have them?"

"Don't know what you're talking about, bud. You're the only one we pulled out of that building." The EMS techs began pushing the gurney into the ambulance.

"We'll be right behind you. I'll see you at the hospital." Claire scrambled away from the truck as the driver closed the rear doors.

"INCREDIBLY, no one was hurt—man or horse—when early this morning, a fire broke out in the D. Wayne Lukas stables at Churchill Downs only hours before this year's Run for the Roses," the television newsman said into the camera.

"Turn it off. I can't take any more of this. I'm surrounded by morons," Mullion said as he poured a shot of bourbon into his morning coffee. "You're sure no one saw you in the lobby?"

"If they did, they didn't suspect anything. My forearm looked normal. I had my sport coat draped over it, and Lopsang walked like he was on a Sunday stroll. Not a hint of a limp. Have you seen his foot? It looks like it had a railroad spike driven through it. My God, he's a tough bastard."

"You better hope so. Nothing good will come of this. What a colossal disaster. Hyperion will compete and security will be tighter than the secret service. Can you give me some kind of reasonable explanation?" He raised his hands, palms up, and looked at Sorenson, who held his bloody broken forearm gingerly in his lap.

"We'd have been caught if Lopsang hadn't started that fire."

"What if Rampage's stable had caught fire? It could have been a bigger catastrophe. You're damn lucky," Mullion said.

"Lucky? You call this luck?" He grimaced and pointed to his broken forearm. "I need a doctor. This is a contaminated open fracture. It's going to get infected."

"Going to a hospital? Another *great* idea," Mullion said, leaning forward in his chair. His eyes widened. "Why don't you write out a confession and stop by the police station on the way?"

"Get a grip. Keep your voice down. I've got to do something. Look at this."

"Don't get blood on the carpet. Go to your room and get in the shower. Clean it up and put something around it. You and Lopsang are going back to Philadelphia. I have people there who can handle this sort of thing with discretion. The transport leaves in a couple of hours."

"You want me to ride with a bunch of horses?" Sorenson asked in amazement.

"You got any better ideas? We're scheduled to fly half the stable to Philly today and come back for Rampage and the rest tomorrow. You and Lopsang will be on that plane. Lopsang will pretend to be one of our stable jocks. He was injured in a training accident. He was thrown and his foot was caught in the stirrup. You're accompanying him home for treatment. Take one of your pills and try not to look so pathetic."

"Easy for you to say. You didn't have your arm almost hacked off by a crazed bitch with a shovel. I need treatment. Fast. This wound is probably filled with horse manure. It already feels infected."

Mullion took a sip of his coffee. "Things will be fine. I employ people for this sort of problem. They'll meet you at the plane and take you to a hospital."

"What about the shipment?" Sorenson asked.

Mullion walked to a mirror, checked his reflection from several angles, and arranged his hair. "It's on the plane."

"It's about time. We're burning cash faster than a Silicon Valley start-up."

Mullion turned from the mirror and began pacing. "It'll be processed, packaged, and distributed in a week. That should solve any short-term cash-flow problems."

Sorenson cradled his arm and tried to smile. "The DEA is doing us a favor. Eliminating the competition. Ours is the only game in town. We practically have the entire black market."

Mullion chuckled. "Screw capitalism, I'll take a monopoly anytime."

Sorenson held out a bottle of pills. "Open this, please. I can't get the damn top off."

Mullion manipulated the top and shook a white tablet into his palm. He held it out for Sorenson.

"Two." He shook another tablet from the bottle.

"Who came up with the idea? You or Ramon?"

"What do you think? But I let him think he did."

Sorenson swallowed the pills. "It's the perfect cover. You maintain a stable and stud farm in Colombia and fly the horses into US racetracks. Thank God those horses eat a lot."

Mullion sat and crossed his legs. He smoothed the crease in his trousers. "By the way, our new director of pharmaceutical development will be making the trip with you today."

"She's on the plane?"

Mullion nodded. "I thought she was staying in Colombia," Sorenson said.

"I want Endovancin production at both facilities. If we rename and market it as a cancer drug instead of an antibiotic, we may be able to sell it in the US. The revenue potential is ten times what the Chinese will pay."

"What about the patents?" Sorenson asked.

"The attorneys tell me we have a legitimate chance. It's worth the risk. If Ramon's men had done their job, there would be almost no trace it ever existed."

"They can still fix that problem." He grimaced. "My damn arm is killing me."

Mullion smiled. "They won't screw it up twice. If we're going to produce Endovancin in Philly, Dr. Jindal must set it up. We can't afford to wait. She'll be on the transport as part of the crew. This way she arrives undetected with a new identity as one of the veterinary staff. It's her job to see that production gets started."

Sorenson winced and cradled his arm. "Security will be crawling all over the airport. Moving a thousand kilos from Louisville to Philadelphia won't be easy."

"That's not your problem." Mullion drank the last of his coffee. "There will be so much happening at the airport and racetrack no one will notice a horse transport taking off."

"I hope you're right," Sorenson said.

"Just make sure you're on the plane and dispose of those bloody clothes in a dumpster on the way to the airport. Now get out of here."

THIRTY-SIX

SATURDAY, MAY 6TH

Louisville, Kentucky

THE BLOOD PRESSURE cuff squeezed like a tourniquet as it inflated. Mark watched the nurse secure the IV with a Tegaderm dressing. The catheter didn't hurt, but when he made a fist it wiggled like a worm crawling under his skin. He looked down at the looped clear tubing taped to his left forearm. Blood backed up several inches into the line. It was cherry red near the vein then faded to a light rosé as it was diluted by the saline.

"Good morning, Dr. Thurman. How do you feel?" the stout nurse asked as she ripped the Velcro and removed the cuff. Her dark gray-streaked hair was knotted in a tight bun situated on the top of her head.

"I feel fine."

"I believe it," she said, recording the blood pressure reading. "One hundred and twelve over sixty-five. Not bad for someone dragged from a burning building a couple of hours ago." She touched his forehead with the temperature probe. "You take good care of yourself."

"I try to."

She glanced at the results. "Your temperature is normal. How's your breathing?"

He took a deep breath and wheezed. "Like an asthma attack." A moment later he was racked by a coughing fit then spit into a plastic kidney basin.

The nurse examined the black-tinged glob. "Good work. Keep that stuff coming up. You're due for another breathing treatment. The respiratory therapist should be by soon. You're a lucky man. It was a wood fire, so there weren't a lot of toxic chemicals in the smoke. The carbon monoxide and hydrogen cyanide levels were low. They treated you with one hundred percent oxygen for a few hours and have tapered it almost to room air."

"So, I can take this off," he said, removing the nasal oxygen cannula.

"No, you can't. Put that back on." She reached up and hooked the tubing behind his ears.

Claire had been dozing in the chair on the other side of the room, dressed in the same jeans she'd worn to the racetrack yesterday. She yawned and stretched her arms above her head. "How is your arm?"

He sat up in bed and looked at his bandaged right forearm, then moved his wrist and fingers. "It hurts."

"What about the rest of you?"

He rubbed his right shoulder and touched the AC joint. He winced. "The shoulder's probably separated, but the clavicle's intact. I thought that ninja might have broken it. Other than that, not bad." He looked back at the nurse. "This is ridiculous. Why am I in the hospital? Get me out of here."

"You can't leave, Dr. Thurman. You're being treated for several serious injuries."

"I feel fine."

"Excellent," she said.

"I want to leave."

"You can't. Dr. Edwards is due on morning rounds. Maybe you can convince him to write your discharge orders." She entered data into a mobile computer terminal and looked at Mark. "Doctors are the worst patients."

"That hasn't been my experience," he replied.

From across the room, Claire shook her index finger and placed it to her lips in the universal sign of *shut your mouth*.

The nurse crossed her arms and stared at Mark. "Well, in my experience, physicians are terrible patients. They think they know everything."

"We do," he said.

"Really . . . you think nurses are worse?"

"I didn't say that."

"You implied it."

"I did not," said Mark as he sat up and tried to lower the bed rail.

"You just stay right there, Doctor. You're not going anywhere."

"Nurse Ratchet, put this railing down."

"I will do no such thing, and it's Cross, Nurse Cross, not Ratchet!"

"Ha! Even better."

"I think you just proved my point, Doctor. Have a nice day." She pushed the mobile computer caddy into the hall and snapped the privacy curtain across the doorway.

Claire frowned and shook her head. "I don't believe it. I told you to be quiet. Now you've pissed her off."

Mark squinted as he moved his injured arm. "How long have I been here? What time is it?"

"Not long," Claire said, looking at her watch. "A few hours. You got here just after six. It's nine thirty. What do you remember?"

"I remember the ambulance ride and being rolled into the ER. Then people poking and prodding. They must have whacked me with some heavy drugs. Things get hazy after that. I remember an ER doc looking down my throat saying he didn't see any burns. I could have told him that. Did I go to the OR?" He held up his bandaged arm.

She nodded. "They wheeled you straight in, cleaned up your arm, scrubbed and bandaged it. He said it might need a skin graft."

"If I need one, we aren't doing it here." They turned as the curtain was pulled aside.

"Hello, I'm here for your breathing treatment." The respiratory therapist assembled an apparatus that resembled a water pipe. He gave it to Mark, who stuck it into his mouth and began inhaling the medication. Water vapor was expelled in a white cloud. He puffed on the device until the RT returned and removed it. He coughed and spit more black sputum into the kidney basin lying in his lap. The wheezing was almost gone.

"Much better. Thanks," Mark said, wiping his mouth.

"Good. I'll be back after lunch," said the therapist as he pulled the curtain.

"I can't stay here. We have to get to the racetrack," Mark said.

"You heard the nurse. Wait for the doctor."

"The battle-axe?"

"Knock it off. Now I know you're feeling better." Claire picked up a magazine and began flipping pages.

A half hour later Nurse Cross entered the room and shut off the IV fluids. "Where's Dr. Edwards?" Mark asked.

"In surgery, but he ordered your discharge." She yanked the tape from the IV tubing and his forearm.

Mark stiffened and looked at the hairless patch of skin where the tape had been. "You got your wish." She removed the IV catheter and placed a gauze pad over the puncture. "Hold this." A moment later she covered the gauze with Coban as Mark removed his finger. She took the half-full IV bag and tubing and placed them in the trash can. "Thank your friend." A man entered the room and tossed a duffle bag on the floor next to the bed.

"John Bristow!" Claire jumped from the chair and hugged him.

"Let's get out of here, Doc."

Mark smiled. "How in the world?"

"Put those on. We can talk in the van."

"Where are we going?"

"The airport," Bristow replied. "Get moving."

"The airport?" Claire asked. "What about the Derby?"

"I'll explain on the way."

———

MARK LOOKED at the gigantic C-130 transport plane parked on the other side of the chain-link fence. Their black Mercedes van turned and stopped at the gate. The sign on the gatehouse read KENTUCKY AIR NATIONAL GUARD, HOME OF THE 123RD AIRLIFT WING.

"I thought we were going to the airport," Claire said.

"We're at the airport. The passenger terminals are on the other side. This is the Air Force facility. We're meeting some of our friends from the DEA." He stopped the van and leaned his head out the window. The uniformed guard stepped over to the vehicle and spoke with Bristow and checked his credentials. A couple of seconds later the gate swung open. The black van proceeded through the entrance. It drove through the parking lot around the Air National Guard Terminal and stopped next to a door at the rear of the brick building.

On the second floor they walked down a lighted hallway and entered a room with a wall of windows facing the airfield. Mark counted eight men, who all turned to face them when the door opened. The men in battle gear wore lightweight dark blue body armor with the yellow letters DEA printed on the back. Two held binoculars and stood next to an impeccably dressed man in a charcoal business suit. He turned and smiled.

"Dr. Hodgson, you look splendid as usual."

"Zachariah," Claire said as she embraced the admiral. "I should've known."

"Glad you both could make it." He looked at Mark. "When I

heard about your escapade last night and that you were in the hospital this morning, I was worried."

"I was, too," said Claire.

Mark shrugged. "It was necessary."

"I'm glad you weren't seriously injured." Jaggears turned to the man on his right. "I'd like you to meet a few of our friends from the DEA. Technically, this is their operation, but it should bring some closure to what we were involved in last month. This is Special Agent James Reightler. He's the DEA team lead. I'll let him take over."

"Thank you, Admiral." He handed Mark a pair of binoculars. "Share these. Focus on the 737 parked next to the general aviation hangar directly across the field." He pointed to a large jet about two hundred yards away. Mark placed the glasses to his eyes and adjusted the focus.

"What about it? It looks like a commercial airplane," he said. "That's a horse transportation service?" He handed the binoculars to Claire.

"Correct. It's a dedicated equine transport aircraft owned by the Bonsantos Corporation. The back two-thirds is fitted with stalls and feed. It flew in from Bogotá this morning. Its itinerary states it will load a dozen horses all belonging to Bonsantos Stables and fly them to Philadelphia. These have been competing in races during Derby Week."

"Legitimate?" Mark asked.

Reightler nodded. "Oh, yes. They own this year's Derby favorite."

"We're aware of that," said Mark. "Are there any horses on it now?"

Reightler shook his head. "They'll be loaded tonight after the races. Bonsantos is one of the biggest agricultural companies in South America. Their corporate headquarters are in Bogotá, where they have a three-hundred-acre stable facility fifty miles outside the city. They began competitive racing ten years ago and have been quite successful. Rampage is their third entry in the Derby."

"Why Philadelphia?" Claire asked.

"Presumably because of its proximity to Baltimore. The horses will be stabled on a farm near the New Bolton Center on the outskirts of the city for a week prior to transport to the Pimlico Race Course to compete in races leading up to the Preakness."

"So, why are the DEA and TSI interested in this plane?" Mark asked.

"Good question," said Reightler as he focused the field glasses. "We think it's transporting more than horses and hay. One of our rapid response teams has been collaborating with the Colombian National Police for the past year investigating Bonsantos. TSI has worked with the CNP for several years. As a result of that collaboration, we believe it's carrying a half ton of opioid. At twelve fifteen today, three units will converge on that plane and we'll find out."

"Why are *we* here?" Claire asked while looking at Mark.

"Because Admiral Jaggears insisted."

"I should've guessed," Claire said.

"Also, you two and Mr. Bristow can identify some of the people who are associated with this organization. You've seen several up close and personal. For now, I want you to stay here while the raid goes down. Afterward, you can take a look at the roundup." Reightler lowered his binoculars. "Any more questions?"

They shook their heads.

"All right, then. It's game time." Reightler gave Bristow a hand radio. "Leave it on this frequency. I'll keep the mic open." He led his men out of the room.

Mark looked at Admiral Jaggears. "You're not staying?"

"I have a plane to catch. I'll see you back in North Carolina."

"Time to finish what we started in Panama," Bristow said, looking at Mark and Claire.

"What *they* started," said Claire.

Mark, Claire, and Bristow stood at the window and watched as the DEA team exited the building. They entered a white van with the 123rd Airlift Wing's insignia on the side. Bristow raised the binoculars to his eyes. He turned to his right and pointed. "There's another van about a hundred yards away parked in front of the next hangar." He scanned left. "There's a third one over there."

"This should be interesting," Mark said, looking at his watch. "It's almost twelve fifteen."

"They're moving," said Claire, pointing to the van to her right. The others accelerated toward the plane a half mile away. "How are they going to get in?"

Mark reached for the binoculars. "There's a ramp attached to the rear exit door on the other side of the plane."

"That's how the horses are led on and off," Bristow said. "It's the only entrance I can see unless a forward exit door is open on the other side of the plane." One of the vans stopped next to the ramp while the other two were stationed near the tail on either side. The men exited and ran toward the plane.

"Go! Go!" came the words over the radio. Two squads scrambled up the ramp and disappeared into the fuselage. Ten seconds later several gunshots cracked over the speaker. "Get your hands up! On the deck! Now! No one move!" Bristow kept his binoculars focused on the ramp. Two minutes later they heard, "All clear. Let's get these guys out of here."

"That was quick," said Mark.

"Look!" Claire pointed toward the plane.

"What the hell?" Mark said as he looked through the binoculars at the plane almost a thousand yards away. "Is that a rope?" A thin line dangled from the front exit door. Two figures slid down.

Bristow picked up the radio handset. "They can't see them. The ramp is blocking the view." The first figure came down fast, fell, and rolled on the ground. He twisted onto his hands and knees and stood up. The second slid down the rope and let go several feet from the tarmac. Both were limping as they ran for a white pickup truck parked next to the plane. Bristow keyed the radio.

"They're getting away," said Claire.

"Reightler . . . Bristow, over." He waited for a few seconds then repeated his message.

"What is it?"

"Two men are escaping. They came down a rope from the forward exit. They're getting into a white pickup truck near the nose."

"Copy. We're on it."

Bristow turned to Mark and Claire and smiled. "Come on." They ran to the door, rushed down the hallway to the stairs, and exited into the parking lot. The van was parked five yards away.

Bristow backed out and accelerated as the white pickup truck sped past them a hundred yards to their right. It went between the Air National Guard Terminal and the 123rd Air Wing hangar. "We've got them," said Bristow. "They'll have to stop at the gate."

"Get on it!" Claire yelled. She placed her hands on the dash as Bristow braked and turned in pursuit. They sped between the buildings and closed the distance as the truck slowed at the guard gate.

"There's a white van behind us. I think it's Reightler," Mark called from the back seat.

A uniformed man stepped from the guardhouse and raised his hand for the pickup to stop.

"He's not stopping," Bristow said as the truck accelerated. The guard dove out of the way as the vehicle crashed through the wooden crossbar. Traffic on the other side of the gate was heavy and moving fast. The pickup didn't slow down and turned left into the path of an eighteen-wheel tractor trailer. The massive truck slammed on its brakes. Smoke came from the tires and the rig began to skid.

"Hold on," said Bristow as he stomped the brake pedal.

A flatbed truck loaded with steel girders slammed into the back of the tractor trailer. The semi jackknifed. The Mercedes van skidded to a halt as the sliding trailer rushed up to meet them. "Hang on!"

Claire screamed and covered her face. The big rig teetered toward them. Bristow slammed the transmission into reverse and the van jumped backward, slamming into the vehicle behind them.

The fifty-three-foot-long trailer balanced on its left-side wheels, and in slow motion, it tipped over. The ground shook like an earthquake.

"Damn!" Bristow hit the steering wheel with the palms of his hands. The gate was blocked and horns blared.

To his left, in the distance, Mark glimpsed the white pickup dodging traffic. It slipped into the far right lane and exited onto the freeway. "Son of a bitch!"

Reightler appeared at the passenger window and knocked. "Everyone all right?"

"I think we're good," said Bristow, looking at Claire and Mark.

"I'm fine," Claire said, shaken. Mark gave thumbs-up.

"Did you get a look at them?" Reightler asked.

Bristow gave him the license plate number. "A short guy was driving. Someone wearing a head scarf in the passenger seat."

"It was a niqab," said Claire. "The entire head was covered. They turned around and all I could see were eyes through the slit."

Reightler walked to the back of the van while speaking into his radio. He returned a minute later. "I notified the Louisville PD. They'll get them. Let's go back to the plane. I want you to take a look at the rest of them."

―――――――

SEVEN MEN SAT on the tarmac a dozen feet away. They stared at the ground with their arms handcuffed behind their backs. One sat off to the side cradling his arm. The team of DEA agents stood guard. "I recognize the one wearing the sling," said Mark. "He was in the stables this morning when the fire broke out. He tried to drug Hyperion."

"What happened to his arm?" Bristow asked.

"Fiona whacked him with a manure shovel when he tried to inject him with something. Don't you recognize him?

Bristow stared for a few seconds then shook his head.

"He's the guy we saw leaving the freighter in Cartagena," Mark said. "The hat?"

Bristow smiled. "N. Sorenson."

Claire's eyes narrowed. Her jaw clenched. In a blink she had crossed the space and was now drawing back her right hand. A snap like the sound of a firecracker drew everyone's attention as Sorenson's head whipped around. "You low-life bastard! Where's Meera?" She wound up for a second strike. Mark grabbed her arm and pulled her to him. "Let go of me! He kidnapped us. He stole the Endovancin files. The son of a bitch tried to sell me into slavery."

"Settle down," Mark whispered in her ear.

"That's assault," Sorenson snarled as the left side of his face blossomed into a bright shade of red. "Keep that bitch away from me or I'll file charges."

Claire twisted and broke away. With feline quickness she leapt forward. Sorenson's eyes widened. He tried to say something as she kicked him in the groin. He bent forward as a scream exploded from his mouth. Her right fist struck his jaw and he crumpled to the ground. The bloodstain on the sling expanded.

Claire shook her right hand and held it to her chest. "That's for Meera."

Bristow stepped in front of Sorenson and squatted down. He shook his shoulder. "Where is Meera Jindal?"

Sorenson groaned and opened his eyes.

"Don't make me ask you again."

"My arm," Sorenson said. "I need a doctor."

Bristow reached out and squeezed the sling.

"Ahh!" he gasped.

"Where is she?"

"Don't touch me! I don't know what you're talking about."

Bristow poked the forearm again. "Hey, Mark, I think I felt a bone crunch."

"Get this lunatic away from me!" screamed Sorenson. He rolled onto his back and tried to push Bristow with his left hand. Bristow grabbed it and bent his wrist downward. "Stop! Please, stop!"

Bristow increased the pressure. "I'm only going to ask one more time. Where is she?"

"She's here, damn it. She works for Telos." Sorenson said sobbing. "She was on the plane."

"Liar," Claire yelled. "She'd never do that. You drugged and kidnapped us. You stole her research."

Bristow eased the pressure on his wrist. "Keep talking."

"She was here. I swear. She was supposed to fly to Philly with us." Tears streamed down his face as a mucus bubble expanded from a nostril. "Let go of me, please. You're killing me. I want a lawyer. I'll make a deal."

Reightler stepped forward. "That's enough, leave him alone."

Bristow stood and turned to the group. "She must have been in the pickup."

"And the ninja with the skewered foot," Mark said.

"The woman wearing the niqab?" Claire asked. "How can that be possible?"

Bristow squatted back down. "Where did they go?"

"I don't know." Bristow brushed his hand over Sorenson's wrist. He winced. "The racetrack, damn it. Mullion is part owner of Rampage."

"That's no secret," said Mark. "We've known that for months."

"Mullion and Ramon Bonsantos are business partners, you idiots. The horse is entertainment. It's a front."

"All right, let's get this guy downtown," Reightler said. He grabbed Sorenson under his uninjured arm and helped him to his feet. "We can finish interrogating him later."

"Not without a lawyer. This is coercion, police brutality," yelled Sorenson.

"Brutality? I'll show you some brutality." Claire lunged forward as Mark swept his arm around her waist and lifted her off the ground. "Let me go!" She squirmed like an angry cat.

"Read him his rights then get him out of here." Bristow looked at his watch. It was after three. "We need to get to Churchill Downs."

"Sir, check this out!" yelled one of the men standing in the rear doorway of the cargo hold. Next to him, on a leash, stood a German shepherd with his tongue out and wagging his tail. "Catch." He tossed a rectangular object about the size of a brick.

Reightler caught it and smiled. "Jackpot."

"There were eight of them in this hay bale," the DEA agent said from the doorway. "There must be a couple hundred bales in here."

"This could be big," Reightler said, holding the package in front of Sorenson's face. "What do you have to say about this?"

"I got nothing to say. What is it?"

"Looks like a kilo of heroin to me," Reightler replied.

"I don't know anything about that. I didn't do anything. I was just catching a ride back to Philly to have my arm treated."

"What happened to your arm?" Reightler asked.

"I tripped going down some steps late last night."

"And fell onto a shovel in a pile of hay and horse manure," Mark chuckled. "I'll bet Fiona picks him out of a lineup, no problem." He looked at Bristow then raised his hand. Bristow gave him a high five. "I wonder how long this operation has been going on?"

"We'll find out," said Reightler. He looked at one of his men. Impound this plane. Treat this area as a crime scene."

"Yes, sir," he replied and walked toward one of the vans.

"Speaking of horses, you're right, we need to get to the track," Claire said as she brushed hair from her face.

"We'll never make the race in this traffic," Mark said.

"Yes, we will," said Reightler. "There are a few more folks to round up at Churchill Downs, and I want to talk to Mr. Mullion. Come on." They rode in the van to the terminal building and got into an unmarked black Dodge Charger. He lit up the vehicle. They drove across the airfield to the other side of the airport and went out an open gate. The siren started wailing as they entered traffic.

THIRTY-SEVEN

SATURDAY, MAY 6TH

Churchill Downs, Louisville, Kentucky

THE TWIN SPIRES towered above as they passed through the entrance gates. Their guest passes dangled from colorful lanyards around their necks. "This way," Mark said, pointing to a sign that read WINNERS CIRCLE SUITES. Claire gripped his hand but didn't respond. "Hey, what's the matter?" he asked as they wove their way through the throng of revelers standing next to the paddock area. Horses were in the stalls being saddled for the next race.

"There he is!" Mark stood on his tiptoes facing the paddock. "There's Worth and Jennifer, and Edgar." Around them several men in seersucker suits talked and laughed with women decked out in spring dresses and wide-brimmed hats. They were sipping mint juleps from straws sprouting from plastic cups. "We didn't miss it. Come on, let's get to the box." He pulled on her hand and turned when he felt resistance. "Hey, where's that beautiful smile?"

They stood engulfed by the crowd as patrons dressed in festive splendor were queued up around them. She put her mouth close to his ear. "I spent days looking for a new dress and hat for this, and now I feel like a stable hand," Claire said as the plume from a woman's hat brushed her face.

"Cheer up. We made it."

Her eyes brightened and dimples appeared. "You're right. No one cares anyway." They showed an attendant their guest credentials and made their way up the stairs. "Too bad we didn't have an extra pass for Bristow."

"I think he wanted to stick with Reightler," Mark replied as he examined the signs and followed them to the exclusive bar and betting area. "They have unfinished business."

"Keep your eyes open," she said.

"We're safe in this crowd. Come on. I want to place our bets."

The owner's suites were packed shoulder to shoulder with resplendent guests. In centuries past, in a different setting, they would've been the equivalent of royal courtiers. Claire took in the display of wealth and privilege. Media celebrities, along with men and women who pulled the strings of political and economic power, surrounded them . . . and they were staring at her. As Mark maneuvered through the parting crowd, she looked down at her worn jeans, flannel shirt, and dusty riding boots. She sniffed her shirt collar and crinkled her nose. The faint odor of wood smoke permeated her clothes. She pulled at his sleeve, stood on tiptoes, and kissed his unshaven cheek.

Mark grinned. "Thanks." He pushed forward, stopping and starting. "Excuse me, excuse me . . . pardon me, please."

Claire stayed close.

Bloody hell. Who cares what these peacocks think?

She peered through the crowd and caught a glimpse of the track just twenty yards away. Beyond it, tens of thousands of intoxicated spectators reveled in the infield.

"Look for box number eight," Mark said.

"How do you know?"

"Hyperion's post position is eight. That's how the owners' boxes are assigned. It should be marked by a flag with his colors."

"There it is." She pointed across the congested area to a blue banner with a corner-to-corner white X and a green border. "Look, there's Stephen."

"I asked Dusty to invite him. Hyperion wouldn't be here if it weren't for him."

"There's Meghan, too," Claire exclaimed.

Mark tightened his grip on Claire's hand as they maneuvered through the crowd. Dr. Stephen Sayre turned as they squeezed through a group of men and women. He smiled then chuckled. "Did the airline lose your luggage?"

"Shut up and hand me a drink." Claire wrapped her arms around his neck. "It's good to see you. There'll be no more comments about my clothes."

He handed her his glass. "I haven't taken a sip."

Mark shook his hand. "We've got some catching up to do."

"You'll be glad to know all your subjects are fully recovered and are back on Morgan Island, happy and mischievous as ever."

"That's great news. I've got a ton of stuff to fill you in on." Before he could start, someone tugged at his elbow.

"Dr. Thurman. Good of you to make it," said Warwick Grant with a broad smile.

"We almost didn't," responded Mark.

Just then a horn sounded. They turned toward the track. Claire pointed to the white tower that marked the winner's circle. A bugler wearing a black riding helmet and red jacket stood on the stage in front of the structure. The familiar "Call to Post" blared from the elongated trumpet. The two-story video boards on either side of the winner's circle and the massive fifteen-thousand-square-foot high-definition Big Board on the far side of the field displayed the horses and riders led by their assistant trainers. The procession began making its way from the paddock onto the track. The images on the smaller screens changed, and the words to the first lines of "My Old Kentucky Home" appeared. The University of Louisville Cardinal Marching Band began to play the Kentucky state song while over a hundred thousand fans sang along. Claire wrapped her arm around Mark's and squeezed.

Applause sounded over the grounds as the band finished. Then, a roar rolled through the grandstand. "Look! There they are," Claire yelled. The line of horses and attendants paraded toward them. Each horse was led by its trainer and accompanied by the families of its owners.

"There's nothing quite like the post parade at Churchill Downs," said Grant, who stood next to Claire.

"He's been through so much and worked so hard to get here. I can't thank you enough." She waved as the line of horses and jockeys walked past toward the starting gate. "There's Worth and Jennifer, and Dusty and Laura."

"It's been an ordeal," Grant replied.

"Hyperion," Mark said, pointing to his right. "Look for the pink saddlecloth when the race starts. That's how you can spot him."

"Rampage is in the sixth position," Grant said. The huge black stallion strode before them. He wore a black saddlecloth with a gold number six matching his jockey's black and gold silks. "What a beast. If he were armored, he'd look like a warhorse straight from the Middle Ages."

"Hyperion isn't intimidated," Claire said.

Grant looked at her and smiled. "By God, I think you're right." Hyperion's head's was held high as he pranced by.

"He doesn't remember a thing," said Claire.

Grant beamed. "If he does, he's not showing any signs. Fiona's got him in great shape. Look at the way his belly tucks up high into his hind legs. Magnificent."

The rest of the field paraded before the crowd. The track announcer called out each horse's name, his jockey, and his owner as the procession moved toward the gate.

Mark looked toward Rampage's owner's box as he was introduced. "Rampage, the number six horse, is today's favorite, ridden by George Barbee and owned by the Bonsantos Stables," said the track announcer. "He's the winner of the Rebel Stakes and the Arkansas Derby." The video board flashed a television shot of Jeffery Mullion in a suit and sunglasses standing next to a beautiful woman straight off the cover of *Vogue*. He stood expressionless, swatting his left palm with a rolled-up program.

Mark scowled and clinched his right fist as the group in box six cheered for the massive black brute. The scowl turned to a grimace as the gesture caused a stab of pain in his burned forearm. He glanced at his bandages then scanned the crowd, looking for Bristow or Reightler.

"The number seven horse is Typhoon, ridden by Avelino Gomez and owned by the Winkler Foundation," said the announcer. "He's a West Coast entry from Santa Anita and this year's winner of the California Derby. Typhoon should give Rampage a true test today. He's the second favorite at two to one. In the number eight position is the darling of the field, Hyperion, ridden by Edgar Contreras and principally owned by Worth and Jennifer Hobbs. Hyperion has made an incredible comeback after suffering a devastating injury in this year's Rebel Stakes at Oaklawn Park just two months ago. It's a miracle he's competing. He's a long shot at seventy-five to one." The parade continued until the twentieth horse and rider passed by. "The final contestant, in the twentieth position, is Black Caviar, ridden by hall of fame jockey Willie Simms. He's owned by Conner and Margaret Pennerash from Louisville and is the hometown favorite. He'll have his work cut out for him today. The last time a horse came from the outside position was in 2008 when Big Brown managed to pull it off."

The horses were now being loaded into the barrier stalls as the crowd of over one hundred and fifty thousand fans focused their attention on the starting line. Mark noticed an attractive woman in a blue dress with a wide-brimmed white hat standing in front of him. Beautiful auburn hair spilled from under the hat brim halfway down her back. Her legs were strong and shapely, and she confidently stood in matching blue high heels. A small purse hung from her arm as she placed her white-gloved hands together in front of her face as if in prayer. "Fiona, you made it back from the parade." She turned around. "You look gorgeous. I'm so used to seeing you in jeans and a ball cap." She blushed and smiled.

"How's your arm? You had us worried. I wanted to come to the hospital this morning, but Hyperion needed me."

"Don't worry. I'm fine." He held up his bandaged forearm. "This will heal in a few weeks. How's our boy doing?"

"He's still stirred up from last night. That was horrible. He could've been killed if that man had injected him," Fiona said.

"We got the guy you chopped with the shovel. You broke his arm. I'll tell you about it later. Did they find the syringe?" Mark asked.

"I don't know. The stable is a total loss, there's nothing left. We had to find another stall to keep him for the day. It's thrown him off his usual routine."

They watched as the horse Black Caviar was loaded. Two seconds later the crowd collectively gasped. "Oh, no!" Fiona said as a horse burst through his gate before the start. "That's Hyperion!"

"Ladies and gentlemen, we have a false start," the track announcer said. Edgar yanked on his reins. Hyperion threw his head from side to side and skidded to a stop. Several attendants ran up and led Hyperion around to the rear of the starting gate.

"Terrible," Grant said. "I've never seen a horse win after a false start."

"Let's pray he didn't hurt himself," Fiona said. They watched as the medical staff performed their examination. They reloaded him into the starting gate.

The track announcer's voice blared from the speakers. "Ladies and gentlemen, once again, we're ready for this year's running of the Kentucky Derby." A second later, the gates exploded open and the horses lunged onto the track. "And they're off! Iron Liege from the number three position bolts into the lead. Rampage is in second on his right with Twenty-Grand in third position."

The pack stormed down the straightaway as the starting gate was pulled off the track. "He seems to be okay," Claire said as the horses thundered past. The jockey riding the horse with the pink saddle blanket was buried back in the pack.

"He's in a blind switch," Dusty shouted over the crowd noise. "Damn! Come on, Edgar. Don't let him get boxed in!"

The horses were packed close like a moving thundercloud raining dirt and sand as they entered the clubhouse turn. Riders stood in stirrups crouched over their mounts as they negotiated for position.

"At the quarter-mile pole, it's Typhoon and Donerail neck and neck in the lead, followed by Iron Liege. Rampage is cruising in fourth on the outside." Mark's attention was diverted to the gigantic video board across the track. "Where is he?"

"There! Third or fourth from the rear," Grant yelled. "He better start making a move." He held his rolled racing program in his fist like a baton and shook it up and down. "Come on!"

"In the middle of the back stretch, Rampage is in second. Typhoon has the lead by a half-length," the announcer continued his call. "Donerail has fallen off into fifth place. Iron Liege is in third with Ben Brush and Aristides coming on strong."

"They're blocking him!" Dusty shouted. "Get to the outside!"

Fiona stood with her hands clasped together, not saying anything.

Claire jumped up and down screaming, "Let's go!"

"They're passing the half-mile pole with Rampage in the lead. Typhoon is holding on to second with Ben Brush moving into third. Aristides, Omar Khayyam, and Eclipse are three astride behind Ben Brush. They're starting to separate."

"Look! Edgar's got him free. He's moving up on the outside," Hobbs yelled, standing on his tiptoes with his fist raised. "Come on, Hyperion!"

"He's got to do something!" said Claire.

"Rampage has the lead to himself. Typhoon is dropping off. Here comes Hyperion on the outside. He's making up ground. Omar Khayyam and Eclipse are neck and neck in third with Aristides in fifth. They're rounding into the home stretch with Rampage in front."

"He's doing it! Come on, Hyperion!" Claire screamed. "Come on, boy!" She began to jump. Hyperion was moving.

"I had no idea he was a stretch runner," Grant yelled over the crowd.

"Here comes Hyperion on the outside. He's passing Donerail and Aristides. He's in fourth place. They're at the quarter pole!" Hyperion was running alone on the outside.

"He's getting faster," said Hobbs. "Show him the whip." As he said this Edgar flashed his crop in front of Hyperion's right eye. The horse accelerated.

"Go!" Fiona shouted.

The screaming crowd almost drowned out the track announcer. "Hyperion is closing. It's Rampage by two lengths but here comes Hyperion!" Just then Rampage moved to his right.

"What's Barbee doing?" Grant said. "That bastard."

"He's trying to cut him off!" Claire screamed.

"At the eighth pole it's Rampage by half a length. Hyperion is closing. Rampage is on the inside. They're neck and neck!"

The two horses ran together. "He bumped him! Cheater!" she screamed. The horses flashed by in a blur.

"It's too close to call!" said the announcer. "A photo finish." Edgar stood in his stirrups with his fist and riding crop high in the air. Hyperion ran with his head up and tail flashing. "Amazing."

Ten seconds later a picture flashed on the video boards and viewing screens throughout Churchill Downs. A great roar went up.

Dusty stood with both arms above his head. "Hyperion hit the wire first!"

Claire turned and leapt into Mark's arms. "I can't believe it! He did it." Fiona and Grant were jumping with their arms raised. Mark glanced at box number six. The people were subdued. Several men were being escorted from the box in handcuffs. Mark recognized James Reightler and several agents with the DEA. There was no sign of Jeffery Mullion.

"Come on," called Hobbs. "You and Claire are with us." He began the walk all racehorse owners dream about. They filed from the box and walked through the tunnel toward the sunlight. As they emerged into the infield, an official greeted them and led the group to hallowed ground. The winner's circle at Churchill Downs. Mark and Claire stood on the periphery and watched Hyperion receive the coveted blanket of roses. They turned toward the podium, where the Kentucky governor stood next to the two-foot-tall solid-gold trophy. He stepped up to the microphone.

"Ladies and gentlemen, we have a final result," said the governor. "Hyperion is the official winner of this year's Kentucky Derby. Congratulations, Worth and Jennifer Hobbs." He shook their hands. "Eclipse held off Omar Khayyam for second place. Typhoon finished fourth, and Rampage has been officially disqualified for illegal contact on the home stretch." A gasp came from the crowd.

"Serves him right." Claire laughed. She put her arms around Mark's neck and kissed him. "It was worth it. We did it."

THE BLACK MERCEDES van stopped in front of the Romano Mazzoli Federal Building. There was little traffic in the city on Sunday morning. Mark, Claire, and Bristow exited and climbed the steps to the entrance. They took the elevator to the third floor and entered the office with the SPECIAL AGENT JAMES REIGHTLER nameplate on the door.

"Good morning," said Reightler. "Congratulations on the win yesterday." He stood in a doorway that led from the antechamber to his private office. "Come on back." He waved them forward and retreated. They followed. "Have a seat." He motioned to several chairs in front of his desk then turned his computer screen around to face them. "Watch this." He pressed a key and a video began. "This is from a police car dashcam taken yesterday afternoon, about half an hour after the airport raid." The image showed a white pickup truck breaking at a police roadblock. The car with the camera stopped behind the pickup. There was no audio. Two individuals exited the vehicle with their hands up as police officers surrounded it with drawn weapons.

"Nice work," Mark said. "Is that the guy who tried to kill me in the barn?"

"I don't know."

"Why's he limping?" asked Mark.

"He won't say, but his right foot looks like someone drove a railroad spike through it."

"Then that's him, but it wasn't a railroad spike, it was a pitchfork tine. He should be charged with assault *and* arson."

"He has been."

The video kept rolling as an officer approached the other occupant of the pickup. The person's face was covered. The policeman stepped forward, cuffed the suspect, then removed the hood. Claire took a deep breath.

"Meera? How could she?"

"Can you identify this woman?" Reightler asked.

Claire nodded. "She's Dr. Meera Jindal, the woman Sorenson claimed escaped from the plane yesterday. We went to graduate school together. She's one of the world's leading pharmaceutical chemists."

"Not anymore," Reightler said.

"Is it true? What he said?" Claire asked. "Is she working for Telos?"

"It looks that way. Let me fill you in on a little background. I'm in charge of a task force that's had Telos Pharmaceuticals under investigation for the past eighteen months."

"You've known about them that long?" asked Bristow.

Reightler nodded. "An informant tipped the police in Huntington, West Virginia, that the local pill supply was coming out of Philadelphia. A couple of arrests in Philly led to more evidence implicating the company. We believe Telos is at the center of one of the biggest narcotic prescription drug rings in the country. From what we've been able to piece together, it started when the CEO, a guy named Jeffery Mullion, approached Ramon Bonsantos. He's a Colombian whose family owns the Bonsantos Corporation, one of the largest agricultural enterprises in Central America."

"Agriculture enterprise?" Mark interrupted. "I take it they're not like Del Monte."

Reightler leaned back in his chair and chuckled. "I don't think so. Ramon's father was a close friend and business associate of Pablo Escobar. He helped Escobar in his early days by allowing him to stash cocaine on his produce trucks. The Bonsantos smuggling operations have since branched out into more sophisticated narcotic operations. The Telos-Bonsantos partnership began about the time the DEA and other federal agencies started to wake up to the magnitude of the prescription drug epidemic. Mullion proposed that his company would produce black-market drugs if Bonsantos could supply the base product."

"How did they pull it off?" Mark asked.

"They set up a black ops production facility outside Philly," Reightler said.

"How could other employees not know about it?" Bristow asked.

"No one knew about it. Bonsantos supplied the skilled labor to run it. All employees were part of their organization. Ramon Bonsantos has been smuggling semiprocessed opioid paste into the States for years. This junk ends up in the Telos facility, where the product is purified and made into counterfeit prescription drugs. They are street marketed as the equivalent of Oxycontin laced with fentanyl called Nirvana. Bonsantos then distributed the product through their network of urban gangs. It was run nationwide."

"Slick," Bristow commented.

"Disgusting," said Claire.

"For a while it worked. Telos used the illegal drug profits to fund their legitimate drugs. They washed the money and funded business operations."

"Like the development of Juvanimab," she said.

Reightler pushed a file of papers across his desk toward Claire. "Another one was going to be your Endovancin after they stole the formula from Electra Pharmaceuticals, who employed Dr. Jindal."

Claire flipped through the documents. "Where did you get these?"

"From Sorenson. He's cooperating," Reightler answered.

"But we were kidnapped," Claire said. "Meera didn't join them."

"We think Dr. Jindal cut a deal after the raid while she was captive."

"Why?"

Reightler shrugged. "Who knows. Everyone has their price."

"Then, she did it under duress. You can't arrest her for that," Mark protested.

"It's not so clear-cut. Believe whatever you want, but she cut a deal and took some of their money. Let the lawyers figure it out. For now, she's state's evidence."

"No way. I don't believe it. Where is she?"

"In a cell three blocks from here," Reightler said.

"She's in jail?" Claire asked. "Why isn't she out on bond? Can I talk to her?"

"Her lawyer's trying to arrange it. Actually, I *want* you to talk to her. See if she'll tell you anything. But you heard Sorenson yesterday. He implicated her."

"He's a liar."

"He claims she agreed to produce the stolen drug. She was supposed to run a new drug factory in Bogotá. Sorenson says China was their primary customer. The Chinese were going to buy tons of the stuff and distribute it worldwide. He said Telos paid Jindal a lot of money."

"I don't believe it. Let me talk to her. I can get answers. I can get the truth. There's got to be an explanation," Claire said. Reightler picked up the phone on his desk. A minute later he hung up.

"You've got your wish. She's at the police station."

"Wait," Mark asked. "Where's Mullion? I saw him at the track yesterday. Did you arrest him?"

Reightler frowned. "He slipped away."

"How? He was right there, ten yards away, in owner's box six."

Reightler turned the computer screen back around and entered several commands on his keyboard. "Check this out. It's security cam footage from yesterday right after the race."

Mark leaned closer and pointed to the screen. "There he is." They watched as Mullion picked up a gym bag and walked out of the cam view as the crowd was jumping up and down. "The race must have just ended. Where's he going?"

"Keep watching," Reightler told him. "It took some time, but we pieced this together late last night." Claire moved next to Mark and they watched as another camera showed Mullion walking down a hallway and entering a women's restroom.

"What's he doing?" asked Mark.

"Keep watching."

The time on the video indicated eighteen minutes elapsed while a dozen or so women entered and left the restroom. Then, a striking woman with long dark hair wearing a black dress and sunglasses emerged. She adjusted her hat as she walked down the hallway out of the camera image. The sequence of video images from different cameras continued, all showing the beautiful woman making her way through the crowd and finally exiting the complex. She stood at the curb and moments later, she entered a black stretch limo that drove away, disappearing into traffic.

"That's a dude—that's Mullion?" Mark sputtered.

Reightler nodded. "We think."

"No way."

"You're sure?" asked Claire, who elbowed Mark in the ribs. "Get a grip, and close your mouth."

Mark shook his head. "A Victoria's Secret model maybe, but a guy? No way."

"We ran the facial features. That is Mullion. *She* caught a flight to Paris yesterday evening. We found an entire woman's wardrobe in Mullion's hotel suite. That's him . . . her."

CLAIRE FOLLOWED an officer into a ten-by-twenty-foot room. Meera was seated with her wrists handcuffed and chained to a metal ring attached to the tabletop. The top half of the back wall was covered with a mirror. Claire pointed to the chains. "Is this necessary?"

"Procedure, ma'am," replied the officer. "I'll be right outside. Yell if you need anything or want to leave."

"Thank you." She sat down across from her friend.

Meera looked up and gave her a tight smile. Mascara streaks marked her cheeks. "Can you tell me what I'm doing here being treated like this?"

"I'm trying to figure it out. Why *are* you here?"

"I don't know. This wasn't supposed to happen."

"What *was* supposed to happen, Meera?" Claire asked. "Your lab was attacked. We were taken hostage. Were you in on all that from the beginning?"

Meera shook her head and fresh tears streamed from her eyes. "No. After they separated us on the ship, Sorenson started talking to me. They realized they couldn't make Endovancin without me. I hadn't recorded all the steps for the synthesis. They started making offers for me to work for them."

"But why? Why would you work for them? They're crooks."

"Because they said they'd kill you if I didn't, and my family, too."

Claire reached out and touched her friend's hand.

"They were going to drug you and throw you overboard. I made them promise they wouldn't harm you."

"Thank you."

"They threatened my parents," Meera said between sobs.

Claire continued in a soft voice as if she were trying to console a child. "If that were all of the story, we wouldn't be here. Sorenson claims you work for them as an employee of Telos and Bonsantos. Is that true?"

"I had no choice," Meera said. She wiped her face on her sleeve.

"You always have a choice."

"You don't know half of it. Once Aaray got sick, our family went broke paying his medical bills. They're destitute. My brother is in college. He would have had to drop out and return home. That's why I'm here. I wanted him to have what I had. To be able to stay and finish his studies."

Claire shook her head. "I don't understand. You didn't have to join them."

"Do you have any idea of the cost of cancer treatment?"

Claire shook her head.

"Hundreds of thousands. That doesn't count my brother's education. They said that if I came to work for them, they would pay the medical bills and provide money so Sanjay could finish college. I would make enough to support my parents."

"But why did you come back? Why leave Colombia?" Claire asked.

"They wanted me to set up a production facility in the States."

"Why, though? Electra would've helped. There are scholarships Sanjay could have applied for. I'm sure Roberts could've done something. Did you ask him?"

Her eyes flashed. "Don't say his name. I'm not sorry if he's dead. It's his fault. If he'd told me about your work, I might have saved Aaray in the first place. We could have tried it on him. My brother might be alive today. My family wouldn't be ruined."

"But Meera, we didn't know Endovancin cured osteosarcoma until after Aaray's death. We don't know if it would have cured his cancer."

"We might have figured it out sooner if he hadn't been so paranoid and secretive. We could have tried."

Claire looked down. "Tell me about Endovancin. How did Mullion think he was going to market and sell it in the United States?"

"I asked him that. He said they had the best attorneys money could buy. They were prepared to fight for the patent rights for years, if necessary. In the meantime he was going to sell it to China. They were going to pay him a fortune."

AN HOUR LATER, Reightler handed her a bottle of water as she came out of the interrogation room. He told her, "I'm sorry, Claire but there you have it. She did it. Her family was financially ruined. Her nephew had cancer and no insurance. He racked up enough in hospital charges that Meera and her parents would have been paying them off for the rest of their lives. On top of that, the brother's future depended on Meera finding a way for him to finish school. Telos agreed to pay the bills and triple her salary. Once her hands were dirty, they controlled her. She had no choice but to do what they wanted."

"But she was coerced," Claire said. "There's got to be some way to get her off. She doesn't deserve to go to jail. She's worth more to society working."

"You may be right. Let the lawyers figure it out. I doubt if she'll do time," Reightler said.

"What about me and Mark? We knew about the drug. Were they going to kill us?" Claire asked.

An eyebrow elevated as Reightler glanced over his glasses. "They already tried. My guess is they'd try again. You were loose ends that had to go," said Reightler. "They almost destroyed the proof that Endovancin existed when they torched the labs."

"But how did they know about Yemassee?" Claire asked. "They couldn't have known we'd used it before."

"The place in South Carolina?" Reightler asked.

Claire nodded. "How did they know we'd be there?"

"According to Sorenson, Coleman told them. Mark mentioned it to Grant during one of the surgeries. Afterward, Coleman called Sorenson, who relayed it to Mullion. We believe it was Ramon Bonsantos's men who set the explosive charges."

"They nearly succeeded," said Mark. "We were lucky to have Evelyn Heinricht's lab as a backup plan."

Claire walked to the window. "Don't forget Rafael. If he hadn't given us the remaining Endovancin, Hyperion and our subjects would have died and there would be no evidence the drug existed. Telos might have been able to bring the drug to market in the US under a different name."

Reightler folded his arms and nodded. "While they continued to make a fortune ravaging the country with their counterfeit prescription drugs. We estimate they're responsible for over fifty percent of the pill traffic in the DEA's Appalachian mountain region."

"What's that cover?"

"West Virginia, Kentucky, and Tennessee. Bonsantos was the perfect racket for them. It has all the legitimate Central American agriculture business connections but was a front for the third-generation drug cartels. The horse racing business allowed them to smuggle over ten thousand kilos of opioid paste into the States since the alliance with Telos. The part ownership of Rampage gave the appearance of a legitimate arrangement. It was almost a perfect setup. We missed it for several years."

"It unraveled all because Rampage clipped Hyperion and almost killed him," said Mark.

"That and Dr. Hodgson's recognition of the miraculous properties of Endovancin. If she hadn't gone to Panama to investigate the drug, we may have never figured it out."

"Was the raid planned not knowing I would be there?" Claire asked.

"Sorenson claims to have been as surprised to see you as you were to see them. They didn't know you'd be there. He recognized you because Dr. Jindal cited your research in one of her scientific articles. He'd checked you out on LinkedIn and had seen your picture on other professional websites. He'd read the papers you and Mark published. It was Sorenson who approached your lab tech and used him as a spy. That's how he figured out the drug worked. Unfortunately, it cost the poor fellow his life."

"Evil people," she said.

"If you hadn't been there, they might have pulled it off," said Reightler. "I hope they get to experience a little hell here on earth in a place called Leavenworth."

"They deserve it."

EPILOGUE

FRIDAY, MAY 12TH

Police Department Firing Range, Raleigh, North Carolina

DETECTIVE JACK INGRAM holstered his gun. He and Mark began walking back to their gear twenty-five yards off the firing line. "How do you like that belt?"

"I'm going to move this TACO back." Mark unhooked his belt. He laid it on the wooden table and began to unfasten one of the AR mag pouches. "My elbow keeps brushing against it."

"When you've got it right, we'll practice two-gun transitions." He began pushing nine-millimeter rounds into an empty pistol magazine. "We tracked down the blonde. Her lawyer made a deal with the prosecutor and she's cooperating."

"Ard's girlfriend?"

"More like assassin," Ingram said.

"She killed him?"

"I don't know. She claims they went on a date. We located a guy who saw them at a bar that night. They got into an argument with him and left. They went back to Ard's place. After that he ends up dead."

"A date? That's a joke. How'd she pull it off?"

"With help. It's looking like she seduced and drugged him. Then, someone took his body to the lab and used his ID for access."

"When were you going to tell me this?"

"I'm telling you now," said Ingram. "Her lawyer just made the immunity deal, so don't get your panties in a twist." He slipped the loaded magazine into its holder on his belt and started filling another.

"Go on."

"We brought her in yesterday, but she wouldn't say anything until her lawyer arrived."

"Poor guy, Ard didn't realize who he was tangling with."

"I'll bet he never had a clue." Ingram finished filling the second magazine and rammed it into the magwell of his pistol then holstered the weapon. "We also discovered he went to the bank and opened his safety deposit box the day he died. There was a handwritten document that indicates he was hired to provide experimental results to a pharmaceutical company."

"Telos."

"Yeah, he was passing information. They promised him acceptance to a medical school and a lot of money."

"He should've kept studying. He was talented and smart. He would've made it."

Ingram crossed his arms. "You ready?"

"Not yet," Mark said, adjusting his belt. "What else did the woman say?"

"She denied killing the kid. She claims to have been hired to seduce him and get information. She said he got drunk and she was able to get what she needed off his phone. He was unconscious when she left him that night. She fingered Sorenson."

"That makes him guilty of kidnapping and murder," said Mark. "Has he rolled over on Mullion?"

"Not yet, but why wouldn't he? You think Mullion would protect him? I'd bet the cartel has him marked. He'll be lucky to testify."

"I hope he gets a chance." Mark inserted a full magazine into the Sig, racked the slide, decocked the hammer, and slipped it into its holster. He began loading 5.56-millimeter rounds into an AR mag. "He could probably write a book about it."

"That's what the DEA's counting on."

"Anything on Mullion?"

"He's disappeared. No trace, so far."

"He's probably sipping café au lait at a table somewhere along the Champs-Élysées."

Ingram chuckled as he walked to the rifle rack and picked up his M4. "He's a slick one, but we'll get him."

"You mean, you'll get her."

"Him, her, it doesn't matter; Interpol is coordinating the search for both. What's up with Claire?"

"How do you know about that?"

"I have more sources than you'll ever know. What's going on?"

"She's taking a sabbatical and going to work with a biotech firm in San Diego."

"Explain. I don't get it."

"Her lab has to be rebuilt. The fire damaged half the building. That's going to take at least twelve to eighteen months. That's a lot of time to waste. She wants to continue her research."

"Couldn't she work at Wake Forest with her mentor?"

"You do have good sources," Mark answered as he stood and filled his M4 magazine pouches then slipped his head and arm through the rifle sling. "She doesn't want to go back there. I guess she feels like she needs a new setting. She won't admit it, but she feels she's been under Heinricht's wing for too long."

"But why is she going to work with her ex-boyfriend?"

"Damn, Jack. How do you know so much?"

Ingram smiled. "It's my job. Sorry about that."

"Yeah, well. Don't be. It's her call. It's a pharmaceutical biotech firm that's doing good work. She wants to study the anticancer mechanism of Endovancin, and identify the mutations that cause the problem. They've given her everything she's asked for."

"Where does that leave you two?"

"It doesn't change my feelings, but I don't know." Mark started walking toward the firing line. "I love her. I think she loves me. Sometimes, two people have to see if their relationship can survive over long distances. I guess this is a test for us."

"You two better work this out. I'm not going to be happy about it if you screw up a great thing."

Mark adjusted his hearing protection and ball cap. "I'll try not to let you down."

They stood next to each other on the line. Ingram slipped on his sunglasses.

They each held their rifle at the low-ready position. "Failure drill," said Ingram.

"Got it."

Ingram glanced in Mark's direction then back to the targets. "Shooter ready?"

"Shooter ready."

"Fire!"

AFTERWORD

Several years ago while exploring ideas for a story that would ultimately result in this book, I happened upon a marvelous HBO documentary titled *Barbaro*. At the time I had only vague memories of the tragic events of his life. If you haven't seen the movie or are unfamiliar with this incredible horse, I urge you to take an hour of your time and watch it. I couldn't pull myself away. It moved me to tears. Then the thought occurred, if fractures could be healed fast enough, an injured horse could be saved. This was the catalyst for the story. Hyperion became my Barbaro. For those of you who may be wondering, the epigraph at the beginning of the book is the inscription on Barbaro's statue that stands in front of the entrance to Churchill Downs.

The horse racing industry continues to come under fire because of the type of injury Barbaro experienced. Sadly, even today these *are* mortal injuries in horses. They have become an epidemic threatening the sport of racing. At the Santa Anita racetrack in California, two dozen horses suffered fractured limbs and were euthanized over a five-month span between December 2018 and May 2019. This is a tragedy. But there's hope—real hope, not some pie-in-the-sky science fiction. The fracture-healing biotechnology I describe is real, and progress is being made every day to bring it into clinical practice. This is the essence of translational medicine–the discipline where transformative medical advances are expedited from the laboratory bench to the hospital bedside. I hope this book stimulates more interest and research into this incredible bone-healing technology. It could save a lot of horses.

Two outstanding equine veterinarians, David Hodgson and Foster Northrop, deserve special recognition for their assistance on this project. Each put up with my many intrusions into their busy lives and answered innumerable equine-related questions. James Reightler was my go-to guy for all things related to tactical situations and firearms. If there are technical errors regarding these subjects, they are my fault.

The manuscript was edited by Christina Roth, Cheryl Castela, and Chantelle Osman. Maxwell Roth designed the cover. I'm grateful for their help and extraordinary talent. However, this book would not be possible without the abiding love and support of my incredible wife, Vicky. She read each version of the story and was an unending source of inspiration and encouragement. I will never be able to thank her enough.

CPSIA information can be obtained
at www.ICGtesting.com
Printed in the USA
FSHW021327140719
59966FS

9 780999 456132